PRAISE FOR
JULIETTE WADE AND *MAZES OF POWER*

"Delicious political intrigue and
—Ann Leckie, Hugo  r of
stice

"The impressively winding plot, logically acute characterizations are sure to hold readers' attention. Wade is an author to watch." —*Publishers Weekly* (starred review)

"A vivid, thrilling journey through a wonderfully realized and wonderfully complex world; and a fascinating look at power and its exercise across different strata of an intricate society."
—Aliette de Bodard, Nebula award-winning author of
The Tea Master and the Detective

"A thought provoking and immersive work of sociological science fiction in the footsteps of genre luminaries like Ursula K. Le Guin, Doris Lessig, Jack Vance, and Eleanor Arnason."
—Tor.com

"Wade, an expert in language, makes the complex society of Varin perfectly comprehensible. The characters are compelling and fully dimensional. Comparisons to the likes of Julie Czerneda, Ursula K. Le-Guin, Joan Slonciewski, and Jack Vance are obvious and appropriate; the book would also appeal to those who enjoy the byzantine politics of, say, Catherine Asaro or David Weber." —*Analog*

"A twisty ride through family drama and tangled politics, *Mazes of Power* carries readers into a world of love and treachery, and doesn't let them go." —Laura Anne Gilman, author of *The Cold Eye*

"A deliciously complex, glittering work of family intrigue and life-or-death politics in a world that's utterly alien, with characters who are all-too human. I loved it."
—Kelly Robson, Hugo award-winning author of
Gods, Monsters, and the Lucky Peach

DAW Books is proud to present the novels of Juliette Wade

The Broken Trust

MAZES OF POWER
TRANSGRESSIONS OF POWER

MAZES

of

POWER

Book One of The Broken Trust

JULIETTE WADE

DAW BOOKS, INC.
DONALD A. WOLLHEIM FOUNDER
1745 Broadway, New York, NY 10019
ELIZABETH R. WOLLHEIM
SHEILA E. GILBERT
PUBLISHERS
www.dawbooks.com

For Tim, Niall, and Eagan,
Janice, Deborah, and Lillian,
and for Myrna

VARIN IS A PLACE WHERE HUMANS HAVE ALWAYS
LIVED ON AN ALIEN WORLD.

IT IS ALSO YOUR HOME.

The Castes of Varin

Grobal–the Noble Race

Arissen–the Officer Caste

Imbati–the Servant Caste

Kartunnen–the Artisan Caste

Venorai–the Laborer Caste

Melumalai–the Merchant Caste

Akrabitti–the Undercaste

The Eight Cavern Cities of Varin

Pelismara

Selimna

Safe Harbor

Erin

Herketh

Peak

Daronvel

Vitett

CHAPTER ONE
Change

Tagaret believed in music the same way he believed in the sky. It was unreachable, invisible, transcendent, and somehow a promise that there had to be more to life than this. Mother had always assured him, when they'd fallen back into that vague, wistful state after the grand concerts were over, that they must be grateful to have been born into the nobility and have their health, too—that no better life could be had in all Varin. With her beside him, he could believe that it was true. But then Father's official appointment as Alixi of Selimna had stolen her away across the surface wilderness, leaving him and his brother behind.

Up there, traveling on the Roads, Mother had seen the sky out her window. She'd told him about it in her very first letter.

> *Vast, bright, deep—Tagaret, I try, but these words fail to describe its full, terrifying beauty. Somehow, the sight of it changes everything.*

He'd shivered over her words and waited to hear more, to hear *how* everything was different now. A beautiful sight couldn't bring back the days before the decline, before the yearly Announcements that cataloged defects and deaths. If it had eased Mother's tears, it must mean something important . . . but she'd never mentioned it again, and after that the notes of hope disappeared from her letters.

Some experiences could change your entire life. Not necessarily for the better.

With yet another Announcement looming, Tagaret clung to the promise in the music. In the five years since Mother's departure, he'd attended every concert, hoping to feel his heart uplifted. Tonight's piece promised to be unlike anything written before: a controversial new symphony, *The Catacomb,* described by advance listeners as an experience that would change the image of the Kartunnen artisan caste, change the meaning of music—change everything.

Tagaret looked down at his ticket: thick paper with looping calligraphy in black and gold. He could imagine himself twelve again, and Mother handing it to him, pointing out his seat while she described the music to come in a voice ringing with excitement . . .

"Change everything," he whispered.

He stepped through the doors into the Eminence's grand ballroom, with his three best friends following behind him.

All the finest people were here. Announcements brought out a bigger crowd than musical events. Politicians, gentlemen, and ladies murmured in anticipation, their jewel-colored suits and gowns glittering in the electric light of the chandeliers. Tagaret led his friends into the right-side aisle, feeling the gossip-hungry eyes evaluate his new height, his poise, and his maturity before moving on.

"Fifth row," he said, as the chandeliers dimmed slightly. He handed extra tickets back to Fernar, Gowan, and Reyn.

"Wow," said Fernar. "Right up front—how'd you get such good tickets to an Announcement?"

Tagaret sighed. "They're for the *concert*, Fernar. My mother's the patron of the concert series."

"Great," said Gowan. "We can look right up at the Speaker of the Cabinet."

Reyn aimed a punch at Gowan's shoulder. "Come on. Tagaret just said, we're here for the music."

"Right," said Tagaret. "Thanks, Reyn." Fernar and Gowan would never quite understand the anxiety he and Reyn felt before Announcements because they hadn't lost parents to leadership positions in the provincial cities.

"Actually, I'm here for young ladies, too," Fernar said, nodding toward the stage. "That's quite a view—let's skim on over there."

Tagaret followed his gaze. A group of girls sparkled near the base of the stage, talking and laughing in a tight cluster. Each was guarded by a man or woman in black silk: members of the Imbati servant caste, marked with the curving forehead tattoos of bodyguards. Jewels inside a wall of coal. The view alone almost pushed Announcements out of his mind, but Tagaret held Fernar back. Someone else had had the same idea: two boys on the opposite side of the stage were pushing toward the group.

"Those boys are Tenth Family," Gowan whispered. "Let's see if they mess this up."

As the boys drew close, the girls' attendant bodyguards shifted subtly, tracking them. Tagaret gulped in sympathy. Surely, they wouldn't be fool enough to speak or touch . . .

A bodyguard moved. In a split second the taller boy dropped, laid out facedown on the floor with the bodyguard pinning one arm behind his back. Girls gasped, and startled members of the crowd pulled back. The bodyguard immediately released his grip and bowed, and the boy's friend helped him to his feet. The downed boy held both hands over his face as he scrambled away.

"Ouch," Reyn muttered. "They'll wish they didn't have to show their faces at school tomorrow."

Gowan snorted. "They've got a lecture coming from their Family Council, too—Tenth Family fools."

Fernar laughed aloud. "Guys, come on, we can do better than *that*. All we'll do is walk up and past. Our reputation will be brilliant for *weeks*."

"So long as the Imbati don't humiliate us," said Gowan.

Tagaret gulped a breath, with a glance at Reyn. "We're fine so long as we all behave. Agreed?"

"Agreed," the others said.

What better opportunity would they get? To catch the scent of the girls' hair or their hand oil—maybe even to have one look him in the eye—oh, yes . . .

Tagaret strode to the front, making sure the others stayed close, and turned into the aisle that crossed the base of the stage. All around, the eyes were watching. Fernar liked other boys to see them be so daring; Gowan liked the attention of politicians. Whichever group was looking, they'd win more reputation if they supported each other shoulder to shoulder.

Two of the bodyguards had noticed them now. So had all the girls. One of Tagaret's cousins in the First Family met his gaze and nodded; the other girls whispered with fingers held before their lips. Though his heart raced, Tagaret carefully turned his eyes downward as he drew closer. Imbati escorts didn't permit much attention to their mistress' faces. He quivered, sneaking glances. Mm, the curve of a pale shoulder. A ruby bodice—long amethyst skirts—graceful hands—a sway of dark braids . . . Then his eyes caught on an arresting pair of brown eyes that had been following his movements, and he gazed at the girl's face a moment too long.

An Imbati woman in black skirts flowed smoothly between them. Mercy—Tagaret swerved off fast before the Imbati could make a move on him. Breathing down the adrenaline, he walked to the stage and looked up at the instruments. Above him was the yojosmei with its priceless wooden frame, and double keyboards of polished stone, where the symphony's composer would soon sit.

Someone else came close and looked up. Not Reyn, Fernar, or Gowan. A girl.

By Sirin and Eyn, why would a girl leave the main group? To see him? Impossible. Surely, she was here for the instruments. But maybe, just maybe, she *had* come to see him, and liked music, too. He leaned toward her without thinking; she had radiant copper hair and a long emerald-green dress that fell over her curves in a slow caress he wanted to follow with his own fingertips. Thank heavens she wasn't any closer, or he'd have been on the floor by now. Her male Imbati escort had graying hair, and looked powerful enough to throw him all the way to the fifth row. But, if asked politely, might he consent to give his Lady's name?

"Tagaret, well done!" Fernar clapped his shoulder, and he jumped. Gowan appeared on his other side. "Guys, we've had cabinet members watching us. Now they'll know who you three are." They already knew Gowan; his father was in the cabinet.

"That's great," Tagaret said. But the girl had disappeared, and Reyn now leaned against the stage in her place. "Where did she go? Reyn, did you see her? The girl with the copper hair?"

Reyn pushed his blond curls out of his eyes with a sly smile. "Sure, I saw her. Copper and emeralds, right? Left the pack to follow you?"

"Did she?" *That* tightened his stomach. He stood on his toes and found her. By the holy Maiden Eyn, she put the other girls to shame. "Look there—at the far corner of the stage."

Fernar frowned. "I think she's Sixth Family."

"Hmph," said Gowan. "Don't bother, Tagaret—Sixth are muckwalkers. Always fraternizing with Lowers, ungrateful for their position in the Race. I don't expect many politicians will be lining up at her father's door."

"How can you say that?" Tagaret protested. "You don't know her."

Reyn took his elbow. "Never mind. Let's go sit down."

Tagaret kept glancing back over his shoulder. The girl was indeed talking to a Lower—a boy wearing a pale gray coat, the mark of the Kartunnen artisan caste. But that couldn't really be muckwalking. Mother had talked to musicians about setting up the concert series . . .

"Look," said Gowan. "It's the Speaker—here he comes."

Tagaret's stomach clenched. He dragged his eyes away from the girl and sidestepped between the brass chairs to his seat. A hush spread through the crowd, and the heavy crystal chandeliers dimmed, leaving Speaker Orn in the spotlight. Orn looked pretty bad tonight, his red face blotchy and exhausted as he lumbered to a microphone at stage center, his Imbati manservant hovering close.

"Ladies and gentlemen, thank you for coming out tonight. This year has been a prosperous one for the Grobal Race across Varin. The Pelismara Society," Speaker Orn gestured across the assembled crowd, "has had a record number of healthy pregnancies carried to term, with only one additional case of hemophilia, and no further spinal malformations or mental disabilities."

Tagaret winced. Please, just let them get to the music . . .

"Births were seen across all twelve of the great noble Families, with the strongest growth occurring in the Third and the Eleventh." Speaker Orn stopped for breath, clutching at the stand of the microphone. "News has also been good from the provincial cities. Only a single death in the Peak Society, and two in the Erin Society. None in Vitett, Daronvel, Herketh, or Safe Harbor."

Beside him in the half-dark, Reyn gave an audible sigh of relief.

The Speaker wheezed and cleared his throat. "Selimna saw—" He broke off, coughing.

Tagaret tensed. The Speaker's manservant stepped forward; her usually expressionless face showed concern. Speaker Orn turned as if to speak to her, swayed—and collapsed. The servant cushioned his fall onto the wooden floor of the stage, then held her hand to her Master's forehead. But she didn't actually touch it.

Never touch the fever-fallen. A childhood warning loomed suddenly in Tagaret's head. "Guys," he blurted, "let's get out of—"

Someone shouted, "Kinders fever!"

The room erupted.

Tagaret sprang up and pushed toward the aisle. Reyn fumbled at his arm, so Tagaret grabbed onto him, glancing back in the half-dark to check that Fernar and Gowan were close behind. A vast, gold-glimmering lady blocked their way.

"Lady, excuse me—"

The lady shrieked. "It's in the air! Heile have mercy, it's in the air!"

Kinders fever in the *air?* Nausea crashed over him. Tagaret forced one shaking hand into his pocket and pressed a handkerchief over his mouth. The Lady wouldn't move and wouldn't shut up. Seeing no bodyguard, he took a risk and pushed by. They managed to reach the aisle, but it was mobbed in seconds. Bodies pressed and bumped. *Don't touch*—but how could he not touch? Tagaret inched his way along the stone wall, pulling hard on Reyn's hand and praying the other two were back there holding on. People surged chaotically—no forward movement though there should have been an exit just past the next column. Then someone raised the lights, and he saw it.

The door was so completely blocked by desperate people that even three Imbati manservants couldn't force it open.

No, no . . .

Tagaret twisted, searching above the heads for another door. There was one behind them, but it, too, was blocked. He couldn't see Fernar or Gowan. Had they been pulled off in another direction? Trampled, gods forbid? How could he search for them in this chaos?

A narrow gap opened among the shifting bodies, and he glimpsed the girl with the copper hair. She was calm, and she was *moving.* He leapt into the gap toward her, dragging Reyn behind, and found himself in a narrow space behind her back. The girl held her Imbati escort by the waist while he cut through the panic toward the windows in the opposite wall.

Those windows didn't open, but it hardly mattered. He had to stay behind the girl, just get there. He climbed over tumbled chairs, around a gentleman who had fainted in his seat, over a body. The one constant in the chaos of movement was the girl's beautiful hair, almost close enough to touch.

Reyn's grip never slackened. The windows drew closer ahead. People pressed inward from both sides—*keep right behind the girl, don't lose her*—

The crowd surged, and Tagaret stumbled onto the hem of the green dress. The girl cried out and fell backward into him. Fragrant sweet copper hair in his face, oh gods, the touch of firm flesh under green velvet, her back against his chest, oh mercy, danger, danger! He tried to shove her back upright, but the escort turned around, dark brows angry beneath his curving tattoo. Tagaret cowered. Reyn screamed. The bodyguard leapt—

Right past them. Tagaret whirled around. A man was charging at them, swinging a brass chair. Tagaret scrambled back but met a wall of people. The bodyguard got one hand to the chair, which swung aside and struck Reyn in the head. Reyn's knees buckled.

"Reyn!" Tagaret shouted. He grasped for him, got a coat sleeve and hauled upward, got one hand under his arm. Reyn's head lolled sideways, and he almost lost his grip. He grabbed again, stumbled—

A crash of glass.

Tagaret looked up. Their attacker was gone, and the bodyguard had just thrust the brass chair through one of the ballroom windows. Before Tagaret's eyes, he pulled it back again—glass rained and shattered on stone—then hurled the whole thing through. He walked over to them, took Reyn's unconscious body easily over one black-silk shoulder, curved his other arm around the girl, and headed out, kicking out broken glass. Reyn's blond head was the last thing to disappear.

He mustn't lose them—

Tagaret ran through the bottleneck crush and popped out into the still air of the night gardens. The panicked crowd dissipated fast: a rush of feet moving outward toward the west wing of the Eminence's Residence, the grounds, and the noble districts beyond. Strong shouts came from farther away in the darkness, and here and there, guards of the Eminence's Cohort appeared, cutting against the flow of fleeing nobles and servants.

"Reyn!" Tagaret shouted, searching the deep shadows. "Can you hear me? Where are you? Gowan! Fernar!" What would he give for daylights right now—for someone to turn on the atmospheric lamps on the cavern roof, just for a minute when they were so sorely needed?

"Young sir," called a voice.

There—shapes in the dim garden, huddled by a bank of flowering shrubs—the Imbati and the girl standing, Reyn slumped on the ground.

"Reyn!"

He fell to his knees at his friend's side. He'd failed them; if he'd just kept them together, this wouldn't have happened . . . "Reyn, speak to me. Are you all right?"

Reyn curled forward, head in his hands.

"That Imbati saved your life. Oh, Imbati, you—" He looked up, but the girl and her bodyguard had vanished into the dark. He couldn't even thank him. "Reyn, I'm so sorry. How bad is it?"

"Owwww."

"Gods, your head, let me see it." Tagaret pressed his fingers through Reyn's hair, searching for lumps, for blood. What if he had to get him to the medical center? He was no bodyguard—how could he lift him? And even if he managed to haul him across the gardens, how many people would already be clamoring for treatment?

"Tagaret, I'm all right," Reyn said. "Aah—"

"No, you're hurt—"

"Sure I'm hurt, but I'll be all right." Reyn's hands grabbed tightly to his wrists. "I'll be fine, Tagaret, I promise."

"May Heile grant you her healing mercies."

The hum of a guard's weapon, and a crash of glass echoed off the cavern roof. More panicked people ran past, killing his momentary relief. So many people still caught in there . . .

"Did you see Fernar or Gowan?" he asked. "Reyn, tell me they're not still in there. Did you see them?"

Reyn's voice was small, cold. "No . . ."

"I have to help them." Tagaret waved down a guard as she ran toward the ballroom windows.

The guard hesitated. "Sir?"

"I need you to find Gowan of the Ninth Family, and Fernar of the Eleventh. Their safety is important to me."

"Yes, sir. If you will describe them, sir."

"Sixteen years old. Gowan has long sandy hair, a round face, and a red jacket; Fernar has short black hair, broad shoulders, and an amber suit with a lace collar. Promise me you'll find them."

"I'll do my best, sir."

"And get them home safely."

"Yes, sir." She saluted with a chop of her right hand to her left shoulder, and ran on.

Now, he should get Reyn home. If he could get him on his feet.

"Reyn, can you get up?"

Reyn didn't answer. Tagaret knelt beside him, felt for his head, and lifted it. The light from the ballroom was at the wrong angle, but a faint light from the opposite direction moved over Reyn's features. A tiny floating spark—one of the wysps that drifted here and there throughout the city-caverns—had come near. Good luck at last. Reyn gazed up at him, looking quite bewildered; the chair must have hit him hard.

"Can you get up? Reyn, please." His voice broke. What if Reyn's injury was more serious than he thought?

Reyn blinked. "I'll try."

Reyn's legs were so unsteady, Tagaret half-carried him through the gardens into the west wing of the Residence. In the spiral stairway, he stabilized them with his shoulder against the curving stone, struggling step after step until he got Reyn all the way up to the third-floor hall. When Reyn's Imbati caretaker opened the door of their suite, she immediately took charge.

"Grobal Tagaret, sir," she said, taking Reyn from him, "thank you for your help. I'm aware of the Kinders scare and will be taking preventative measures. If you will, please go straight home and bathe."

Instantly, every particle of dust on his skin felt infectious. Tagaret sprinted downstairs to his suite, slapped his palm against the lock-pad and rushed in.

"Young Master Tagaret, thank heavens you've come home."

That wasn't their irritable caretaker, Das—it was the First House-man, Imbati Serjer. Tagaret had never been so relieved to see him. Serjer was the most constant of their Imbati, distant yet fond, almost like a much older brother. Anxiety made wrinkles in his crescent-cross Household tattoo.

"What's wrong, Serjer?" Tagaret asked. "Is it the fever?"

Serjer leaned his head to one side, an understated but chilling Imbati gesture of discomfort. "Sir, Gowan of the Ninth Family has sent word that he and Fernar of the Eleventh Family are safe. Unfortunately, I must inform you—Imbati Das just resigned from the House-hold. I'm terribly sorry."

Varin's teeth.

His brother had done it again.

None of the caretakers ever stayed. Nekantor drove them away, one after another, with his particular habits, his constant insults, and his flagrant disrespect for the Imbati customs of personal space. And if he ever got to Serjer—not Serjer . . . Tagaret took a deep breath. "Serjer, I apologize for any offense my brother may have given to your person this evening."

"Not to worry for me, young Master, I am unscathed."

"Oh, thank heavens. Please, consider yourself off-duty unless there's some emergency."

"Thank you, sir."

Tagaret strode across the sitting room but checked cautiously through the double doors before entering the private drawing room. His brother was nowhere to be seen. When he reached the door to his rooms, he found the lock broken—Nekantor again, gnash him! But there was still the lock on the door of his private bathroom. Tagaret shut himself in, filled the marble tub, and scrubbed his body with a vengeance.

What if Kinders fever really had been in the air? They said the first symptom was fatigue, then dizziness, then the fever that could blind and deafen even when it didn't kill, and the hives that could stop you breathing, drop you dead on a stage in front of hundreds of people—mercy, how long would it take to know you had it? Everyone said people with stronger blood could recover, but how strong *was* his blood? How strong *could* it be, when all twelve Great Families numbered how directly they were descended from the Great Grobal Fyn? Should he trespass into Father's office for the genealogy records, to see how many cousins he really had in the Pelismara Society? Would it make any difference?

There had to be *something* he could do—

There was a scraping sound. Tagaret dropped his hands into the water, fury rising as the handle of the locked door began to turn.

"*Nekantor!*" he bellowed. "Don't come in here!"

Nek came in anyway. "Or what? You'll call the trashers up the chute to kidnap and incinerate me?" He was dressed to perfection in a pale brown day suit and had a horrible eager light in his eyes. "Have you heard the good news? The Speaker of the Cabinet just died of Kinders fever. You know what that means, don't you?"

Panic in the ballroom, a girl in a green dress, an Imbati bodyguard, a crazed man with a chair, Reyn injured, death stalking him in the bathtub—! Tagaret clenched his teeth. "I already know what it means." Nek might be two years younger, but he schemed like a forty-year-old politician.

"It means everything will change." Nekantor began pacing a tight pattern on the bathroom floor, every second black tile from the tub to the door and back. "I've worked it all out. By tomorrow the Heir will have appointed Father to the Speakership; by tomorrow evening he'll receive the radiogram; he'll be back here in Pelismara within the week. We won't need Imbati Das anymore, so I fired him."

An indignant protest died in Tagaret's throat. Nek didn't have that kind of authority—but he'd driven Das to resign, so the result was the same. And that wasn't the worst of it. Father coming home? Father, with his cruelty and his devastating surprises . . . the thought chilled him despite the hot water.

"You're insane," he snapped. "Get out of here."

"We won't be the sons of the Alixi of Selimna anymore, we'll be the sons of the Speaker of the Cabinet. The First Family will advance to an unrivaled position. And then the Eminence will take fever and die, and there will be an Heir Selection, and you know what that means . . ."

Only Nek could sound so delighted when predicting death. Maybe this would shut him up; he grabbed a towel from the rack and tossed it to the floor, hiding the next black tile.

Nekantor jerked to a stop, staring at the spot. "Take it off."

"Get out of my rooms, Nekantor."

Nek's jaw tightened, and he clenched his fists. "Take—it—off."

Tagaret swallowed, but he couldn't afford to back down, not here on his own territory. "Get out."

Nekantor gave a feral snarl, snatched up the towel, and threw it in his face. Didn't run out, though—first he stepped on the black tile, then wheeled and stormed out yelling, "Serjer! Serjer! Idiot Imbati, where are you?"

Gods, not Serjer . . . Tagaret held his breath, but let it out again when the First Houseman gave no answer. Who knew how Serjer had stayed faithful all this time? His steadfastness was more precious than ever. Thank all mercies he'd excused him for the night.

Tagaret climbed out of the bath, wrapped himself in a towel, and dragged his desk chair over to blockade the bedroom door. That felt like action. It was something, anyway—a start. Tomorrow he could ask Serjer for a better lock. And figure out another way to hear *The Catacomb*.

It wasn't enough, though, when *everything* was wrong. The only people with the power to effect change were politicians, but wading into politics would mean having to use distasteful skills that Father had drilled into both of them since birth. The ones Nekantor loved, and had clung to after Father left. Tagaret's mind shied from the idea.

On the other hand, if Nek was right, something important really *had* changed. Tagaret slid open the drawer at the bottom of his wardrobe, full to rustling with handwritten letters. There was a photograph here somewhere—there. Mother wearing her sad smile, sitting straight as a queen with her hair flowing down like a red-gold river, and white-haired Imbati Eyli standing guard behind her shoulder.

After five years away in Selimna, Mother would finally be coming home.

CHAPTER TWO

Tested

The Speaker's death last night, like the tumble of a stone from the roof of some forsaken cavern, had the entire Imbati Service Academy holding its breath, listening for worse.

Not the best conditions for an employment interview.

Imbati Aloran sat in his dormitory bunk and tried to focus on the papers he'd prepared, but intermittent whispering in the main aisle wrecked his concentration. Clumps of students had gathered, murmuring about Kinders fever. Some were fully dressed in maroon Academy uniforms; others wore nightgowns; a few, diverted from the showers, were wrapped only in bath towels. Most of the talk centered on how lucky they were to have been born outside the inbred confines of the nobility.

This was a disaster indeed, if it could make self-respecting servants gossip like nobles.

Aloran pushed his hair behind his ears and tried again to focus, but a voice spoke, tuned to private pitch.

"Aloran, may I join you?"

Kiit, he would happily admit. He nodded.

She ducked gracefully under the top bunk beside him. Ready for class, with her long braids still damp. "Forgive me if I'm interrupting," she said. "I thought perhaps you looked—nervous."

Aloran shrugged. "I have my first interview today."

Kiit smiled. "I *knew* one of them would ask you in! You'll do wonderfully." Her eyes grew cautious. "Were you aware that you're still face-naked?"

Aloran hissed in a breath. *Now* he remembered his interrupted routine. To appear at an interview unmarked would be to fail before he began. He went to the mirror he shared with his bunkmate and painted the small black circle between his eyebrows. Then he combed his dark hair into its ponytail which, thanks to Kiit's precise trimming, fell just outside his collar. He shut both makeup brush and comb back into his box of implements.

"Much better," Kiit said, when he turned around. Her eyes moved over him enticingly. "You sure look different in black."

Aloran flushed. The black silk suit was new, and it *felt* different. Freer, smoother, more professional. Older, too, as though he deserved a real manservant's lily crest Mark, not just a circle of paint. Scary how much he liked it.

"May I ask you a question?" Kiit said.

"Not now, please. I should study."

Kiit's brown eyes lit, and her mouth curved—that look of mischievous intimacy that meant she'd ask him even without permission. "Have you had any new employment inquiries? Which one is this?"

"That was two questions, sweet."

"I love you."

He could only smile when she said that. "I love you, too. Lady Tamelera of the First Family; and no."

"First Family?" Kiit exclaimed. "What an opportunity! You'd have your entire Academy debt paid off in less than a year. You'd—" She frowned. "Lady Tamelera. She's the Lady Alixi. You'd have to move to *Selimna?*" Abruptly, she appeared to realize she'd asked another question, blushed, and said, "I hear it's beautiful there. The daylights are gold. Though the city-caverns are colder."

Aloran looked down and left: the gaze-gesture code for apology. "I probably won't get the position," he said. But it would be amazing if he did. Four current family members; three castemates in the Selimnar Household, and four here in Pelismara. A very generous salary offer and incredible prestige. . . Unfortunately, the First Family had included no portrait of Lady Tamelera, which made it difficult to imagine himself in her service. "More important than the money," he said, "I want to find the right person."

"*Imbati, love where you serve,*" Kiit quoted. "You're such an idealist—if a nervous one."

"I'd be less nervous if everybody weren't chatting."

He wasn't the only one to object. A lilting provincial accent had risen above the general murmurs—the voice of Min, a younger student who'd traveled from the Safe Harbor sand caverns to enter the Gentleman's training at the Academy.

"Come, fellows, talk won't tame the waves," Min said. "It's consequences we must think of. Political alliances'll shift now. And, should the fever spread, there may be fewer service positions."

Aloran frowned. Min had always seemed earnest and rather affectionate. Coldness wasn't like him.

"Gentleman's servant," Kiit remarked.

He nodded. That was certainly the Gentleman's training talking. Gentlemen's servants were experts in politics but knew far less about health—a serious problem in the current situation. He glanced at Kiit, set his papers aside, and went over to the group.

"Allow me to explain something," he said.

Maybe it was the black suit, but all eyes turned to him. Best would be to teach them the lesson of ten, required memorization for members of the Lady's training like him and Kiit.

"Say this year brings a new variant of Kinders, inoculants fail to anticipate it, and ten Imbati contract the fever," he said. "Of those, only one will face the most severe symptoms—anaphylaxis, sensory loss, or death. Two will miss one week of work or instruction and require a doctor's care for complications. Six will not need a doctor, and one will be entirely asymptomatic."

"You're generous with information," said one of the twelve-year-olds.

"That's not all of it." The second half always chilled him to the core. He took a deep breath. "If the one Imbati with no symptoms comes into physical contact with any Grobal, and ten of them subsequently contract the fever, all will die without a doctor's care. Seven will experience rapid-onset anaphylaxis and require immediate intervention to prevent death. Even if these survive, four will die of fever, and one will survive with sensory loss." He looked at each member of the chastened group. "You might be the one to unleash death on those whom we are sworn to protect. That shame would be on the Academy forever."

Min gaze-gestured gratitude. "May I ask you a question, Aloran?"

"Yes."

"Wouldn't past inoculants still give them some protection?"

"The Grobal inoculation rate is too low, in part because they have an abnormally high allergy rate," he said. "*We* are their wall of safety, and therefore we must be vigilant. I'm even potentially a risk to the Lady who will interview me today."

That got to the core of it. No wonder he was nervous. Once the group dispersed, Aloran returned to his bunk, counting breaths to steady himself. He must under no circumstances touch the Lady . . .

"You were right to tell them," said Kiit.

She'd been right, too. "Kiit," he said, "I can't believe Lady Tamelera would agree to see me while the source of the fever remains unidentified."

Kiit nodded sympathy. She offered her hand palm-upward, inviting him to touch.

That sped his heart for a different reason. "Afterward," he promised. "I'll come and find you."

Imbati Ziara the Health Master, who advised him, had requested that he present himself at her office before his interview, so Aloran left the dormitory four minutes early. Centuries of foot traffic had worn concave paths into the limestone here; he walked past three ceramic catchpools which gathered water from drip-chains heavy with calcite, their origin points invisible on the cavern roof. Aloran crossed to the main Academy building and entered between columns whose capitals were carved with golden flames. Once inside the arched hallway, he went to the third bronze door and knocked.

A castemate opened the door. It wasn't Master Ziara. This new woman was a full head shorter, with white hair and a faded lily crest tattoo that put her at about seventy. Nothing was faded about her expression, however, which suggested the strength of an antique weapon: well-oiled, experienced, and sharp.

"Master Ziara has been called away to duty," she said. "I am Tamelera's Eyli, of the Household of the First Family."

Lady Tamelera's *body servant?* Sirin help him, was the Lady herself in the Health Master's office? He swallowed a gasp and bowed. "Tamelera's Eyli, sir," he said respectfully. "I am Aloran, at your service."

"My Lady has not accompanied me today," the senior servant said. "I am to interview you in the Hands classroom."

"Yes, sir."

Thank the gods—there could be no danger of accidental infection. But how strange that the family would ask a servant to interview her own replacement . . .

Tamelera's Eyli walked ahead of him, quickly, with an unusually delicate gait. She pushed through the bronze door of the Hands classroom and faced him at the center of the mats, turning her back to the long metal shelves of bowls, balls, papers, and other practice instruments.

"All right, young one," she said. "What's wrong with me?"

That was *anger*. His heart lurched into his throat. Had he done something wrong? He fell into a deep bow. "I don't mean to offend you, sir."

"It would be easier if I could afford manners, Aloran," Eyli said. "This is a matter of great importance to my Mistress, and since she will be unable to evaluate you herself, I must be harsh. I will ask questions and give orders without redress."

"I am yours, sir."

"My question, Aloran. Evaluate me."

Aloran took a deep breath. He walked around her, studying her stance, her face and breath, the subtle contours of muscle and bone against her black silk garments. "You have at least one compressed vertebra in your upper back," he said. "Perhaps an old injury; it does not hamper you significantly. You have severe arthritis in your knees, but your hands are unaffected. You have no obvious vision or hearing problems, but your balance is slightly impaired."

"Then it would be getting time I retired," she muttered. "Give me evidence for your assessments."

He gulped. "Your posture, sir. And the way you walked as we came here."

Eyli attacked with another question. "Why do you want to take my position with Lady Tamelera?"

So she *was* being forced out. Despite her aggression, though, her voice softened when she said her Lady's name. That was more intriguing than anything he'd seen in his papers.

"I wish to work for someone I can serve faithfully," Aloran answered. "Someone who understands the bond that can grow between a mistress and her servant. I won't presume to ask what it is about your Lady that moves you, but if she were gracious as well as noble, then I would vow service to her without reservation."

Eyli stared at him wordlessly. Would she send him away?

Without warning, she jabbed a hand at his stomach.

Plis' bones! Aloran managed to deflect it, but then she tried to hook him with a foot, and suddenly they were fighting. Or, *she* was fighting. He was mostly defending—Eyli was certainly capable of hurting him, but he didn't dare strike back. She'd adapted the moves cleverly to compensate for her knees. Dodge, leap, deflect, deflect . . . Eyli's gaze left him for a second, as if she'd glimpsed someone at the door. He chose not to attack her for it.

Silk swished behind him.

Aloran whirled and met Master Ziara's foot coming high; he got one hand to it and spun away. He dodged Eyli's next jab, and deflected a quick pair of blows that Master Ziara attempted to land on his neck and shoulder. Panting, he kept his feet and arms moving while they both assaulted him. What did they want him to do? Surrender? Surely not—but would they really prefer him to attack? Mind whirling, he began to retreat across the mats.

Master Ziara dropped her fighting stance and reached one hand toward Eyli. A signal. The senior servant drew herself up as stiffly as an iron bar and fell sideways.

Gods. . . !

He lunged forward. Found contact and pulled Eyli in, twisting so he hit the floor first. She landed full on top of him.

No, what had he done? She wasn't his mistress, she was a *castemate*. Such an offense to her person!

"Please forgive me, sir," he panted, setting her on her feet and retreating fast. He began a breathing exercise to calm himself from the exertion; it didn't help with the embarrassment.

"No broken bones," Eyli remarked. "Ziara, Aloran gave only scant evidence for his physical assessment."

Master Ziara inclined her head. "Pardon me, sir, if I guess that his assessment was nonetheless correct."

Eyli let slip a brief gaze-gesture of assent. "You have further business?"

"New public information," said Master Ziara. "Two decrees from His Eminence Indal, issued five minutes ago; disseminate to all castemates."

"Proceed."

Master Ziara took reciting stance, holding one hand flat at the small of her back, and turning her eyes upward.

Aloran thought quickly. This was a lucky interruption. If he'd assessed Eyli's health correctly, then maybe he was also right about her love for her Mistress. *Something* was hidden behind Eyli's aggression and unwillingness to speak. Could she be under oath of silence? But if she were, how could he learn more about Lady Tamelera?

"First," Master Ziara intoned, "every person present at the concert panic must be subject to health checks and interviews. Second, because the orchestra was present, the Kartunnen caste has become suspect as the fever source, and therefore no Grobal shall have contact with any Kartunnen until the source of the Kinders fever has been identified." She dropped her stance. "Unfortunately, that includes doctors."

Aloran managed not to stare. Health checks, but no contact with *doctors?* That took the Grobal ignorance and fear of science to an entirely new level.

"And," Master Ziara added, "from the Academy Headmaster, two items. First, we have a team working to determine which variant of the fever claimed Orn's life; second, we request volunteers of the Lady's training to conduct health checks on the concert attendees. Answers to be delivered to the Headmaster's office at your earliest convenience."

Eyli frowned. "Ziara, my young Master Tagaret will have been there, but I'm not permitted to contact him until tonight. If you would be so kind?"

"I'll take care of it."

"Thank you."

Aloran sent his own gaze-gesture of gratitude to Master Ziara as she left the room. Thanks to her, Eyli had just suggested a perfect way to learn more. "Sir," he said. "May I make a request?"

The senior servant returned her attention to him. "Yes?"

"With your permission, may I observe Lady Tamelera's sons?"

Eyli studied him for a long moment. "Good idea," she said. "Grobal Tagaret and Nekantor are currently in role-play session at the Grobal School. Observe them; and when you have satisfied yourself, report back to me."

Maybe this hadn't been the best idea. Role-play was one trial he'd thought he'd finally left behind. The path toward the Grobal School brought a familiar dread, and once the wardens had let him out through the Academy's front gate, Aloran was grateful for the excuse to run.

At this hour, the Plaza of Varin bustled with a whirl of tourists, mostly Lowers unaware of the fever scare. Merchants wore necklaces of silver and chrysolite; miners wore heavy black belts and stained clothes; artisans had painted lips and wore gray coats. Here and there a few Highers of the Arissen officer caste stood out in rust-red uniforms. In comparison, the Imbati bureaucrats who crossed between the columns of the Courts on the plaza's east side or the Old Forum in the south, or who whispered past the massive steel cylinder of the Alixi's Elevator at the southeast corner, provided a welcome touch of sanity.

On the north side, at the Residence gate, a pair of Arissen in the orange uniforms of the Eminence's Cohort passed Aloran in. He crossed the rock gardens and circled behind the Residence's west wing to the classical stone building that housed the Grobal School.

No more running.

He entered through the glass doors. It was unsettling to pass by the familiar door of the ladies' play hall and approach the gentlemen's hall instead—ladies he knew firsthand, boys only by horrifying report. May the Twins stand by him.

He slipped inside. This room was the mirror image of its neighbor: high smooth stone vaults, walls decorated with paintings and embroidered hangings, a floor carpeted in deep Grobal green. But where young ladies gathered at brass tables near the walls, giggling over notes or pets and laying verbal traps for any Imbati who dared approach, the boys roved the room in gangs. These gangs surrounded Academy students or sent individual boys out to accost Imbati and bring them back.

Aloran struggled against an urge to retreat. A voice spoke beside him, and he nearly jumped.

"Aloran? May I help you?"

It was Min, looking alarmed to see him.

Aloran bowed. "Employment interview," he said. "I've been asked to observe the sons of a prospective Mistress, Grobal Tagaret and Nekantor of the First Family."

Min gaze-gestured an offer of information. "Fair trade, for earlier," he said. "Gang behavior predicts political success. Grobal Tagaret captains a mixed-family gang of four. He's a leader but not a crowd-dominator, and reaches across boundaries. Grobal Nekantor plays a dangerous first mate to the crowd-dominator of his gang, but leads the group in intellect. Both promise to float servants high, as expected with their parentage."

"Thank you," Aloran said.

A round-faced boy started coming toward them, carrying a blue-feathered kanguan on his shoulder.

"You'll excuse me," said Min. "Find Grobal Tagaret at the back, sitting under the Great Grobal Fyn." With a quick two steps away, he intercepted the boy with the kanguan. When he spoke again, all emotion had vanished from his voice. "Min, at your service, sir."

"Come, Imbati," said the Grobal boy. "You'll serve us."

Aloran could only watch, while an ache grew in the back of his throat. The boy's gang surrounded Min, poking him from all directions, ordering him to the floor and back up again, then forcing him to hop over a tripping foot. Min's professionalism was impressive—not only had he selflessly put himself at risk to redirect the boys' attention, but he stayed calm through the entire thing.

Aloran wasn't about to waste good information. He moved cautiously toward the back wall. There, the embroidered image of a young, prominent-nosed Grobal Fyn—the father of modern Varin—towered over his male descendants. Directly below the wall hanging, four boys lounged at a brass table, only one of them actually in a chair: a slim, long-boned boy with a classic Grobal nose and hair the reddish-tan color of sandstone. That had to be Tagaret. His posture was earnest, and a smile played on his lips. Perhaps his mother was like him . . .

Aloran dared a few steps closer.

"I found out there's going to be another concert," Grobal Tagaret said. "Tonight. On the fourth level, concert hall at Tesrel Circumference and Yinnari Radius."

"You're proposing we go to a Lower's venue?" asked a boy with long hair, leaning against the table.

A dark-haired boy crossed his arms. "With the fever out there?"

"The fever's not *out there*," Grobal Tagaret said. "Speaker Orn never went to a Melumalai concert hall."

"Then why should we?" the long-haired boy asked.

"Just to get away with it?" suggested the dark-haired boy. "For the reputation?"

"But nobody of any importance will be there."

Grobal Tagaret's cheeks flushed. "It's for the music, Gowan. And I can think of one person who might go."

A blond boy standing behind Tagaret laid one hand on his shoulder. "Copper and emeralds? Surely her parents would never allow her to defy the Kartunnen ban."

"I have to see her again, Reyn. If there's any chance at all—"

The dark-haired boy laughed. "Make sure to leave a few ladies for the rest of us."

Grobal Tagaret snorted.

"Hey," said Grobal Reyn suddenly. "Look at that Imbati watching us."

Discovered. Aloran's heart pounded, but he swallowed all expression off his face and humbled his head. Now he'd learn whether these boys were like the others.

Grobal Tagaret of the First Family stood up from his chair and approached. He was surprisingly tall—six feet at sixteen, far taller than any of the other three—but he wore it without apparent self-consciousness. "Imbati," he said, "you must be a visitor. What's your name?"

"Aloran, sir."

"I find it interesting, Aloran, that you come wearing black and don't offer yourself to our service."

Aloran gulped. "My apologies, sir."

"Wait, I know him," said Grobal Reyn, walking toward them.

"My sister has seen an Imbati Aloran. You should hear her go on: 'Oh, his muscles! He could pick me up, just like a doll!'"

Grobal Tagaret flicked a glance at him. "That's interesting. Thanks, Reyn." He squeezed his friend's shoulder, and Grobal Reyn leaned into his hand. Perhaps more than friendship was at stake between those two. "Sometimes I wish *I* could be Lady's," Grobal Tagaret said. "At least I could get close to the ladies."

The other boys laughed.

Aloran hid a smile in his heart. Self-deprecating humor, and generous indulgence of a stranger Imbati's attention—both very hopeful hints of his mother's temperament. "Grobal Tagaret, sir," he said, "if you will permit me to ask?"

"Yes?"

"Is your brother with you?"

The Grobal boy grimaced. "Aloran, Nekantor is never *with* me."

Oh, dear . . . Aloran bowed low. "I have offended, sir. I beg your forgiveness."

But Grobal Tagaret didn't chastise him. "Aloran, you don't want to know Nekantor," he said. "Most people don't want to know him, but Imbati particularly. He's over near the door, if you're bent on finding him. Dark jacket, looks a lot like me. In Benél's crowd—but don't get too close."

"Thank you, sir."

"You are dismissed."

Aloran took two steps backward before straightening from his bow. That had gone so well! He headed back toward the entry door with more confidence, weaving between the gangs. Despite the warning, he couldn't leave until he'd found Grobal Nekantor. Family resemblance might show in both sons.

There.

The boy stood in a gang of almost ten who had waylaid Anin, one of his bunk neighbors. Grobal Nekantor's physical resemblance to Tagaret was striking: a few inches taller, and he and his brother could have passed for twins. But there the resemblance ended. Even from afar, this boy felt—wrong. The other members of his gang were reckless and excited, but even standing still, Nekantor possessed more frantic intensity than any of them. An anxiety disorder certainly; maybe also something more. His eyes moved too fast, sharp and dangerous. 'Don't get too close' seemed like very good advice.

Anin, pale-faced, tried to maintain composure inside the predator circle while Grobal Nekantor whispered into the leader's ear. The leader pulled a kuarjos piece from his pocket and threw it at her. She tried to catch it, missed, and Nekantor slapped her across the face.

Aloran gasped.

The gang laughed as Anin tried to swallow her pain—and it got worse. The dangerous eyes leapt over to him. Though they were the same brown as Grobal Tagaret's eyes, they still felt black. Aloran froze under them.

Grobal Nekantor left his group and stalked up, scowling. "You're different, Imbati," he said. "I don't know your name."

Aloran tried to speak calmly through a clamped throat. "I am Aloran, sir."

"Come with me, Aloran. You'll serve us."

Chills ran down his back, but he bowed. "I'm terribly sorry, sir. I am unable to serve you. I am of the Lady's training, and I'm here doing research."

"Research—ha! You're not doing research. You're just unwilling."

There was no appropriate reply.

Grobal Nekantor snorted. "Come watch Anin. Watch how a real servant behaves, and then you'll have your chance."

Mai help him, he couldn't let Anin suffer it again. He blurted, "I can offer to braid your hair, sir."

That gave the boy pause, but only for a second. "My hair?" he demanded. "My hair—Benél!"

That hadn't been the best idea. The gang diffused and recoalesced around him. At least Anin was able to slip away.

The lead boy's eyes were blue, and blunt as fists. "What, Nek?"

"This Imbati said he could braid my hair. How dare he try to play a game with me! How dare he speak to me as if I were a girl!"

"Are you trying to play a game with your superiors?" the leader demanded. "Speak, Imbati."

Aloran bowed again, as humbly as he could. "Your pardon, sir. I am of the Lady's training. I am here for research, but I am unable to meet a gentleman's needs."

Grobal Nekantor narrowed his eyes.

The leader grabbed Nekantor by the back of the neck and gave him a little shake. "Come on, Nek, it's a waste of our time if he's for ladies anyway. He probably has a girl's brains." The other boys laughed, and the gang's attention shifted. Aloran moved away fast, but he could still feel Grobal Nekantor's gaze burning his back as he left the hall.

Once out of the School, he ran through the grounds and back to the Plaza of Varin. The crowds had diminished, opening a gap at the center of the plaza where the glowing white trunk of a shinca tree emerged rootless from the rock and warmed the air all around. Its steady invulnerability soothed his panic. He stared up at the shinca's bright column, which vanished among stalactites and atmospheric lamps on its way to the surface five levels above.

How could two brothers be so different? What if the Lady was like Nekantor instead? Why had Eyli allowed him to observe these boys if she knew it would just confuse him?

Something was clearly wrong in this house. Only the Lady should have mattered, but she was out of reach, unable to show him whether she was kind or merciless. Were money and prestige reasons enough to pursue this?

But he had to. If word got back to the family that he'd abandoned the interview, their bad word could ruin him.

Aloran forced himself into a breath pattern. Think—the real problem here was lack of information. Eyli divulged so little; chances were good she was under oath of silence. Could she have granted his unusual request purposely, to circumvent her oath? If he appealed to her directly, perhaps she might do it again.

He returned to the Academy, steeling himself for the risk. He entered the Hands classroom with deliberate force, startling Eyli up from the Hands Master's chair. "Eyli, sir, may I ask you a question?"

She'd opened her mouth to greet him, but now she hesitated. "What sort of question?"

Aloran forced himself to say it. "Are you under oath of silence regarding me?"

Eyli stared up with piercing eyes. "Answer me first. What did you learn at the Grobal School?"

"That this branch of the First Family is full of contradictions," he said. "That Lady Tamelera is kind, and that she is angry. That she is brave, and that she is anxious. That she loves others, and that she drives others away."

"Aloran, sit down."

He obeyed and discovered that Eyli was sitting, too. She didn't take the Hands Master's chair, but sank down on the mats instead. Everything about her manner had changed.

"I *am* under oath," she said, in a voice full of pain. "But I will tell you what I can. The most important thing is this: our inquiry was not initiated by my Mistress, but by Master Garr, who has just been appointed Speaker of the Cabinet."

That was disturbing. "Her partner, sir?"

"Garr is callous. He knows nothing of my Lady's needs, but believes he cares for her well. He likes to surprise her. I do everything in my power to stop him, and yet I fail." Her voice quivered. "In the matter of my replacement, Master Garr coerced my silence, saying that if I broke the oath he demanded, he would not permit me to participate in selecting the best candidate. He made me return to Pelismara a day early, and lie to my beloved Mistress when she asked why I must leave her alone with him. Even convince her it was no trouble for me."

"But it *is* trouble for you," Aloran said. What emotion her Mistress brought forth in her—it was mortifying, yet strangely stirring. This woman had known the perfect love of mistress and servant. In the face of that, who could remain untouched? "I wish I could know her as you do."

Eyli gaze-gestured apology. "She often speaks generously with me about her feelings, but I can't speak to how she will treat someone new. I advise care; she doesn't demand the oath of silence often, but she expects it as a rule."

"My heart is as deep as the heavens," Aloran said. "No word uttered in confidence will escape it."

Eyli nodded. "If I've been rude to you, it's because the two previous candidates were so precisely what the Master would have wanted.

I was trying to protect my Mistress from you, Aloran. But you've defeated me. You already know more about her than you think."

Aloran shook his head. "Sir, I'm sorry. I was merely guessing."

"As you were with my health assessment?"

"That was different, sir."

"I don't think so." She looked at him gravely. "In order to reach my Mistress, you will first have to pass review with Master Garr. Say anything you need to in order to satisfy him, but beware of his manservant, Sorn. Sorn is very much his master's man."

Aloran stared at her. Triumph and confusion whirled inside him. He'd *passed*. She was asking him to move onto the next step—and the job had just moved to Pelismara. But did he want it? If the sons were opposed to one another, and so were the parents? "Sir," he said. "I haven't decided . . ."

"Please," Eyli said. "When the Master contacts you, please consent to his review. I've loved my Mistress since she was born. I don't know how I could retire if I weren't sure she was getting the best. This much I can promise: if she accepts you, she will protect you."

CHAPTER THREE
Breaking Rules

The scariest part of Tagaret's health check had been his examiner: the Health Master of the Imbati Academy, built like a cave-cat, with whisper-gentle fingers and eyes like iron under her bodyguard's tattoo. The one time he'd looked directly into her face, he'd become certain she knew every detail of his evening's planned disobedience.

You couldn't ask someone like that to hurry up so you could get on with it. When at last Imbati Serjer escorted her out of his bedroom, Tagaret followed to the entry vestibule and stopped Serjer before he could disappear back behind his small door.

"Serjer? I'm going out to a concert, all right? I'm already late."

Serjer nodded. "Master Ziara has cleared you, young Master."

Was that all? Thank the gods for Serjer—by this point, Imbati Das would already have been issuing demands. "Thank you. It's . . . on the fourth level."

Serjer nodded. "Sir, if you are concerned for your safety, may I request the address?"

Tagaret took a step backward. "My safety, at a concert? You're not expecting another fever scare?"

"Pardon me, sir," said Serjer, "but there are no venues frequented by the Pelismara Society on the fourth level."

"Oh." This was about the Lowers, then. "Well, it *is* a concert hall run by Melumalai. But there will be Arissen, right? Guards or police?"

"Arissen would be unlikely to let merchants hire them, sir. It's possible a few might take interest in music."

"Would Imbati go?"

The crescent cross rose between Serjer's eyebrows. "Music lovers, perhaps, sir."

But no one marked to the family. "Kartunnen musicians are no danger." Tagaret shook his head. "Venorai laborers—no, they wouldn't go, would they?"

"I don't believe so, sir," Serjer replied. "If they did, they would keep to their own groups."

"The Melumalai who run this won't get paid if people aren't safe, will they? How dangerous are people who want to hear a symphony?"

Serjer bowed. "I'm sorry, sir. I didn't mean to worry you."

And there was still one caste left. "Akrabitti?" He frowned.

"I can't imagine they'd risk their safety just for music, sir."

"What? *Their* safety?"

Serjer leaned his head to one side. "Young Master, I believe you said you were late?"

Oh, no . . . Tagaret almost bolted right out, but stopped himself. "Bless you, Serjer. Please protect yourself while I'm gone."

Rather than wait for the Imbati of the Conveyor's Hall to lower his skimmer's control column for use by a seated driver, Tagaret hopped into the footwell as an Imbati driver might, punched buttons, and took off with a tight grip on the handlebars. He had a lot of scandal to court tonight before Father could stop him! After nightfall, the ramp to the fourth level was a bright spine of limestone rising out of the dark neighborhoods; he swerved onto it so fast that the skimmer's leading edge chipped rock before its repulsion plates could adjust position.

Not just late, but *very* late, gnash it—what if he missed *The Catacomb*?

At the top, he punched through the tunnel of reinforced rock that converted roof to floor and shot down Yinnari Radius. These neighborhoods felt more cramped than the fifth level, because buildings of only two stories nudged up against a cavern roof that bulged low overhead.

The intersection at Tesrel Circumference was a roundabout, in a spot where the cavern roof abruptly curved higher. The large concert hall stood at its center, built around a shinca tree. Cylindrical stone walls and a domed roof showed it to be a converted church of the Celestial Family; it advertised its current function with garish neon tubes in the shape of orchestral instruments. Tagaret parked beside a statue of Heile the Merciful playing the foot-drum and pipes. Not a single Arissen was to be seen. He ran in through automatic glass doors into the deserted foyer, then looked around in shock. Inside was worse than outside, all glass and mirrors and painted steel. The place reeked of the new money of the Melumalai merchant caste.

Tagaret approached the box office, where a young female Melumalai panicked at the sight of him and bolted from her seat. A moment later a merchant emerged from a side door—most likely the proprietor, since he had large golden chrysolites set into his silver castemark necklace.

"May the reign of His Eminence Indal extend a thousand years!" he exclaimed.

This man clearly didn't realize that nobles didn't need the formalized greetings Lowers used among themselves. "Ah, mm, Melumalai," Tagaret said. "I'll need to purchase a ticket—and I'm looking for three friends. Are there other Grobal here tonight?"

The Melumalai grinned. "There are six, including yourself, sir! No need to purchase. Your friends have taken care of it."

"Thank you." But *six*? He shivered to think of two pairs of eyes, possibly Family enemies who might report them for breaking rules. If Sirin's hand was kind, though, could those two be the girl and a companion? "Has *The Catacomb* played yet?"

"No, sir. It will play after intermission; if you would be so kind as to wait . . ."

"I'd never interrupt the music." Tagaret moved away, pushing past a velvet curtain into the curving corridor that wrapped around the central hall. Spirit globes still hung from the ceiling here, commemorating departed souls; they and the marble statues created an atmosphere of strange solemnity. A wysp drifted along the passage. It illuminated first a statue of the holy Lovers, Sirin the Luck-Bringer welcoming home Eyn the Wanderer; then the Twins, Trigis the Resolute embracing his despairing brother Bes the Ally amid the desolation of ice—

And then the figure of a Kartunnen, who stood by the side doors, listening.

Could it be? The same Kartunnen boy he'd seen talking with *her*? A thrill ran through him. "Kartunnen?"

The Kartunnen gasped. Just a boy, really, not much older than he was, but the fellow quivered as if torn between hiding behind the Twins and running for his life.

"I'm sorry," said Tagaret. "I didn't mean to scare you."

"Thank you, sir. You're terribly kind." The boy, whose lower lip was painted light green as if he were a member of the orchestra, spoke in an extremely precise and cultured voice. He had long reddish-blond hair pulled back, showing a shiny burn scar on his left cheekbone. Even his nose was intriguing—prominent enough to belong to one of Tagaret's own cousins.

Tagaret swallowed. He was breaking the ban. *Muckwalking*. And *she* had done exactly this! "The music," he said. "When I think of the complexity, the ineffable inspiration . . . I don't know how you do it. Is it the blessing of Heile on the Kartunnen? What's your secret?"

The boy blushed. "I—well, in fact, sir, I don't know why I can do it."

"Seriously?" It was like being served an empty plate. Tagaret opened his mouth to ask more, but the hall doors opened, and a strange crowd pushed them in different directions. Melumalai wore solid browns, greens, purples—at least ten unregulated colors topped with caste necklaces of silver and chrysolite. Kartunnen had painted lips and wore fanciful patterns underneath their variously styled gray coats. They all seemed at once colorful and drab. Tagaret couldn't place what it was they lacked until he returned to the modernized foyer and a cluster of Imbati parted before him. That was it: the shimmer as they moved. Tillik-spider silk evidently was expensive enough to sift Higher from Lower all on its own.

It had certainly sifted his friends. Reyn stood with Fernar and Gowan in a clear space amidst the crowd, the three of them glowing in suits of ruby, topaz, and sapphire, laughing amongst themselves. Tagaret joined them with relief.

"Hey," he said, thumping Reyn on the back. "Sorry I'm so late; the check kept me back."

"Ours went fine, obviously," Reyn said. "How was yours?"

"Well, they let him out," said Fernar. "Guess he's not going to die."

Tagaret shuddered. "Yes, you're stuck with me. Checked by the Health Master herself."

Gowan hummed in amusement. "Who did you expect? Imbati Aloran from today's play session?"

"Ha, ha, Gowan. Have you seen anyone else here tonight?"

"Lowers," Fernar grunted. "This is some serious muckwalking. We'll be lucky if we get any reputation at all."

Reyn looked up at Tagaret and winked. "It's not all bad, though. They have a bar."

The bar stood opposite the box office, a gaudy construction of mirrors and brass, tended by Melumalai. Tagaret said, "You know, Fernar, they'd probably sell you anything you asked for."

Fernar broke into a grin.

Tagaret led them toward the bar, scanning around him as he walked. Lowers, indeed—Father would have a fit if he could see him now!

Suddenly a vision emerged from the hall: luminous as a goddess, her hair braided into a high crown that exposed her perfect neck, her gown shimmering in diaphanous green. He hissed in a breath. "Copper and emeralds!"

The others glanced at each other.

"Are you sure about this?" Gowan asked. "Sixth Family?"

Reyn shrugged. "Gowan, it's not like he'll actually *get* anywhere with her. He'd end up on the floor first."

Don't think about that. Tagaret set his teeth. "Reyn, can I get you a drink?"

"Sure."

Fernar laughed. "Ooh, Tagaret wants a girl! Go, Tagaret."

Fernar could laugh all he wanted, but this was serious. They were way out of bounds right now—this was a real chance to get close. And with Father coming home tonight? He'd be a fool not to take it.

Of course, he had to go to the bar first. Order something innocuous; if she came any closer, she mustn't see him drinking anything with a suggestive name. Lowers cleared the area as he approached. He placed his expense marker on the counter before a nervous-looking Melumalai.

"Vitett Ice, no liquor—uh, two of them, please."

"Yes, sir."

He tried to keep his eyes on the Lady, but he couldn't help noticing that the Melumalai bartender didn't mix a Vitett Ice anything like members of the Household did. He jittered and danced—his style was so distracting that by the time the Melumalai returned his marker and handed him the drinks, she was gone.

Gone! He scanned the crowd, holding the chill stems tightly. Could she have left? Or gone back in? Oh, by Sirin and Eyn, *how could he have taken his eyes off her?*

"I beg your pardon, sir," said a deep, smooth, Imbati-sounding voice behind him.

He turned. She was *here*, her eyes half-veiled by long demure lashes but still a perfect match to her dress, a single lock of copper hair trailing down in front of her ear, her hand resting delicately atop her escort's closed fist. Fernar liked to say that beauty from afar meant flaws close up, but he was *so* wrong. She was a miracle, the very Maiden Eyn descended from heaven.

Tagaret wrenched his eyes off her, forced them onto the escort who had addressed him, and managed to say, "Good evening, Imbati."

"If you will permit me to introduce myself," the escort suggested.

"Please do." His heart raced. Gods, would he really learn her name?

"I am Della's Yoral, of the Household of the Sixth Family."

Della. He couldn't help but glance, and found her looking up at him with intense, curious eyes, white teeth gently biting at her lower lip. Instantly, his heart was thumping hard enough to leap right out of his mouth. He struggled to look at her Yoral.

"A pleasure, Yoral," he said. "My name is Tagaret, of the First Family."

"The pleasure is mine, sir."

His turn; but what more could he say? "Thank you for saving my friend," he blurted, then flushed. Far too personal in a place like this.

Yoral inclined his head, and smoothly changed the subject. "It's a wonderful concert, isn't it, sir?"

"Oh—oh, yes."

"Kartunnen Tromaldin has really brought the Pelismar Symphony to a new level, I believe."

Now *that*, he could agree with. "The shiazin section seems much more spirited under his direction."

"And in only two years at the baton."

Della nodded her own agreement, and for a split second it was as if he'd spoken to *her*. Words bubbled out of him. "I can't wait to hear Kartunnen Ryanin's *The Catacomb*—" He choked off the rest, but it rang in his mind. *Can you, Della?*

"Certainly, sir," the Imbati said. "Worth going out of your way for."

Tagaret tensed—but perhaps the Imbati meant no criticism, since he'd brought his Lady well out of her way, too. He sneaked a glance at Della and couldn't tear himself away. He had to stop—but her smile, and oh, her eyes—

Control yourself, or you'll end the night flattened by an Imbati.

Yoral said, "If the tone has sounded, perhaps we should return to our seats."

He hadn't even heard it, and now she'd be taken away. Gods help him. "P-perhaps your Mistress would like a drink," Tagaret stammered, "since I've kept her from getting her own. Vitett Ice—no alcohol, of course." He offered up the crystal flute delicately, since any inadvertent touch could only upset the Imbati and ruin the whole thing.

Yoral considered, with a glance to his Lady. "Thank you very much, sir." He solemnly transferred the drink to Della. "Excuse us, please."

"Certainly, Yoral."

Tagaret rejoined the others, trembling. As they pushed through the main hall doors, Fernar jogged his elbow. "So, what happened?"

"Her name is Della."

Fernar spluttered. "Her escort *spoke* to you? Lucky!"

"I still can't believe it."

Gowan looked jealous but shrugged. "I'm not surprised," he said. "You watch; more people will want your attention now that your father's been announced as the next Speaker."

"I've been expecting it," Tagaret admitted. But he would stay in this strange world as long as he could.

The inside hall was broad, lit by recessed electric lights around a domed blue ceiling, and also by the shinca trunk he'd seen from outside, which was embedded in a side wall. Carved into the stone beside it was an image of Father Varin kissing life into the world; the matching image on the opposite wall depicted Mai the Right in male embodiment, guiding virtuous souls into the gentle hands of Mother Elinda, and sending evil ones to be gnashed in pieces by Varin's fiery teeth. At the front of the hall, where the altar had once been, a curtained stage now stood. Tagaret took his seat in the front row as the lights dimmed; a cover slid over the shinca, revealing faint silver constellations in the dome overhead.

Reyn touched his arm and whispered close to his ear. "You gave *her* my drink, didn't you."

"Sirin and Eyn," Tagaret swore under his breath. "I really did." He could imagine her drinking it, the pale blue liquid slipping across her full lips and down her throat. It filled him with wanting.

"Don't worry," Reyn murmured. "I forgive you." His hand squeezed, and when Tagaret half-turned, Reyn kissed him at the corner of his mouth.

Tagaret's whole body jerked in shock. Vitett Ice sloshed over his fingers. What in Varin's name? Had Reyn just. . . ?

"You all right?" Reyn whispered.

"F-fine," Tagaret managed. But was he? His heart pounded, and shivers chased down his legs. He could see Della's curious green eyes so clearly, and her lower lip, soft, with her teeth pressing into it—but suddenly he could also see Reyn, gazing at him in the dark of the garden. He took a gulp of Vitett Ice so large it pained his throat.

The stage curtain rose, and the conductor took the podium. At first, his racing heartbeat seemed louder than the music. A whispering in the shiazin section was answered by a low rumble from the golbrum, and then the sound layered into complexities that reached into his guts and pulled. At the yojosmei, with his pale gray coattails hanging below the bench, Kartunnen Ryanin readied hands and feet at the keyboards. Silver light from the shinca broke over the orchestra, so clear that each instrument appeared distinct.

The yojosmei turned feral.

Indignant murmurs arose behind him, but now Tagaret's heart pounded for a different reason. This piece changed the meaning of music. Its dissonant beauty enveloped him in layer after layer of darkness, burying him in the lightless adjunct caverns outside the city where he had no privilege, no power. Around him, he heard dripping water, the rattle of falling rocks, and the cries of an enormous crowd that wandered desperately, often fighting each other in the search for escape, but never finding it.

Finally, the last melodic hiss of the shiazin waned and died. The lights came up, but still his mind lay buried in the heavy dark. The others clapped politely; Reyn nudged his shoulder. Tagaret set down his unfinished drink and stood up blinking. Much of the audience appeared to have walked out in protest, but Della and her Yoral were still sitting in the front row, only ten seats away.

"That was—amazing," Tagaret said.

"Not exactly uplifting," said Gowan. He rose and headed toward the exit.

Tagaret nodded. "You're right."

"Interesting," said Reyn.

It was more than that. It was shattering, like sudden rockfall. When they reached the main foyer, Della and Yoral emerged from another house door. Tagaret clenched his fists to will her closer, and as if she'd felt his desire, Della looked up. In her eyes he recognized the dark secret that the music had given them to share.

And then, Yoral was approaching him.

"Excuse me, sir. I presume you enjoyed the concert?"

"Yes, indeed, Yoral, very impressive," Tagaret replied. The others weren't on polite automatic; only Reyn managed to keep himself from staring at Della. The Imbati raked steely eyes over Fernar and Gowan, and they caved in a step, pretending they hadn't been looking, though they had been.

The escort turned back to Tagaret. "I would be remiss not to thank you for your generosity, sir."

"It was my pleasure," Tagaret said, not quite remembering what he'd done to deserve thanks. Then a motion snagged his eyes—Della's fingers tightening over her Yoral's knuckles. When he looked up, her soft, perfect mouth was opening.

"The Vitett Ice is my favorite drink," she said. Her voice melted over him like warm honey, melting him with it until he was liquid down to his knees. It felt like drowning. "What's your favorite drink, Tagaret?"

He glanced in panic at Yoral, but the Imbati was looking away. He had to answer her. "Th- the same."

"We must speak of this music sometime," she said. "You and I."

Yes, oh, please yes! "I would love to."

"Good night, Tagaret."

"Good night—Della."

As she walked away, her name still tingled on his tongue. The others were staring; Fernar shook his head. "What a night for you."

Tagaret exhaled. Disobedience felt better than he'd ever imagined. "Don't tell anyone I talked to her, all right?"

"Excuse me, sir," said a voice that wasn't Yoral's.

Tagaret turned around.

The Imbati who'd spoken wore a high-necked sleeveless dress in black with hints of blue, and kept her blonde hair in several braids to the front and back of her broad shoulders. He could hardly have failed to recognize the most famous Imbati in Pelismara, even if her Lady hadn't been leaning on a cane beside her—smaller, subtler, in a gown of shimmering feldspar gray that accentuated matching strands in her tight-curled hair.

Lady Selemei of the First Family, and her Ustin.

Lady Selemei was notorious, a widow who had appropriated her late partner's manservant, and used Ustin's insider knowledge to become the first ever lady cabinet member. Father hated her for it—he said she'd stolen the seat meant for him.

"Cousin," Lady Selemei said, "did I just see you with a young Lady?"

Oh, no . . . Tagaret shot a panicked glance at Reyn.

Reyn drew himself up, tugging the hem of his ruby-red coat. "She approached us, Lady," he said. "I think you'll find your cousin was quite polite."

Lady Selemei smiled. "I'm sure you're correct. May I speak with Tagaret alone for a moment?"

"Certainly. We'll wait for him right here."

"Then I'll return him to you shortly."

Thank the Twins for Reyn. Reassured that he wouldn't be dragged straight to the Arbiter of the First Family Council in disgrace, Tagaret followed Selemei and Ustin around the left side of the foyer. The Lady walked at a measured pace, her cane precisely placed with every other step. She stopped before a statue—armor-clad Mai the Right, female this time, subduing her belligerent brother Plis the Warrior—thereby claiming the deity's penetrating gaze and infallible judgment for her own. Then she set both hands atop her cane and gave Tagaret a smile that made his ears burn.

"I'm sorry, Lady," Tagaret said. "I wasn't trying to put anyone in danger. I dragged my friends here. I had no idea Lady Della was here until intermission, I swear by Sirin and Eyn. I only came because I had to hear the music."

"So did I," said Selemei.

He blinked. "You did?"

"Surely you must remember that I'm a friend of your mother's? I was surprised and pleased to see you here, and thought I might renew our acquaintance."

"Oh." She *had* called on Mother, before; sometimes he'd stood by the gaming table to watch them play kuarjos, or keyzel marbles. But it seemed a lifetime ago. Why wait five years to approach him? He sneaked a glance at the deity, but Mai didn't share any divine insight.

"Are you excited to see your father again?" Selemei asked. "I imagine he'll be offering you political opportunities."

Tagaret winced. "Not exactly. I hate politics."

"Dear me. Well, I meant no offense. I felt that way myself for a long time." Her ironic, considering gaze was so much like Mother's. Maybe she was sincere. Joining the cabinet, and keeping herself there, would have been hard work. Why would she have had time for an absent friend's child?

"It's not you, Lady," he said. "It's just—no matter what you want to accomplish, you can't escape the political spelunking. I'm sure you know that."

"I do."

"Everyone's fighting to get on top, when they should be worrying about the Grobal Trust and our charge to care for Lowers. Not to mention the health of the Race. How can we sit idle while doom dangles over our heads?"

"Precisely why everyone hopes this fever incident won't bring on an Heir Selection," Selemei agreed. She smoothed her skirts with one golden hand. "Well, it's been a pleasure, but I've kept you from your friends too long. Do give my best to your mother. Ustin, please return him."

Thank all the gods. He found his friends wringing their hands in an anxious clump in the center of the foyer. Reyn stepped firmly between him and the Lady until she and her servant had left the hall. No one said anything until they reached the skimmers parked out front.

"Is she going to get us in trouble?" Fernar asked.

Tagaret shook his head. "I don't think so. She was nice. She was a friend of my mother's . . . before. I hope I didn't upset her when I said I wasn't interested in politics."

"Politics?" asked Gowan sharply. "What did she say?"

He shrugged. "Asked if I was excited to have Father home."

"Oof," said Reyn.

"She wants something from you," Gowan said. "Politicians *always* want something."

"But she's family. And she isn't like most politicians I've met."

Fernar laughed. "Of course not, Tagaret! She's a Lady."

"Don't let all that talk of 'Lady's politics' fool you," said Gowan. "She stopped being a Lady when she took a gentleman's servant—and a gentleman's place. I don't imagine family means much to her if she can walk out on her own children."

That put an uncomfortable face on it. "Gowan, stop," Tagaret said.

"I told you people would seek you out," Gowan insisted. "She knows the position you'd be in, in an Heir Selection. She'd know this was her last chance to prime you for influence before you came under your father's protection."

"That's enough." Tagaret shuddered. Both the 'position' and the need for 'protection' were Father's fault, and Father would be home in less than an hour. The thought made him want to just drive away—but there was no safe way out of the politics and distrust, just as there was no safe way out of Pelismara. Reluctantly, he accompanied his friends back to the level rampway, trying to think only of Mother.

They checked in their vehicles at the Conveyor's Hall, then walked back along the Grobal School to the Residence. Fernar and Gowan both lived on the second floor, so they went there first. As he and Reyn returned to the stairs, Tagaret sighed.

"I'm not sure I want to go home, Reyn."

"Want me to come with you?"

"That would be great." Reyn would still be here, in spite of the change—thank the Twins. Downstairs in the first-floor hall, he added, "Thanks for saving me tonight."

Reyn didn't answer. Tagaret glanced over his shoulder and caught him with a strange look on his face. At once, he remembered the darkness, Reyn touching his arm, and . . .

He flushed, and his stomach tightened. "Reyn, what's wrong?"

Reyn pushed his blond curls out of his eyes. "I don't want you being nice just to be nice."

"What?"

"If you don't want me with you, don't pretend you do."

Tagaret blinked. "But I do—I mean, why wouldn't I? Because you—" His voice failed.

Reyn looked away. "You have that girl. Now your friends are just inconvenient."

As tense as he was already, mention of Della brought the wanting back in a flood. Guilt came with it. "Reyn, I don't *have* her. You're certainly not *inconvenient*."

"I was tonight."

"How can you say that? You kept Selemei from dragging me home in disgrace. If I could pick anyone to brave Melumalai with, it would be you."

Reyn glanced up. "That's all very well to say."

"Have I ever lied to you? You had it right: it's not like Della and I can go anywhere. I have no power, no position, certainly nothing my father would *permit* me to offer to hers. Sure, I want to *see* her." To hear her voice again, to feel that rush that echoed in him now. "But it won't change anything."

Reyn stared at him hopelessly. "Tagaret, it already has."

"How, Reyn? What has it changed?"

Reyn grabbed him by the shoulders and kissed him.

Great gods! It felt so good—Reyn's lips were his, then hers, confused and irresistible. Tagaret pulled him closer, and Reyn's arms locked around him. Every unattainable dream pressed into a desperate, breathless instant.

"Reyn," Tagaret gasped, "if someone comes—"

Reyn nodded. Tagaret slapped the glass recognition pad to unlock the door of his suite, and together they crossed the vestibule and sitting room at a run, ignoring the First Houseman's greeting. But as they entered the darkened drawing room, something moved.

Tagaret smacked the light switch in sudden, choking fury.

The lights exposed Nekantor, sitting in the corner by the entrance to the back-bedroom hall. There was no doubt what he'd been up to—messing with the door again. He hated it. *He hated it!* Anger strung his gut tight from jaw to belly—he hated the anger, too.

"Nek! Leave my door alone!"

Nek narrowed his eyes, conceding nothing, denying nothing. "You saw that Imbati today, Tagaret. He's after us. He's an information gatherer; he's sent by Eminence Indal because he knows the Heir owes our father a favor; he's going to hand us over to Arissen assassins."

Tagaret gritted his teeth. "Aloran's no danger, Nek; he's too young. He's not marked to anyone's service, so he can't be sent."

Nek's glance flicked away toward the window at the end of the hall, then returned. "He wants Father's Sorn's job—he knows Father is coming home, and he's planning to knock him off, and take his place."

"Nek, if he were anywhere near certification, we would have seen him before." Though he *was* old enough . . .

Then it really struck: if Reyn's sister knew him, *Aloran was a Lady's servant.* Mother's Eyli *was* getting old. But Mother loved her; she'd never send her away. Why had Aloran come to find them?

"He wants something from me," Nek said. "He doesn't want to braid my hair."

Tagaret scowled. Why was he arguing anyway? Nek would make up his mind his own way, and would never take advice. He wasn't stupid—he was abominable.

Tagaret turned his back on his brother. "Varin's teeth, Reyn. I'm sorry."

Reyn wouldn't meet his eyes. "I should go."

"But, Reyn . . ." His stomach flipped. Reyn shouldn't go—but what would happen if he stayed?

"It's fine, Tagaret. I'll see you tomorrow, all right?"

"All right." Mechanically, Tagaret walked Reyn out front and said goodbye. Then he ran to his room and locked the door.

CHAPTER FOUR

Like Father, Like Son

Nekantor stared at the locked door for a long time. Tagaret had locked it. He'd locked it because he couldn't face the truth, that an Imbati was pursuing them for reasons unknown. But Tagaret always locked the door. Tagaret wanted to keep secret games.

The door must not be locked.

Nekantor left the wall and sat beside the door again. The lock was brass, bright and new on the bronze door—heavier than the last lock, and it would be harder to unlock. Each lock was heavier than the last. Tagaret would get a palm lock if he could, trying to keep his secret games, but palm locks couldn't be bought; no one could make them anymore. And so Tagaret would lose again, because now he would pick this lock, just like the last one, and the fourteen before that. Of course, Tagaret would be angry. But Tagaret was harmless even when he was angry, and the door must not be locked.

Imbati Aloran, now—he wasn't harmless. Was he harmful? Well, but he wasn't harmless; he was different, and unexplained. Presuming to appear in play session to spy on him and Benél, claiming to be doing research? *Research?*

Unacceptable.

He and Benél had spoken about it afterward. In private, after the other boys had left, they'd tried to understand Imbati Aloran. Benél was good; Benél was strong, very strong, able to keep seven boys in thrall to the First Family. But there were a lot of things he didn't understand, which was why it was important to explain things to him. When he understood, he was powerful.

But this time Benél wasn't the only one who didn't understand.

Unacceptable.

How to explain Imbati Aloran? Not an assassin for Father's Sorn, nor an information gatherer, because he wasn't marked to service. Tagaret was right—infuriating. The will of gentlemen was the reason why Imbati lived and moved. How could Aloran do *anything at all* with no will behind him? Gnash Tagaret! He'd made this harder on purpose.

And he was trying to hide behind the locked door.

Nekantor took a wire from his pocket and put it into the lock. It felt like a tight lock, with not much movement in the wire. Benél would come tonight, soon. When Benél came, he'd stand beside him, speak in his ear, and go with him wherever he was going. All the others might squabble amongst themselves, but one thing didn't change: Benél listened to *him*, and all the others followed where Benél led them.

A sudden sound: the front door again. Thieves? Assassins? Benél didn't have his palm coded; you couldn't open a palm lock with a wire.

But then, Imbati Serjer's obsequious voice: "Welcome back, Master, Lady."

"Oh, Serjer, it's so good to see you again."

"Thank you, Lady."

"Serjer, help us get this luggage in."

"Yes, sir, right away."

That's who it was. Father and Mother, scheduled to arrive tonight, for good, after five years and a voyage up on the surface. They wouldn't like him at Tagaret's lock. He removed the wire. He gritted his teeth. Gnash Tagaret for locking the door—the door should not be locked.

"Tagaret! Nekantor!" Father's voice called from the sitting room, full of power like boulders grinding. Oh, he remembered that power: the stones that had once framed the world. Nekantor moved away from Tagaret's door as Father came in through the double doors.

Father was fat, and his hair was gray. Fifty-seven, and he had power, won in countless power games—but it took Kinders fever to give him the prize of his career. Speaker of the Cabinet now, and soon he'd be in the confidence of the Eminence Indal, so the Eminence Indal would listen to him. Garr was already in the secret confidence of Herin, the Heir to the throne.

Herin of the Third Family owed Father everything. All the Pelismara Society knew the story of how Dest of the Eleventh Family had been assassinated during the last Heir Selection; Dest had been Herin's most powerful rival. It was Father who'd made that happen—but even after picking the lock on his office and searching the files, Nekantor still couldn't guess how he'd done it. The Arissen police had never tied it to him and never would. Nobody could play power games like Father, and now he stood with his mouth at the ears of both the Eminence and the Heir. That was power.

"Father," Nekantor said. "Welcome home. Congratulations on your promotion."

"Nekantor," said Garr. "Good to see you, son."

"Nek, love, how are you?" Mother's hand messed the hair behind his ear.

He shook it away. "I'm fine, Mother." Mother was pretty and didn't have power. She got him servants who were no good. Imbati Aloran—she was trying to get him Imbati Aloran as a servant? No, Imbati Aloran worked for ladies. That was it: Imbati Aloran could work for Mother. But Imbati Aloran played games, and no one should hire an Imbati who played games.

No matter. He could play games better than any Imbati, if it came to that.

"Where's Tagaret?" Mother asked.

Nekantor lashed a glance at the locked door. "In his rooms. Locked, in his rooms." He fingered the wire, in his pocket.

"Tagaret!" Father shouted.

The lock clicked open. Ohhh, so satisfying, like slipping into warm water. Tagaret came out and shook Father's hand. Tagaret was taller than Father, and thin, and his hair was not gray. But Tagaret was harmless, too stupid to take part in power games, and wouldn't listen when things were explained to him. Only three in his gang, and he refused any talk of becoming Heir—how absurd.

"Father, it's great to have you home," Tagaret said. "Any trouble on the Roads?"

"None on the Roads," said Father. "But we were delayed having to use rampways into town. I'm starting to think they'll never get the Alixi's Elevator fixed."

"That's too bad. How was the trip, Mother?"

Father grunted. "Your mother and I slept most of the way. How's school? Have you been reporting your grades to the Arbiter of the First Family Council?"

Tagaret scowled like a baby. "Of course I have, Father. School is going fine."

Enough silliness. Nekantor stepped forward. "Father, the *important* news is that the Kinders fever hasn't become an epidemic. Its source is still under investigation. The Eminence Indal is in fine health. His partner has not achieved another pregnancy. But the Heir Herin's partner has carried their second child to seven months, so it looks good."

Father glanced over. "Thanks for telling me, Nek. I'll have to congratulate him."

Serjer and Father's Sorn crossed to the master bedroom carrying luggage. Mother's Eyli crossed empty-handed. Useless Imbati. Imbati Aloran played games, but he could carry luggage at least.

"The surface is always a nervous place, Tagaret," Mother said. "But I'm so happy to see you—look at you, you're taller than me." Tagaret hugged her, and she hugged him back tight.

"I missed you so much," Tagaret said. "I'm so glad you'll be back for our birthdays."

Father clapped his hands together. "We would never have missed your political debut, anyway. I've been planning it for months. You're going to burst onto the scene with the entire First Family behind you."

Tagaret was harmless and did not know how to plan. With Tagaret's stupid attitude, it would be a lot of work. But Father was back. Father would explain things to him. Father would make him listen.

No sign, yet, of Benél. Nekantor looked down to where the gold watch on his wrist said two minutes to nine. "Benél will come in a few minutes," he said. "I'm going out with him."

Father frowned. "You can't go out tonight, Nek," he said. "We've just gotten back. It wouldn't be appropriate."

"Well, but if he's already got it planned," Mother said.

"Nonsense, Tamelera. You're not going, Nek."

Not going. But he *was* going; he was going out tonight. As soon as Benél came, he would go with him. "I'm going," he said.

"Nekantor—" said Father.

Tagaret and Mother made uncomfortable faces. He wanted to scream at them.

"Master, a message," Serjer announced, striking his messenger pose, turning his eyes Higher to relay the voice of his betters. "To Garr of the First Family. May we stop by tonight to welcome you back and discuss cabinet strategy? In anticipation, Fedron of the First Family."

Mother shook her head. "Well, as we've just gotten back—"

"That's great," said Father. "Any time before ten is fine."

Mother dropped her hands into her skirts. "But, Garr, it's not appropriate."

"Show some sense, Tamelera," said Father. "This is the cabinet we're talking about."

"But you *just said*," Mother said, closing fists. "This is our first night with our sons in five years!"

Now, this was interesting. Nekantor smiled. If tonight involved cabinet members, staying home might not be so useless after all. "Father," he said. "I'll stay here if I can be part of your meeting. Strategize about you claiming your place at the head of the First Family. You'll have to show Fedron he's not in charge of us anymore."

Father scowled. "Nekantor . . ."

Then the doorbell rang, and Father waved them all toward the sitting room.

Nekantor ran, so no one could touch him. If this was Benél, then he would go with him.

Sorn opened the door like a good Imbati, and Benél was here, smiling. Oh, it felt good. It always felt good, when Benél smiled.

"Benél!"

"Nek!" Benél said—and to Father, "Good evening, sir. Nek's coming out with me and the fellows."

"I'm afraid he's not," said Father. "We've just gotten home."

Benél stopped smiling.

No. Nekantor grimaced. His chest was hot, it twisted—he was going out with Benél tonight, and Benél was strong, and *he would go with him.* "I'm going with him," he said. "Benél and I are going out tonight, with friends. We had it planned."

"Why don't I show you how I've arranged my rooms, Mother," said Tagaret. They didn't have power; they ran away. They disappeared through the double doors—

And Tagaret's lock clicked.

The door must not be locked! He *had* to go out, away from the locked door. Benél was strong, and he would go out with him tonight. It was planned!

"Nekantor," Father said. "Tonight you're staying home with us."

Nekantor stared him in the eye. "Oh, so I *do* get to strategize, then?"

"Don't be ridiculous; this is men's business."

Nekantor frowned. Secret games—he closed and opened his hands. Father was not harmless like Tagaret. "Well," he said, "if you can play games with your little gang, I don't see why I can't play with mine."

Father's face darkened, and he turned away toward the front door. "Good night, Benél," he said stiffly. "Tonight's not a good night."

"Good night, sir," said Benél. "I'm sorry, sir."

Nekantor hissed under his breath. It was definitely not a good night. Father made it a miserable night. Father had power, and wouldn't let him strategize, and wouldn't let him go out tonight. But *Benél* was going out tonight, and here—in the suite—*Tagaret's door was locked*. It should not be locked! It was too tight in here—too tight in here already, and Father turned with a breath, and was going to bind him tighter. Nekantor shoved through the double doors, ran down the hall, and locked himself in his rooms, so he wouldn't feel the door that should not be locked, so he wouldn't feel Benél going out when he did not go out. He hunted the bedroom, searching, touching, checking. Was anything wrong? Anything? No, nothing—here, there was nothing wrong, except that he was not going out.

His father banged on the door. "Nekantor!"

There was no need to answer. Father had power, but he didn't have the key, and he couldn't open a lock with a wire. He'd give up soon enough and go play with his own gang.

Nekantor sat on his bed and hugged his knees, staring into the calming perfection of the window shade that hung exactly straight. There had been one that hadn't, and he had destroyed it—cut it in pieces with a knife, until it was not a window shade anymore. That had fixed it.

Tap. Tap.

A sound, behind the perfect window shade. He pulled it down carefully, so it rolled up perfectly. Benél's hand, outside the window.

Ahh, Benél was here, and tonight they were going out together. Nekantor opened the window very quietly; he could play games as well as anyone. Outside, Benél was smiling. It felt good.

"Come on, Nek. Get down here." Benél was very strong, and caught him when he jumped from the windowsill.

Nekantor carefully straightened his trousers, his shirt, his vest, then followed Benél out into the grounds. The other seven gathered, telling stories and sharing rumors as they headed out into the city. Nekantor walked beside Benél, listening, remembering. He whispered plans into Benél's ear, so Benél could understand.

When Benél understood, he was powerful.

CHAPTER FIVE

Resistance

Not until the lock clicked did it really hit him. *Mother was here.* She held him, and despite how much smaller she suddenly seemed, the warmth, the softness, the comfort were exactly the same. It pulled the last five years right out of him.

Tears rose in Tagaret's eyes. "Oh, Mother, I can't believe it . . ."

"Tagaret, my love, my darling," she murmured into his neck. "I'll never have to leave you again, I promise. Your father has always wanted this—the provinces couldn't possibly offer him better."

Tagaret closed his eyes. "Don't say that, Mother. We'll be together because *we've* always wanted this, not because it's convenient for *him*."

"Of course, darling. We—"

Father banged on the door, and Mother winced.

"Mother," Tagaret said, "What if I don't answer? Just for a few minutes."

She gave him a tighter squeeze. "Well, I'm afraid the cabinet members *are* coming, and you *do* have a debut to think of."

"I know that . . ."

She smiled. "But I'm sure you can impress them."

Father banged again. "I hear the doorbell. Tagaret!"

"Coming, Father." He and Mother went out arm in arm.

"Garr," said Mother firmly, "A short visit only, please. We have family to think of."

"Tagaret," Father said. "Enough clinging."

Tagaret clenched his teeth. He'd tolerate this business because it was necessary, but he wasn't letting go. Father and Sorn led the way, and Imbati Eyli opened the doors for all of them to the sitting room.

They were just in time to see Serjer admit Grobal Fedron—and Lady Selemei.

Tagaret held his breath. Fortunately, Lady Selemei gave no sign that she'd met him earlier.

"What a pleasure," Father boomed. "Fedron, just the man I wanted to see. Come; explain to me the increase in the Pelismara Division's harvest safety budget. Wysp problems, or Venorai theft?" He drew Fedron toward one of the sitting room couches, ignoring Selemei as if she were as invisible as the visiting manservants.

He could do better than that. "Welcome to our home, Lady Selemei," Tagaret said.

"A pleasure, Tagaret," the Lady replied. She shifted her cane into one hand and extended the other one to Mother. "It's just wonderful to see you again, Tamelera—the collective intelligence of the Pelismar ladies declined precipitously with your departure."

Mother took her hand. "That's kind of you to say. I owe you a game of kuarjos, or perhaps dareli, if we can persuade Keir and Lienne to join us."

Lady Selemei's eyebrows shot up. She took one step toward Mother and whispered in her ear.

Mother cried, "Lienne *Fell?*"

Without thinking, Tagaret tried to move between them. "What?"

Mother drew him back again. "It's all right, Tagaret. We had a friend—actually a childhood cousin of mine—it's true I hadn't heard from her. Now Selemei tells me she's Fallen to take an Arissen man as her life's partner. Almost two years ago. And no one told me."

"Fedron and I sent a radiogram to Selimna," Lady Selemei said softly. "I'm sorry; I assumed it had reached you."

Tagaret nearly choked. "Your cousin turned her back on the Race, and Father didn't *tell* you?"

Mother glanced fury toward Father, but her voice came soft and sad. "I can't believe Lienne is gone. She was so bright, so noble. I never imagined—and think of her children . . ."

That was a cold thought. To have your mother abandon you to become Lower—change herself into something unrecognizable? Losing Mother to the provinces seemed nothing in comparison. Tagaret wrapped his arm around her shoulders.

"It was a tragic loss," Selemei said gently. "We can still play dareli with three."

Mother was clearly distressed. "Well, the cards would play differently," she said. "And you're busy, with the cabinet's business . . ."

"I'd love to tell you about it," Selemei said. "I think you'd find it very interesting—for example, the role the Imbati caretakers play in supporting unconfirmed children."

Fedron called from over by the couches. "Lady Selemei, we need you!"

Father added, "Tagaret! You, too."

Tagaret didn't move. Gnash it. Gnash Father.

"I do hate to leave Fedron unprotected," Lady Selemei remarked. "Perhaps we should *all* join them?"

"Tagaret!"

"Mother, do please join us," Tagaret said. "Just for a minute."

"All right, love."

Father and Fedron were posturing at each other, chests thrown out like rival kanguans. Fedron looked visibly relieved when Selemei went to his side.

"Tamelera, come stand by me," said Father.

"I'm with Tagaret," Mother replied coolly.

Father frowned.

Tagaret held back a smile.

"Cousin," Fedron said to Selemei, "I've just been telling Garr how critical it is to maintain our First Family front just now."

"Mm, yes," Lady Selemei agreed, and glanced at Mother. "Tamelera, you've seen how influence patterns shift when a family isn't unified, haven't you?"

That was clever. 'Influence pattern' and 'unify' were terms from dareli, but now they sounded like real politics.

Mother seemed gratified. "Well—"

"Tamelera, this is men's business, not Lady's politics," said Father.

Mother's smile vanished.

"*Father*," Tagaret protested. That was more than just rude; Father would never have allowed *him* to speak that way to a cabinet member, especially an ally.

Lady Selemei's hand tightened on her cane, but she gave a light laugh. "You know, Fedron has always appreciated my support—haven't you, Fedron? Three votes add up to a lot of power—if we don't blunt our impact or lose a cabinet seat due to family infighting." Sweet, but deadly accurate—she obviously understood the consequences if Father removed her.

"This is about *influence*, Garr," said Fedron. "You're here, aren't you? And you're Speaker now. Set the past aside. The Fifth Family has gotten daring lately, and your arrival means we can act against them."

"Hmph," said Father, and spoke over his shoulder. "Serjer, get drinks for five. Looks like we'll be here a while."

"Wait," Tagaret began, but Father flashed him a look so dangerous he gulped. *Mother had said.* She'd *said*, only a few minutes! Tagaret looked to her, pleading.

"Make that four, Serjer, please," said Mother. "I hope you'll all excuse me, but I'm tired after the day's travel. I'll leave you to your business meeting."

"I'll take you to your rooms," Tagaret said quickly.

"You'll do nothing of the sort," Father growled. "You have responsibilities here. You need to prepare for—"

"I've *been* preparing for my debut," Tagaret said. "I've done everything you asked for five years."

"Well, then show me you're ready. Show Fedron you're ready."

"And Selemei, too, Father. There's no better ally than family."

"And Selemei, too, then." Father looked him in the eye, and the corners of his mouth twitched upward. "Serjer, bring drinks for four."

W hat had happened to Mother?

By all rights, she should have helped him hold his own against Father, but since their arrival she'd been giving in constantly. Tagaret found himself abandoned, unable to visit friends, forced to entertain Father's constant stream of guests. He knew this had to be about finding a political mentor, even if Father liked to act all mysterious about it. But with each new visitor, he found himself setting to more and more grimly, for not one of them showed any interest in asking bigger questions. Mother did nothing but watch him get more and more frustrated.

Was retreat her only strategy? Did the anger he saw in her eyes mean nothing?

Today he'd gotten stuck in a maddening conversation with Benél's father, who had stopped by still wearing his green Adjudicator's robes. How many times was one required to express polite relief at the lack of new fever cases? Evidently, as many as demanded by a man of importance.

At last Tagaret was able to flee to his rooms; he locked the door before Father could invite anyone else.

Immediately, there was a knock.

Not again . . . He was steeling himself to unlock the door when he realized the knock had been too restrained, and from the wrong side of the room. He turned. "Serjer?"

The First Houseman appeared from beneath his curtain. "I'm sorry to disturb you, sir," he said. "I've received a private message for you."

Who would send him a message? To judge by the tilt of Serjer's head, nobody innocuous. Tagaret held out his hand, but Serjer took reciting stance, with eyes upturned and one hand behind his back.

"To Tagaret of the First Family," he said. "I extend my invitation to you to attend an informal tea and yojosmei concert at the Club Diamond, Barell Circumference and Kyaral Radius, at 2:00 afternoon on Soremor 15th. See you there! Sincerely, Lady Selemei of the First Family."

"Selemei!" Tagaret exclaimed. A private overture from her was not a good sign. She had to be using him to get to Father somehow. His debut was tomorrow—too close for this to be nothing. What did she want? His gut said to ask Mother, but Mother hadn't even seen her for five years. "Serjer," he asked, "*See me there?* Selemei just expects me to show up?"

"Young Master," said Serjer, "you needn't attend. The Lady has no means to compel you."

But she did. How brave he'd felt, breaking the Kartunnen ban, muckwalking, talking to Della . . . Lady Selemei was too sharp to keep his secret out of kindness. If he didn't show up at this tea, she'd go straight to Father. Mercy, how deftly she'd trapped him!

"Serjer, what can I do?" he asked. "I can't beat Selemei on my own, but Father would kill me for having spoken to her alone in the first place, and Mother never helps. She sits back and lets Father insult her. I can tell she's angry, but she does nothing."

"Young Master," Serjer said softly, "I don't wish to presume."

"Please, Serjer. I trust you."

Serjer gave a faint smile. "Sir," he said, "I don't recommend sending any reply to Lady Selemei's message. As for your mother, this is nothing new for her. Currently, I believe she considers your future success. She endures much for your sake—we of the Household admire her selflessness in this."

"That's—kind of you." But disconcerting, too. "Serjer, you're not saying this is my fault, are you?"

The First Houseman's face colored. "I don't know."

Tagaret stared at him, trying to read the statement one way or the other, but his voice had been toneless and unemotional, and his eyes were inscrutable under the crescent-cross tattoo.

Gods, he wished he could talk to Reyn.

Instantly, the memory of their kiss flooded over him, heating his limbs and tickling deep in his stomach. At school, such thoughts were easy to avoid; school was school, and he could count on Fernar and Gowan to tempt him with talk of Della. But to see Reyn alone? Now?

Who else could talk to him about all this?

"Serjer," Tagaret said, "I'm going to Reyn's. Please don't tell Father where I am unless you absolutely have to."

Serjer bowed. "Of course, sir."

Tagaret walked coolly up to the third floor, pretending all was like before, coming over after school. He politely greeted Reyn's caretaker, Imbati Shara, who escorted him through the double doors into the Ninth Family's private space.

Reyn's ten-year-old sister Iren peeked out from her room at the end of the hall, with her bodyguard behind her. She was always alert to visitors. Tagaret waved, and she waved back.

But today, this place seemed too familiar—plush ocher couches, paintings of the Safe Harbor sand caverns, and all. It was too full of Reyn. They'd wrestled here, played keyzel marbles, draped themselves on the couches to do homework, sat side by side and talked about their parents until silence overcame them . . .

"Young Master Reyn," Imbati Shara called at the open door to Reyn's rooms. "Tagaret of the First Family, for you."

Tagaret couldn't take another step. His throat closed up.

"Tagaret?" Reyn's voice said from inside.

"Yes," he managed. "I'm here." He went in and leaned back against the door as it swung shut.

Reyn was working at his desk; he hooked one elbow over the back of his brass chair, frowning. "Are you all right?"

There was a reason he was here, and it wasn't Reyn's concerned mouth, or the way it made his heart pound. "Not really," Tagaret said. "Trouble at home. Can we talk?"

"Of course." Reyn patted the corner of the desk.

He'd sat there plenty of times. Now the idea of being so close nearly chased his thoughts right out of his head. He didn't move.

Reyn frowned. Deliberately, he stood up, walked across the room, tied back his bed-curtains, and sat down cross-legged on the blue covers.

Tagaret slid into the chair facing him. It was too hard to look at him, though; instead, he glanced aside at the portrait of Reyn's father and mother, Alixi Faril and Lady Catenad of Safe Harbor. They stood arm in arm, smiling.

Tagaret took a deep breath. "It's my parents again. To start with."

"Well, Varin's teeth. That's no good."

That sounded like the same old Reyn. Tagaret glanced over at him. Reyn was picking at a button near his knee.

"It's worse, now, though," Tagaret said. "They're living with me, so I'm in the middle of it."

"I'm sorry."

"Father has to run everything and everybody," he said. "And Nek defies him, so he jumps on me and Mother. My debut's the only thing I hear about, and I can't go anywhere anymore because I have to greet all Father's boring guests, while he ignores Mother completely. He talks about her to her face, talks *for* her, talks *over* her—" The familiar ugly feeling grew inside him; his fists closed all on their own. "Name of Plis, sometimes I could punch him in the face! I keep thinking she'll stand up to him, and sometimes she looks like she's going to, but then she either caves in or leaves. I swear, he treats her so much like an Imbati, she might as well be crossmarked."

Reyn winced. "Gross, Tagaret, don't say things like that."

"All right, not *really*. But I think it would take a vote of the joint cabinet to make him stop." He sighed. "Sometimes I think you should have gotten your parents back, instead. At least you would be happy."

"I'd never take your mother from you," Reyn said softly. "Why don't you talk to her about this?"

If only he could. Painful silences appeared to have swallowed everything they'd once talked about. "I can't."

"You always could before."

"In *letters*. I couldn't tell her what I'm telling you. Gods, I almost didn't tell *you*." What had he been thinking? That he'd cut himself off from his best friend and write letters? He shoved himself out of the chair, walked to the bed, and sat beside Reyn. "I'm an idiot, Reyn. I'm sorry—what I really want is a way to change this myself. I should just have ignored Father and come over here after school."

Reyn shrugged. He seemed to have lost his voice.

"Maybe if I can convince Mother to speak *with* me," Tagaret said, "we can get Father to listen."

Reyn nodded, the tiniest motion. "Maybe."

"And guess what—you remember how Lady Selemei saw me with Lady Della? Well, now Selemei's invited me to a tea on Soremor 15th. I should talk to Mother about that, too. Reyn, you're the best." He leaned against Reyn's shoulder.

Reyn put his hand on Tagaret's knee and squeezed.

Tagaret caught his breath. The touch resounded inside him like a hammer-strike on the golbrum. Twins stand by him! Here he was on Reyn's bed, and Reyn was looking up at him, close enough to kiss if he wanted . . .

If he wanted . . .

Reyn said, "I think you should go talk to your mother now." He stood up, went to the bedroom door, and opened it.

Tagaret flushed. "Thanks, Reyn."

Reyn smiled. "Any time you need me."

Tagaret walked home slowly, taking deep breaths. He had to shake off the feeling before he talked to Mother, but it was harder than he'd imagined. Thinking of Della only made things worse. He went to his rooms to be alone.

Except the lights were on. And Mother stood in the center of his bedroom, with Eyli behind her.

"Mother?" Tagaret stopped in place, cheeks burning. "I, uh, I'd been thinking I'd come see you . . ."

"I know I've intruded, love, and I'm sorry," Mother said. "I've got a surprise for you. First, a little something for your birthday tomorrow— I hope you like it."

Hanging from a silk ribbon on the finial of his bedpost was a new suit: long slate-green trousers with dark pearl buttons, and a fascinating jacket of mottled blue, green, and white, with short sleeves styled into slight flares at the elbow. That was a fashion the Pelismara Society had never seen—a choice that said 'Mother' all over.

"That's innovative," Tagaret said. "Is it a Selimnar style?"

Mother beamed. "I commissioned it from a textile artist I'd been working with. The jacket uses both tillik-silk and plant fiber. The sleeves make sense when you see the matching shirts."

Imbati Eyli went over and reached beneath the suit, coming out with a pair of white silk shirts. They had long cuffs that fastened up to the elbow with white pearls—just right to be shown off by the jacket.

"Thanks, Eyli," Tagaret said. "Mother, it's amazing. I'll wear it for my debut."

"When you wear it, I want you to feel that I'm with you," said Mother. She came to him and stroked his shoulders. "I know the world you're entering will place demands on you, but remember, success doesn't have to come on your father's terms."

When *she* said it, he could believe that he'd actually find a way through all this. Her eyes were bright now, her smile daring. Was that why she'd acted so meek? Because she'd been planning this? Father had been going on and on about making an impression on his birthday. *This* would certainly surprise him.

Tagaret grinned. "You know how to inspire people, Mother. I

wish you could have heard *The Catacomb* with me. It's like nothing ever written by a Kartunnen's hand."

Mother frowned. "I thought the Residence concert was interrupted?"

"I heard it at a Melumalai venue," he admitted, and before she could object, added, "Mother, it was for you. I *had* to hear it."

"Oh. I suppose . . ."

He might as well confess everything now; that was what he'd planned. "Mother, I need to ask your advice."

"What about?"

"I talked to a girl at the concert. Lady Della—she approached me first, Mother, I swear. Her bodyguard allowed it."

Mother caught a shocked breath. "Darling, please tell me you didn't run afoul of the Imbati. Were you hurt?"

"No, no," he said quickly. "The problem is, Lady Selemei saw me there, and now she's sent me an invitation to tea. Soremor 15th, just after your birthday. If I don't go, I think she's going to tell Father."

"Surely not . . ." Mother frowned. "But no. Before, I'd have sworn Selemei would never put a young lady's reputation in danger, but she's playing on the men's side these days. I'm not sure anymore." She sighed. "Selemei used to invite *me* to tea."

"I guess you could come with me."

"But we don't even know what kind of event this is." Mother turned to Eyli and extended a hand to her, palm-up. "You'll help us figure this out, won't you, Eyli? Maybe you could ask her Ustin?"

Eyli laid her hand on top of Mother's. "I'll help as much as I can, Mistress."

Tagaret stared at their touching hands. The gesture was obviously formal—but it was also intimate, because *Imbati didn't touch.* "Mother, what's this?"

Mother blushed. "Darling, listen. You don't know what it was like living in the Selimna Society while the need for safety kept you behind. Not a single child among all two hundred of us? It was like living without a future. I needed someone to confide in—and the acquaintances I had were too casual. Eyli was the one I could talk to. I came to see her differently, like a mother. Now that we're home, I pray you will understand that."

Tagaret nodded. He looked over Mother's shoulder at the old, faithful Imbati, trying to see her differently.

Eyli had tears in her eyes.

His heart seized. Something must be terribly wrong—what could make an Imbati *cry*?

"Anyway," Mother said. "Time is wasting, and we need to go."

"Why?"

"Tonight, I'm taking you to see the sky."

That was a jolt! Tagaret gaped at her, the words of her letter bubbling up in his mind: *vast, bright, deep, terrifying* . . . "M-mother," he stammered, "are you sure it's safe?"

"Oh, yes." Mother leaned toward him. "I even tested it for you. On our way here, when your father and Sorn were sleeping, *I went outside*."

"What?!"

"I couldn't have done it in daylight. The wilderness crowds around you, and the colors are brighter than seems possible—the sky feels like it's going to suck you right up! I'd never put you through that."

The thought turned his insides to jelly. "Mercy . . ."

"But at night it's not too different from the city. The wysps give a bit of light, and the stars are like crystals on a high cavern roof." She squeezed his arm. "I saw Mother Elinda, shining full in the sky. The Road is made of soft grass, and everything moves, and the air has this *taste*—I can't describe it. That's why you need to see it for yourself." Her face glowed, as if she thought nothing of walking out of the Residence and driving straight up the rampways into the roofless wilderness.

"Mother," Tagaret breathed. "You're so brave."

"Oh, no. Brave, no." She glanced about the windowless walls of his room, twisting a lock of red-gold hair in front of her ear. "Darling, there are so few times in our lives when we're truly unwatched. If you let one pass you by, it might never come again."

He shivered, but she was right. What if he'd never spoken to Della? And what if he really *could* see the sky? He took a deep breath. "Well, if—"

His door shuddered against its new lock. "Tagaret, are you in there?"

Father.

Mother's hands flew to her mouth. Eyli, though, looked like the world was ending. *This* was what was wrong. Not Mother's plan, but somehow, this. What was Father up to?

"Tagaret, answer me!"

Tagaret exhaled. Slowly, he went and answered the door. "Yes, Father. I'm here."

"Good." Father pushed in, forcing him to step back out of the way. "I need you to—oh, hello, dear."

"Hello, Garr," said Mother evenly.

"Well, since you're both here, there's been some news. The source of the Kinders fever has been found."

Tagaret set his teeth. He was *not* going to pretend curiosity.

Father wrapped an arm around his shoulders, immobilizing him. "It wasn't the orchestra; it was Kartunnen . . . *professionals*. Orn was patronizing that whorehouse everyone's been talking about!"

Mother looked utterly disgusted.

"Father!" Tagaret protested.

"Anyway, Tagaret, I need you for something. Come with me to my room."

"Now?" He sneaked a glance at Mother. Imagine it: not just spirit globes, but real stars. Moving air, and Mother Elinda shining, maybe even Heile and her six siblings arrayed across the heavens . . . "I'm busy. Mother and I, we're planning something."

"I'm afraid it can't wait." Father started dragging him out of the room.

"Father, stop!" Tagaret cried.

"What is it, son?"

"Mother and I were having a—a private talk! You can't just barge in like that—and I can't believe you'd mention prostitutes in front of her!"

Father pulled him into the drawing room and shut his door. "Son, you'll see why this is important. After all, once you've had your birthday, you'll be choosing a servant. And of course you both had to hear the Kinders fever news. No point in trying to protect Tamelera; she'd have heard worse rumors if she hadn't heard the truth from me. The fact is, Orn was an idiot."

Tagaret almost laughed in disbelief. "You're insulting the dead now?"

"Complimenting the living, my boy!" Father laughed. "You're ten times the man he was. I know you're too smart to risk yourself with Lowers for sale." He pulled Tagaret's ear to his mouth, confidentially. "It's so important for boys your age to have *close* friends, like Reyn."

"Varin's teeth, Father!" Tagaret tried to throw him off.

Father only clamped tighter. "Understand me, Tagaret. Play with whomever you like—it will make for good political influence later. But anyone *else* gets word of you wasting your value to the Race, and you'll wish you were no son of mine."

Varin help him—Father was a beast! When Imbati Sorn opened the door of the master bedroom, Tagaret simply went in. It didn't matter what this was about. The faster he got in, the faster he could get out and go back to Mother.

In his parents' room, the chairs from the lounge corner had been pulled out into the middle of the floor. Between them stood an Imbati—Aloran, the one from the play session.

No tattoo on his face for now, but maybe not for long.

Dear gods.

Father grinned. "Now, don't tell your mother," he said. "It's a surprise."

CHAPTER SIX

Un-Imbati

Grobal Tagaret was not the person he'd wanted to see.

Aloran fought the urge to tense his arms and shoulders. *Distance yourself*, the lesson said. *Measured breaths relieve the body. Relief of the body calms the mind. The calm mind is observant and prepared.*

Eyli's pleas had been too moving to deny, but he'd never imagined this. The luxury in the house was undeniable—walking in through the sitting room he'd even noticed an extravagant game table and chairs of inlaid wood—but contrary to the romantic suggestion of the Master and Mistress' shared bed, the atmosphere of conflict here was stifling.

Grobal Garr made it worse with every word. He hadn't mentioned the Lady once—not even to hint that she might have concerns relevant to the hiring of her own servant. The task of pleasing such a man put him only two breaths away from panic, yet he must hide all emotion from Garr's Sorn, who had stayed watching while the Master stepped out.

And now, to face Grobal Tagaret, too?

Yet, perhaps this was better. The boy might divulge information about his mother that his father had not.

Grobal Garr gestured expansively with the arm that wasn't clamped around his son. "This is Imbati Aloran," he declared. "Aloran, my elder son Tagaret."

Grobal Tagaret glared at him, body rigid, mouth trembling.

That look felt like a knife in his side. Yet Eyli had asked him to be here; and even if she hadn't, the Lady still deserved his best effort. Aloran bowed deeply. "It is my pleasure, young sir." And to please the father, added, "If I may presume, sir, a very promising-looking boy."

Grobal Garr chuckled. "Yes, indeed, very promising. He'll reach seventeen tomorrow."

"Congratulations, young sir," Aloran said.

Grobal Tagaret didn't answer.

"Don't you see why I brought you, Tagaret?" Grobal Garr asked. "It's perfect practice for choosing your own servant. Besides, if we like Aloran, he'll be a present for your mother's birthday, so he'll be your bodyguard, too, until you find your own. You might as well help me test him."

Judging from the outrage on Grobal Tagaret's face, his father's birthday surprise wouldn't stay secret for long. Would the boy devise some test to reflect that outrage? Would there be any chance for *him* to show his good intentions?

Grobal Tagaret shrugged off his father's arm. "*Fine*," he said. "Just what I needed, an Imbati lesson." He lay facedown on the floor, provoking a frown from his father, but no visible reaction from Garr's Sorn. "Aloran, pick me up."

Was that all? Aloran's skin prickled with relief. The unconscious fallen was a familiar challenge, pair-practiced a thousand times with his bunkmate, Endredan, and easier still when he knew the 'victim' had sustained no injuries. A fine opportunity to communicate good will. Slipping one hand under the Grobal boy's near shoulder, he rolled him into his arm, then lifted his knees and carried him to one of the lounge chairs. "Please excuse my imposition, young sir," he murmured.

Grobal Tagaret looked at him.

He should have sent some signal, but under Sorn's sharp gray eyes, he could do nothing. Aloran lowered his eyes. *Young sir, please understand. I promise to love where I serve.*

"Oh, Tagaret, well done!" cried Grobal Garr. "Quite an ingenious test of his physical abilities. All right, what's next?" He had walked over near his wooden dresser; he picked up a white ceramic rabbit that sat upon it and brought it with him back to the chairs. "Escort duties."

Aloran kept his breathing level. "Yes, sir."

Grobal Garr sat heavily, turning the rabbit over in his fingers. "Frankly, Aloran, when we're out in public, I find my Tamelera receives more attention than she should. How do you propose to address this problem?"

Aloran struggled not to react. More attention than she should? What did *that* mean? It was none of her partner's business how she was escorted. All he could think to do was fall back on an early lesson, from the days before he'd rejected becoming a nurse-escort.

"The Lady dictates our direction, sir," he said. "I scan the surrounding gazes. Lowers' attention is unimportant and will add to the Lady's appearance of attractiveness. Female attention creates the illusion of jealousy, and thus should be considered an enhancement to the Lady's reputation. Male attention is undesirable. Any gaze to the face merits a discouraging glance; three seconds of continuous attention necessitates a shift of position to break the gaze with my body."

Grobal Tagaret looked really angry now.

Grobal Garr nodded. "And if there is an unwanted verbal approach?"

"A noble lady will not immediately respond to verbal advances; usually there is a slight pause, into which I can interpose myself as the primary speaker."

"A systematic plan," said Grobal Garr. "Tagaret, what do you think?"

"They do that for *schoolgirls*, Father," the boy said.

"Now, son, ladies are ladies, and must be treated with the same respect no matter what their age."

Aloran couldn't stop a twitch. Did he really call his ignorance of her wishes *respect?*

Grobal Tagaret exploded. "I can't believe you! Mother *loves* her Eyli—how could you take her away without even telling her?" He pointed a shaking finger at Aloran. "And now you're dragging this poor Imbati into it when he doesn't know any better?"

Aloran felt heat in his face. The young Master was wrong. He *did* know better—or he should have. By coming here, he'd made himself complicit in a scheme to hurt the Lady he was trying to serve. It was repugnant, un-Imbati. To have Grobal Tagaret defend him only made the shame worse—and it would be a miracle if Sorn didn't notice it.

"Tagaret," Grobal Garr growled, "don't make me sorry I included you. If you care for your mother at all, you'll fix your attitude right now."

Grobal Tagaret clenched his jaw. "*Here's* a question that will really help my mother—Aloran, how will you protect Lady Tamelera from Kinders fever?"

Test her for allergy, and then decide. . . ? But if he said that, he'd be lucky to get away with merely confusing them. Hopeless as it was, he had to answer, "Young sir, the safety and well-being of my mistress is my first concern. Kinders fever is transmitted by touch. I will allow no one to touch her."

"So, there you go," said Grobal Garr. "An excellent answer, Aloran."

"But Father," Grobal Tagaret protested, "aren't you even going to ask Mother before you go and have him marked?"

"Of course I am, on her birthday. Aloran, that'll be all for now—I'll let Serjer show you out. Serjer!"

Aloran held still. The sooner the First Houseman appeared, the sooner he'd be able to escape this. But seconds passed, and Serjer didn't answer.

"Serjer!" Grobal Garr called again. "Where could he be?"

Aloran held his breath. Presumptuous even to think it, but could he be lucky enough to have the young Master show him out? Just the smallest moment where he might be able to apologize in private?

"Shall I go get Serjer for you, Father?" Grobal Tagaret asked. Too sweetly—chances were better he'd go straight to his mother.

"No, stay with me a moment," said Garr. "Sorn, you may show Aloran out."

Sorn came to life with a bow. "Yes, Master."

Aloran surrendered his last chance and followed Sorn. The steel-haired servant stalked more than he walked—clearly, he was assiduous in maintaining combat readiness. Something about his carriage hinted of arrogance, though; or one might say, it bore a disconcerting similarity to his Master's.

In the entry vestibule, Garr's Sorn made as if to let him out, but stopped with his hand on the door handle.

"Oh, Imbati Aloran," he said. "That was well done."

Hearing a fellow servant call him by caste name raised the hairs on his neck. Aloran swallowed. "I can only do my best, sir."

"Oh, you did perfectly. It's good to know that our Lady's servant may finally know his place."

What? Aloran looked into the senior servant's face, and a conviction hit him in the stomach: something was wrong with Sorn. His tattoo might be Imbati, but the nobility that had seeped into his posture had taken over his words, suggesting even worse corruption deep inside. *Very much his master's man . . .*

Sorn's mouth bent into the shadow of a smirk. "You're excused," he said, and opened the door.

Aloran had never felt so grateful for the protection of the wardens at the Academy gates. He hurried to Master Ziara's office, and almost smiled in relief when she answered his knock.

"Come in," said Master Ziara. When the door clicked shut, she added, "You've chosen a good moment to stop by. We've identified the fever: it's the Selostei 19 variant, contagion rating medium, against which this year's inoculant has shown seventy percent effectiveness. The Speaker contracted it from a Kartunnen—that's how it hopped the Imbati wall. But the wall itself remains intact."

"Thank you, sir." That was reassuring, at least.

"I take it you've just completed your review."

"Yes, sir." Aloran tried to untangle shame from suspicion so he wouldn't blurt out wild accusations. "I think Grobal Garr liked me, but I'm not meant for *his* service. I'm certain now that Tamelera's Eyli is being forced out. Lady Tamelera needs someone she can trust, but I have no idea if she'd want my services."

Master Ziara gaze-gestured sympathy. "This inquiry is problematic, but you may yet meet the Lady. We won't know until the family contacts us again."

"I understand." He took a deep breath. "Sir, I have to tell you. Something strange happened while I was there, with Garr's Sorn."

Master Ziara's eyes widened, flicking unexpectedly toward the intercom station on her desk. But she spoke calmly. "He's the head of your prospective Household. I'd understand if you were nervous of him."

"It was more than that." How could he share what he'd sensed without looking like a fool? Evidence. She would ask for evidence. "Sorn called me by caste name. He said he wanted me to know my place."

Master Ziara pressed her lips into a slight frown. "Graduates of the Gentleman's training don't always value our skills as much as their own."

"Yes . . . yes, I know." He sighed; he'd seen such attitudes before, but they had never rattled him like this. "That would make more sense than what I thought . . ."

She waited, watching him.

Aloran cleared his throat. "Sorn seemed wrong. Un-Imbati. He held me back in the vestibule and for a second I thought he might do something—unpredictable." *Horrible*, his gut whispered. But for that he had no evidence at all.

Master Ziara responded gently. "Aloran, this is a Household which clearly suffers much pressure. It may be that Sorn struggles in his leadership of the group as well; we can't know at this point. After a difficult review, you might have been sensitized to such things."

That was a very reasonable explanation. Wrong—but reasonable. He sighed. "Thank you, Master Ziara."

"I'll let you know as soon as I hear the family's response."

"All right."

He left her office slowly. After observing those Grobal boys, he should just have trusted his instinct and stayed away. Tonight had been too great a risk, for so little learned. But now, Grobal Tagaret would tell his mother of the scheme, and that would be the end of it.

Light footsteps tapped behind him. He glanced back, half-expecting Kiit. Instead, it was Master Ziara, hurrying away down the hall.

Where was she going so fast?

On impulse, he followed, just far enough to see her disappear into the Headmaster's office. Could she be seeing the Headmaster about what he'd told her?

He stopped himself.

Here he'd been accusing Garr's Sorn of un-Imbati behavior! What would he do, eavesdrop at the Headmaster's door? No; he should go straight home before he did something stupid.

Aloran took the orange-lit path past the catch-pools to the dormitory. The night's review still echoed in his mind. He had learned one thing: the sons bore little resemblance to their father, so their mother was probably tall and thin. And since Grobal Garr's temperament seemed to match Nekantor's, maybe she was like Tagaret. Kind, but angry.

Wait.

He'd said that to Eyli, and she'd told him he knew more than he realized. He'd said other things, too . . . what had they been? Instantly he was torn, appalled that he'd let Grobal Garr suck him in, yet desperate to win through to the Lady. He began a breath pattern; confusion tangled to a knot in his stomach.

He needed to see Kiit. In the dormitory, the ceiling lights were dimmed, but a few smaller lights remained along the rows of bunks—one of them, Kiit's reading light. He walked over and checked for her bunkmate, Jeris, but the top bed was empty. Even better.

"Aloran?" Kiit patted the bed beside her.

He ducked in and pulled down the upper coverlet so it gave them some slight privacy. Kiit was beautiful in the shadowy light, face-naked and ready for bed.

He forced himself to address public information first. "The fever news . . ."

She nodded. "Already received."

Thank Heile. "My review . . ." he said, and stopped. How could he tell her? He'd never before envied her frankness, but he could have used it now. Maybe if she weren't watching him . . . "Uh, may I brush your hair?"

"Of course." Kiit fetched her brush.

Aloran brushed slowly. The tangles divided across the brush and fell away, and the words sighed out. "It was bad. I didn't see the Lady."

"Oh, Aloran. I'm sorry."

He kept brushing.

After a while Kiit shrugged. "It's only one bad experience, though. You did say you thought the Lady was worth the risk."

"The Lady—" His moment of tantalizing insight revived, and indignation came with it. "Kiit, the Master *hides* her. He says she needs to be *protected*, and then he—" His voice failed. *He uses me to hurt her.*

"Well, the ladies do need to be protected," Kiit said. "Or we would have no vocation."

Aloran shook his head. Years of dry lessons on caste decline and demographic pressure turned ugly when they became real. Imagine her, having to stand constantly amid Grobal Garr, Tagaret, and Nekantor. How could *anyone* survive in that position?

"Kiit," he said. "What should I do if they *don't* reject me? What if they call me back?"

"*Do?*" She turned to face him, wrinkles creasing her unmarked brow. "Aloran, you feel so strongly you'd risk your reputation to avoid these people?"

His throat tightened. "I don't know. What if it's worth it?"

"Then fail," she said with a shrug. "Show emotion; trip; startle and drop something—whatever you must. You're too good to be ruined by one refusal."

Aloran shuddered. If he failed to appear, the Academy would be blamed. If he deliberately underperformed, he could hurt his chances at another job. But if he took the position, he could end up corrupted just like Sorn, Mai forbid.

"I'm not sure, Kiit," he said.

She gave a smile of sympathy and offered her hand, palm-upward.

Oh, yes. Gratefully, he pressed his hand to hers, savoring the tingle of permission. He put his arm around her.

Kiit switched off her reading light and began kissing down his neck.

Apparently, she wanted more than comfort. Her first touch had already roused him; he didn't suppress the urge, but undressed quickly and joined her under the coverlet. Kiit's skin was smooth, and she pulled him hard against her. He drank her avid kisses. As she took him in, the evening finally released its grip on his mind. He thrust urgently, thoughtless of anything but her, holding his breath to take his climax in silence.

Afterward, he turned to lie with his face toward the metal struts of the upper bunk. Kiit's silken head rested against his shoulder, and he listened to her breath slowing naturally.

Before long, Kiit's bunkmate Jeris returned. She knew, of course. Jeris lay with her own girls; so did his own bunkmate, Endredan, who was chosen of Mai. Dormitory life was like that; everyone knew about everyone else. But they'd never intrude or gossip, because they knew what *respect* really meant.

Thank all the gods he had been born Imbati.

CHAPTER SEVEN
Age of Choice

I t should have been a nightmare, except that it was true: Mother sobbing, on her knees beside her Eyli on the floor, and the old, faithful Imbati crying, too, clinging to Mother's hands, begging forgiveness for the failings of her age.

Tagaret hated himself for causing it. But he'd had no choice—or had he? Was it worse to hurt Mother with the truth, or to hide it? Either answer seemed to turn him into Father.

He would never be like Father. Today he had to prove it.

With grim determination—and quite a lot of one-handed buttoning—he dressed in his new suit. For safety's sake, he asked Serjer's approval; Serjer caught a button he'd missed, and reminded him that his first obligation wasn't school, but his meeting with the Arbiter of the First Family Council.

Right.

It wasn't so bad. Arbiter Erex was a good place to start—he might be stuffy and traditional, but he gave excellent advice, which was why the First Family had chosen him to safeguard the Family's reputation into the next generation. Tagaret jogged inward across the central halls of the Residence and into the arched corridor on the east side, where cabinet members and Family Councils had their offices. The Arbiter's small, intense manservant, Imbati Kuarmei, was waiting outside Erex's door. She bowed, and let him in.

"Tagaret!" Arbiter Erex said. "Congratulations." He was only slightly taller than Kuarmei, and the thin hand he extended across his steel desk had clubbed fingertips—a symptom of his congenital heart condition.

Tagaret shook his hand. "Good morning, Erex, sir."

"I've been looking forward to this day. And you're certainly look-ing the mature gentleman! Who's the artist behind that handsome suit?"

Tagaret smiled. "It's from Selimna, sir. I'll ask my mother for the name."

"So kind of you. Unfortunately, I don't think it would suit me near as well." Erex tugged his sober, amber-toned sleeves, and motioned Tagaret into the facing chair. "I know we must get you off to school, but this won't take long. Here's your new expense marker, if you'll give me yours, so you'll be able to purchase alcohol whenever it's appropriate."

Tagaret couldn't resist asking, "Not 'whenever I like'?"

"Seventeen is the Age of Choice," Erex said primly. "I expect a young gentleman of your age to make good choices."

"I understand, sir." He fished his marker from his pocket and handed it over. The one Erex gave him in return was darker green, with a Grobal insignia in the corner. "Thank you, sir."

"The good news is: no more homework, no more grades. How-ever, you'll only switch to half-time school attendance after you find an assistant position, either in the Pelismar Cabinet, the Family Coun-cil, or the Courts."

Confirmed: that was why Father had been introducing him to everyone. Mai knew Father probably already had someone all lined up, and would want credit for 'surprising' him. "Do I have any choice?" Tagaret asked.

Erex smiled reassuringly. "A boy with your connections? In fact, your problem will be too many to choose from. Several parties have already expressed interest by asking to sponsor you at upcoming events. From the cabinet, Fedron you know already; also Doret of the Elev-enth Family, and Caredes of the Eighth Family. There are others, but you might as well start at the top."

That was more helpful than Erex probably realized. It implied Fa-ther was making people compete for favor. So the decision might not yet be final. Doret was a cousin of Mother's, but, unfortunately, also an old-friend-turned-crony of Father's. Caredes, he had no idea—but who except Father's allies would dare to express public interest? "Who are the others? Do any of them want to ask questions?"

"I'm not sure what you mean."

"Is there anyone who actually listens to new ideas, or will they all just tell me what to do?"

"They will *teach* you, young man." Erex looked almost flustered; the way he laid his hand on his chest made Tagaret feel guilty for asking at all. He changed the subject.

"All right, then, what about ladies? I can be betrothed now, right?"

"Ah." Erex tapped his blunt fingertips together. "Tagaret, I arranged a betrothal for your cousin Inkala just yesterday, but in fact, partnerships depend on the political success of the gentlemen who offer them."

Inkala was almost his own age. "Sir," Tagaret asked, "how old was the gentleman you matched with her?"

Erex sighed. "Young Tagaret, let me just say that finding an assistantship is your best step toward gaining the required status." He offered his hand again. "Feel free to come to me for advice any time you need it. Oh, and I'm afraid I haven't yet received your birthday letter from the Eminence; I'll have my Kuarmei deliver that to you later today."

"Thank you, sir." Tagaret walked out with a sigh. Alcohol was one thing, but he had zero chance with Della, and politically, it was a choice between Father's friends and Father's other friends. No choice at all.

"Tagaret!" voices cried. "Congratulations!"

Reyn, Fernar, and Gowan?

His three friends grinned, pulling him forward into birthday hugs. Tagaret tried to pretend Reyn's arms felt just like the others', but they didn't at all. He cleared his throat.

"Wow, guys? How in Varin's name did you find me here?"

Reyn laughed. "Asked Imbati Serjer. Nice coat, by the way."

"What's it supposed to be?" asked Fernar.

Tagaret looked down at the mottled colors and shrugged. "Mixed fiber, I think."

"It's the ocean." Reyn ran one finger down his sleeve. "My parents have shown me photographs."

Mother really *did* want to make a statement. "Wow, Reyn. Thanks for telling me."

"To business, then," Fernar announced. "Tagaret, this way." He turned back toward the central section, and Tagaret found himself being herded along by the other two.

"Where are we going?" he asked.

"It's a surprise."

"What kind?" When they entered the foyer that stood outside the Hall of the Eminence, Tagaret recognized a figure beside the golden statue of a former Eminence. "My cousin Pyaras?"

Gowan coughed in surprise. "Not exactly."

"Happy birthday, Tagaret," Pyaras called, in the high sweet voice that had now become incongruous. Pyaras was only eleven years old, but lucky in his blood—taller and stronger than most boys of fourteen. Everyone said he might make Heir one day.

"Pyaras, what are you doing? Going to see Erex?"

Pyaras' strong dark brows knit. "No. Looking for you."

"Well, that's sweet." Tagaret went to him and clasped his cousin's head against his shoulder. Pyaras squeezed back with the strength of a vise. "Oof. You came all this way just to wish me happy birthday?"

"No," Pyaras said. "I want to join your gang."

Tagaret glanced at the others. "Look, Pyaras. That's nice of you, but it's not a *gang*. These are my friends."

Pyaras huffed. "Just because I'm your cousin means I can't be your friend?"

"I didn't say that; of course, you're my friend."

"It's just that we're going somewhere right now," Fernar put in.

Pyaras scowled.

"To school," Tagaret reassured him. "Why don't you come with us?"

So they walked Pyaras to school, but there were things you couldn't talk about with an eleven-year-old. Especially since today was boys-downstairs-and-girls-upstairs, and the first-floor corridor was humming with lascivious whispers about Speaker Orn and the notorious Kartunnen house. Calls for 'punishment for whores' made him want to cover his cousin's ears. Pyaras was unhappy when they left him, but accepted a promise to see him after school. It was troubling; there must be something going on.

"Sorry about that, guys," Tagaret said. "We should get to class, too."

"Good idea," said Reyn.

"Let us know how it goes, Fernar," said Gowan. He jogged away toward the end of the tile-floored hall, where bronze classroom doors were starting to clang shut. Reyn hesitated a second longer, and then followed him.

Fernar grabbed Tagaret's arm and pulled him into a curtained window alcove.

"What?"

"Shhh!" Fernar waited until the hall quieted, then whispered, "I found something for you. *Her.*"

"*Della?*" His whole body flushed at the idea. "Holy Sirin, we can't."

"Can't we?" Fernar ducked out and bounded away toward the brighter illumination of the central marble staircase.

Tagaret flung himself after. Fernar was fast; taking the steps two at a time, Tagaret barely managed to catch his coattails before they hit the top. "Fernar, wait, we'll get in trouble!"

"No, we won't." Fernar winked at him. "We're not going to see *her*. We're going to see Imbati Yoral. If you're worried about being caught in the hall, then try to look short and female for a minute."

Right now he was feeling anything but female. Tagaret dragged his fingers off the stone banister, his blood humming from his head all the way into his toes. If he could just take one look into the classrooms—*Della*—but no, he mustn't . . .

Three doors down, Fernar steered him toward a large staff room with a circular window in its door. He'd only ever seen the place empty, but now it was filled with Imbati escorts, sitting here and there on sofas or chairs, most reading, but some actually conversing. He gulped.

Fernar reached past him and knocked.

Every head in the room turned; more than thirty tattooed faces looked straight at him.

"Fernar!" Tagaret hissed. "What are you *doing*?" Oh, were they in trouble now! Or was *he* in trouble—probably none of them could see Fernar at all. He tried to scrape together something like polite calm as the nearest escort, a grave elderly woman, came to the door.

"Yes, sir?" Obviously, evaluating him before deciding to turn him in.

Tagaret stood as straight as he could. "I am Tagaret of the First

Family," he said. "If I may, I would like to speak with Della's Yoral, of the Household of the Sixth Family. I apologize for the inconvenience."

"Please wait inside the door," she said. "With your friend."

"Thank you very much. *Come in*, Fernar." He stepped across the threshold. Some of the escorts went back to their reading, but none resumed talking. At the back of the room, Della's Yoral stood and came forward with a short bow.

"If I find you have approached my Mistress alone," he said, "you will never speak with me again."

"We haven't," said Fernar.

Right, but Yoral would never take their word for it. Tagaret grasped at a random inspiration, and cleared his throat, imagining Imbati Serjer to find the pose, eyes up and one hand behind his back.

"Della's Yoral of the Household of the Sixth Family," he intoned, "I extend my invitation to meet with you, and anyone who may accompany you, in the south vestibule of the Grobal School, this afternoon five minutes after the end of classes. Sincerely, Tagaret of the First Family."

He risked a glance and caught Fernar gaping, Della's Yoral in what could only be called a strenuous effort not to look—something. Amused, hopefully, rather than insulted. The escort was silent for a painfully long moment.

"Tagaret of the First Family," he said at last, without a trace of humor. "Perhaps, instead, the north vestibule. My ability to meet will naturally depend upon the convenience of anyone who may accompany me, and thus I may not be able to respond properly to your invitation. Would this be convenient for you? Sincerely, Della's Yoral of the Household of the Sixth Family."

"I accept your terms," Tagaret whispered.

"Then you will excuse me."

"Oh. Yes."

It wasn't until they were back in the shelter of their window alcove that the adrenaline caught up, and Tagaret started shaking. Had he really been that brave? Or stupid? Would Della actually come, or would she merely laugh? He fell back against the wall with both hands on his head. "Oh, great heavens!"

"I can't believe you!" Fernar exclaimed. "You looked just like an

Imbati—I thought he'd kill us for the insult, and now you're *meeting* him? You offer him a drink, and he lets Della *talk* to you? How do you get away with this stuff?"

"I have no idea, Fernar. None. It's the luck of Sirin, or something."

"Well, can I come with you, then, in case she has a friend?"

Tagaret scoffed. "And break Yoral's trust in me? Of course not. Fernar, I will tell you one thing: you have to make the Imbati happy."

"Are Imbati ever happy?"

"Oh, come on. Of course they are." Fernar had obviously never lived alone with servants. "Just promise you won't follow me."

Fernar snorted a laugh. "Fine—I can't wait to tell Reyn and Gowan about this."

Tagaret swallowed. Reyn wasn't going to be happy at all.

School was interminable. In spite of his guilt over Reyn, every thought of Della sent him into embarrassing swells of anticipation, drowning out the Schoolmasters' lectures. When the final bell rang, Tagaret sprang up and wove northward through the press of exiting boys to the end of the corridor. Outside the first set of glass doors, he stepped against the wall, and glued his eyes on the place where the marble stairs disappeared above the landing.

Please let her come, holy Eyn, please . . .

As the flow diminished, a hand tugged at his sleeve. Tagaret jumped. It was Pyaras, looking frantic. "Tagaret, I've been looking everywhere for you. You promised to get me!"

"I'm sorry, Pyaras," Tagaret said. "It's my fault—something came up." Thank Sirin, they had a minute before the girls came down. Pyaras wasn't like Fernar, but he could still cause Yoral to abandon the meeting.

"I have to join your gang, Tagaret," Pyaras said. "I *have* to—Benél's boys are after me!"

Tagaret looked at him hard. "Seriously? Nek would never threaten his own family."

"Not Nek," said Pyaras. "It's different boys every time, but always Yril and Grenth of the Twelfth Family. Please, they're coming."

Tagaret glanced back through the doors into the main corridor. It was true; a group of boys was on its way, with Yril of the Twelfth Family in the lead. But he couldn't afford a fight right now. Even if they didn't get caught by the Schoolmasters, he'd lose his chance to see Della, and Yoral would feel sorely insulted. Maybe he could get Pyaras out of reach, then duck back in before the girls came down . . .

But he'd broken his promise once already. And Pyaras was family.

Tagaret set his hand on his cousin's shoulder and braced himself as the double doors opened.

"Heyy, Pyaraaas . . ."

In stalked Yril, followed closely by his big cousin Grenth and the gang's other two enforcers.

"Hello, Yril," Tagaret said firmly.

Yril stopped and his eyes narrowed. Sizing him up. "Oh, hey, Tagaret."

"Any particular business you have with my cousin?"

Yril's eyes flicked furtively back toward the hall. He stood straighter. "What's it to you?"

Another gang member came in—Jiss, his name was. That made five of them, and trouble, except that Yril's glance suggested something else was coming. Better keep him talking.

"I'm concerned for Pyaras, naturally," Tagaret said. "Something *I* could help you with?"

A reckless smile peeled across Yril's gaunt face. "Maybe so. You're looking lonely today."

"He's not!" Pyaras cried before Tagaret could hush him.

Yril laughed. "Little Cousin's too big to shut up. Too bad he's too small to matter."

Pyaras growled.

But Yril was right. Reyn's absence was a cold space at his back. Fernar's physical strength would have been awfully welcome. Gowan was no heavy, but his connections made for effective threats, so at five apiece it would be about even. Right now, it was Yril and friends against the First Family—but maybe that was why Yril had targeted Pyaras in the first place.

Tagaret put his other hand on Pyaras' shoulder, holding him down. "Making a move on the First Family, are you, Yril? Testing your support by abusing a boy of eleven, well, that certainly shows your courage."

Yril said nothing; Grenth and the others shuffled feet. Another gang member pushed in, with a silver-eared limeret perched on his shoulder.

Six to two—*if* these boys were all taking Yril's orders.

Tagaret scanned the exits. The gang already blocked the main hall; on the stairs he and Pyaras could be run down with no witnesses, but out on the grounds their humiliation would be public. He'd have to take a chance that Yril hadn't yet consolidated his support.

"Nekantor!" he shouted. "Ho, are you there? First Family! Benél!"

Yril flinched.

And the last three boys walked in.

Benél strutted chin-first—he was no longer moody and quiet like before he and Nek teamed up. With Nek by his ear and a wiry fellow named Losli at his elbow, gnash it if he didn't look just like Father trailing a pair of cronies.

Benél looked around, frowning. "What's going on here?"

Yril made fists. "I'm just—"

"He's been roughing Pyaras," Tagaret said loudly. "With friends. Seems unlike you to target a cousin."

Nekantor's eyes sharpened in a way so familiar it made him sorry for Yril. "Ohhh," Nek said. "Is this your ploy, Yril? You really are an idiot."

"I'll show you who's the idiot!" Yril snapped. The gang's focus shifted, bodies taking sides. Tagaret relaxed his hands on Pyaras' shoulders.

Pyaras charged.

"Pyaras, no!" Tagaret cried.

Pyaras hit Grenth in the stomach so hard that the larger boy wheezed and doubled over. Shock splashed outward through Benél's gang.

Mercy, get out, get out, get out—

Tagaret dived in, grabbed Pyaras under the arms, and dragged him backward through the outer doors.

"Run!" he shouted.

He swerved away from the Residence—that was too obvious a route, and without cover. Instead, he headed straight north, crashing across gravel paths and jumping short hedges. A quick glance showed Pyaras catching up, a furious Grenth some distance behind. Ahead, the arbors and fountains of the City Garden beckoned with a sound of water. His lungs started to ache. He dodged around the Safe Harbor fountain, a sandstone basin and pinnacle entwined in blue glass. Pyaras overtook him as he reached the Erin fountain; he pulled Pyaras down behind its drenched basalt mass and stopped, listening for Grenth's footsteps.

"I can't *believe* boys! They care more about fighting each other than they do about anyone else."

That voice. Tagaret tried to force his breath quiet. That was the voice that sang shivering melodies in his sleep. Could he be imagining it?

"Mistress, you made the right decision."

No, that was Imbati Yoral. And the presence of a bodyguard would easily explain why Grenth had broken off pursuit. "Pyaras," Tagaret hissed. "Can you get yourself home from here?"

Pyaras flashed a grin. "So am I in your gang now?"

Varin's teeth . . . "It's not up to me."

Pyaras raised his eyebrows.

"All right, I'll talk to the others, but I can't promise!"

Pyaras' lips twitched in amusement. He peered through the arbors, then nodded sagely. "Good enough."

Tagaret tried to straighten his clothes. The coat had stood up to the run better than he expected; he could only hope the shirt wasn't a total mess. He walked out between the Peak and Selimna fountains. Della and her Yoral had just passed his position, heading toward the north grounds gate. Della must live outside the Residence, where the cavern roof was lower and the less well-connected families had their homes.

Sixth Family, Gowan's warnings nudged. *Muckwalkers.*

But today, making his own choices mattered even more than it had before.

"Pardon me," Tagaret called. "Yoral—"

The Imbati turned, fast as fire.

Tagaret instinctively stepped backward. "I apologize," he said fervently. "My younger cousin came under threat, and he ran to me. This put you in danger, and I'm sorry. I entirely understand if you decide you don't wish to meet." *But please don't hurt me . . .*

Della was watching him now. If he could just look straight at her, he would gaze all day. He turned his open hands to the Imbati, pleading silently.

"Grobal Tagaret, sir," said Yoral. "It appears that this morning, you came directly to me."

Tagaret nodded. "Yes, of course."

The Imbati took Della back on his arm, moving closer. In the corner of his eye, Tagaret could see her anxiously biting her lip. "You understand," Yoral said, "that allowances depend entirely on context and company."

What should he say to that? His throat tightened at the word 'allowances.' He risked a glance—Della's eyes came to his. Her vivid green attention sent a rush down his body. She smiled, soft lips pulling back over white teeth. If only he could shout it aloud in praise: Della, Della!

"Tagaret," she said.

"Della," he blurted. He couldn't have stopped himself—it was hard enough keeping the volume down. He sneaked an eye to Yoral, but the Imbati now stood impassive.

"He means," Della said, blushing, "if I'm with friends, or my family, you have to talk to him, still."

"Oh. Of course."

A wysp, drifting by the gate, cast glimmers in Della's hair. She wrung her hands. "I'd been planning what to say to you," she said. "But there were those boys, and I didn't . . . I think I'll get it all wrong."

"You couldn't possibly."

She caught him with an intense look. "*The Catacomb*, Tagaret. You remember it?"

"I'll never forget it."

"Neither will I. Can you tell me—" She glanced away abruptly. "Did you hate it?"

Doubt whirled in his stomach. Had she *hated* it? But how could that be? She'd stayed to hear it out . . . "Uh, n-no," he stammered.

"Oh, thank Heile."

Seeing her shoulders relax was such a relief that his knees felt weak. By Eyn's grace, he'd passed her test. "I'm awed by the inspiration behind a piece like that," he said. "Kartunnen are so different from us. I wish I could understand how they do it."

"You're not just saying that?"

The intense look was back: that was a dare, an invitation to cross a line he couldn't see. He shivered and leaned slightly toward her. "I *love* music. Sometimes I think—" His voice cracked. "What I mean is, do you think Kartunnen might have stronger feelings than we do? To create feelings in us so easily?"

"I don't think so at all," she said. "But then, I've met Kartunnen Tromaldin."

Tagaret gaped. "You've met the conductor of the Pelismar Symphony?"

Della retreated slightly. "I'm sorry."

"No, please don't be. You're very lucky." It was Tromaldin whom Mother had met, back when he was playing lead shiazin and the concert series was only an idea.

Della's lips curved. "Well, I'll remember that, if it seems likely to happen again."

Yoral glanced at his watch. "Please excuse us, sir. We're expected at home."

"Of course," Tagaret said. "Goodbye." He looked at his own watch and panicked: birthday party in six minutes. He turned back to the Residence and ran.

By the time he reached home, there were already voices in the dining room. He managed to cross the sitting room and lock his door without being discovered, flung himself into the shower, scoured dry, and with Serjer's help, changed into the second shirt Mother had given him. Checked himself in the bathroom mirror—combed his hair—all right, ready or not.

Warily, he cracked open his bedroom door.

A man's quiet voice spoke from nearby. "Tagaret, is that you?"

Not Father; not Nekantor. That sounded like . . . "Arbiter Erex?"

"Please excuse the intrusion," Erex said. He cast a glance at the doors where the noise of partygoers seeped through.

"Sir, are you feeling all right?" Tagaret asked. "I thought you said your Kuarmei would bring my letter."

"Oh, yes! I am well." Erex smiled. "You're kind to ask. In fact, I thought you might like my company at the party, since Garr has invited certain individuals I mentioned to you this morning."

"*Individuals?*" Gods, was Father putting him up for public auction? "It's kind of you, sir, but no thanks—I'd like to handle this myself."

Erex nodded. "One warning, then," he said. "Caredes of the Eighth Family is looking for you. You'll know him by his eyes. Expect him to speak of the negative."

"I understand. Erex, will my father get mad at you for warning me?"

Erex shrugged. "Not if you don't tell him."

Tagaret laid his hands against the double doors to go out, but stopped and turned back. "What about Lady Selemei?"

Erex's brows pinched. "She's not on the interest list."

"I mean, what I'm asking is, she's family, so can I consider her an ally, like Fedron does? Or is Father right to think she's a danger?"

"Oh, an ally, most definitely." He glanced to one side. "Still, don't trust her overfar."

"Why not? What does she want?"

Erex lowered his voice. "She has *attempted* to end ladies' duties as we know them." But then he smiled. "Not to worry, though; that was years ago. We've got her well in hand at this point."

Do you really? For an instant, Tagaret was tempted to tell Erex everything about the tea invitation, to beg for his assistance, but there was no time. Father was waiting for him outside these doors. "Thank you, sir," he said, and pushed through.

If not for Erex, he'd have expected mostly cousins in the sitting room. Instead, the space was as crowded as he'd ever seen it, with gentlemen and ladies both—no visiting manservants, though he spied both Serjer and Premel moving among the guests. Nek was here, too, showing no signs of the confrontation with Yril. He stood, as always, slightly to one side, wearing a disconcerting half-smile and not touching anyone.

"Here's Tagaret!" Father shouted.

The room erupted into applause. There were cries of "Tagaret!" and "Congratulations!"

"Thank you," Tagaret said. "Thank you all for coming. This is a very big day for me—and I hear, also for my cousin Inkala, who was betrothed this morning." The crowd applauded; from some distance in, Inkala waved gratefully. Not far from her stood Pyaras, and his father, Administrator Vull, who must have felt the occasion was special enough to step out of his bureaucratic work. And there was Caredes of the Eighth Family. Erex wasn't kidding about the eyes—Caredes' bulging gaze must indicate some sort of glandular condition. Beside him, Mother was showing her pleasant face, with only her severely braided hair to hint at the will required to maintain it.

Tagaret sought Father's glance. A frown had darkened his face, maybe in reaction to Mother's Selimnar suit. The only plausible way to stop him was to control the topic of politics before he had a chance to. Tagaret cleared his throat as he turned back to the crowd. "I know I've got some important career decisions to make now, and I'm looking forward to talking to all of you individually. But before I do, I'd like to thank Father and Mother for coming back from Selimna." He indicated them, and the crowd burst into applause, particularly Fedron and Doret, who had moved to the front. Father puffed with pride and inhaled as if to launch into his own speech, so Tagaret added quickly, "And special thanks to Mother, for giving me the music that kept me alive while they were gone. I'm planning to continue to support the concert series she started—I'd really like to see *The Catacomb* return to the Residence under more happy circumstances."

There was a burst of applause, enthusiastically led by Amyel, Gowan's father.

"All right, son, that's enough," Father growled, drawing closer. "On to business."

"You mean assistant positions?" Tagaret muttered back. "Shouldn't we negotiate those privately with interested individuals, so we don't look like Melumalai in front of our guests?" He met Father's gaze, trying not to waver.

Father narrowed his eyes, almost like Nekantor. "Fine, then. Let's get started." He pulled Tagaret toward the four cabinet guests. Tagaret kept his head up and apologized to the people they bumped as they went. He glimpsed Erex following at a discreet distance; also Nekantor, staying nimbly out of harm's way.

"Tagaret, congratulations," Fedron called. "Nicely done, Garr, nicely done."

Right, of course, his age was Father's doing.

"Yes, indeed," Doret of the Eleventh Family agreed, raising a glass of yezel that surely wasn't his first. "The Race is grateful for your gifts of these two handsome sons."

What a pair of tunnel-hounds. Tagaret waved down Serjer, who with a sympathetic glance, offered a silver platter of food to the cabinet members. Fedron and Doret were quieter with their mouths full of lake-bass roe on crackers.

Gowan's father Amyel brandished a cracker in one hand. "Young Tagaret, I'm glad to hear you won't be abandoning music," he said. "The series is a worthy project and an excellent organizational experience if you increase your own responsibility."

He'd never thought about it that way. "Thank you, sir," said Tagaret.

"You won't have time for that *and* your assistantship," said Father. "Unless you're offering, Amyel, and can allow him the time?"

Amyel demurred.

Caredes of the Eighth Family hadn't taken any food; his bulging eyes scanned Tagaret up and down. "No diseases?" he asked.

Thanks to Erex's warning, Tagaret managed to smile. "No, sir. I'm well, thank you."

Caredes shook a bony finger. "That fever's still around, you know. Anyone could die, any time. You, me, him—" He flipped his thumb at Amyel, who shrugged amiably. "*Anyone.*"

"I'll be cautious, sir. Thank you for the advice."

A stir began across the room. People pulled back, opening an aisle between Tagaret and the front entrance of the suite, where a tall man and his servant now stood under the awed stares of the guests.

"It's Herin," Arbiter Erex almost sighed. "The Heir."

The Heir was worth staring at. His skin had a deep golden tone; his hair was two shades darker, and he wore it curled tightly against his head. In a gold velvet suit he practically glowed.

"Tagaret of the First Family," he said. "I bring your birthday letter from the Eminence Indal. Congratulations on your Age of Choice."

CHAPTER EIGHT

Playing Games

Nekantor watched, his heart racing.

Power hummed around Herin, drawing every eye in the room. *This*, now—this was the *real* game. Nothing like Yril's feeble attempts to play, abusing a boy so young it was practically a joke, trying to sneak support away from Benél. Yril had whined something about giving him Tagaret as a gift, but Benél had got him in a headlock, and then all the others came in line. As if Yril could give them supremacy against Tagaret's gang—ridiculous. He couldn't give them something they already had.

The Heir took five steps into the room with his head held high and his glimmering shoulders thrown back. Nekantor sneaked forward, dodging skirts and suits, edging close enough to feel that electric power. Father shook Tagaret out of stupid paralysis and shooed him forward.

"So, young Tagaret," said the Heir. "Congratulations to you."

Tagaret bowed submissively. "Thank you, sir."

Now the Heir's servant produced the letter from the Eminence Indal, and the Heir handed it to Tagaret. See the power rub off on the eldest boy of the family, letting him share the center of the room? That was Father's doing; only Father could have swayed Herin to come to this party. Meanwhile, Arbiter Erex stood off to the side gaping like a cooked fish. Erex would never stand in the center of a room.

Benél could have, if he were here. He would know how—Benél was powerful.

"Thank you so much for coming, Herin," Father said. Garr, the second-best player in the room. The very fact that the Heir stood here was his victory. Garr and Herin shook hands, their eyes locked, each man vying for the upper hand. The Heir was handsomer than Father, more perfectly dressed—so easy on the mind—but he broke away first. He pretended decisiveness in the release, but really it was weakness. Father knew he was owed, for the assassination that had put Herin ahead of all his rivals, and Herin knew it, too.

"And who's this?" Herin asked, turning so the power came warm as heat. Nekantor straightened in it. His bones hummed.

"My second son, Nekantor," said Father. "Nekantor, the Heir, Herin."

Nekantor bowed, smiling. He had information on Herin: *the Heir's partner has carried their second child to seven months, so it looks good.* "It's a pleasure to meet you, sir," he said. "The Race awaits your latest gift, with honor for your partner's endurance."

"Thank you very much, young man." Herin preened and puffed, then turned to Father. "She grows and grows, and makes no complaints. The child moves. It bodes well."

"May Heile and Eyn keep them both," Father said.

"Excuse me, Herin, sir," said Tagaret. "May I offer you a seat and something to eat?"

Nekantor looked at his brother. Unexpected—and not a bad move. That would keep the power near them longer.

Herin chuckled. "I don't mind at all, young Tagaret. Thank you."

The fluster was awful. Father shouting, Imbati scurrying, guests moving about making noise—oh, the chaos! Nekantor breathed hard. The patterns of power in the room broke and churned. It made his chest hot, made him want to scream—but *that wasn't a good move.* Nekantor clenched his fists. He backed to the wall and stared at his watch.

Yes, the watch. It was gold, with a polished circle of glass on top, gleaming and perfect. Perfect, perfect, and it counted seconds one by one, pulling his eyes into its slow pattern while tick, tick fell like ripples into his mind. He let go his fists. He touched the buttons on his vest, top, middle, bottom. He straightened his cuffs, looked back to the watch. Tick, tick . . . better, better. He would not scream. He would stay in the game.

The noise of fuss slowly diminished. Nekantor glanced up and back to the watch. Cataloged the glimpse in his head: a pattern of guests, Heir, Father, Tagaret. Not too much motion. Tick, tick . . . Safe enough. He sneaked between the skirts and suits to a place beside Father at the Heir's right hand. A cushioned brass chair had been brought for the Heir to sit in. Herin held a mushroom pastry, and gold sparkling yezel in a crystal glass. He was gold, all gold. Attention ran down the crowd to him and he drank it with his yezel, in sips.

"Garr, my compliments to your Household. The food is delicious." He beckoned to Tagaret. "Young Tagaret, I have some advice, in return for your kind invitation."

Tagaret took a step forward. "Yes, sir?"

"Always be careful of accepting gifts or favors." Herin looked out across the crowd. "When you accept a gift, you accept an obligation along with it." He lifted his sparkling yezel, and toasted the guests, who aahed and murmured because they did not have power.

And now, for accepting his gift, they all owed him.

That was well done—Herin made his game of favors look easy. He accepted the offer of food from Tagaret, but he cast aside obligation to Tagaret by thanking Father. Easy to thank Father, because food became insignificant before the favor of murder which outweighed all others. Herin then singled out Tagaret to award advice and won obligation from the entire room.

But—strange weakness—the advice the Heir gave was to teach his own game. Only a fool would drop jewels where anyone might pick them up.

His loss. It was a good game, and easily learned. Nekantor scanned the room. What kind of favor might snare Amyel of the Ninth Family, or Caredes of the Eighth, or Arbiter Erex? What favor might the Heir himself accept? And what about Father?

Something about giving him Tagaret as a gift.

An ugly memory. Nekantor caught it and closed it in his fists: Yril, in a headlock, making stupid excuses to Benél.

But not just making excuses. *And not stupidly.* Yril had been playing the game of favors, right under Benél's nose. Failing his coup, he'd try to win obligation from the boy who had power.

He'd failed there, too. Benél knew his own cousins better than that.

But Yril. How *dare* he? A headlock was insufficient—he must be taught a lesson before he tried again. Before he caught Benél alone, with no one to explain things to him. There were plenty of reasons why Yril deserved punishment—and Grenth, too, who'd followed him. And Pyaras also, for making the whole gang look weak.

Nekantor growled in his throat.

Father growled louder.

Was he being scolded? He looked up, but Father wasn't looking at him; he'd been clearing his throat to speak.

"Herin, I must say, when I first heard that Orn had met misfortune, I wasn't sure if I should leave Selimna, but you've certainly made it worth my while. It's a pleasure working with you."

Herin obviously didn't like it. He smirked at Father out of the corner of his eyes. "A pleasure, indeed," he said, "but you've missed something, Garr. It wasn't *misfortune* that Orn met."

Nekantor grimaced. He had *that* information on Orn. Orn had met a Kartunnen whore.

The crowd in the room shuffled and tittered. They'd listened, toadying to please Father, and when the Heir turned a countermove, were caught in the struggle. Nekantor scanned around, but the other cabinet members were nowhere to be seen—too afraid to get between the big players. Now they would miss the fun of watching.

Father shrugged. "I'd say Kinders fever was misfortune enough for any man."

"For all the Race, you mean." Herin handed his yezel to his servant and stood, looking around at the crowd. An interesting move: now he'd claimed the crowd against Father, and they shivered under the power radiating from him. "Those Kartunnen know they'll survive infection, so they think nothing of risking *us* with their negligence. It's more than irresponsible. It's criminal! Don't you think someone should teach them a lesson?"

Father scowled. Amusing, how he hated to be topped. More amusing was how useless Tagaret was—he'd conceded completely, dropping his face into his hands. Father would never do such a thing. Two more seconds, five at the most, before he'd turn his own countermove. Nekantor waited. One, two, three—

Garr stepped into the Heir's circle and stood by his side. "Certainly, Herin. But who would do it? I've spoken with the police. They say it's a licensed establishment and they have no grounds to close it. No grounds! Who would dare teach them a lesson after that?"

Herin tossed his head. "I would—if it didn't mean such a terrible risk to the nation."

An idea struck, so perfect that Nekantor laughed out loud.

Faces whipped around to stare at him. In the silence, a lady tittered. Then the entire crowd burst into laughter.

They thought it was a *joke?* Nekantor threw his head back and laughed harder. Fine, let them think so if they wanted!

Really, it was an opportunity.

The Heir and Father both wanted those Kartunnen whores taught a lesson, or why bother with this competition of rhetorical questions? It was all posturing. Oh, oh, who would dare teach the filthy whores a lesson? Who, indeed? There they both were, eyes only for their own power struggle, stupid for this moment to one simple and obvious fact:

They were both asking for a favor.

Nekantor walked out of the party, to his rooms. He circled, touching, checking, making sure nothing was out of place. But when everything was perfect, he didn't stop pacing. He watched the moves unroll in his mind. Go get Benél; go get Losli, and Losli would fetch the others. Take skimmers down to the Kartunnen neighborhood. Yes, this would be a good game.

He had to wait until the party guests left; Father would never let him go out before dinner. Frustrating, but it did give him time to plan. When his dinner plate was perfectly empty, he left the others at the table and went back to his rooms. He put a wire and a fresh handkerchief in his pocket. He walked out again through the empty sitting room where the Imbati had tidied away the party. Now the game could begin.

The first move was to get Benél.

It wasn't easy to go out. Nekantor went into the vestibule. He counted buttons on his trousers, his shirt, his vest, three times before he dared to touch the door handle. Remember, it wasn't really going out alone; he was going straight to Benél's, and Benél's suite was only fifty-seven paces away. He held his breath and dived out.

He walked fast, breathed when he had to. This was the hardest part: just get to Benél's. Wall curtains could hide assassins—he touched each one as he passed by. Fifty paces managed now. Fifty-five.

He rang the doorbell, then banged on the door, and snapped at the Imbati who opened it.

"Let me in. I'm here to see Benél."

"Sir," the Imbati said, bowing, "I'm afraid the family is still at dinner." Maddening creature, he stood on the threshold, blocking the way to safety inside.

Nekantor growled. "Let me in, gnash it!"

"Sir—"

"Remeni, it's all right, I'm finished." Benél's voice, beyond the curtain. The idiot servant bowed away.

Benél pushed through the curtain. Benél was here: the first move of the game, done. Nekantor gulped air. It was all right—Benél was powerful, and his powerful hand came, grasped the back of his neck, shaking gently. "Hey, Nek."

"Hey, Benél," Nekantor said. He was always safe with Benél, and Benél was smiling at him; it felt very good. "I have a project for us, tonight."

Benél nodded. "Sure. Do we need the boys?"

"Yeah."

So the second move of the game was to get Losli.

They walked together to Losli's suite. Benél's hand stayed tight on his neck all the way. Losli was small and fast, with the heart of a follower and a good head. When they told him they'd be hitting the whorehouse, he frowned.

"What about Arissen?" he asked. "If your dad and the Heir want this done, does that mean they're getting the police out of the way?"

"No," Nekantor said. "So you'll be lookout, Losli. You'll warn us when the Arissen come near."

Benél grunted. "Arissen should be the ones getting this done; not us. They're bigger and stronger."

"They won't, though," Nekantor said. "They said they had no grounds." He shuddered. The whores presumed to contaminate their betters—that should be grounds enough. "But if *we* do it, then it's a favor for Father and the Heir both."

Losli pinched the bridge of his nose. "We need fists for this. Definitely Tindamer and Dix, but I don't see how we can get along without Grenth, and that means bringing Yril, too. After today, I'm not sure."

Nekantor nodded. "They need to be punished."

"Grenth won't be able to stop *Arissen*," Benél said. "Not if Pyaras can fold him over, Nek."

Losli slapped his forehead. "I didn't mean Grenth should fight Arissen . . ."

But maybe he should. Nekantor grinned. "That's it!"

"What?"

"It's perfect. Grenth and Yril will help us get our job done, and then when you give the alarm, Losli, tell *them* last." Who knew that Arissen could be so useful?

Losli nodded.

"What about Pyaras?" Benél asked. "He can't start thinking he can humiliate us in public."

Nekantor licked his lips. Maybe Arissen could be useful again. He sighed dramatically. "But, *Benél*, didn't Pyaras' strength impress you? He's so big, it's—it's *unrefined*. Makes you wonder if his blood is really of the Race . . ."

"Nek," Benél said, starting to chuckle. "No one humiliates like you."

So that was the second move done, and by the time they'd finished the third—fetch the others—and the fourth—take skimmers uplevel to the Kartunnen neighborhood—the entire gang was laughing about Pyaras the little Arissen. Yril and Grenth laughed loudest. They were angrier because Pyaras had turned their coup on them. Nekantor didn't need to laugh, just leaned close to Benél's ear as he drove. Delicious anticipation bubbled in his stomach. Passing the Arissen insult to Yril and Grenth had been an excellent move. While laughing, they trusted, and thus they opened themselves for their own reward.

"All right," said Benél, pulling their skimmer to one side of the narrow road where the whorehouse stood. "I'm parking here. Jiss and Losli, here behind me; Dix, on the other side of the door, Grenth and Yril behind him—and Tindamer and Drespo at the back."

Nekantor extricated himself hesitantly from their seat. This Lowers neighborhood was all one thing or all the other: the broad circumferences were mostly sidewalk, covered with disarranged furniture and pointless statuary that made his skin crawl; the radius streets were narrow with no sidewalks at all. And now the door of the establishment had no number. It itched at him.

But it would be all right, because Benél was here. He was safe with Benél, because Benél was powerful—and together they had a game to play. Now that they were here, the first move was to get in; the second, to sweep through the open spaces; the third, to identify doors to be unlocked or broken; the fourth, to deal with the inhabitants behind . . .

Benél climbed a pair of steps and knocked on the unnumbered door, which swung inward. Nekantor followed him in—then stiffened. He tried to retreat, but the others piled in behind.

The entryway was a high-ceilinged room with no corners, and tiny bright lights hanging at random heights above. Every curved surface fluttered with glittering shreds of cloth, as if there were a fan somewhere, blowing across them so they never stopped moving. Wrong, all wrong! No place to rest his eyes except on the two women, and *they*—his stomach twisted—they were *crossmarked*.

He tried to breathe, shallow breaths with no air in them.

"Welcome, Gentlemen." The woman who spoke was dressed in green velvet, presuming to imitate a Lady. Her breasts were bare, and her nipples stared at the walls like rock-toad's eyes. The other had assumed an Imbati appearance, with a false tattoo painted on her forehead. When he tore his eyes off it, he discovered her sheer black dress hid nothing.

"Benél," he whispered. "Benél!"

"Go!" Benél shouted. He jumped at the disgusting creatures and knocked them down. They screamed. The boys charged. Nekantor was knocked to one side and another, and then they broke through a door behind the fluttering and disappeared into the space beyond.

Nekantor stood, trying to breathe.

The fluttering wouldn't stop, closing in on him with every breath. There was screaming. The gong-metal sound of doors hitting walls. Crashing and breaking. He couldn't find his buttons or his watch.

Losli ran in. "Nek, come on! We've got some doors that won't open."

Nekantor tried to answer.

"Nek, you all right?"

He should go with Losli. There was a game to be played. There was a wire in his pocket. But the fluttering, and the filthy Lower females . . .

Losli ran out. A minute later he reappeared with Benél.

Benél was here.

Nekantor gasped, "Benél . . ."

"Come on, Nek, we need you." Benél's hand came, grasped the back of his neck, and pulled him through the fluttering wall into a long, curtained corridor. Doors swung open at intervals, with fighting inside. More screaming. Benél brought him to a door that was shut.

Locked.

Yes, doors must not be locked. There was sex behind this locked door. Nekantor knelt and put his wire into the lock. It was an easy lock, no harder than Tagaret's seven locks ago. A scraping, and he twisted the wire, and then a click—ohh, so satisfying.

The door swung open.

The room within was a riot of multicolored cushions—no place to rest his eyes except on the two men. Both stood on the defensive. A tall, broad-chested one with gleaming skin and muscles took shelter behind a smaller, slighter one, who held a pillow over his parts with one hand.

"You will not come in here," said the small man firmly. "In fact, if you do, I will personally make sure each of you fails to achieve a career in politics."

Politics?

Slowly, Nekantor dragged his eyes from the nude body of the male prostitute onto the small man's face. Almost unrecognizable from this afternoon.

Erex, the Arbiter of the First Family Council.

"S-sir?" Benél stammered. "What in Varin's name are you doing here?"

"My business here does not concern you, young Benél," said Erex. "Stay away from us. I won't let you touch him."

"But—"

Erex's voice quavered slightly. "You may consider that I have my hand upon your school records at this moment. Your father would be very disappointed if you were to fail again."

But his hand wasn't on school records. Nekantor knew where it had been. On the body of the man who stood behind him. The thought made his jaw tighten and his stomach burn. "Varin's teeth . . ."

"Close the door, young Benél," said Erex.

Benél closed the door.

Nekantor stared at it—no relief. The knowledge of sex writhed and squirmed in his head. The chaos of destruction echoed all around. Panic climbed his nerves. He turned to look at Benél. Benél's face was perfectly familiar; yes, he was safe with him. "Benél," he murmured. "What do we do now?"

Benél shook himself. "Never mind that room, Nek. There are more."

He didn't want more. He wanted Benél to grab him and shake him. "Benél . . ."

Benél's hand came, not on his neck this time, but tight around his shoulders. "Stay close to me."

They stumbled down the debris-strewn hall. Doors swung open and shut. A whore crossmarked in Arissen red fled from one of the rooms with Tindamer pounding after. Drespo appeared with a rip on the shoulder of his jacket.

"There's another locked door down this way," he said.

Benél pulled Nekantor there. Nekantor didn't want to open the door. The door was locked. He set his teeth and tried to turn away from it, but it was locked, and it reached hooks into his mind. A locked door. The door must not be locked. If he unlocked it . . . sex . . . but it must not be locked.

His hand shook as he put the wire into the lock. Twisted.

The door swung open.

The walls of this room were black, all black, hung with shackles and straps of dark leather. In the center of it stood a woman whose naked skin was marked with uneven black smudges. The only garment she wore was a dark gray hood that hid most of her face.

The undercaste mark.

"Trasher!" Nekantor cried.

"Akrabitti filth!" shouted Benél. He leapt at her, fists swinging. She dodged, grabbed a pair of manacles off the wall, and threw it in his face. Benél roared in pain.

Nekantor screamed.

The trasher was coming at him. Gods, don't let her touch! He leapt backward and smacked into someone, whirled, but it was only Grenth. Grenth and Yril ran after the filth-marked whore. Then Benél was here, wrapping an arm around him again. Benél held a handkerchief over his mouth.

Nekantor gasped, "Benél, that Akrabitti—she—"

"I'm a fool," said Benél. "She's not undercaste. She's a Kartunnen dressed up, gnash her. Let's see if we can get out of this for a minute."

A few steps farther on, they found stairs leading upward. The stairs were quieter, calmer, and did not flutter. It wasn't enough to cool the chaos, but it might lead to better. At the top of the stairs was a locked door. Nekantor put his wire into the lock, and twisted.

The room inside was rich, with a green carpet and velvet curtains held back by golden ropes. It was also empty. Benél pulled Nekantor in and closed the door.

Nekantor stood still. There was a bed here, with smooth pale satin covers. A low set of brass shelves with cut-glass bottles and small crystal glasses. A glass-topped makeup stand, with a tall mirror over it.

The mirror. Nekantor walked to it, laid his hands on it. Pleaded with it. Smooth clear glass, and it should have calmed him, but the bed loomed inside it, whispering of sex. He could see Benél moving there, pushing his hands among the glass bottles. Benél grabbed one and came nearer. Reached below Nekantor's right elbow and set two glasses on the stand.

Nekantor looked down. Two crystal glasses, and Benél's hand, and something else on the table beside it.

A ring. Too reflective for silver. Platinum, then, and smooth, a perfect smooth circle that pulled his mind in, spun him, soothed him.

Benél poured from the bottle. "Nek, here, this will help us both feel better."

Nekantor looked up from the ring and back down. Cataloged the glimpse: Benél, his lower lip swollen, holding a glass of luminous clear brown liquid. He wasn't ready. He *wanted* to look at Benél, but he still needed the ring.

"Benél," he said. "Don't drink. Wash your hands first. This is a fever house."

"Oh, right." Benél moved away. "I found the bathroom," he said.

Nekantor put his hand over the ring. He closed his fingers, felt the smooth perfection of it. Brought it with him through the door to a red marble room where Benél stood, pouring water over his hands and splashing it on his face. Nekantor bent to the water also, washing his hands and the ring with them. Finally, he was able to look up again.

Benél gave him a glass. "Chatinet," he said. "My dad drinks it. You'll like it." He put the glass to his lips and tipped his head back. The liquid vanished into his mouth.

Nekantor looked at the glass. Sniffed it, took a sip. His lips burned, but it was sweet. And a glass should be full or empty, so he took another drink. Tipped back his head for the last drops, and warmth hit him in the stomach. Now the glass was empty. He rolled the ring around his hand and put the empty glass down on the red marble.

"Benél, we have to get out of here," he said, shaking his head. "This place . . ."

Benél came, put his arm around his shoulders. "It's awful," he said. "I didn't know it would be so bad for you, but you're right. It's disgusting."

Nekantor nodded and rolled the ring around his hand. Benél's arm was tight around him, and Benél's lip was hurt. Gnash that whore, for doing that to Benél. Benél's lip was swollen and soft. He didn't want to look at it—he couldn't stop looking at it. The chatinet was gone, but the heat in his stomach wasn't. Dizziness buzzed behind his ears. He lifted one finger and touched Benél's hurt lip.

Benél hissed a breath in, slowly.

Someone banged on the door, slammed it open. Nekantor took his finger back, hid it against his stomach.

Losli.

"Arissen!" Losli panted. "Let's go!"

Go. Oh—mercy, yes—finally to escape! Nekantor ran down the stairs, faster, faster, up the hall. No eyes for the destruction or the open rooms. Escape was all that mattered—the last move in a game that had gone all wrong. The others' footsteps pounded behind him. He burst through the fluttering room, out the door. Lights in the narrow street—shouts. Benél slid into the skimmer's seat and punched the controls, while Nekantor climbed straight over the seatback and in. Before he was even fully seated, the skimmer lifted, and they were away. Benél drove like he was crazy, hopping the sidewalk and weaving along the streets, then hurtling down the rampway to the fifth level.

No sirens.

He and Benél arrived first at the Conveyor's Hall. Jiss and Drespo came in just behind, then Losli driving alone, and Tindamer and Dix jammed into a skimmer too small for the two of them. No sign of Grenth or Yril.

Nekantor took a deep breath and laughed. Benél laughed, too. They climbed out of the skimmers, and Imbati took them away.

"Home, everyone," Benél called. "And everyone wash."

Tindamer snorted.

"Not to worry," said Losli. "I think I'm going to bathe for a day."

"My jacket is ruined," moaned Drespo. "And we lost Yril and Grenth."

"Home," Benél repeated.

Nekantor watched them all go. Benél's hand came to the back of his neck, shook him gently.

"That means you, too, Nek," Benél said. "What's that you're holding?"

Nekantor opened his hand. The ring gleamed in the bright light of the Conveyor's Hall. With everything around him no longer in chaos, it was no longer perfect. There was something engraved on its inside surface. He lifted it and peered in.

To Yanun my love, Indal

"Indal," he murmured. There was only one Indal. "Benél!"

Benél frowned. "What?"

Nekantor looked up. The truth fell into his mind like a stone, and its consequences spread further, further, further. His heart raced. "It's wonderful news. The Eminence is going to die."

CHAPTER NINE

The Mistress in Person

Aloran moved with his softest, most professional step along the public hall toward the suite of Grobal Garr and Tamelera of the First Family. This would be the last time. Tonight he'd finally meet the Lady herself, but he must fail before he allowed himself to work for her.

Selfish, the voice of condemnation whispered. *Selfish as a cat.*

But he'd already hurt her, just by getting involved. He should withdraw so he couldn't hurt her more.

Grobal Garr will pick someone worse.

Kiit thought he was doing the right thing. And his entire life was at stake—weren't those sufficient reasons?

Selfish Imbati. Love where you serve.

He wanted to grit his teeth, but chose not to. *I serve the nation, too, don't I? How can I do that if I'm miserable?*

The Lady is more miserable.

Of that, there was no doubt. He stopped at the bronze door of the First Family's suite and allowed himself a sigh. Eyli said Tamelera had strengths—but Eyli had loved her since childhood, and perhaps saw her differently. What person could live among these men and not be diminished?

Aloran rang the bell. *Please, anyone but Garr's Sorn.*

The door opened on a different man tonight: a heavier man, light brown hair sifted through with gray, marked with the crescent cross of the Household. "Aloran, you are well come," he said. That was the rocking sea-level accent of Safe Harbor, even more distinctive than Min's. "I am Premel, Keeper here."

Aloran bowed. "I'm pleased to make your acquaintance, Premel, sir. Thank you very much for receiving me."

Premel soberly escorted him in. "The Mistress occupies the dining room at the moment," he said. "You're waiting in the Master and Mistress' chambers until they're pleased to enter, such time when the review will officially begin."

"Thank you, sir."

Strange, to walk through their richly appointed sitting room and private drawing room with a sense of distance rather than curiosity. Premel left him alone in the Master and Mistress' chambers, and this time he found his eyes drawn to the paintings. One was a scene of Selimna: Kartunnen musicians playing on the sidewalk under golden daylights, while mosaic grain fields billowed across storefronts behind them. Another was a portrait of a huge crowd with a plaque reading: The First Family. That had to be some Kartunnen's additive fabrication, for surely no artist would be able to capture eight hundred and four people within any reasonable period of time. Aloran scanned for the Lady's likeness, but the faces were too small. If he looked closer, he'd risk not making it back to the center of the room when he heard them coming.

His stomach wavered. Was that how he should fail tonight?

No, it probably wouldn't be enough.

Muffled voices filtered into the room: first Grobal Garr's unmistakable bass rumble, and then a woman's voice, *her* voice—sweet high notes of distress. A strident cry came right outside the door:

"An Imbati?! Garr, how *dare* you!"

The door of the chambers sprang open and slammed into the stone wall. The Lady blazed in the doorway, bare arms flung outward, her silk and jewels gleaming like the battle armor of Mai the Right. Her livid eyes paralyzed him.

"None of your tantrums, now, Tamelera," said Grobal Garr, stepping in to one side. "This is Imbati Aloran. Excellent medical training, bodyguard's training, and all the rest. Quite satisfactory, to my mind."

Grobal Garr was different tonight. No longer powerful, but an old, fragile, thirsty man, drinking the anger that gave his partner twice his life, and using it to rouse a slow, salacious smile. Aloran couldn't stand to look at him.

Lady Tamelera swept forward to fill his vision.

He held his breath. She was so close he could have traced the blue star patterns in her irises—oh, mercy, he'd looked her in the eye! But he couldn't tear his gaze away. Clearly, the Lady was in complete control of herself, and not at all surprised. His heart shrank.

"*Satisfactory*," she hissed. "You propose to give me a *man*, and call that satisfactory? Think I have too much companionship in my life, do you? It's not enough that I've lost Lienne to the Arissen and Selemei to politics—now you have to surround me entirely with *men*?"

"Of course not, love," Grobal Garr said. "He's simply the best."

Lady Tamelera glared at her partner, then whirled and came in again. Aloran cringed. Her heavy skirts caught and tugged against his ankles; her merciless gaze raked him head to toe. She hesitated a split second, and then raised two fingers, her jaw hardening. Heile's mercy, she was going to pinch—Aloran clenched his teeth, his entire body quivering, waiting for pain.

He felt nothing.

The Lady's lightning fingers plucked edges and folds of his clothing, missing him entirely. He tried to find another breath.

"Tamelera!" Grobal Garr barked, now clearly outraged.

"Imbati Aloran, the best the Academy has to offer," she sneered. "He's certainly a finer specimen than *you*, Garr. I'm surprised you want to have him around as a measuring rod for your own physical decline."

Her partner's face flushed red. "See here!"

"Oh, so I've gotten it wrong? Instead, he's supposed to treat me for *my* deficiencies, is that it?"

"Dear, you're not seventeen anymore—"

"And you're not forty!" she snapped. "But you have other means than offspring to buy *your* reputation. So, Aloran, are you going to restore my fertility?"

Holy Eyn, was *that* why Grobal Garr had asked so many questions about his medical training? What could he say? He took a terrified breath.

"Stop!" Lady Tamelera commanded. "Don't answer that."

Aloran bowed his head. "Thank you, Lady."

She leaned close, hissing in his ear. "I've had a *friend*, you understand that? Even if you replace her, you will never *have her place*."

"No, Lady."

She strode away toward the window. On the stone sill sat a pair of ceramic rabbits—the white one, he'd seen in Garr's hand at his last review. She picked it up, gazing across the room at Garr. Her voice turned singsong-sweet. "So, darling, do you want me to ask him questions?"

"As many as you want," Grobal Garr replied.

The Lady whirled and flung the rabbit.

Aloran flinched. The rabbit came so close to his head that it flashed white in the corner of his eye. It smashed on stone behind him.

"Forget it," the Lady said. "I won't pretend that you care what I think. I've seen him. I'm sure I already know what he's capable of. Anything I don't know I'm sure you've already checked. Why do I need anything else?"

"See now, dear? That's better," said Grobal Garr.

"Come now. We'll drink a toast, to thirty-five years of me, and eighteen of *us*. It might help my mood." Ignoring her partner's proffered arm, she swooped past him out the door, and called sharply, "Premel!"

Grobal Garr stroked his chin with a sickening smile, and followed her out. The door swung shut.

Aloran stood alone, shaking.

The door opened slightly, and the First Houseman peered in. "Aloran," he said softly. "Let's take you out."

Aloran crept silently behind Serjer to the front door. Heile be merciful—let nothing change the Lady's mind and bring her back! On the threshold, he mustered enough manners to bow. "Thank you, Serjer, sir."

"I'm so sorry," Serjer said. "I had a feeling it might happen this way. Good night."

"Good night."

Aloran walked back to the dormitory and sat motionless on his bed, trying just to feel the steady routines of life progressing in near-silence around him. The reality of Lady Tamelera was shattering. The violence of her eyes—it was as if they'd burned holes right through him. Imagine what it would have been like, after a month: with so many holes, there would have been nothing left of him at all. Thank all the gods she'd never given him a chance. He cupped his face in his hands and took a deep breath. Then he let it out slowly, as if just learning the exercise for the first time. Another breath—this one easier, and easier then to fall into the pattern.

When he raised his head again, Kiit was beside him.

"Kiit—" he whispered, with difficulty. "She hated me."

Kiit's eyes widened, but then she shrugged. "Well, if she thinks she does, so much the better—but she can't really hate you. She doesn't know you."

He shook his head.

Kiit leaned in closer. "My heart is as deep as the heavens, if you want to tell me."

"We should be completely alone."

She considered for a moment, then stood and led the way out.

The wysps were numerous tonight. One airborne spark floated just outside the dormitory, two between their dormitory and its neighbor, and another in the shadowy gymnasium, where Kiit drew him down by two fingers onto the soft padded floor of the bodyguard's training area.

"Aloran, may I ask you questions?"

"No, not yet. First, I'll tell you. I'll tell you—what she looks like." If he could push Lady Tamelera away, maybe he could evaluate her at arm's length rather than trapped in her gaze. "She's exactly the same height as me."

"A Grobal woman, five foot ten?"

He nodded. "It *is* unusual. She has blue eyes—" *Eyes, boring into him.* He shook his head. "She wore her hair up. Her Eyli is very skilled. Maybe it would reach to the small of her back. Sandstone red shading to gold, with no gray. She has the Grobal nose."

Kiit raised her eyebrows. "Unattractive, then."

"No, not really. Just maybe—distinctive. It's a handsome enough face." He shook his head. "Grobal Tagaret must have told her about me. Sirin and Eyn, she wasn't supposed to be so powerful. She—" Nearly sucked into it again, he looked away. The nearby wysp drifted slowly up to the high ceiling and vanished into it.

"She frightened you," Kiit whispered. "You—I can hardly imagine it. None of the Grobal girls ever frightened you." She caught a horrified breath. "She didn't touch you, did she?"

"No—no." That was the strangest, and still inexplicable. If she had wanted to dissuade him and anger Grobal Garr, why hadn't she actually touched him, or hit him with that rabbit? "It's so horrible," he said. "She hates her partner, and he deserves it. You just can't imagine how much she hates him, and all he does is smile."

Kiit grimaced. "Well, at least they told you no."

"They didn't say anything at all. Their First Houseman apologized to me."

"But at least you did what you needed to, to be disqualified. Facing that, it wouldn't have been hard to blush, or shake, or turn away."

"I—I shook all the way home," he said. He tried to laugh, but his eyes felt hot with tears.

"It's no shame to you," Kiit said softly. "Listen to me, Aloran. You've done what you needed to do. It's time to leave this behind. Isn't it?"

He dragged in a breath. "Yes. I guess."

"The sooner you let go of it, the sooner your life will come back to normal. Everything is going to be all right."

Aloran nodded. The review he could let go of, but the holes still burned.

CHAPTER TEN

Lady's Politics

Now he knew what would happen if Mother stood up to Father. The whole house had seemed to vibrate, long into the night. Tagaret struggled to sleep, woke late, and stared at the ceiling vaults, wishing he didn't have to move.

Wishing he'd never told Mother. Or that Father had never found Imbati Aloran. Or even that Mother and Father had never returned from Selimna at all.

The past held no solutions. But what did the present offer to end Mother's misery?

He wanted Reyn.

Reyn, who always had his back, who always understood what he was going through. Who hadn't spoken to him since his birthday, since Fernar set him up with Yoral.

I hurt him.

Admitting it put a desperate ache in his chest. He couldn't help wanting Della. But he'd known how Reyn would feel. His body shivered in the tangle of memories. Mai help him, why was it suddenly so complicated? And today was Soremor 15th, when Lady Selemei would attempt to capitalize on his indiscretion.

Really, he should never have approached Della in the first place. It was too dangerous, too hurtful to everyone.

He needed Reyn.

Tagaret showered and dressed, but hesitated before leaving his rooms, and had Serjer bring in breakfast instead. The whole house felt brittle, as if any misstep might cause a rockfall. Best would be to escape the house entirely and not return until afternoon.

Did he dare risk facing Lady Selemei? What would she do to him if he did not?

Cautiously, he ventured out. The drawing room was empty. Tagaret cracked open the double doors—and found Father on the nearer couch, sitting with his back to him. He and Sorn formed a perfect blockade of the only exit.

And then Nekantor's voice spoke up. "Father, Tagaret's at the door."

Varin's teeth.

Father shifted on the couch and looked back. "Tagaret, come in," he said. "I need to talk to you and your brother, both."

So much for stealth. Tagaret took a deep breath and joined them. Nekantor had apparently been pacing out of sight, near the dining room door.

"Glad you're finally up, Tagaret," Father said. "You have a meeting today. Caredes of the Eighth Family, at two."

Tagaret gulped. *The same time as Lady Selemei's tea?*

This was it. To obey, he'd have to confess, and throw himself on Father's protection. Maybe the punishment wouldn't be so bad—after all, Father always insisted that Selemei wasn't worth taking seriously.

But he couldn't do it. He would far rather join a plan to 'end ladies' duties as we know them.' In fact, why should he let Selemei frighten him? He would go to her tea; he would argue for her support of a law to protect Mother; and he *would* get a vote of the joint cabinet to make Father stop!

For a heady moment, the word *no* stood on his tongue, poised on the verge of an explosion. But then he thought of something safer.

"Father, I can't. I'm already meeting someone at two. Amyel of the Ninth Family."

Father looked skeptical. "Amyel approached you personally?"

"No—but you said I should take initiative and use my connections." Tagaret held out both hands, praying Imbati Sorn wouldn't pick out fictions from truths. He had to escape!

Father glanced over his shoulder, but Sorn remained silent. "Hmph. Sorn, contact Caredes and request a postponement; whatever's most convenient for him." Sorn bowed and vanished through the vestibule curtain. "Tagaret, have a seat."

Tagaret closed his eyes. Of course it wouldn't be that easy. He sighed and edged into a chair.

Nek continued to pace.

"Be careful with Amyel," Father said. "Let him offer a sponsorship if he likes, but it's too early to pursue a permanent position with him. Friendly as he seems, you can never quite predict what he's going to do."

Nekantor turned his head. "Meaning Father has yet to bring him in line."

Father glared. "Nekantor . . ."

"I'm sure you can do it, Father."

Father smiled stiffly. "And one more thing, Tagaret. About your friends, Yril and Grenth of the Twelfth Family."

That sounded suspicious. "They're not my friends."

"Neither should they be. I'll have you know, that brothel has been shut down, the employees are under arrest for crossmarking, and the head of the Twelfth Family Council has barred Yril and Grenth from all public events for the next month. They're an embarrassment. I won't hear of you associating with them."

Tagaret glanced at Nekantor; he was smirking.

Gnash Nekantor. "What lies has Nek been telling you?" Tagaret demanded. "I've *never* associated with Yril and Grenth—they're in *his* gang, not mine. They were probably acting on *his* orders. I'd expect Nekantor was in that brothel himself."

Father looked startled. "Nekantor?"

Nekantor shuddered and started straightening his clothes. "Father, you wanted the whores punished," he said. "They have been. Grenth and Yril were stupid enough to get caught, so they got what they deserved. What does it matter who else was involved? Would you like to know the two reasons why the First Family wins?"

Tagaret stared at his brother. Varin's teeth—Nek *had* been responsible. He'd *been* there. It was disgusting, and Father didn't even chastise him.

"What reasons?"

Nekantor smiled. "First, because Herin asked for the favor, and the First Family got it done. Second, because we know the truth before anyone else. The Eminence has been there, and that means he's going to die."

"What?!" Father lurched to his feet.

"*Nekantor*," Tagaret protested. How many times had he heard *that?* "Father, may I please go now?"

"Where are you going?"

"To Reyn's. He's Ninth Family; he can help me with Amyel. You're not taking Nek seriously, are you?"

Father had a gleam in his eye and breathed way too fast. "If there's any slightest chance, we have to be prepared," he said. "Your entire life could change, Tagaret. You haven't seen an Heir Selection."

It would have been alarming, if it hadn't been so ridiculous. "Father, Nekantor has been predicting Indal's death since the age of twelve."

Father glanced behind him, as if wishing he hadn't sent Sorn away. "All right, then. I'll allow it."

"Thank you." Tagaret ducked behind the vestibule curtain and knocked on the door to the First Houseman's hall, holding his finger to his lips as Serjer opened it. Serjer bowed, touching his hand to his heart and then his mouth.

"I'll be at Reyn's," Tagaret said, then mouthed in a half-whisper, "And Selemei's tea, at two. Tell only my mother."

Something not quite a smile flickered in Serjer's eyes. He held open the front door.

That was a narrow escape—imagine if Father had tried to send Sorn with him. Tagaret feigned a stroll at first. The suites hallways were less busy on weekends than school mornings, but a few neighbors were out, strolling beneath the arches or leaning on the deep window-sills that overlooked the flower gardens. No one here knew where Nekantor had been. And despite his earlier dismissal, the thought of Indal at the whorehouse refused to leave him. No, Nek couldn't be right; and anyway, if Indal did die, *he* could just become Heir and fix everything. *So there, Father.*

The second he was out of sight in the spiral stairway, Tagaret climbed the steps as fast as he could.

At Reyn's suite, Imbati Shara greeted him, and took him into the back. Tagaret looked for Reyn's sister, but her door stayed closed.

"Young Mistress Iren is visiting a friend this morning," Shara said. She knocked on Reyn's open door. "Young Master? Tagaret of the First Family, for you."

Tagaret held his breath for Reyn's welcome, but there was silence. Then, "I'll be right out."

Could it be that bad? But Shara hadn't turned him away.

"Do sit while you're waiting, sir," the Imbati said.

Tagaret moved toward the ocher couches, but his nerves were wound too tight to sit. A few moments later, Reyn emerged. He wore a loose silk house-jacket and a deliberately nonchalant expression.

"Hello, Tagaret," he said. "How's Della?"

That burned. "Reyn, don't," Tagaret said.

Reyn said nothing.

"Please, I'm sorry. Fernar and Gowan started that, and I couldn't *help*—well, I mean, Della's not my friend." Oh, holy Bes, that was all wrong. He tried again. "I know I hurt you. I didn't mean to. I want to talk to you, like we did before."

"Before?"

Tagaret nodded. He sat and patted the place beside him.

Reyn came closer, but he didn't sit down. "You having problems again?"

Gods knew he was; he always was. But that wasn't it. He caught Reyn's sleeve. "Reyn, sit with me. I swear to the Twins, I'm sorry."

Reyn didn't move.

The desperation rose in his throat. Tagaret sucked a huge breath, to keep it from turning into panic. "Reyn, I miss you. You're the best friend I could ever have." He grasped Reyn's hand.

Reyn's fingers closed tight on his. The warmth of them expanded under his skin. Tagaret pulled, and Reyn sat slowly beside him, looking almost scared.

He couldn't blame him. Looking down into his friend's face, he felt as if they dangled over a ledge. "Reyn?"

Reyn kissed him hard.

Oh, gods, yes.

Tagaret pulled him in tight, and Reyn's hands escaped around him, down to his waist, across his back and up under his jacket. Hands of fire, sending heat straight to his center. He stood, pulling Reyn's body against his, and Reyn's tongue sneaked between his lips. He pursued it. Reyn's mouth was softer inside than outside. *A vision of her soft lips parting* . . .

Tagaret pulled back, panting. "Wait."

Reyn's hands loosened, but his gaze intensified. "Why?"

Trigis and Bes—they had to stop. He'd never use Reyn like Father said, for politics, but was he using him anyway? "M-my clothes," Tagaret mumbled. "I have that appointment with Lady Selemei, and I told Father I'd be seeing Amyel, too, so I can't go home to change."

"That's an easy problem to fix." Reyn glanced at the open door of his rooms.

Tagaret understood instantly. The biggest shock was the flush of urgency that bubbled up in him at the thought. He pulled Reyn closer without thinking. "But, Reyn," he breathed. "I don't want—you could get in trouble if anyone found out."

"We're alone here." Reyn put a hand on his waist.

"I don't want to hurt you."

"What *do* you want?"

Della—but Della was impossible, and always had been. There was no one like Reyn, no one surer in his trust.

Before he could think too hard, Tagaret bolted for the bedroom and started to undress. He hesitated once at the sight of Reyn doing the same, but Reyn moved to him swiftly, eager lips and hot skin making it easy to respond, strong hands caressing until Tagaret gasped aloud.

In the swoon of pleasure, he could almost forget his doubt.

At lunch, Reyn held his knee under the table. That touch unlocked waves of memory intense enough to push all other thoughts out of Tagaret's mind. He pressed his hand over Reyn's and leaned against him, sneaking kisses when Imbati Shara stepped out. Eating became secondary; even peril kept a respectful distance.

Not until the caretaker respectfully inquired about his afternoon obligations did he remember himself. Tagaret laid out his challenges, and Reyn sensibly suggested that he should try to meet with Amyel while they still had time, in case Father decided to ask him questions. Unfortunately, when they attempted to make the arrangement, Shara informed them that both Gowan and his father were out.

So they'd have to take on Lady Selemei first.

Walking to the Conveyor's Hall, he and Reyn kept at a carefully agreed distance—but once they'd skimmed out into the streets, he loved how Reyn wrapped one arm around his waist. He drove up the stone spine to the fourth level and turned east.

The Club Diamond stood in a section of the city-cavern where the roof soared high enough to accommodate a building of four stories. It was easily recognizable by its height, and its vertical rows of diamond-shaped windows. Out front, a crowd of Arissen in bright rust-red spilled from the sidewalk into the street.

Tagaret sucked in a breath and braked. "Something's wrong."

"Are you sure?" Reyn asked. "They look pretty relaxed, for Arissen."

Tagaret examined them more closely. Maybe this wasn't an emergency. Most of the Arissen weren't in full uniform, and a few wore white with punctuations of Arissen red. He parked the skimmer and approached a young couple at the back of the crowd—both solid blocks of muscle in red shorts and white sleeveless shirts.

"Excuse me. Arissen?"

The woman snapped into a salute, chopping her open right hand to her left shoulder. "Sir."

"Is everything all right, here?"

She grinned. "Oh, yes, sir. This is the Soremor open wrestle-off. *I'm* going to win." Her companion burst into laughter and punched her; she shoved him back. "Well, I confess, sir, I'm fourteen-to-one. But I'm definitely going to beat *him*."

"A wrestling competition?" Tagaret asked. "That's all?"

"Yes, sir."

Arissen life must be more careless than he thought, though it hardly seemed worth Falling for. "Plis' strength to you both," Tagaret said. "Please excuse us; we have an engagement inside."

The young man raised a hand to his mouth. "Castemates, review!" he shouted. "Grobal to the door!" The effect was impressive. Every Arissen, uniformed or not, snapped to attention and stepped back, opening a straight path to the club entrance. Tagaret waved thanks, and he and Reyn hurried in.

The foyer inside was small, which explained the crowd in the street. Four doors lined the facing wall; the Arissen had lined up in front of the rightmost one. As they entered, an old Melumalai woman hurried up.

"Pardon, sirs, pardon. You are destined for the Lady's tea concert, are you not? Elevator on the left, if you please, sirs." She trotted ahead, pressed the call button, then bowed them into the elevator.

The confined space brought Reyn wonderfully close to him. It also recalled Tagaret to the risk he had to take. Lady Selemei had already trapped him once—what if something went wrong, and Reyn were caught? "Reyn, I'm putting you in danger here," he said. "You should stay outside and meet me afterward."

"But I want to be here." Reyn touched his sleeve. "To brave Melumalai with you again."

Tagaret's skin tingled. "But this is Lady Selemei. The risk—"

"Will be cut in half." Reyn looked up seriously. "Listen. With me here, people won't conclude you represent your father, or the whole First Family. And my presence as witness may limit Lady Selemei's ability to pressure you."

He wanted to kiss him. Instead, he nodded. "You're the best." A tone sounded, and the elevator doors opened. Selemei's Ustin stood in the hall outside.

"Welcome, young sirs," the Imbati said. "Follow me, please."

At the end of the hall, they entered a broad space that was mostly dark. Spotlights illuminated a yojosmei at the center, and round tables around the edges of the room, where people spoke quietly.

The slow tap of a cane drew nearer, and Lady Selemei walked up, her deep blue gown separating itself only slowly from the dark. "Cousin Tagaret. I'm so pleased to see you here."

Show no fear. "Thank you so much for inviting me," Tagaret said. "May I introduce Reyn of the Ninth Family?"

"Reyn." Lady Selemei offered him her golden hand, and Reyn kissed it. "A pleasure to meet you."

"The pleasure is mine, Lady," Reyn said.

"Consider yourself welcome here. Bringing a friend is not against the rules."

What? Tagaret cleared his throat indignantly. "There are *rules?*"

Lady Selemei looked at him. "In a Lady's world there are always rules, Cousin."

That hurt. He thought instantly of Aloran's systematic techniques to isolate Mother—of Mother's shrieks echoing around the doors . . . "I'm so sorry."

"Don't worry," Lady Selemei said. "My rules are simple. First, you allow me to seat you as we enter. Second, you must speak to the people you sit with, and do so civilly. Third, you must respect our guest artist with silence, and not switch tables while he is playing."

That didn't sound bad. Tagaret glanced at Reyn, who shrugged. "I believe we can do that."

"Then I know just the table for you."

They followed her, threading between the pools of light. When Lady Selemei slowed, Tagaret shook his head in disbelief. He knew every person here: Arbiter Erex and his partner, Lady Keir; Amyel of the Ninth Family—and Gowan.

"Would you all be so kind as to look after our newest guests, my cousin Tagaret, and Reyn of the Ninth Family?" Lady Selemei asked.

"Of course, Selemei," said Amyel.

"I told you he'd be here," Gowan whispered.

"Tagaret!" exclaimed Arbiter Erex. "I admit, when I saw Gowan here, I started wondering if you might attend. I believe you've met Keir, my lovely partner?"

"Yes; it's been a while," Tagaret said. She'd been the youngest of Mother's gaming friends, maybe twenty-five, with golden skin, dark eyebrows and black hair in a tower atop her head. "It's a pleasure to see you. I hope you'll think to visit our home soon—my mother would love to see you again." He glanced cautiously at Erex, but if the Arbiter wished to deliver any warning, he couldn't tell.

"I'd be happy to," said Lady Keir.

"Keir, darling," Erex said, "Did you know? Reyn is the son of the Safe Harbor Alixi."

"Ah? I've always wanted to see Safe Harbor. I love the idea of red-banded city-caverns," she said politely, but didn't offer her hand. She flashed a smile at Lady Selemei. "Thanks for bringing them."

"Enjoy your tea," said Lady Selemei, and tapped away into the dark.

Amyel laughed. "Well, Tagaret, Gowan told me you'd need him here. I guess he was right."

"I couldn't be more grateful, sir," Tagaret admitted. Only Fernar was missing. "Gowan, how did you know?"

Gowan shrugged. "Reyn told me. I figured we'd be stronger together than we would separately."

"Absolutely." Tagaret took his seat. "Amyel, sir, I'm very happy to see you. I hope you'll forgive me—I had to tell my father I was discussing a sponsorship with you, so he'd let me leave the house."

"Is that so?"

Tagaret flushed. "Sorry, sir. I don't mind telling him it won't work out. But if I hadn't seen you at all, it would have been awkward."

Amyel chuckled at that. "I see your point. Garr of the First Family must be handled with care."

A Melumalai server laid down cups of tea; Tagaret lifted his and inhaled the warm steam.

"Quite correct," Arbiter Erex agreed. "In fact, I'm amazed Selemei would invite Tagaret under his father's nose. It's a risky move."

Tagaret looked up. "She invited you, too, Erex, sir."

"Ah-ah-ah." Erex tapped his clubbed fingers together. "She didn't, in fact—she invited Keir. I'm just lucky my partner enjoys my company enough to bring me along."

Lady Keir laughed. "Erex, you're a dear." When she looked at Tagaret, her brown eyes were serious. "You never know who to expect at these events, so my partner makes an excellent ally. And Selemei always invites the most intriguing ladies."

Gowan leaned across the table. "Yes, but what is she trying to *do*?"

Tagaret looked at Erex, but the Arbiter said nothing. Risky to answer such a question when Ustin might be listening—though surely many of Selemei's guests asked the same.

Amyel rubbed his chin. "I've attended twice now. There's never any political discussion, but several charity projects have begun here, and there are always interesting people—for example, see over there? Cabinet Secretary Boros of the Second Family is here today, with his partner, and his son Menni."

Tagaret looked. He recognized Menni, who had been a few years ahead of him in school. Menni's mother had deep brown hair, while the Cabinet Secretary himself was golden-skinned and bald as a marble. They were holding hands.

Father never holds Mother's hand.

"It's quite natural," Amyel concluded. "Being a Lady, Selemei hasn't grown up getting to know the people she works with. Sensible, really, to invite them to tea."

Tagaret nodded. *Especially if you want to change ladies' duties as we know them, and can't become Heir.*

"Try it," said Lady Keir. "For Melumalai tea, it's quite good."

Tagaret sipped his tea. He waited for Lady Selemei to return, but as minutes slipped past, the conversation never waned. It was great to have Gowan and Reyn both here. Amyel was unfailingly friendly. Most striking, though, was the ease that Erex and Lady Keir enjoyed together. They never touched, but despite their age difference, they obviously liked each other. Tagaret couldn't stop a pang inside.

The light dimmed above their table.

"Excellent," said Amyel. "Time for the concert."

Over the yojosmei, the spotlight intensified, drawing reflections from its double rows of polished stone keys, and a man in a flowing gray coat walked out of the dark.

Tagaret hissed in a breath. *Kartunnen Ryanin.*

He'd never imagined seeing the composer so close. Ryanin's large frame was spare, his hair graying in a receding streak from each temple. His eyelids were painted black, and his green lower lip sparkled. He had large hands, and long fingers that caressed the upper keyboard with loving familiarity as he sat down. Once he began to play, there might as well have been nothing else in the room. His fingers and feet flowed like water, creating visions that no one had ever imagined. However Ryanin had arrived at this new style, it was amazing to hear. Della would have loved it—he must tell her.

Except that he'd probably never speak to her again.

All too soon, it was over. Ryanin bowed to the applause of the guests, then walked out the way he'd come, with a receding flutter of his gray coat. The music left behind a darkness that was more enticing than forbidding. Tagaret stood up.

Reyn reached for his arm. "Where are you going? To look for. . . ?"

"Shall we come with you?" asked Gowan.

"It's all right," Tagaret said. "I don't want to cause a stir. I'm not going far; just to look at the yojosmei."

He approached the instrument cautiously, gazing at the spot where Kartunnen Ryanin had sat, and the glimmering rows of agate keys, narrow above and wide below. It made him think of that other Kartunnen—the boy he'd seen at the edge of the Eminence's ballroom and spoken to at the Melumalai concert hall. When he looked up again, Lady Selemei was standing beside him.

"It's lovely to see you up," she said. "It was a wonderful concert, I think."

She'd been watching for him to move. Tagaret's stomach clenched, but he took a deep breath. Reyn and Gowan were nearby; and it was better that he'd drawn her out into view, since she was less likely to attempt anything dangerous while people watched. "Yes, indeed," he said. "Kartunnen Ryanin is brilliant."

"I'm glad I engaged him." Lady Selemei gave a modest smile. "Glad, too, that none of my guests have walked out. But gladdest of all that you came today. You're more unusual than I gave you credit for, young man."

"How so?"

The Lady shrugged. "Most of my visitors don't leave their table until they've attended more than once, and none of them have ever gone to the yojosmei."

"I like music," Tagaret said. "What I *don't* like is playing games."

"I can see that," the Lady agreed. "That's why I invited you."

"Really?" Tagaret held his voice quiet with effort. "If that's why you invited me, then why do I feel like you're playing with me now? My mother says you wouldn't endanger a young lady, but it looks like you'd still use one in order to get me here."

Lady Selemei thought a moment. Then she faced him, placing both hands atop her cane. "I apologize, Tagaret."

"What?"

"Cousin, I've always protected and supported ladies, but to achieve success in the cabinet, I need the support of men. Not just any men will do. When I saw you with that young Lady, I acted impulsively because I wanted to learn about you and test how far you'd go to protect her. But it's true I put myself in a bind. If you'd been another sort of man, she would have been in danger. I used her unfairly." She looked up, and the glimmer of a smile danced on her lips. "Fortunately for me, I was right about the sort of man you are—perhaps because I've raised two sons of my own."

"Lady Selemei, does this mean we can speak frankly?"

"I believe so."

"I need your help. My father's had me talking to lots of people, but he controls every last one of them. I need to know what your 'Lady's politics' is really about. Your guest list shows you're not just interested in courting my father's enemies." How could he explain what he really wanted without endangering anyone? "Is it . . . the kind of politics that would help my mother?"

Selemei nodded, with such sadness he felt certain she knew. "You realize, of course, that telling you my goals would be a serious risk."

He raised his eyebrows. "It's a serious risk for us to be speaking at all."

"How about this?" said Lady Selemei. "An exchange of risk: I tell you precisely what motivates my politics, and you allow me to sponsor you at your next public event. Just one—a concert perhaps, or a party."

"I don't know . . ." She'd certainly be better than Caredes, but Father would flip!

Lady Selemei leaned closer. "Think about your answer while I tell you mine. Lady's politics is simply politics as executed by a Lady. You know your mother, and you've met young ladies, so you know we have to do things quietly. In a direct confrontation, we always lose."

Tagaret nodded.

"But it's not like that in all of Varin, is it?"

"No . . ." The evidence of that was just outside the club door, where Arissen men and women laughed together, waiting to wrestle one another.

"Ladies have wits. And we have the means to arrange for our own protection, given the chance. Your mother, for example, has excellent wits."

His mind filled in the rest: . . . *though Father never gives her the chance to arrange for her own protection.*

"I work quietly now, young Cousin, in the hope that one day my two youngest daughters will be able to choose their own partners— boys their own age, whom they love. If I can get enough help and influence, the change might come soon enough for you and the young Lady I saw you with. Now, is that worth one event? You decide."

Tagaret looked her in the eye—passionate, intelligent, so much like Mother. "One," he said.

Lady Selemei started to smile, but turned and frowned at the sight of Imbati Ustin approaching fast. Someone was following her. Someone small, with white hair . . .

Mother's Eyli.

His stomach lurched. Had Father found them out?

"We're leaving, young Master," Eyli said grimly. "With Reyn. Now."

That was the caretaker's tone, that would brook neither question nor denial. Tagaret hurried back to the table. Amyel was on his feet, manservant on the alert, with Gowan and Reyn beside him; Erex and Keir stepped aside, letting the five of them run behind Eyli toward the exit.

"Tagaret," Reyn hissed, "What's going on?"

Tagaret shook his head. "Some emergency. . . ?" He pushed out the concert hall doors, and gasped.

The corridor outside was filled with Imbati, all pressed flat against the wall to let their party through—theirs, and one other. A hand stopped the elevator door from closing, and Menni of the Second Family slipped in with his manservant. Reyn moved closer; the silence in the tiny space shivered with fearful questions that Tagaret didn't dare ask.

At the bottom, Arissen were waiting for them—Arissen out of uniform, maybe redirected from the wrestling crowd. Menni and his servant boarded one skimmer; Amyel and Gowan took a second, with Amyel's manservant driving. Tagaret crammed himself beside Reyn into the third, while Eyli reconfigured the controls so she could drive. The three Imbati moved out as a team, driving in formation with the Arissen.

"Tagaret," Reyn whispered. "Was Nekantor right?"

"I hope not."

They hit the rampway down, and the formation strung out. Tagaret felt like he'd left his stomach at the top. What if Nek *was* right? Was that the reason for this escort? Was every boy between twelve and thirty in danger now?

"Tagaret . . ." Reyn whispered.

"We'll be all right." Surrounded as they were, he couldn't hold him, but he could feel Reyn's body all down his side, even sense his fearful heartbeat. "We'll be home soon."

Reyn's fingers sneaked into his; he held them tight.

In the Conveyor's Hall, the Household was out in force. Several of them surrounded Menni as he left on foot. Amyel and Gowan left with probably seven more. At least ten Imbati surrounded their own skimmer—Tagaret put his arm around Reyn's shoulders.

"Imbati," he said, "Let him come with me."

"Your pardon, young sir," said a Household woman. "You must each receive an escort home. We have been so instructed."

Reyn looked up with terror in his eyes. "It is, isn't it. Indal is dead."

Gods help them. What else could this be? Only the death of an Eminence could cause this kind of massive mobilization! Suddenly, he wanted nothing more than to be alone with Reyn, to hold him, to feel them both safe and alive.

"Imbati Shara will know for sure," Tagaret said. "If Indal is dead, then you should go with them, Reyn. Get home, where you'll be safe."

"But you—"

"I promise, I'll get home as fast as I can."

Five Household servants took Reyn; another five escorted him and Eyli across the grounds, into the first-floor hall of the suites wing. Serjer had the door open before he or Eyli could touch it.

Inside, Mother was shrieking.

The awful sound reverberated through the open doorway. Anger—that was familiar—but also a terrible note of grief. Mother had known where he was. Did she think he'd been hurt?

He rushed in through the curtain. The sitting room was a disaster. Paintings and curtains had been torn off the walls. Mother stood near an upended gaming chair with her hair in disarray and her face streaked with tears. Nekantor was in a corner with his back to the wall, staring at his watch. Father stood red-faced near the dining room door with Sorn behind his shoulder.

"Tagaret!" he barked, striding forward. "About time!"

"You bastard!" Mother screamed. She picked up the keyzel marble set from the gaming table and flung the stone board at Father, toppling the table and sending marbles everywhere. "You can't take my Eyli. You can't do it!"

"Behave yourself, Tamelera," Father growled. "Indal is dead. We have far more serious worries now. We need another bodyguard, and we need him *this instant*."

Tagaret looked between them, unable to breathe. *Indal was dead.* Nekantor was right.

Reyn, be safe . . .

Mother clenched her fists. "Why? You need *another* servant who can run off and kill people for you?"

Sorn twitched. Tagaret turned his head in surprise, but the moment was gone. It couldn't have been, though. Sorn never lost composure—never looked like anything but a statue carved in stone.

He turned back just in time to see Father reach Mother and backhand her across the face.

"Leave her alone!" Tagaret roared. "What in Varin's name is going on here?"

Mother ran from the room, sobbing.

Tagaret tried to follow, but Father stepped into his way.

"We have more important business now, Tagaret," he said. "It's time for the Pelismar Cabinet to pick the next Heir, and I swear on Plis' undying bones that it's going to be you."

"Gnash the cabinet. I'm going to Mother. Let me past!"

"Caredes will no longer do—nor will Amyel. They'll have too much interest in their own Families' candidates, and we can't trust them. Fedron will be your sponsor now. The Accession Ball is in two days. We've got to make you look so incredible that every Family will know you're the candidate to beat."

Nekantor appeared beside Father, a disconcerting glow in his eyes. "Imagine it, Tagaret," he said. "The First Family will advance to an unrivaled position. You're going to win, and I'm going to help you."

"Get away from me, Nek," Tagaret growled. "I don't want your help."

Father thumped a heavy hand on his shoulder. "Don't make a mistake, son. Nekantor has some good ideas that we can execute by the time of the Ball. I can't wait to see you walk into the ballroom with me and Fedron! This is going to be the most important event of your life."

Tagaret clenched his teeth. How satisfying it would have been to throw Father's manipulations back in his face, to tell him he'd promised 'the most important event of his life' to Lady Selemei. But Father would be livid, and wouldn't let him by to see Mother, who was far more important. He lowered his head and pushed past Father, into the back of the suite.

He'd get his satisfaction when he saw Lady Selemei face-to-face with Father at the Ball.

CHAPTER ELEVEN
Marking

After that disastrous review, Hands class seemed anticlimactic. Ball-handling felt so pointlessly innocuous that Aloran raised his arm and shot a ball hard at his partner, Katella. She caught it, of course. Katella was the Hands Master's prize student.

"Nice throw," she said, and fired it back at him. For an intense minute they pelted balls at one another. "You're mixing Hands with Combat today," she remarked. "Is this some special skill you're developing?"

"You never know—" he caught and flung back another three balls, "—when you might need to catch something thrown at you hard. Happened to me in review, and I wasn't ready." Caught a fourth beside his head. Hadn't caught that rabbit. It had missed him by pure luck.

Katella frowned and threw again. "Some review. A good mistress would protect you."

The next ball hit him straight in the chest.

Maybe it wasn't luck. The rabbit had missed, and those pinches that made no sense—they made perfect sense if she'd intended to *protect* him.

Eyli had promised: *If she accepts you, she will protect you.*

As if in answer to his thought, there was a knock on the classroom door. Balls dropped to the mats, bouncing unevenly into silence. Even before she walked in, he knew it would be Master Ziara. His insides were suddenly vacant.

"I call out Aloran, to be Marked Tamelera's Aloran of the Household of the First Family."

Aloran stared at her, struggling to find his lungs again. Then he realized his classmates were bowing to him, and forced his feet to move. The greatest honor at the Academy—the most prestigious position imaginable—the most terrifying Lady in all of Varin.

"Congratulations," said Master Ziara.

"Thank you, sir," he said, in a half-whisper. How could this be happening? He'd failed so badly—how could it *not have been enough?* He returned his classmates' bow, then followed her out.

Master Ziara strode at a stiff pace down the stone hall toward her office. "We have much to do before I accompany you to the suite as witness," she said. "Your move has already been arranged. Your appointment with Artist Orahala is at four thirty-two afternoon."

Less than an hour? Had a Marking ever been scheduled so fast?

"Master Ziara," he said hoarsely.

She turned to look at him.

But what could he say? He didn't want this. Lady Tamelera didn't want it either, but she'd already paid his Marking fee and first month's salary, or he couldn't have been called out. Why had she accepted him? How could he face her? Yet he must be hers: Tamelera's Aloran. Tamelera's burden.

Master Ziara stepped away again. She brought him into her office and locked the door. "Aloran, there's more," she said. "The Eminence Indal is dead of Kinders fever. Herin of the Third Family is now Eminence of all Varin."

His manners failed. "What? It hopped the wall *again?*"

Master Ziara kindly ignored his rudeness; she took up a scented cloth from her desk and held it out. "Wash your face for the Artist while I speak to you," she said. "There is some special information you need now."

Aloran took the cloth, but tremors began in his stomach. New information now must be privileged, not public—and therefore, not to be shared until the Marking was certain. He took a deep breath. "My heart is as deep as the heavens. No word uttered in confidence will escape it."

Master Ziara smiled. "Thank you. Allow me to explain. You are being Marked into a position which has just greatly increased in importance. Grobal Tagaret is expected to be a prime candidate for Heir, so Grobal Garr wants you bodyguarding both your Lady and her son, at least until he has his own bodyguard assigned."

"I understand." His classmates would give anything to be so fortunate. Aloran lifted the scented cloth and rubbed it across his face. The cosmetic circle between his brows marked the fabric with a black smear. He folded it and wiped again, carefully, and then again. When no pigment remained, he shivered.

Master Ziara politely averted her eyes. "There's more," she said. "The Academy considers Garr's Sorn to be dangerous. He is suspected to have played a role in the murder of Dest of the Eleventh Family in the last Heir Selection, and with a new Heir Selection now upon us, I fear we may see him act again."

Aloran swallowed. That explained her reaction when he'd reported the senior servant's strange behavior. "May I ask—am *I* in danger from him?"

"You might be, if you were to discover him in illegal activity, or if you should chance to uncover any details about his past actions."

He shook his head. "Well, I wouldn't neglect my Mistress to serve the Courts."

"Would you not?" she asked, suddenly intense. She leaned both hands on her desk. "What about the nation of Varin, then? I would not request this of you, Aloran, if not for your unique position. Will you swear, for the sake of Grobal lives at risk, to keep a place reserved in your heart for the service of the nation above that of your Mistress?"

Only yesterday, he'd protested he must serve the nation—but this request was frightening. How deep must be their suspicion, that the Academy would ask a student to stain his vow of service and hide secrets from his own mistress?

"Master Ziara, I'm sorry," Aloran said. "I will need every bit of my strength to vow myself to her already."

Master Ziara's face melted with unexpected sympathy. "Then I won't press you there. Would you swear instead to watch Garr's Sorn, and report to the Academy any information you might find?"

"I don't know," he said. "To put myself in danger—"

"To serve," she said. "No more than that."

The call of vocation was strong—but to dive past a warning marker was to invite rockfall, and Garr's Sorn was suspected of the ultimate transgression. "I can't promise."

"I understand," said Master Ziara. "Come with me."

Together they walked out the front doors of the Academy building. No one was around to see him face-naked in public. Probably they were in class, reviewing the complex procedures of legal election—and illegal assassination—by which the Grobal selected their Heirs. The gate wardens with their diamond-within-diamond tattoos bowed to him.

"The children of the Academy are always welcome to return," they said.

Aloran bowed. "Thank you, sirs. I have been grateful for your protection."

He was grateful, too, for Master Ziara's company, or he might have been too unsettled to remember the way to the Artist's chamber. In by the service entrance beside the Residence's main doors, along a Maze hall, then up all the way to the top of a spiral stairway to the third floor and along the hall again. They were two minutes early. He waited, but could not find the rhythm of the breathing exercise, to keep calm. Lady Tamelera's blue eyes arose in his memory, burning hot—or maybe so cold they burned, irises sharp, needles of ice around a bottomless black center.

"It's time," said Master Ziara.

Aloran went in.

The room was dim, with cornices lurking in the corners of the ceiling. The only light came from a shadowy metal arm descending from the roof. Its bright circle illuminated a reclining chair and a metal table bearing the Artist's tools: vials, swabs, a simple black pen, and of course the instrument itself, molded in steel to fit the Artist's hand.

Artist Orahala appeared from behind a curtain, dressed in white to match the rope of her hair curling into a fossil seashell atop her head. The manservant's tattoo on her forehead was the only anchor for her strange lightness. Her face, expressionless, held a thousand lines of past expressions to give her joy, grief, anger, and love at once. "Aloran," she said.

He'd dreamed of this moment. He bowed, in awe and horror.

"Please sit down."

The chair whirred and moved, until she had him looking up into the light. Her hand descended bearing the ephemeral scent of alcohol; a swab whispered over his skin, trailing cold in its wake.

"The Mark must suit the wearer," she murmured, raising her pen.

"A firm center, to reflect a strong spine." The pen stroked down his forehead to the bridge of his nose. He tried to breathe calmly. "The curves of the chevron must reach with the tall man's poise." A stroke up to his hairline, then another. "Grace in the eyebrows reflected in the arcs. You do not pluck your eyebrows, Aloran."

"No, sir."

She nodded. "An arc may be strong over a black brow but must be lighter than the brow itself."

This line felt swift and cold. He tightened his hands on the armrests of the chair, but words escaped him anyway. "Artist, what if it's wrong?"

Orahala paused. "It isn't wrong," she said. "It simply is." The pen drew two shorter facing curves, down his forehead to the bridge of his nose where all the lines converged. Then her hands disappeared; pads came to rest against the top of his head and behind his ears, pinning him motionless. Though her face was lined, the Artist's hands were as steady as the immovable shinca trees.

"But her partner inquired without her permission," he whispered desperately, while slow spirals tickled above each eyebrow. "She was given no choice. She hates me. How can I make the vow to her when she hates me? The money isn't important—is it really too late to give everything back?"

"*Imbati, love where you serve,*" the Artist said. "Nothing else will matter." There was a hum. The device glittered in her hand—he shrank away from it.

"Artist . . ."

"She has selected you, Aloran," Orahala said. "This will not be the last time in your life you must accept the inevitable. Taking the Mark in a mistress' name is like accepting the partnership she will choose for you. It is a commitment. Love, if it comes before, is simply luck. The love that comes after is yours to make. In the name of Lady Grobal Tamelera of the First Family."

Aloran closed his eyes. "In the name of Lady Grobal Tamelera of the First Family."

The needle didn't hurt so badly, but the tears welled up anyway. It lasted forever, the needle returning and returning while he wept, unable to stop. In the end, the cold touch of the ointment was a shock.

Every tender line of the Mark felt burned into his skin with perfect, permanent clarity. The Artist put a silk handkerchief into his hand and released him from the chair. He dabbed the cloth lightly on his wet cheeks, afraid to touch his face at all.

Outside the room, everything seemed completely unfamiliar. Master Ziara pacing downstairs ahead of him was no longer his advisor. This hallway would be his way home. Serjer at the door was now his colleague in the Household of the First Family.

"Welcome, Aloran, sir," Serjer said. "Master Ziara, welcome. The Mistress is ready for us." There were signs of disturbance in the house; the sitting room looked as if it had been disarranged and hastily put back together, and Serjer seemed nervous. The First Houseman led them farther in and knocked at the Master and Mistress' chambers.

"Come in." That was Lady Tamelera's voice as he had first heard it: sweet, distressed, and delicate, barely audible behind a door. *Don't let it change.*

The Lady was sitting with lowered eyes, in the same chair where he had placed her son at the Master's review. A paper contract lay beyond her on her writing table. Aloran forced himself to walk close, to kneel at her feet. The hem of her dress was light blue, embroidered with fine stitches in white. Beneath it showed the toe-tips of her white silk shoes.

The vow began with 'Mistress.' *Mistress, don't hurt me. Mistress, forgive me for not being what you wanted.* His tears rose again, but he swallowed them. This was the beginning of his duty.

"Mistress," he said. "The Mark upon my face I have taken in your noble name. Thus I kneel before you to offer my duty, my honor, my love, and my life to your service. Upon your loyal servant, pray you bestow a touch, the seal of your hand upon this, the vow of my heart."

She didn't move. No anger in her today, but fear, like an animal cornered. Heile only knew she was as dangerous. She glanced past him, uncertainly. "I've signed the contract," she said. "Must I?"

"Anywhere it please you, Lady," said Master Ziara.

Would she touch the Mark? He tried not to cringe while she studied his face. She lifted her hand toward that bare and vulnerable path into his secret self, and he held his breath—but she laid her hand instead upon his cheek.

"Ziara as Academy witness."

"Serjer as Household witness." In the corner of his eye, the two crossed to the writing table and signed their names.

"With your permission, Lady," said Master Ziara.

Lady Tamelera nodded. "You may be excused."

Aloran remained on his knees. The door shut almost inaudibly, a mark of Serjer's skill. Alone with her and helpless: this was the way it would be, except when it was far, far worse.

"I'm sorry, Aloran," Lady Tamelera sighed. "I—well, I suppose it's that I've never done this before."

He lowered his eyes and kept silent. How could he have reassured her, even if it had been his place?

"I'll give you some time," she said. "An hour, to settle in before your duties start at dinner. It's not much, I know. My Eyli—" she choked off the words and cleared her throat. "Eyli said you were quick, and I could train you on the job. I won't need service in the bath. I've mostly been doing it myself anyway, to spare her knees."

"Mistress," he murmured, casting a cautious glance up. She grimaced—mistake. Try again. "Lady. I am yours to command."

She looked away toward the window. In profile, her face was both fragile and sharp, as glass already broken once. "I'll need you to watch Garr, so he doesn't surprise me," she said. "His Sorn will try to stop you."

He couldn't stop a shudder. "Yes, Lady."

"There will be no night duties; I have no disorders."

"You are healthy, Lady," he said. "I'm certain of it."

"Try not to—" She winced. "Never assume that an order from Garr is an order from me."

"No, Lady."

"I think that's everything."

If only it were. He cleared his throat.

"Yes?"

"Lady, I have been told the Master wishes me to bodyguard young Master Tagaret," he said. "May I consider that an order from you?"

"Yes, whenever Tagaret and I are together. The Accession Ball will be the first major danger." The thought seemed to upset her. She crumpled in slightly upon herself, looking away to the window again. "I'll be alone now. You are excused."

"Thank you, Lady."

He gathered himself, stood, and left through the door to the drawing room.

Serjer was waiting for him. "Allow me to take you out of the public rooms, sir," he said. "I should introduce you to our Maze."

"Yes, please." Finally, shelter from the gaze of noble eyes.

Two curtained doors led out of the entry vestibule, one on either side as they faced the front door. Serjer indicated the one on the right. "Through this door is the lesser Maze, with my personal space, the Keeper's space, and the caretaker's space," he said. "The caretaker's position is currently unfilled. From the caretaker's hallway you can access the boys' rooms. Nekantor's rooms are farthest at the end of the hall, and if you value your person, I recommend you leave his door alone."

Good idea. Aloran nodded.

"On the other side here is the main Maze entrance. Let's go in." A straight narrow hall ran along the inside of the suite's front wall, lined with neat, shadowy shelves. "Shelf lights switch on here when you need them," Serjer said, indicating an illuminated switch, and when the shelves changed to smooth metal, "this is the backside of the pantry cabinet—we access it from the kitchen on the other side."

At the end of the narrow hall, where the Maze turned a sharp left along the side of the suite, there was an exit into the main Residence hallway. Serjer entered numbers at a keypad on the wall. "Put your palm here, please, sir."

Aloran pressed his hand to a panel of glass; a red light flashed briefly behind it.

"Now you'll be able to get in here directly without using the front door. All unaccompanied staff must enter here, including the Residence Household when we request their services. Please inform me if you need them, and I'll contact the Household Director by intercom."

"All right."

Serjer led him down the side corridor. "Premel is our Keeper; he's out ordering groceries at the moment, but he'll want to discuss your meals later tonight or tomorrow. He and his partner Dorya have three children; their youngest just entered the Academy. Premel's most often to be found here in the kitchen—" He indicated the first door they passed. "Then down here are the laundry and bathroom, which we all share, and this door is Sorn's room."

Aloran's throat tightened. He'd have to pass Sorn's room to get to his own? But he should have remembered: the Master had the right side of the bed, and the Mistress the left.

"Sorn's partner is Fedron's Chenna, who serves the Master's closest cabinet ally; she stays here some nights, so don't be surprised if you see her, but they have no children."

"May I ask a question?" Aloran said.

"Yes, sir."

"What time does the Master wake?"

Serjer smiled a little. "At seven. If you wish to watch Sorn, he wakes at six sixteen."

Smiling like that, Serjer probably had no idea what the Academy suspected of the head of their Household. "You are generous with information," Aloran said.

Serjer inclined his head. "And here's your room, at the end." The room was small, but a window with a deep stone sill allowed light in from outside. It was empty except for three moving boxes, an unmade bed, and a simple polymer dresser beneath the window. "I'll get you some sheets this afternoon," Serjer said, "but usually you'll get your own from the laundry room."

"Oh, I can get them."

"You were Marked today, sir," Serjer said matter-of-factly. "I'll get them. For now, I invite you to eat with me. It's best to have something in your stomach before attending the family dinner."

Food. He hadn't even noticed he was hungry. "Oh, thank you, sir," he sighed.

Serjer smiled again. "You do not owe me sir anymore, Aloran. I owe it you."

"Ah. Maybe we could both forget about it?"

"In private only." Halfway down the hall, Serjer added, "And I will give you a chance to reconsider when you have healed."

When Aloran finished eating, he walked down the Maze hall to his room. Serjer had made the bed with stiff white sheets in precise corners. Aloran sat and closed his eyes, breathing deeply. The Mark was sensitive and conscious, grasping his face like a hand—it refused to let him relax. Finally, he got up, changed from his Academy uniform into a black silk suit, and began emptying his moving boxes.

There wasn't much. His implements, atop the dresser. His Body reference books, on the deep stone windowsill for now. His medical treatment kit, in the bottom drawer. His clothes, in the other drawers.

He was unprepared.

Tears welled up in his throat, but he forced himself to breathe. This was a job—the one he'd spent his whole life training for. Time to do it.

He'd have to buy more black suits. To find a coverlet for the bed. And more importantly, to purchase an armor-vest and combat rounders for the kind of bodyguarding they wanted.

The Accession Ball, now—that was a real worry. Every member of the Pelismara Society in a single room pressing hands, when one of their own had just died of Kinders fever? If only he could offer his Mistress an inoculant—but even if she would permit the suggestion, and were not allergic, there was no time for it to take effect. With that kind of contagion risk, he'd be tempted to wear his treatment gloves.

Gloves.

That wasn't a bad idea—Kartunnen sometimes wore cloth gloves for fashion. But if his Lady were not to consider them beneath her, they would have to be handmade to match what she wore to the Ball.

He found his service speaker and flicked it on, but heard only silence in his Lady's chamber. If he opened the small door with the crescent-moon handle, he could go and study her wardrobe. But if she were still there, sitting quietly, she would be angry because she wanted to be alone. Lady Tamelera, angry.

He opened the door into the Maze and went looking for Serjer.

He found the First Houseman in the laundry, pressing and folding napkins. "Sorry to interrupt," he said. "May I ask you a question?"

Serjer nodded. "Certainly."

"Do you know what the Lady plans to wear at the Accession Ball? I need to make gloves to match, and I don't have much time before my duties start."

The crescent cross between Serjer's brows lifted slightly. "I don't imagine you'll have time for shopping now, but if you can specify a list, I'll pass it on to the Residence Household for you. As to her choice of wardrobe . . ." He switched off the steam press. "Our Mistress appre-

ciates art. She had a collection of custom gowns made while in Selimna, and I imagine she'd choose one of those. They may be difficult
to match, however, because they're patterned after the sky."

Had he heard correctly? "The *sky*."

Serjer's mouth quirked a little. "Yes, she has unusual tastes. The
gown she's wearing today is the midday gown; I've seen her try the
dawn gown and the sunset gown, though she hasn't worn them publicly. Since Mother Elinda will be invoked at the Accession ceremony,
I suspect she'll choose the midnight gown. Would you like to see it?"

"I don't want to interrupt her—"

Serjer's brows pinched. "I think we must," he said. "I'll give you all
our measurements for her, but we've never measured her hands."

Of course not. Aloran closed his eyes for a deep breath.

"Aloran," Serjer said gently, "what you saw—she *was* angry, but
she was mostly performing for the Master. She is kind to us."

"Thank you for telling me." He would grasp at any small hope—
but he wasn't one of them. The Artist scolded in his mind: *The love that
comes after is yours to make.* "Serjer, would you—could you, come
with me?"

"Of course." Serjer fetched a measuring tape from a metal drawer,
then accompanied him down the hall and knocked on the crescent-
moon door. Thank Heile. He couldn't have mustered the courage on
his own.

The Lady's voice issued from the service speaker. "You may
come in."

They went in. The Lady sat facing them, body tense and arms
crossed. Bowing, Aloran tried not to look like he was terrified. He did
study the gown she wore, which was a masterpiece: flowing silk in a
vivid, hand-dyed light blue, with patterns of fine white embroidery
that rippled and swirled across it. *That* color would be impossible to
match.

"Pardon us, Mistress," Serjer said. "Aloran has an innovative idea
for your wardrobe at the Accession Ball, and—as it happens—I do not
possess sufficient measurements to aid him."

At the word 'innovative,' interest sparked in Lady Tamelera's eyes.
"What is it, Serjer?"

"Aloran?" said Serjer.

Aloran cleared his throat. "I perceive a danger that Kinders fever may be passed among those gathered at the Ball," he said. "I would like to measure you for gloves to match whatever gown you have chosen."

"Gloves!" the Lady exclaimed. "Now that's something I've never seen in the Pelismara Society."

Did that mean no? Aloran bowed.

But she seemed genuinely intrigued. "Serjer," she said, "show him the midnight gown, please. *Gloves*—they'd be shocked!"

"Indeed, Mistress," said Serjer. From the broad wardrobe against the wall, he pulled out a floor-length sleeveless gown of black silk. What elevated it from Imbati to breathtaking was a profusion of tiny diamonds recreating the starry night from hem to shoulder.

"I'd *like* to shock them," the Lady said. Her hands were less confident than her voice. Her long, shapely fingers shook slightly when she held them out.

Aloran hated to touch her, but it was impossible to take the measurements properly any other way. He winced inside with every slightest brush and kept his eyes lowered, praying she wouldn't be too angry at his lack of precision. Serjer kindly noted down the measurements.

As he rolled the measuring tape, Lady Tamelera said hesitantly, "If . . ."

Aloran stopped rolling. He waited, but she didn't continue. After a moment, he murmured, "Yes, Lady?"

She cleared her throat. "If it's a health issue, I believe—I believe we should measure Tagaret's hands also."

"Yes, Lady."

"Serjer, could you run and get him, please?"

Serjer bowed but didn't move. "Would you permit me a presumption, Mistress?"

"Yes?"

"Aloran wishes with all his heart for you to accept his service."

Aloran flushed and nearly dropped the measuring tape. *Oh, don't let her be angry . . .*

Lady Tamelera pulled her hands back against her stomach. "Ah, Aloran—" Her voice sounded very small. "I believe Tagaret is in his rooms. Could you please fetch him for me? And, ah, ask him to bring the suit I gave him for his birthday."

He bowed. "Yes, Lady."

This time, Serjer stayed behind. Aloran walked out the public door into the drawing room and peeked to the right down the hall. One door down there—that would be the one to avoid. Which meant the door directly across from him was Grobal Tagaret's door—or, young Master Tagaret's, since he'd be the *young Master* now. It stood slightly ajar. Aloran raised his hand to knock—

And found himself face-to-face with Nekantor.

CHAPTER TWELVE

Priorities

What in the name of Varin's teeth was an Imbati doing here?

"Listening!" Nekantor snapped. "How dare you?"

"Young Master, if I may—" the Imbati said, bowing low, but not before the black hair and broad shoulders gave him away. Gnash him, it was the Imbati from the play session—the one who played games.

"Do you think you can play a game with me, Imbati?" Nekantor demanded. "You care about what I say to my brother? What did you hear?"

"Pardon me, young Master," the Imbati said. "I heard nothing. I came to see young Master Tagaret. May I please speak with him?"

Nekantor growled. Worst thing about Imbati—deflections, deflections. This Imbati had heard Tagaret say he didn't care to become Heir, because Tagaret refused to say anything else.

Tagaret's voice approached behind him. "Nek, what are you doing? Who's there?"

Nekantor never took his eyes from the Imbati. "I'm accosting a spy," he said—and see, how the Imbati flinched when he said the word 'spy!' Oh, yes, this one had been told to learn something. Something important—to learn whether Tagaret wanted to become Heir. That information had to be important to someone. *Someone* would want to know that Tagaret had no priorities at all and couldn't see the value of the prize in front of his face.

Benél always listened.

"Mercy, Nek," said Tagaret at his shoulder. "Leave him alone. That's Mother's new Aloran."

Nekantor scowled. "Imbati, raise your head."

Slowly, the Imbati obeyed. Black hair. Dark eyebrows, and above them the manservant's mark, new and raised with pink edges. Proof of loyalty.

"Fah," Nekantor said. Distasteful, that Tagaret was right. Mother would never send *her* servant to find out if Tagaret wanted to become Heir; she'd just ask Tagaret. "He was *listening*, though, Tagaret. Aloran was listening to us."

Tagaret made a small exasperated sound. "What did you need, Aloran?"

The spy will give himself away with his face—but Aloran answered without flinching. "Young Master Tagaret, your mother wishes to see you, and requests you bring the suit she gave you for your birthday. May I help you with it?"

"Fah," Nekantor said.

"No need," Tagaret answered. "I'll get it. Tell her I'll be right there."

"Yes, young Master."

And so the Imbati turned, walked away, and returned to Mother's room.

Nekantor growled in his throat. Loyalty or not, Aloran played games.

His brother's voice came behind him again. "Nek, move."

Nekantor turned around. Tagaret was carrying his suit over his arm as if he were strolling out to some party.

"How can you pretend there's nothing going on here?" Nekantor demanded. "You and I should be back in Father's office, right now. We have important business to plan."

Tagaret made a face. "Plan it yourself, Nek."

That was enough. Gnash Tagaret, and gnash the Imbati, too. "Fine! You go play with Mother and her new toy." He shoved out into the sitting room and went straight into Father's office without knocking. "Father, Tagaret is a complete waste of time," he declared, then stopped.

Father wasn't in his chair; he was lying on the couch. The couch was new and different—unacceptable. It hadn't been there before Father left, or when Father was away. And now was the time for Father to be *back*. It was *not* the time for him to be lying down.

Father knew as well as he did that Heir Selection was the best game of all. The vision rolled out in his head: twelve Families, twelve candidates, each following his own little line toward a center point where only one could remain. Once the candidates were confirmed and the voting rounds began, the little lines would twist and dance—and be marked with blood.

Just minutes ago, he and Father had been planning. They'd narrowed down the most likely candidates for each Family, identified basic strengths and weaknesses, talked about how to make sure the First Family's candidate was strongest. Only the strongest candidate could stand at the center, beneath the hand of the Eminence Herin himself— and here was Father, *taking a nap?!*

"What in Varin's name are you doing?" Nekantor snapped.

Father sat up slowly, wincing. "What is it, son?"

"The First Family must have the best candidate."

"Oh, don't worry," Father said. "Fifth and Third will be Tagaret's toughest rivals. Fifth will probably choose Innis, even though he's almost thirty-one—Tagaret will make him look old. Third has Foress and Vant, of course, but Xemell has the best health—and he's fourteen. Tagaret can beat him just by looking mature."

Nekantor scowled. "Not if he won't try. Benél would do better."

Father laughed, and his fat body quaked. "You woke me up to tell me that?"

Nekantor set his teeth. "Benél knows how to hold power, Father. He leads."

Garr rubbed a hand across his forehead. "Don't be ridiculous," he said. "Benél is only an Adjudicator's son, and he'll never even rise to his father's position. Tagaret can outthink him in his sleep."

Nekantor closed his fists. "Not—if—he—won't—*try.*"

Garr leaned forward and grasped his shoulder with a heavy hand. "Well, that's why we're working on him, isn't it."

Nekantor jerked away, but Father's handprint stayed, sticky on his shoulder. "Then maybe you should be *working on him* instead of taking a nap!"

Father frowned. "I'll do as I like, Nekantor. Now, you go find something useful to do."

Nekantor stared, then whirled and walked away. Gnash Father, too! Do something *useful*? As if he hadn't been working out the moves of Heir Selection ever since he found the ring? Even going to Benél's would be more useful than staying here.

He couldn't go to Benél's carrying a handprint.

He went to his rooms, stripped off his clothes, and tossed them out the laundry chute. Picked out new ones from his dresser and put them on, closing each button in order. Trousers, one button; shirt, seven buttons; vest, three buttons to make eleven. He fastened his belt, straightened his cuffs, and moved from there into the circle.

He checked the door, running his finger along the crack between bronze and stone. Checked his desk—all the drawers closed, the chair pushed in until it touched. Checked the window shade, perfect, then ran his hand up the bed and tapped the bedside table three times. Veered left to avoid the curtain on the wall and went to his wardrobe, pressing its doors shut and also each drawer beneath, caressing its brass handles. Checked the bathroom door, and back to the main door to close the circle. Ahh, yes, now everything was perfect. Ready to go out.

Nekantor went to the front vestibule and considered the door handle. It was safer today in the halls than it had ever been—he'd be no target for assassination, because everyone knew Tagaret would be the one chosen. Only fifty-seven paces. He held his breath and dived out.

Luck was with him. Benél's Household Imbati was quick to open the door.

"Young sir, what are you doing out at a time like this?" the Imbati said. "Hurry in, and I'll get the Master."

Nekantor stepped in, frowning. The Adjudicator was home? He waited, straightened his cuffs, and checked his buttons. This wouldn't be a hard game, though; if the Adjudicator questioned him, he could always say Father had sent him.

Instead, it was Benél who came to the vestibule, smiling wide.

"Nekantor—Varin's teeth!" Benél turned to the Imbati. "Remeni, Nekantor won't stay long. Don't bother Father with this when he's so busy."

The servant looked uncertain but bowed his head. Benél was good with servants.

Nekantor followed him in. This suite was exactly the same as his: all the walls and doors in the right place, exactly the same place. Only the furniture was different. And Benél's rooms were in the same place as Tagaret's rooms, but Benél's door was open: he had no secret games. All the games that were important, they played together. Benél brought him in and locked the door against any others. It was their citadel.

"I can't believe you came out," Benél said. His hand came to the back of his neck, shook him.

Nekantor smiled. "Plenty of people are in danger, but not me. Not today."

"Lucky you." Benél turned away and prowled around the room. When he passed his desk, he kicked at its legs. "I hate being closeted like this! Father has hardly spoken to me."

"Why? Is he planning your candidacy alone?"

Benél stopped and stared.

"Why does everybody think it's a joke?" Nekantor demanded. "It's not a joke. My brother is an idiot who can't see the value of what's in front of his nose. *You* have power. All the boys know it. They follow you because they want you to give it to them, too. You should be the First Family's candidate."

Benél's face turned red, but he smiled. "I'd like that," he said. "But the First Family is strong. We have a lot of good possible candidates." He shrugged. "I'm sure other Families are fighting over the same problem right now."

Nekantor nodded. The Twelve Great Families loomed all around, each one fighting over who would enter the game—who would become the focus of power, and the target for death, the boy who walked that twisting path to the center. "It's a good game," he said. "They're fighting, but I know who they'll pick."

Benél was watching him. "I bet you do," he laughed. "Let's have a drink and you tell me about it." His lip curled into a smile.

That was a smile full of secrets, secrets to be shared inside their citadel. It felt very good.

Benél got down on the floor beside his dresser and reached underneath, found a bottle and a small glass. He poured the glass full. The liquor was luminous brown—chatinet, like in the whore's bedroom.

In the whore's mirror, the bed whispering of sex, and Benél moving, pushing his hands among glass bottles . . .

Nekantor sucked in a breath; it came out again as a laugh.

Benél looked through the liquor at the lamp beside his bed. "I found this in Father's office," he said. "Last week you liked it. Didn't you?"

Chatinet put warmth in his stomach and made him dizzy. "I liked it," Nekantor said.

"All right, then." Benél came and offered him the glass.

Nekantor didn't take it. Benél's clothes were rumpled, from getting down on the ground. They were all wrong, and had to be fixed. He tugged on the silk at Benél's shoulders, straightened his vest. Took his belt and realigned it with the button on his trousers.

Benél laughed. The glass in his fingers jiggled a little.

Nekantor took the glass from him, drank a sip. Chatinet invaded his throat and nose. It was sweet, and burned, and smelled like the whore's room, like sex and secrets. "Tagaret won't be our candidate," he said. "He can't be."

"Why?"

"Simple. He doesn't care."

Benél's eyebrows lifted. "How can he not *care*? It's Heir Selection, for Plis' sake."

"See, that's why my father has to choose you." Nekantor lifted the glass and drained it, because a glass should be full or empty. The chatinet ignited in his stomach.

Benél took the glass, filled it, and raised it high. "Here's hoping you can do it." He tossed his head back; muscles moved in his throat.

"I'll *make* him listen," Nekantor said. "We'll play the game together." The pattern of the greatest game of all rolled out across Benél's brown silk carpet, and Nekantor stalked around it, while the fire in his stomach diffused and spread. He stopped at one spot on the tasseled edge. "Ninth Family is easy. They'll think they have to choose between Reyn and Gowan, but Gowan is the one with cabinet blood. They'll choose him." He pointed across to another spot. "Twelfth will choose Yril."

Benél snorted. "After we got him disgraced? How can he be an Heir candidate if he's closeted from attending the Accession Ball?" Benél sat down at the center of the carpet, bottle in one hand and glass in the other. He held his head high; his back was straight and his eyes gleamed. Power radiated from him like the heat of a fire. How could no one else see it?

Nekantor looked toward the spot on the carpet's edge where Yril would stand, and shook his head. "Nevertheless, they're too divided over the others. Yril's the only one with both intelligence and tenacity, not to mention good health." He pointed across the carpet. "We'll see Fernar coming from the Eleventh. Xemell from the Third, Menni from the Second."

"You're amazing." Benél laughed a little and poured again. "A genius."

"It's why we belong together," Nekantor said.

Benél's face reddened. He smiled, slow and broad, and sipped his drink.

Oh, that smile felt good. Nekantor's ears burned. The chatinet put warmth into his legs. "I plan, and you carry the power," he said. "We are like Plis the Warrior and his adjutant on the fields of Melu."

"No, we're not."

Nekantor cast him a glance. "No?"

"Not really." Benél studied his drink.

Nekantor stared. Neither full nor empty, the glass put hooks into him, pulling him toward Benél. He bent down and snatched it, drained it fast. Chatinet slithered down his throat. His skin tingled where Benél's fingers had touched his.

Benél's hand grasped his ankle, stopping him before he could walk away.

"We're Trigis the Resolute and Bes the Ally," Benél said. "Sit down; I'm sure you can still see the pattern from here."

Nekantor sat down. It was true. From the center, he could see all of it, and in the swirling fumes of chatinet the lines did their dance of intrigue and assassination. Sangar of the Eighth Family, Herm of the Seventh, Innis of the Fifth. Some would die. All would lose, except for one.

Benél's hand landed hot on the back of his neck. Tightened. Shook him.

"Thanks, Nek."

Nekantor looked at his face, very close now. Benél's lip was almost healed, from the whore that had thrown the chains at him. "What for?"

Benél's hand released slightly, moved, pushing down toward his shoulder. It tensed his muscles and shivered him. Benél said, "For thinking I could be Heir."

"You will be."

Benél swooped in, and for a second Benél's lips pressed his.

Nekantor gaped. Benél's hand tightened on his shoulder, moved again. Feel the power there—so much power! Nekantor raised his hand and touched Benél's face. Power leapt through the touch like an electric shock, and Benél surged suddenly. Benél's mouth, hot and urgent, sent power exploding outward; Nekantor fell on his back with Benél all over him.

"Benél! Honey, dinner's on the table; where are you?" A lady's sickly-sweet voice.

And suddenly Benél was gone, taking everything away. Nekantor gasped for breath. Benél shut the bottle and quickly pushed it and the glass back under his dresser.

Nekantor struggled up. Hissed desperately, "Benél!"

Benél's hands lifted him, set him on his feet. "That's my mother— we have to get you out of here before they find you."

"No," Nekantor said. His body shook, and the room shook, everything still submerged in chatinet and Benél's mouth. "I have to stay with you."

"No, you have to get home before your father misses you at dinner." He looked around frantically. "I know—here."

Benél's hand grasped the back of his neck, dragged him behind a curtain into darkness.

Nekantor's throat shrank tight. "Benél!" he croaked. "What are you doing? This is the Lowers' hall!"

"This way, quick."

Benél dragged him stumbling forward, around a dark corner. Chatinet made the shadows sway. They clung to his clothes and pressed inward toward his skin. Benél's hand on his neck wasn't enough to keep him safe. He couldn't breathe. He couldn't breathe!

And suddenly Benél's hand pushed him through another door, stumbling into light. Walls draped with curtains, and green carpet under his feet—the vestibule? Benél pushed him out the front door.

He was alone in the hall. Alone, except for the clinging shadows.

Nekantor ran. No counting, no touching, just trying to keep his feet moving straight—the bright light of the hall tugged at the shadows but couldn't chase their taint away. He flung himself home and straight to his rooms. Tore off all his clothes and climbed into the empty bath, poured water over himself. His skin was flushed red. Had the shadows burned him?

Benél hadn't meant to take him through the Lowers' hall. He'd been forced to. It was the Lady's fault—Benél would never have done it if he'd had any choice. And if he were here now, everything would be all right. Benél's hands could rub shadows away. Benél had power.

Nekantor scrubbed himself with soap and poured more water, hot. It scalded, but now the flush was from the water, not from the creeping shadows. He dried himself and covered up the evidence with clothes, one careful layer at a time. He would have been safe if Benél were here.

Benél's hands, Benél's damaged lip—

Benél was in their citadel, fighting off the Lady's invasion. But he should have been here.

Benél's arms, Benél's mouth—

It was too tight in here.

Nekantor went into the bedroom and tried to start the circle. No. Impossible to stand still. Too hurried, too shaky, and circling dizzied him. His mouth still tasted of chatinet and Benél.

Too tight in here.

And when he went out into the drawing room, he found the locked door.

The door was locked. It was in the right place, exactly the same place. He should have been inside it, with Benél, but instead Tagaret had locked the door. The door must not be locked!

A wire was no good for this lock; hours of work hadn't cracked it, and the hooks reached deep. Nekantor stalked the drawing room. What he needed was—there. A large split geode full of amethysts, awkward but good enough. He hefted it, cold, rough, heavy, in his hands. Back to the lock, and he slammed the stone into it. His knuckles stubbed—the geode slipped out of his fingers and thudded to the floor.

The doors from the sitting room burst open.

"Nekantor!" Father shouted. "Varin's teeth—what are you doing? Get away from that door!"

"No!"

Father's rough hand gripped his shoulder, spun him away from the lock. Father growled, dangerous with power. "You'll do as I say. The entire family has been at the table waiting for you."

"But the door," Nekantor protested. "The door must not be locked! It's wrong. You don't know what Tagaret does in there. He plays secret games—and he doesn't even care—he doesn't deserve a citadel!"

Father's fingers dug deep as claws, grinding his bones. "What in Varin's name is wrong with you?"

"It's wrong!" Nekantor cried, heat overflowing from his eyes. "It's wrong! The door must not be locked!"

Fists bunched on his collar and pulled him up into growling teeth—and suddenly the growling stopped. The fists shoved him backward into the stone wall. "Drunk!" Father shouted. "Drunk! I should have known."

Nekantor gasped, limp. Father's fists hung him from his clothes, dragged him to his rooms, flung him on his bed. Then Father slammed the door; its vibrations shook outward, undoing everything that had once been right.

Nekantor sobbed and shook. He didn't dare open his eyes to see everything wrong, all wrong. He felt with his hands, found the edge of the bed, the smooth surface of the bedside table, and on it, the whore's ring.

The ring was round, and smooth, and perfect. He followed it with his fingers, around and around. It was more than perfect; it was his own piece of power, the key that had opened the ultimate game, and let him see the pattern before anyone else.

He followed it with his fingers, around and around.

Around and around, in the blind dark.

CHAPTER THIRTEEN
The Accession Ball

Father called this a day of opportunity—and it was—but the 'most important event of his life' had just turned his friends into enemies, and a handshake into a threat of death. Tagaret struggled not to cringe at the excitement of the crowd. Half the First Family had now packed into the suite, including at least six of the Family's eligible males. Erex had charge of the younger ones, Father of the older, but Father was shamelessly playing favorites, and Tagaret could feel the glares of the men in their twenties. No Lady Selemei, so the major standoff was still to come.

"Tagaret, good luck tonight!" Yet another overenthusiastic middle-aged cousin offered a handshake, then hesitated.

Tagaret tugged tight his white, pearl-buttoned gloves, and smiled when the man decided to thump his shoulder. "Thanks."

"Stop messing with those gloves, or I'll take them," Father rumbled.

"Father, they're for safety."

"Young Tagaret," said Fedron, "we need you to look serious, not *artisanal*."

He would have given anything for Reyn right now. Searching for a friendly face, Tagaret waved to his cousin Inkala, who came and lifted his hands consideringly.

"How do *you* think they look?" he asked.

"Perfectly good!" Inkala giggled. "On your *mother* . . ."

"Come on!"

Mother's gloved hand touched his arm. "Come over here a second, love," she said. "You don't have your mourning scarf on."

Any excuse for a break. He let Mother take him aside, threading through the crowded dining room and stopping just inside the kitchen's swinging doors. When Keeper Premel saw them, he bowed and stepped out.

"I'm sorry, Mother," Tagaret said. "I know it's important. I know what the Heir's power means. It's just that I can't stand it."

Mother kissed his cheek gently. "I know, love." She found the long, moon-yellow mourning scarf he'd stuffed into his pocket, and knotted it around his right arm just below the elbow. The ends fluttered down to his knee, whispering of Mother Elinda's gentle comfort—but it was impossible to feel comforted, knowing how Indal had died.

He tugged at his gloves again. Mother's were midnight black with diamonds, like her dress, and came up past her elbows. Which raised the question—

"Mother, where's Aloran?"

Mother blushed and hugged herself. "I told him to meet us at the vestibule as we go out."

"Father will complain again."

She raised her head defiantly. "You think I care a pin for what your father thinks?"

What a question. Tagaret decided to be honest. "Mother, if you *really* didn't care, don't you think you'd realize that Aloran has vowed himself to *you*, not Father? It's no defeat if *you're* the one giving the orders."

Mother looked annoyed. "I'll concede the point, Tagaret. But here's the problem: he's a man. He doesn't disappear into his black the way he should. I turn, and I *see* him, and he's a *man*. Now you'll tell me it doesn't matter."

Tagaret shrugged. No point lecturing her on something she'd told *him* a hundred times. And bringing up Father's bias for male bodyguards wouldn't help at all.

She squeezed his arm. "I'm trying, love. I've written to Eyli, and she assured me again that she vouches for him, so I *am*, I promise. But you need to try, too. Whether you're the First Family's candidate matters less to me tonight than that the Pelismara Society sees you behave as the man you are. Do I need to ask Erex to take you in his group?"

That made his cheeks burn. "No. I'm sorry."

Mother lifted her head. "Thank you, Premel, for permitting our intrusion." She took Tagaret's arm. "Here's an idea. Why don't you walk in with Pyaras? You need the company, and Erex would like a break from handling him."

"But Pyaras isn't eligible," Tagaret said.

Mother nodded. "And if *you* tell him that, he might believe you."

So they found Pyaras and joined the mass procession of the First Family, at least the portion of it that answered to Father, walking in between orange-uniformed Arissen toward the central wing and the Hall of the Eminence. Father and Fedron were at the front, side by side, accompanied by Sorn and Chenna. Tagaret came behind with the other eligibles, doing his best to smile. Pyaras was definitely upset about something, but his energetic presence made it easier to ignore Nekantor stalking the edge of the group, and the prospect of Selemei's imminent appearance. Mother walked on Tagaret's left, smiling at everyone's compliments for her gown and gloves; Aloran followed so quietly it seemed impossible even she should notice.

"Tagaret," Pyaras said suddenly. "Am I in your gang? Did you ask?"

Oh, no. "Sorry," Tagaret said. "I hadn't yet—but with the Selection on, it's just you and me anyway. First Family first, and all that."

Pyaras' dark brows knit. "I should be eligible, you know. Everyone always said so. I'm big enough!"

"It's not about being big, Pyaras."

"But I'm *almost* twelve! My blood is pure!"

Tagaret frowned. "Of course it is. Who says otherwise?"

Pyaras flushed and mumbled, "People call me 'Arissen' at school. Don't tell my father. Grenth started it, because I hit him."

"Varin's teeth." Tagaret squeezed his cousin's strong shoulders. No way had Grenth started it, though; that kind of subtle retaliation was pure Nekantor. "I'll let you join my gang, all right? I'll tell the others. You don't need to ask again."

Pyaras hugged him so hard his feet came off the floor.

"Pyaras, calm down," Father growled. "You'll cause trouble in security."

Tunnel-hounds were on duty outside the Hall of the Eminence. One approached them now, trotting on small dark paws, snuffling their feet and knees with its eyeless head and broad, sensitive nose. Whether it was trained to sniff poisons or sense energy weapons, it apparently found none in their party.

Fedron eyed the animal and shrugged. "Tunnel-hounds didn't save Dest from assassination last time. He was downed with a simple projectile. I worry about precedent."

Tagaret scanned the heavily guarded foyer for assassins. "You think they'd try it again?"

"No one would do it at the Ball," said Father. "Besides, projectiles are so uninspired."

"Permit us, sirs?" Two Arissen guards approached, carrying tunnel-hounds. An upper-body check was unpleasant, but tolerable in the name of safety. Pyaras actually crooned to the hound and offered it his fingers, but when the guard smiled at him, he scowled.

The Arissen passed them in.

Tagaret sucked a breath. Potential enemies packed the Hall of the Eminence, glittering in their finery from the wall hangings all the way to the stage with the wooden throne, while mourning scarves in grieving yellow whispered, *death*. To be on guard, he needed his eyes open. And to be the man Mother wanted everyone to see, he had to stand gracefully, making the high mosaic vaults his portrait frames, and the crystal chandeliers his spotlights. More and more eyes watched him as the Great Families entered through doors around the Hall. From this vantage point he couldn't clearly identify either Ninth Family or Eleventh. Sixth seemed like it might be in the far corner.

Reyn. Gowan. Fernar. Della. They were with him now only as a haunting ache. He exchanged glances with the cousins around him, but only Pyaras smiled.

Soon after they arrived in the First Family's assigned area, a reverent voice sang a single clear note that cut through the murmuring gossip. The crowd hushed, and the lights dimmed, revealing the stately form of the Voice of Elinda upon the stage. She stood with arms reaching forward, her deep blue sacramental robes overlayered with a yellow funereal cloak. A silver moon-disc shone upon her chest. When silence was at last complete, she sang the prayer:

"All with eyes in this place, hear me, gaze and turn your faces upward! Though ages pass, the heavens still show us the inevitable way: the Silent Sister spins and circles beneath our feet, and her holy siblings dance with her around our great Father."

Tagaret turned his face up. In the mosaic arches above, tiny gold tiles hinted of the stars. Mother had tried to lift him up to them, but had managed only to bring their likeness down, in the diamonds across her gown. "Father Varin," he mumbled. "Source of all life."

"Today we honor Indal of the Fifth Family," said the Voice of Elinda. "He rose in brightness, and grew to glory, Eminence of all this land which takes our great Father's name. Nightfall came too quickly upon him." She raised her arms high, and her sleeves fell into great curves like those of Mother Elinda herself.

Tagaret loosened the scarf at his elbow, and nudged Pyaras to do the same. They raised their scarves as arms rose across the Hall, sweeping the room in yellow.

"All honor to Indal of the Fifth Family as he sets in this life," the Voice of Elinda said. "Let him find his way to our great Mother's arms and take his place among the stars."

"Honor to Indal of the Fifth Family," rumbled through the crowd.

"Indal of the Fifth Family, we release you into our Mother's care."

"We release you."

Tagaret let go. Scarves twisted and fluttered to the carpet. Better if the fever could be banished so easily.

Now a man's baritone began to sing—the Voice of Varin rising. First to appear out of the crowd, though, was the Heir. Pyaras grabbed Tagaret's arm excitedly. Herin climbed slowly onto the stage, shining out across the Hall in a suit of regal white silk. The Voice of Varin, wearing the gold disc of Varin upon his chest, mounted the steps behind him. Herin stopped at the center of the stage, and the Voice of Varin wrapped the white-and-gold drape of the Eminence around his shoulders, fastening it on his right shoulder with a shining pin.

"The day of the Eminence Indal has ended," the Voice of Varin declared. "The day of the Eminence Herin has begun. All hail the Eminence Herin!"

"All hail the Eminence Herin!" The enormous shout pounded in Tagaret's body.

The Eminence Herin raised his arms to the assembled people, who fell into silence. "It is with a heavy heart for my friend Indal that I take this responsibility upon myself," he said. "And now I wish to dedicate myself to my people."

Behind him, the throne looked less like the work of an artisan and more like an ancient vine that had grown out of the stage. Herin sat down upon it, stroking its burnished arms as if delighted by their curving, twined shape. The Voice of Elinda and the Voice of Varin moved to places on either side of him.

"What does that mean?" whispered Pyaras.

Tagaret had a general idea, but looked for Mother—she'd seen an Accession before.

"It's for all the Varini," Mother explained softly. "Herin has officially assumed the Grobal Trust on behalf of the Race, and now the Lowers will accept his leadership."

An Arissen walked up onto the stage. He cut a powerful figure in his bright rust-red dress uniform, wearing the feather-crested helmet of a military Division Commander. He saluted before the throne. "I am Revett of the Pelismara Division, and I speak for the Arissen," he said. "I give my people into your Trust." He crossed to the Eminence's other side and went to a small table at the back of the stage, where two Imbati, a male warden and female bureaucrat, watched him sign something. Then he returned to the front of the stage and stood proudly looking out.

Somewhere behind Tagaret, a singsong whisper came, "Arissen Pya-raas . . ."

Pyaras made a strangled sound, and whirled.

Gods, not in front of everyone! Tagaret flung his arms around him—for a second Pyaras struggled—then by Heile's mercy, Pyaras subsided with a gasp, burying his face in Tagaret's coat.

"You're all right," Tagaret murmured. *Gnash Nekantor.* "They're wrong. Don't listen to them."

Pyaras fought tears. "I hate them," he whispered. "Arissen—I *hate* them!"

Don't let Father notice . . . Tagaret patted his back. "Just don't listen."

By the time he looked up, three more Lowers had come onstage. A small, graceful and dignified Imbati man with long white hair and the faded tattoo of a manservant, and a sharp-eyed Kartunnen woman with a purple lip and pale gray academic robes both stood at the front looking out. A huge Venorai woman now presented herself to the Eminence. She was obviously a surface worker, for her skin was a striking sunmarked brown. She wore a laborer's thick black belt over a gaudy tunic. Blinking at it, he realized the design was a print of flowers.

"I am Kitrin, elected leader of the Venorai Union, and I speak for all of us." Her powerful voice made the room seem small, and only got louder as she added, "I speak for the ones who give you your brass, your orsheth, and your food." Murmurs of dismay and disapproval ran through the crowd. "I give my people into your Trust."

She strode off toward the signing table, and her place was taken by a Melumalai man who seemed meek in comparison. The weight of his silver-and-chrysolite necklace spoke louder than his words. "I am Odenli, chairman of the Melumalai Banking Syndicate, and I speak for the Melumalai. I give my people into your Trust." He, too, went and signed his name.

Only one left. A nervous shiver ran down Tagaret's back. He searched behind Odenli—there? No; that wasn't a dark gray hood, just a shadow in the crowd. The stairs to the stage stayed empty.

The Akrabitti were missing.

Herin didn't seem to notice. When the Melumalai returned to the front of the stage, he stood and raised a paternal hand over the glimmering line of Lowers. "With the spirit of the Great Grobal Fyn as my guide, I pledge myself to the Grobal Trust," he declared. "Giving to each according to need, the hand of the Grobal shall guide the land of Varin."

The Voice of Varin and the Voice of Elinda cried out again, "All hail the Eminence Herin!"

"The Eminence Herin!" boomed the crowd.

As the echoes died, Nekantor said sharply, "That was wrong. The pattern was broken."

"Hush, Nekantor," said Father. "Now, everyone stick together and watch your step; we're moving to the ballroom."

Tagaret took Pyaras' shoulder and walked with the crowd toward the broad archway on the right of the stage, careful not to step on fallen mourning scarves. But for once, Nek was absolutely right. "It *was* wrong," he said.

Pyaras looked up. "Really? Why?"

Tagaret shook his head. "Herin can't have assumed the Trust for all the Varini when the Akrabitti were missing." In fact, now that he thought about it, everything about those Lowers had been wrong. The beautiful silk costumes. The scripted words. None of them looked anything like the Arissen wrestlers, or Kartunnen Ryanin, or the Melumalai bartender. Only that Venorai woman had showed a glimpse of her true nature, and she'd won no favors from the crowd.

Pyaras made a face. "Who'd want to see a *trasher*, though?"

"Pyaras," said Mother, chidingly.

"Well, they don't."

"It's not that." Mother lowered her voice. "It's the *ashers* they don't want to think of."

Tagaret shuddered. Mother was right—he didn't want to imagine the people who now held what was left of Indal. After the mourning moon had fallen, no one wanted to think about endings anymore.

They walked out of the deep archway into the ballroom, where an orchestra was playing. The crowd spread out, moved faster—began to speak of eligibles, and candidacies, and dealmaking. The hungry talk of Selection drowned the music, chattering on the stone walls, the windows, and the wooden floor.

Father beckoned and smiled, and people swarmed inward, armed with questions. Tagaret tried to watch the older eligibles' example, but before long it was too much, and he simply had to answer on his own, with as much enthusiasm as possible. *Yes, I'm seventeen now. My health report was excellent; Father's Sorn has it if you'd like to see. Of course, who wouldn't be excited? Yes, it was hard when Father was away. He was still my political mentor, though; we wrote letters twice a week. I've worked with him intensively since he returned. No, I haven't attended a cabinet meeting. Yes, we discuss them at home.* The envoys of rival Familes might compliment, but they couldn't disguise their appetites, and their smiles were full of sharp teeth. Even with Imbati Sorn, Aloran, and Chenna tense on the alert, he felt nowhere near safe—and Lady Selemei might appear at any moment. Maybe she was somewhere near even now, trying to be brave enough to face Father. Tagaret tugged his gloves tighter.

"That's it!" Father barked. "I've had it." He trapped Tagaret's wrists and yanked his gloves off.

"Father—" Tagaret gasped. His hands felt cold, and his stomach churned. "Father, please. I need those."

"Don't be ridiculous. It's time you got serious here."

"Tagaret," said Pyaras. "Look who's coming."

Mercy, not Selemei . . . Tagaret turned in a panic, but it wasn't. A rush of relief weakened his knees. "Reyn!" he cried. "Fernar!"

"It's great to see you," Reyn said. In his eyes was a tinge of that desperate look he'd had when they were separated in the Conveyor's Hall.

With the sensation now expanding in his stomach, he probably looked the same.

"You're looking official, Tagaret," Fernar grinned. "The portrait of an Heir candidate."

Tagaret found a smile. "So are you." Someone had styled Fernar's dark hair, and he looked poised and confident. On impulse, Tagaret hugged him—and Fernar clasped solidly back, a proof that Selection hadn't quite changed everything. "How in Eyn's name did you escape the Eleventh Family?"

Fernar laughed, thumping him on the back. "Guile, fifteen rival eligibles, and a borrowed manservant."

"Oh, well done!" Tagaret released him and embraced Reyn.

"I miss you," Reyn whispered.

Oh, gods, yes. Tagaret didn't trust himself to speak, just nodded. He forced himself to thump Reyn on the back, then reached out to include Fernar in a huddle. "What a mess," he said. "When do we all get to be together again? Where's Gowan?"

"In the center of attention, of course," said Reyn. "No one's so eligible as he!"

"Lucky him."

Fernar shrugged. "He's always been more about politics than the rest of us. It serves him well right now."

"I'll give you that," Tagaret said. "Look, I should tell you—Pyaras here needs our protection, so when all this is over, he's going to join us awhile. I hope you won't mind." Pyaras, who had been hanging nearby, smiled shyly.

"He *is* good in a fight," said Fernar approvingly.

Reyn stiffened. "Tagaret—it's Lady Selemei!"

Tagaret straightened fast, grasping at Reyn and Fernar's hands for support. His heart pounded in his ears. Lady Selemei and her Ustin were still a few paces away. The Lady had handed her cane to her servant, and had clasped the hands of a man from the older eligible group; he had her eyes, and was smiling broadly at her. Nekantor drew near, as if thirsty for impending conflict. Father bristled.

"Tagaret," said Fedron. "Be polite with her, now."

Fedron must have meant the warning for Father, but Father lumbered toward Selemei, showing no sign that he'd heard.

"Selemei, keep out of this," he said.

Lady Selemei smiled, with a nervous glance for Tagaret, and held out one hand so Ustin could return her cane. "I'm sure it's only natural for a Family's cabinet members all to be present," she said. "I only thought I'd give Brinx my good wishes."

"Which shows you have no respect for the First Family's strategy."

"Garr, please." Arbiter Erex stepped away from his group of younger boys. "I don't believe direct confrontation is part of our strategy."

Tagaret blinked. *Direct confrontation.* Selemei had said something at the tea: *In a direct confrontation, we always lose.* That was why she hadn't come earlier, and why she hadn't approached him first. She'd told him she needed the support of men. *He* was the one who needed to be brave enough.

He took a deep breath.

"Lady Selemei, thank you for coming," he said loudly. "Father, and Fedron, I have a wonderful surprise for you! I've asked Lady Selemei to act as my sponsor tonight."

Fedron's mouth fell open. Father spluttered, "What?!"

"Why, congratulations!" Reyn exclaimed.

"Tagaret, that's great news," said Fernar.

Lady Selemei nodded to them. "It's so kind of you both! I must say, Fedron, I was honored when Tagaret suggested it. I'm excited to have the opportunity at an occasion like this."

"*Tagaret . . .*" Father swelled threateningly, on the brink of explosion. "*You're not serious.*"

A bubble of fear tried to burst in Tagaret's throat, but the only way out was forward. Seeing that Father's hand had loosened around his white gloves, he snatched them back and put them on again, tugging them on tight. "Yes, yes, I am. Quite serious. Lady Selemei is the best possible sponsor for me tonight, even if you don't see it."

Father started to crack. "Even if I—!"

"He's right," said Nekantor.

Tagaret stared. Had *Nekantor* just said he was right?

Father seemed just as stunned. "What are you saying, Nekantor?"

Nekantor calmly straightened his vest. "I'm saying that the First Family can only be hurt if we are perceived to have a rift between our cabinet members. If Tagaret is seen escorted by Lady Selemei, the First Family demonstrates unity and our cause is strengthened."

Lady Selemei relaxed into a demure smile. "I had no idea there was such an astute bit of strategy behind your invitation, Tagaret," she said. "But I am happy to oblige."

Father chewed his lip. "Fine, go ahead. Good to see you applying yourself, Tagaret." His eyes added, *We'll talk about this later.*

"Tagaret, I would very much enjoy a walk around the ballroom with you," Lady Selemei said. "May we, so that we can meet some of our competition?"

And leave behind his friends? But Pyaras had Erex to look after him, and Reyn and Fernar were already being missed elsewhere—besides which, he'd do anything to get away from Father.

Tagaret said his goodbyes and began to walk. The crowd still felt dangerous, but it was totally different to be moving, and to be with Lady Selemei and Mother, guarded by Ustin and Aloran instead of Chenna and Sorn. Even the way the Lady held her cane lent an additional sense of protection.

"You know," Tagaret said, "I think I might actually enjoy this evening."

"I'm not surprised," said Selemei. "It's not every day you get handed a shortcut to your deepest desires."

He conceded a nod. "You're right, of course. I could really make some changes if I were Heir—but this feels like a cut through the adjuncts. Lots of cracks and pitfalls to die in."

"You'll have people looking after you."

People like Father and Nekantor. Tagaret winced. "That's worse, though. They all want to control me. I'm not sure it's worth it."

"Not sure it's worth it?" Lady Selemei asked, looking at him sidelong. "On the contrary. You must not have thoroughly considered it."

"Selemei," Mother scolded.

"It's all right, Mother." Tagaret looked hard at Lady Selemei. "We're allies now, aren't we? What do you mean, I mustn't have considered it?"

Lady Selemei raised her eyebrows. "Perhaps you didn't realize the Heir has his pick of the Families, to take any partner he likes."

Tagaret stopped breathing. The air had become a bath of electricity; his entire body prickled.

Della. What if she were no longer a dream? What if she could be real? *Sirin and Eyn!*

"Then let's walk," Tagaret said. "Let's show our First Family strength."

CHAPTER FOURTEEN

Dangerous Trespasses

When it was all over, Aloran shut the crescent-moon door behind him and stood still a moment. The private silence was a relief, but his body quivered with fatigue after hours of vigilant tension. The boys had gone back to their rooms and the Master to his office with Grobal Fedron, attended by Sorn and Chenna. Lady Tamelera had dismissed him again and gone to bathe alone.

Home safely—but not really safe.

Even with his Lady and young Master Tagaret wearing gloves, there had still been so many unprotected hands, shaking, patting, touching. Contagion rating medium, with that kind of exposure . . . If the Master himself didn't contract Kinders fever, someone close to the family surely would. Now was the time to act, or he might find himself helplessly standing by when someone died at their dinner table.

He had a few minutes—it might be nearly midnight, but Premel wouldn't serve Household dinner until Sorn came off-duty, and no doubt Sorn and Fedron's Chenna would be occupied in the Master's office for a while.

Aloran locked his room. He jogged from the Residence into the Academy, and went to the Body Sciences building.

Ezill the pharmacy warden bowed as he walked in. "Good evening, Aloran. I suppose the Residence medical center is too busy for your comfort tonight."

"It hadn't occurred to me to go there," he admitted. After only two days, no matter how intensive, he hardly felt he belonged to a noble house. "Please tell me I haven't lost my privileges here."

"Of course not. I must remind you, though: now that you're

marked, your access to medications will depend on which expense marker you're using."

"Ah, right." Aloran scanned the carefully labeled bottles and tubes along the glass shelves. Special green labels marked those medications—like mood stabilizers and contraceptives—whose use by the Grobal was subject to strict regulation. Fortunately, those weren't what he needed to treat the onset of Kinders fever. He wrote down his order and set down the expense marker that the First Family had provided.

Ezill looked at him hard. The pharmacy warden didn't possess the certifications his clients did, but he knew his inventory well after so many years. He whispered low, "May I ask?"

"I estimate we'll see a spike in fever cases about three days from now," Aloran answered. "You may want to increase your stock."

Ezill gave a deep, private frown as he turned away with the order slip. He reached for an adrenaline delivery tube.

A voice echoed over from the treatment area. "Aloran?"

Kiit's voice? What would she be doing here at this hour? Dismay chilled Aloran's fingers. When he turned around, he discovered Kiit sitting in a chair beside one of the treatment beds. Her dark hair was unbound. She didn't look injured, but there was something about her eyes . . .

He shook his head. "Kiit, may I ask you a question?"

Instead of granting permission, she lashed his own question at him. "What happened to you?"

Aloran flushed, suddenly aware again of the Mark grasping his face. "That should be evident."

Kiit stared at him. "You're working for *her?* After everything we talked about?"

She had always been blunt, but the questions stung. "Imbati, love where you serve," he replied. "I can hardly object now, can I."

"Aloran, that's not fair! Why didn't you tell me?"

He swallowed. Mai's truth, he hadn't given her a thought—but he'd hardly had time to breathe.

"Aloran," Ezill said behind him. "Your order."

When he turned to collect the pouch, Ezill murmured, "Kiit took a bad fall in combat today; she's here on concussion watch."

Kiit had never handled injury well. Maybe frustration was making her aggressive—and irritability was a symptom of concussion. He should try not to take insult. Aloran breathed himself calm; then he walked to Kiit and bent to her ear. "Kiit," he said, "It happened very suddenly. I can't imagine why she chose me, when she doesn't want me. I'm *trying* . . ."

Explaining it was a mistake. The words laid open an abyss inside him, filled with pain and helpless anger. To find someone worthy of true devotion was all he'd ever dreamed of—and now to be sent away, over and over? It hurt in places he hadn't known he had. Should he tell himself it was better to be sent away than to get close to someone who could burn him with a glance? *How could he even be asking himself that question?* Shame rushed through him, hotter than his Lady's eyes.

Kiit touched his hand.

Aloran jerked away. "Kiit—"

"What—you pleaded for my advice, and didn't take it, and now that you're seeing the consequences, you don't want me anymore?"

"No . . ." He couldn't handle questions; he had no answers. He gazed at her, trying to find his lovely Kiit again, but all their intimacies and confidences fell dimly into the gulf of hurt. "I have to go."

"You can't. I don't even know where to find you."

He frowned. "Of course you do. It's no secret; the suite of Grobal Garr and Lady Tamelera is easy to find. Our Keeper will be insulted if I'm late for dinner."

"You can be late this once, Aloran. I thought love meant selflessness."

She might as well have slapped him. The very accusation was so selfish that suddenly he was shaking with fury. "So did I, Kiit. Whose love do you mean, exactly?"

She dared to say it. "Yours."

"How can you say that to me?" he demanded. "*I'm* so selfish, but you won't even give enough to understand that I gave up *myself* when I took the Mark? I've been working since morning and haven't eaten since midday. You have no right to insist I reserve *anything* for you."

He shouldn't have said that. Kiit hugged herself with both arms, and her eyes went cold. "I see," she said. "Goodbye, Aloran. Congratulations on your new position."

Heart empty, Aloran ran back to the Residence. He rushed to tuck the medicines in his dresser drawer, but by the time he came out to the kitchen the Household had started to eat without him. The oval kitchen table had been expanded to seat six; feeling very obvious, he took a stool from the stack in the corner and sat beside Fedron's Chenna.

"My apologies," he said. "I had an emergency errand at the pharmacy."

"Really," said Sorn archly, from the head of the table. "Yet the Lady never sent you there on foot assignment—that much I know. It was selfish, Aloran."

Selfish. It couldn't be, when all he ever tried to do was serve. His throat ached. He glanced at Keeper Premel, sitting beside his partner Dorya. Premel looked more hurt than angry; the man's feelings were easy to read, maybe because of his training outside the Academy, or because of his provincial origins. An odd Safe Harbor idiom that Min had joked about popped up in Aloran's head.

"I blame the tides," he said.

For an instant there was shocked silence. Serjer's eyes widened. Then Dorya gave an audible snort and started chuckling. Keeper Premel's shoulders quaked with laughter. Hope awoke in Aloran's heart, and for a moment, he could imagine truly being one of them . . .

"Silence!" Sorn snapped.

"Oh, Sorn," said Fedron's Chenna, not bothering to hide a note of amusement in her voice. "Just let him be. Go on, Aloran, eat."

Aloran cast her a gaze-gesture of gratitude. Chenna was severely beautiful in her Accession Ball finery. She and Kiit could not have been more opposite. Chenna's figure was streamlined; her hair, the pale color of unbleached tillik-silk, was short at the nape but long at the top, braided into an intricate crown. He found himself analyzing how the style had been executed, then remembered his food and took a bite. Instantly, his mouth watered, and his stomach yawned. He ate faster.

"You're lucky, you know," said Chenna. "I wish Premel were Keeper in our Household. All we get is Imbati one-pot."

Aloran looked at her again. She couldn't be much over thirty—hard to believe she could be Sorn's partner, despite the gold-and-diamond band hidden among the glittering rings on her fingers. He gave a nod to the greens, tender potatoes, and morsels of berry-garnished marshfowl remaining on his plate. "I'm grateful."

Sorn paused in his consumption to remark suppressively, "It is only our Master's generosity."

"I differ, sir," Dorya objected. "The Master pays, but meal creation falls to the Keeper."

Aloran didn't dare speak. He cast a gaze-gesture of thanks in the Keeper's direction and took another bite. For a few moments, silence continued, but then Fedron's Chenna spoke again.

"I know this feels like Varin's teeth right now, Aloran, but it will get better."

Was his dismay so easy to read? Surely it was, for a Gentleman's servant. Aloran sneaked a glance at Sorn before he replied, carefully, "Ah?"

"Especially once young Master Nekantor decides you're just a piece of furniture."

"*Chenna . . .*" Sorn glared at her.

She gave a subtle shrug. "That's how it happened for me, at least."

Aloran looked around. For some reason, all eyes at the table were suddenly focused on him, as if waiting to see how he would reply. He cleared his throat. "You're generous with information, Chenna."

Sorn pushed back from the table. "And *you* can do better, Aloran," he said, wiping his mouth. "I expect you'll remember that tomorrow."

"Yes, sir." When the senior servant walked out, he sighed.

Chenna rested her silverware across her empty plate. "I guess, while he was away with the Master, my partner forgot what a talker I am." She stood up, extricating her skirts from her stool with a deft flick. "Good night, everyone."

At last, Aloran was able to return to his room. He sat on his bed, took the tie from his hair, and began slowly combing it out.

Someone knocked on his Maze door.

Aloran set down the comb. Who could be calling at this hour? Don't let it be Sorn— Cautiously, he opened his door. "Yes?"

It was Fedron's Chenna.

Her appearance had drastically changed. Her startling light hair, kinked by the style she'd worn, now floated down past her shoulders. She still possessed the lean athleticism of an experienced bodyguard, but she'd changed into a nightgown of silver-blue silk, revealing subtle curves he hadn't previously noticed.

"Sorry to disturb you so late," she said.

Aloran took a breath to gather himself. "Not at all. I didn't realize you were staying tonight. May I be of service?"

Chenna glanced to one side, maybe checking the hall for Sorn. "I have information to discuss."

"Then, please, come in."

Unfortunately, he had no chair for guests. He sat down on his bed, and Chenna sat beside him, closer than he expected. Her eyes moved over his face with singular intensity. It was said a Gentleman's servant could never really stop working. He tried to keep his expression blank.

"I'm sorry Garr's Sorn is giving you so much trouble," Chenna said.

Aloran couldn't help his surprise. "*Garr's* Sorn?"

The graceful spiral lifted over Chenna's left eyebrow. "I often refer to him formally," she said. "He is my adversary. He comes to my bed only because Grobal Garr sends him to spy on me."

Aloran exhaled slowly, amazed that she would choose to take him into her confidence.

Chenna looked at her hands, now bare of all their rings. "We were pledged to partnership eight years ago," she said. "At first, I tried to stop him observing me for Grobal Fedron's secrets. Then I realized my time would be better spent trying to steal Grobal Garr's. The best thing I learned during his five years in Selimna was how not to let him swerve me from my goals. So I don't think I should let him intimidate you, either." In an oddly soft gesture to follow such shocking frankness, she raised one graceful finger and touched her neck, just behind her ear.

Aloran shook his head. What *was* this? Was she trying to help him, or obligate him to her for a gift of information? His eyes couldn't help but follow her pointing finger, and he remembered the short-cut strands of her hair, now hidden like an intimate secret at the nape of her neck. He breathed down his physical response to that thought, and turned aside, so his hair fell in a curtain between them. "Chenna, I'm terribly sorry."

"*Imbati, love where you serve* is a cruel commandment," she said. "But you already know that, I think."

His body went hot, then cold. He shouldn't let her test his calm like this. It wasn't entirely her fault: the Academy was strange to him now, and Kiit appeared to be over. Worse, the more he devoted himself to his Lady, the more painful her dismissals would be—not to mention the inevitable failure he'd face trying to protect her from her own family. "Chenna, I'm sorry, but I can't—"

"I'm here because I can help you protect Lady Tamelera," Chenna said.

Aloran winced. Reading faces seemed a lot like reading minds. Tempting him with such a hope was either kind, or terribly cruel. He looked directly into her sloping eyes. "The information you hinted of?"

She nodded. "Sorn has stolen something that belongs to your Lady."

Aloran's heart pounded. That wasn't a gift—it was a snare. Duty would demand he identify the stolen object and return it, no matter what the risk. But if Chenna thought a Lady's servant couldn't detect ulterior motives, she was mistaken. "You want something from me in return for the information," he said. "Otherwise you would tell me, not taunt me."

"True." A smile curved her lips. "I think you know what I want. I've seen you looking at me."

His eyes dropped to her curves before he could stop them, robbing him of any denial. Every detail of her posture spoke of the strength and grace of her greater experience. He breathed to relax his body, but maybe because of his fatigue, it wasn't as easy as it had been when he'd practiced detachment at the Academy. "This isn't right," he said. At least she hadn't touched him.

"I won't trespass without your permission. One kiss, and I'll tell you what Sorn stole."

"He must know you're here."

"He does, and he doesn't care. Partnership is only obligation; love is the jewel locked in the heart. Besides, he feels certain he already knows what I'm offering you."

What *was* she offering? Aloran measured his breathing. If Sorn didn't know she was here about information, then what he *thought* she was offering had to be sex. Was it? He managed not to look down again, but remembered his earlier glimpse well enough that it didn't matter.

One kiss . . .

Her lips were already quite close, at a good distance for sharing secrets. He simply leaned forward to bring them together. The kiss lingered longer than he meant it to. There was a faint scent of berries on her breath.

Chenna smiled. "It's the key to Lady Tamelera's diary," she said. "He copied it the night of your Marking."

"But how am I supposed to get it away from him?" The words escaped all on their own. This might be his chance to prove to Lady Tamelera that he belonged to her, to get her finally to accept him. But now the snare had entirely closed. Chenna would certainly demand more for an answer to *that*.

Sure enough, she held out her hand, palm-upward: the request for permission to touch.

His skin prickled, but he refused to place his hand on hers. "What will I win, Chenna? I could find a way to take the key on my own."

"I admire your courage," she said. "But the key is in Sorn's room, in the top drawer of his desk. And I can keep him out of the room long enough for you to be certain you'll get in and out safely."

She knew about Sorn. He was suddenly certain of it. Maybe she'd even been asked for an oath by someone at the Academy—but whether she had or not, she knew Sorn was dangerous, and she knew the value of her offer.

He didn't have to take it. He could go straight to Lady Tamelera in the morning and tell her that Sorn had the key; if she asked Sorn for it, he would have to give it to her—

But if he did that, Lady Tamelera would be hurt, and as the one who had delivered Garr's 'surprise,' he would be responsible. He wouldn't be sucked into hurting his Lady again.

Chenna was offering a real way out. And what she asked in return was . . . not undesirable. It wasn't as though Kiit would care now.

"One thing, Chenna," Aloran said. "Your silence on all that happens between us."

Chenna raised three fingers. He watched them press the skin over her heart and rise to touch her lips. Then she extended her hand again.

All right.

With a deep breath, Aloran placed his hand on hers. Her breath caught in her throat. He reached for her neck, finding the short hair at her nape. She answered by grasping his chest with both hands.

After that, it was easy not to think, just to undress and let it happen fast and silently. Chenna's body was all muscle, her movements confident and effective—she seemed to find him as easy to arouse as he found her. She reached climax with a fierce grip and a shuddering sigh, and he came close behind.

Not until he rolled away from her and she began to dress did he wonder: was this what it meant, to give his love to a mistress' service?

"I'll need four minutes to get Sorn out of the room," Chenna said. "Don't move until then. I can give you three more minutes before he comes back; try to be out in two." She slipped out the Maze door.

Aloran dressed, carefully counting the seconds. A long-practiced skill—it helped him regain some composure. No point worrying about Sorn, and how Chenna might get him out of the room after midnight. He should think only of what he had to do. Using the Maze door would be a bad idea: he might be seen in the hall, and Sorn's Maze door would likely be locked.

When he had counted three minutes, Aloran opened the crescent-moon door. He stepped out into noble territory.

The utter blackness of the Master and Lady's chamber was layered with the sounds of their sleeping breath. The Lady breathed a deep gentle rhythm, while the Master struggled and snuffled.

This would have been easier if he'd thought to pace the measure of their bed. When he reached the corner post, the Master stopped breathing. So did he. His heart hadn't yet calmed enough—it sounded far too loud—

Grobal Garr exploded into a gasp, and the Lady's breathing lost its peaceful pattern. Would he wake? Apnea would explain some of his fatigue and irritability. Luckily, he began to snuffle again.

As soon as the Lady's breath resumed its rhythm, Aloran moved quickly to the curtain on the Master's side. He reached behind it, turned the door handle silently, and hesitated. What if he walked in and found Sorn? But his four minutes had already passed, and his remaining two would run out quickly.

He slipped in.

The room was unoccupied, lit only by a small lamp on Sorn's steel desk, which stood against the right-hand wall. Sorn kept a large collection of neatly arranged mementos: a small glass pyramid, two hair combs, several gold-and-silver game pieces, and at least twenty buttons of various shapes and sizes. On the stone walls were taped sketches, portraits, and tiny scraps of fabric. Aloran pulled down his sleeve, so he wouldn't have to touch the desk directly, and opened the main drawer. Lots of papers, a stack of business cards—no key. He pulled the drawer farther out to check the inside corners.

Was that it? No, the glint of metal had come from a strange object about the length of his palm—a bolt of sorts, mostly smooth steel but with a tip like a screwdriver. He left it alone. Glanced around. Not enough time to check the narrow file cabinet in the corner. He frowned back at the desk, then realized Chenna might not have meant the *main* drawer.

He closed the main drawer and opened the uppermost of the side drawers. There it was: a small key in the near corner. Just in time—

He stopped himself with his fingers nearly touching it. Fool, fool! If he took the key, Sorn would *know* his privacy had been breached. Was this a trap?

Every instinct screamed at him to run. He closed the drawer fast and hurried back toward the door into the Master's chamber. Sorn might return any second. The handle didn't turn silently enough, and the smooth-swinging door was too slow . . .

When at last he got the door shut, Aloran stood for a second in the blackness. The sound of the Mistress' sleeping breaths was oddly reassuring. He crept back the way he'd come, then systematically stripped the disarranged covers off his bed.

Never again. Chenna was too close to Sorn. Whether she *meant* to harm him or not didn't matter; it was just too dangerous.

The image of the tiny key stuck like a needle in his mind. Sorn had trespassed. He must not be allowed to keep the key—but there seemed no way to take it back. If he told his Lady about the key, he would be acting as Garr's messenger; if he took it back himself, Lady Tamelera would guess *he* had trespassed, the moment she saw the key in his hand. Either way, she would hate him for it.

Heile's mercy. What could he possibly do?

CHAPTER FIFTEEN

Unexpectedly Concerning Lowers

Tagaret woke with a gasp. There had been some dream—Della beckoning, a stalker in the shadows, pain, then darkness— He'd told Father he wanted the First Family's candidacy. He hadn't told him what he'd planned to do with it. But the 'shortcut' now seemed twenty times as dangerous as it had last night. Father had said everything would be different now. Gowan and Fernar would be rivals; the Great Families would try to beat him, or failing that, to kill him. No one could be trusted.

Would Fernar's Family really try to kill him? Would Reyn's?

Maybe he shouldn't have agreed. Maybe he should have walked out, refused Della's dangers so there would be someone left to trust . . . but he *had* to change things, to help Mother, at least . . .

"Young Master Tagaret?" came a voice. "I believe you're awake?"

Tagaret sat up. "Serjer? What is it?"

The First Houseman stepped from behind his curtain. "A visitor, young Master. The Master and Mistress are still sleeping, but Reyn of the Ninth Family asks for you. Forgive me—I had to admit him, for safety, and I thought you might wish to see him."

That woke him up. "Yes—thank you, Serjer."

Serjer entered, took shirt, underwear, and trousers from his wardrobe and laid them on the bed. "Then I'll bring him to you in a moment, sir."

Tagaret jumped into his clothes, fumbling with the buttons. He was tucking in his shirttails when the knock came; he rushed to unlock his door.

Reyn stood there, wearing a relieved smile. He looked fantastic—blond curls perfectly arranged, dressed in his ruby suit with the lace collar as if he were going to a party. "Sorry if I woke you," he said. "I thought Serjer might send me away."

"Of course not. Get in here before someone sees you." Tagaret grabbed his shoulders and pulled him in. "How in Varin's name did you get permission to come over?"

Reyn raised his eyebrows. He fingered one lapel. "Got Imbati Shara to bring me. Can't you tell?"

Tagaret laughed. "Yeah, she made you all—" *Fancy*, he was going to say, but the wry curve of Reyn's lips caught his eyes, and he lost the word. He bent and kissed him, letting the feeling pull his body to Reyn's, up against the door.

Reyn made a small ecstatic sound and grabbed him by the back of the head.

Just shut the lock—

He managed it, then staggered backward toward his bed, pulling Reyn with him. Reyn's hands were already tearing at his buttons, and Tagaret pushed under the ruby silk, found Reyn's back, then his chest. Chest to chest they fell together and fought out of the rest of their clothes. He knew what was coming, and Reyn pressed against him, waking a crazy thirst that shook him from head to foot.

He heard a knock.

Tagaret froze, panting, arms locked around Reyn as if he might be stolen away.

The knock came again, almost apologetically from the curtained door.

Tagaret gulped air and tried to speak in a controlled voice. "Not now, Serjer."

The reply was muffled—but it didn't sound like Serjer. "Apologies . . . an urgent message . . ." A folded paper nudged under the door.

Reyn's warm body was far more inviting than a walk over to the door of the servants' Maze. Tagaret pushed Reyn's hair back and kissed him, but finally sighed. "I'd better check it."

Reyn put a kiss on his chest. "All right."

The air felt cold. He kept his feet on the carpet while plucking the paper from the stone threshold. He brought it back to the bed.

"Sirin and Eyn," Tagaret swore.

Reyn pushed up on his elbows. "What?"

Tagaret couldn't answer; guilt had stolen his voice. He sat beside Reyn, staring at the paper:

> *Enwin and Pazeu of the Sixth Family will be at home at two afternoon on Soremor 18th, Herin 1.*

"Sixth Family!" Reyn breathed. "They're expecting you? *Today?*"

Tagaret suddenly felt very naked. "I don't know why they want to see me."

"I know why."

He did, too: *Della*. And now that Father was pushing him as a candidate, he'd certainly allow him to go. Tagaret glanced at Reyn, at his slim body and his sober face. "Reyn, I don't know what to do. You tell me. What should I do?"

Reyn looked away, but shrugged. "I shouldn't lie to myself. Everyone partners; we've always known that. It's for the good of the Race."

Was it for the good of the Race that he'd walked with Lady Selemei last night? No, it was for Della. *Della, Della*—but where did that leave Reyn?

Tagaret took a deep breath. "Sure, everyone partners. I just didn't expect a chance at it *now*. I might not get it anyway, you know."

Reyn was wringing the message between his hands. He looked down in surprise. "Tagaret, there's another message."

"Another?" But it was true: now Reyn held two wrinkled papers in his hands. They must have been back to back, somehow. Tagaret took the second. It was on lighter notepaper, in precise handwriting:

> *Young Master Tagaret—*
>
> *Garr's Sorn has taken possession of a key belonging to Lady Tamelera. He keeps it in his room. I regret that, due to my position in the Household, I am unable to restore it to her myself.*

The message was unsigned. It sent shivers down his back.

"Sorn has stolen a key from my mother," he said.

Reyn scowled. "Your father should fire him immediately."

"Father probably ordered him to steal it." Outrage surged up in him, and he seized Reyn's hand. "Reyn, I would never have gotten through Mother moving to Selimna if not for you. I couldn't *live*—I mean, I would never do anything to—" He couldn't finish.

Reyn lifted his hand and kissed his fingers. Then he turned away and started putting on his clothes. "Come on. I bet we can get it back if we take him two on one."

Even when they were both fully dressed, Tagaret couldn't help thinking they'd have been better off in armor. He had to hope that Father wasn't yet awake, so they could get Sorn alone. He pressed his service call button.

A moment later, Serjer stepped in the curtained door. "Yes, young Master?"

"Thank you for your message," Tagaret said. "We'll need to talk to Sorn if you want us to get it back."

Confusion shaded Serjer's eyes. "I believe what you received was the Sixth Family's message, sir," he said. "Sorn is currently in his own room, attending upon your father's awakening."

Wait. Had Serjer *not* been the one to send that message? "Serjer, who sent the second message?"

Serjer looked at him intently. "I couldn't say, young Master."

Tagaret glanced at Reyn. He'd noticed it, too: Serjer was oath-bound. Tagaret hated to press him, but there were few things in the Household that the First Houseman didn't know, and this was important. Maybe if he used a different approach . . . "Serjer, who delivered a paper to my room a moment ago?"

Serjer answered promptly. "Aloran, young Master."

Aloran—now, *that* made more sense. But Aloran was of equal rank with Sorn. Why wouldn't his position in the Household allow him to take the key back? It didn't matter, really; the request was clear.

"Well, apparently, Sorn has stolen a key from my mother," Tagaret explained. "He's been keeping it in his room. Can you help us?"

Serjer's eyes widened, and his jaw clenched. "Absolutely, young Master," he said. "I think you would be best served if I were to take you directly to him."

"*Directly?*" Reyn exclaimed.

"Are you sure?" asked Tagaret. "You'll allow us in the Maze?"

"Meet me at the kitchen entrance," Serjer said, and disappeared behind his curtain.

Tagaret looked at Reyn; Reyn shook his head.

"Well," Tagaret said, "all right, then." His mouth felt dry, but he led Reyn out, locking the door behind them.

"We'll get in trouble," Reyn murmured.

"If Father finds out." He would, though, wouldn't he? Sorn would tell him. Tagaret frowned. "This is for my mother. I won't be mad if you don't come with me."

"I won't leave you."

When they arrived in the dining room, Serjer beckoned from the kitchen doors. Tagaret entered on tiptoes. The kitchen wasn't unfamiliar, but he'd never been permitted in this far. The hall beyond was so narrow that Reyn had to walk behind him with hands on his shoulders.

"Here," Serjer said, indicating a door on their left.

Tagaret took a breath and blew it out. No hesitation—he must show only confidence. Keeping Reyn on his left, he faced the door and knocked so hard his knuckles stung.

Sorn opened the door irritably, but at the sight of them, dropped a gray curtain of calm over his face.

"Sorn, you've taken my mother's key," Tagaret said, holding out his hand. "Give it to me at once."

Sorn said nothing.

"Give it to me, or I'll come in there and take it!"

And something astonishing happened. The gray curtain shifted; Sorn paled and took a step backward. He might even have tried to close the door on them, but something—Serjer's foot?—blocked it open. Then, abruptly, he calmed and said, "Yes, sir." He fetched something from inside his desk.

Tagaret looked down at the small steel key Sorn placed in his palm. One more violation of his mother—rage gave him strength, and he shut his fist over it. "Don't you dare do that again. Reyn, let's go."

They passed out again through the kitchen. Serjer didn't come with them.

"Your First Houseman really loves you," Reyn said. "I would never be permitted in our Maze for any reason."

"I'm lucky," Tagaret agreed. He'd have to make sure Serjer met no punishment when word of this got back to Father.

Strange—maybe Sorn had been too embarrassed to tell Father what had happened. Father had made no mention of Serjer or the key, only sent him off to Della's house with a lecture on political spelunking that Tagaret now felt perfectly free to ignore. He walked out the north grounds gate, dressed in a shining suit of peridot-green, with Aloran behind his left shoulder.

Going to see Della at her home with official permission—what could possibly be better?

The city today was a whirl of excitement. The northbound radius hummed with skimmers, and the broad flagged sidewalks of the mercantile circumference thronged with people of many colors, bustling in and out of shops, or underneath the stone archways that marked the entrance to specialized Melumalai or Kartunnen shopping courtyards. A mixed-caste group stood listening to a musician play shiazin. Tagaret breathed deeper, drinking it in.

"Young Master," said Aloran.

Aloran speaking to him spontaneously? Maybe he would ask about the key . . . "Yes?"

"Please don't change your speed, but we're being followed."

Followed? Tagaret almost jerked to a stop, but Aloran's firm hands against his back kept him moving. He whispered hoarsely, "How do you know?"

"Don't look, sir. An Akrabitti has maintained a fixed distance behind us since we reached the circumference."

A trasher? How could that be? "But we've scarcely walked a block since then."

"Young Master, real Akrabitti keep to their own back alleyways. They rarely use circumferences, and then, only fearfully. This one moves like an Arissen, and I expect he is armed like one."

Tagaret gulped. Maybe they should have arranged a skimmer, but it hadn't occurred to him to use one for a trip so short. "Should we hurry? It's not far—we could cross the street—"

"Pardon me, sir, but that would give him a clear shot at you. I'll thank you instead to turn into the next courtyard and enter the first open shop. Can you do this?"

Tagaret nodded.

The distance to the next courtyard, measured in panicked heart-beats, felt far too long. He walked to the marble column at the corner and turned left—this was a Kartunnen courtyard with an unbroken curve of glass-fronted shops, and a fountain of a man bathing in a riv-ulet that fell from the roof above. For a scary second, he couldn't dis-tinguish doors in all the glass, but then a chrome handle presented itself, and he hurried inside. The shop sold clothing: pairs of manne-quins, noble and Imbati, stood on either side of him. The proprietor came forward with her gray coat billowing.

"Welcome, sir. How may I please your tastes?"

Tagaret took a breath, but Aloran spoke in his ear. "Stand with the mannequins between you and the windows. Speak to her about any-thing you like until I come for you." He didn't go out again, vanishing instead into the back of the shop.

Tagaret cleared his throat, and identified an amber-colored suit in a sheltered spot. "Thank you, Kartunnen. Please, tell me about this suit over here—" But he couldn't keep his mind on the Kartunnen's voice; the possible arrival of an assassin dragged his attention to the people passing the front windows. A Melumalai man, two Kartunnen women, an Imbati woman . . .

There. A hulking figure in dark gray, his head hidden in a charcoal-colored hood, walked along the storefront and gave a single, seemingly casual glance inside. Tagaret's stomach rolled; he tried to keep the mannequins and the Kartunnen proprietor between himself and the windows, without looking like he was hiding.

The man had taken only two steps beyond the shop door when suddenly he lost his footing and fell backward onto the sidewalk, hood slipping to reveal clean-cropped dark hair. He was up again fast, fling-ing up one arm defensively. Something too small to see hit the shop's front window with a sharp crack. With his other arm, the man pulled an Arissen energy weapon.

"Mercy!" Tagaret cried. The shopkeeper screamed.

The man fired a bolt toward the entrance of the courtyard, but dropped his weapon with a grimace as another small object cracked into the shop window. He pulled a knife, but in a blur of black Aloran was on him, kicking the knife from his hand and sending the Arissen weapon after it, far across the courtyard. Aloran landed at least two blows to the side of the man's head. The crossmarked Arissen rolled away from the attack and came up again with another knife, but Aloran whirled away from it, lashing out with one foot and striking the man in the face. The Arissen stumbled to his feet, still with the knife in his hand but with blood streaming from his nose; Aloran kept back out of arm's reach, one of his hands raised in a blocking posture, the other cocked as if to throw something.

The Arissen turned and fled. Aloran pursued him.

Tagaret stared after, hardly able to breathe.

He couldn't have said how much later, Aloran reappeared and started gathering up and pocketing small objects from the ground outside. At last he walked in, with his hair disarranged and his face sweaty. He looked up with concern.

"Young Master?"

Tagaret tried to say he was all right, but nothing came out. Then he looked down—and discovered a fluttering hole in Aloran's shirt, right in the center of his chest, its edges still smoldering. He hiccuped, and his knees wobbled; Aloran's hand took a firm hold of his elbow.

"Kartunnen," Aloran said, "I'm sorry for the inconvenience. I'm pleased that I didn't break your windows."

The Kartunnen answered tremulously, "May your honorable service earn its just reward, sir."

Aloran handed her a card. "When the police come, please direct them to the weapons; I believe there is a knife in the fountain, and a bolt weapon on the far side. I hope they will contact me, but I'm afraid we must go, or we shall be late for an appointment."

Tagaret understood vaguely when they left the courtyard and crossed the circumference into the neighborhood beyond. He managed to stumble along some distance farther, but soon found Aloran backing him up against a wall.

"Young Master," Aloran said softly. "The danger is over. My armor vest served its purpose, and I am uninjured. I believe you would wish me to continue escorting you to our visit with the Sixth Family."

Tagaret nodded, but his voice still wouldn't come.

"Master Tagaret, watch me for a moment. Breathe with me."

He nodded again. Hard at first to keep his eyes away from the hole in Aloran's shirt—the hole the Arissen would have preferred to put in his own back. But more and more he watched the Imbati breathe in, breathe out, and tried to follow. Whether he got it quite right or not, after a minute or so the vagueness at the edges of his vision began to retreat, and he realized they were standing against the outer wall of a Grobal home, just to one side of an iron entry gate.

"Aloran," he said. "Is this their house?"

"Yes, young Master. Shall we go in?"

Tagaret took one last deep breath and rubbed his face. "Yes, absolutely."

They were welcomed in a white-plastered entry hall by several members of the host's Household, who wore uniforms in an unusual combination of black and pale green. Some kind of silent communication passed between the Imbati, but Tagaret didn't feel right leaving it alone after what had happened.

"Not to bother you, Imbati," he said, "but my man encountered some trouble and is in need of a shirt. I would be happy to recompense you if you could provide him with one." He hadn't been in any shape to purchase one in the Kartunnen shop.

One of the women bowed to him. "Immediately, sir." To Aloran she said, "If you would come with me."

Aloran looked him in the eye for a split second before following her down a corridor on one side—Tagaret felt it as gratitude. Even safe inside these walls, he got a chill watching his bodyguard walk away.

"Tagaret of the First Family, I'm so pleased you could come."

Tagaret turned. A door had opened leading farther into the house, and a man stood in it, wearing a smile but wringing his hands nervously. He had cheerful wrinkles around his eyes, and curly nut-brown hair going to gray; a female manservant stood behind his shoulder. He must be Della's father, Enwin of the Sixth Family. Intriguing yojosmei melodies floated in from the space behind him.

Tagaret bowed. "No more pleased than I am to be here, Enwin, sir," he said. *Alive . . .* He cleared his throat before his relief could turn into an inappropriate laugh. "Is there to be music?" Della had said something about music, hadn't she, when they'd spoken before about meeting Kartunnen?

Enwin chuckled—friendly, but still nervous. "Yes, Della told me you loved music. She and her sister worked hard to convince me you would enjoy visiting us today. Come this way."

"Of course." That was strange. How had he not known that Della had a sister?

Enwin led him through a sitting room and along a corridor whose windows gave out onto a courtyard garden, with real climbing vines on the walls, silver-lit by a shinca trunk that pierced upward. Ahead, the melodies beckoned. Finally, Enwin opened a door, and music burst over them.

Such music! He'd thought it must be a group, but it was two people: they sat with their backs to him at a yojosmei made of exquisitely carved wood. All four of their hands and feet moved with joyful abandon. For an instant, Tagaret startled—was that Della, *playing?* But though the girl had the same gorgeous copper hair, this person was far too small, maybe only nine or ten. A gray-coated Kartunnen sat beside her, shoulder to shoulder, so they swayed together to the music. And to one side, clapping along, stood a Lady with an elderly manservant, Della and her Yoral—and *Kartunnen Ryanin?*

Tagaret managed not to gape. But Kartunnen Ryanin *himself*, visiting a private home?

"Tagaret of the First Family," said Della's mother, still clapping. "Come in. I hope you'll forgive us for starting early, but Liadis keeps her own time. May I offer you something to eat or drink?"

"Ah—mm, no, thank you, Lady," said Tagaret.

Della cast him a longing glance that struck his heart and set it racing. Today her dress was a deep blue-green color that made him think of his own ocean coat.

"Sir," said Imbati Yoral. "Would it please you to meet our guests?"

"Yes, Yoral, thank you." This whole room was wondrous and impossible. Live plants grew everywhere; three or more wysps floated overhead amidst mobiles of gold and crystal that hung from a sculpted plaster ceiling; and a young Grobal Lady appeared to have received the blessing of Heile just like a Kartunnen. Also, he could walk right up to

Della and not strain too hard to keep his eyes away from her because it was so easy to stare at the unpainted face of Kartunnen Ryanin.

"You may shake Ryanin's hand if you wish," said Lady Pazeu.

Tagaret offered Ryanin his hand, incredulously. Music buoyed him higher and higher. "Well, certainly. Such a pleasure to meet you in person, Ryanin. I love your work."

The famous composer had a lined face and dark mysterious eyes that spoke of inner inspiration—but he had a very warm smile. "I'm honored, sir."

He was honored, too. Ryanin's fingers brought masterpieces like *The Catacomb* to life—who would have imagined he'd ever actually feel their grip on his own hand?

"This is just amazing," Tagaret said. "I confess, it's not at all what I expected."

"You're kind," said Enwin behind him. "Most would call it eccentric. Or disgusting."

Tagaret shook his head. "I don't think so. How in Heile's name did you decide to train your daughter in music?"

"We didn't decide," said Lady Pazeu. "*She* did. Liadis breathes music like air. She would die without it. Della, why don't you take Tagaret to the yojosmei and introduce him."

"All right, Mother."

He turned toward Della instinctively—her voice was like water after a long thirst. Della came to him, smiling; he walked eagerly beside her, her shoulder only inches from his arm. They went to the yojosmei where the two were still playing.

The Kartunnen at the yojosmei looked up, and his eyes widened in alarm. He had long, reddish-blond hair, and a burn scar on his left cheekbone. It was the boy—the same one he'd spoken to outside *The Catacomb.*

"You?" Tagaret said.

The Kartunnen boy sat open-mouthed in shock.

"Vant," said the girl beside him. "Play, play—why did you stop?"

Della flitted around and embraced her sister, her hands on her shoulders and her cheek beside her hair. "Liadis, look. Someone's here to meet you. This is my friend Tagaret. Tagaret, my sister Liadis. She's just turned fourteen."

Fourteen? She was so small . . . Tagaret turned away from the Kartunnen boy and searched for an escort to greet, but couldn't find one. There were two Imbati caretakers standing by the far wall, but—

"Tagaret, Tagaret, I'll remember that," Liadis exclaimed. "Nice to meet you, Tagaret, do you sing?"

He had nowhere to look but directly at her—and instantly understood why he'd never heard of her existence. Something wasn't right. Maybe it was her eyes, or her turned-up nose, or the long lips, smiling broadly over unusually small teeth. A defective, Father would call her, too weak in her blood for civilized society. Then it hit him like a blow to the stomach: Father would say that a mental defect had Lowered her, or she would have no interest in music.

He would never be like Father.

He smiled at Liadis. "Nice to meet you, too, Liadis. I'm sure I don't sing as well as you'd like. But I think you play the yojosmei beautifully."

"This is *my* yojosmei," Liadis said, grinning infectiously. "Daddy bought it for me. And sometimes Ryanin and Vant come to play with me, and the wysps like it when we play, and come to visit. Vant has a Grobal name, did you hear that? And Ryanin has very big hands. And Della dances, don't you, Della. Tell him what we did yesterday."

Della kissed her sister's hair, then turned her green eyes straight to his, as though she had permission. "We played and danced for an hour, Tagaret. You should have seen it."

"I can imagine it," he said fervently. "As if I'd been here." One sister with fingers and feet dancing upon the yojosmei, the other twirling under the leaves, the gold and crystal, with the wysps lending their surreal light.

Della blushed. She was so beautiful he almost reached out to her. But though the rules surrounding Liadis were obviously different, they couldn't be *that* different.

"Vant, you haven't said anything," said Liadis. "Tagaret, Vant is Ryanin's apprentice. Vant, say hello."

"Hello, sir," said the Kartunnen boy, in his strikingly cultured voice. "Liadis, I'd prefer to play."

"Oh, yes, let's play," she agreed. "Let's play our *Catacomb* duet."

Without another word, they began to play—something that was

obviously an arrangement of the orchestral *Catacomb* for yojosmei, so dark and complex he scarcely believed it could be played by young people. Liadis rocked forward and back. Vant was more still, but his head was bowed, his eyes closed, his hands and feet moving with force and drama as if the music grew straight out of his soul.

One of the wysps near the ceiling drifted down and moved in a lazy spiral over them. In the spell of its light, only the four of them were here: Della, unescorted, gazing straight into his eyes in a way that made him quiver, and her Heile-touched sister shoulder to shoulder with a Kartunnen who for some reason had a Grobal nose to match his Grobal name.

When the song ended, he wanted to clap but stopped himself because no one else was clapping. Aloran had returned; he appeared refreshed, now wearing the black and green of the Sixth Family Household. With hardly a pause, Liadis launched into another complex piece. Kartunnen Vant stood up, and one of the Household offered him a drink, while Kartunnen Ryanin sat and began to play.

"Young Tagaret," Enwin said quietly. "On these days, the concert never ends. Vant and Ryanin take turns so Liadis doesn't wear them out. She will sleep all day tomorrow. Perhaps you would enjoy a tour of the house?"

"Forgive me," said Tagaret. "I don't want to leave the music."

"What if *I* take him?" asked Della.

He stared at her. Could he be so lucky?

"Oh, do let her, darling," Lady Pazeu said to Enwin, taking his arm. "This kind of opportunity comes so seldom."

Della's father pinched his lip, but then he nodded.

Yoral took Della on his arm and walked out into the corridor. Heart racing, Tagaret beckoned to Aloran and followed. They entered the silvery garden courtyard, which smelled intriguingly of dirt and flowers. Della didn't seem inclined to carry the tour any further; she sat down in a brass chair at a small table. Tagaret joined her. The shinca cast its aura of warmth against his back. His knee was so close to hers . . .

"Liadis," Della said. "She's why."

Tagaret glanced up at Yoral, who stood behind her. The stern Imbati nodded permission, so he looked back at Della with relief. "She's *why?*"

"Why my father studies Lowers," Della said. Her fingers played nervously with the edge of the brass table. "You can see that, can't you? It's not muckwalking, really. It's about—"

"It's about the music," Tagaret agreed. "Your sister is blessed of Heile, that's clear."

Della looked at him seriously. "Not just the music, though. I mean, it's not wrong for me to care for my Yoral's happiness, is it? Nor you for your man's. The Grobal Trust is for all of them."

For Aloran. Tagaret looked over his shoulder. Aloran's eyes were lowered. Even having just saved his life, the young Imbati was too respectful, too shy to be breached. That didn't mean he didn't deserve to have someone care for his happiness.

"I wonder," Tagaret said. "I know it's a strange request, but might I speak with your Yoral for a moment? About a personal matter?"

Della blinked in surprise. "Really? Yoral, would you permit it?"

Yoral didn't look much startled; but then, he was Imbati. "If I may ask that Aloran briefly watch my Mistress, then I am willing," he said.

"I will," said Aloran.

The other side of the shinca seemed a good enough place so as not to take the older servant too far from his Lady. Tagaret took a deep breath. Yoral looked up at him with obvious curiosity.

"It's not about Della," Tagaret said. "It's about—" He lowered his voice. "Aloran." Then he explained, carefully, about his mother and Aloran, about the key, and the anonymous note. When he was finished, Yoral considered for several seconds.

Finally, he murmured, "Sir, how long has young Aloran worked for your mother?"

"Three days or so."

Yoral nodded. "That explains some of it. Household rank often counts for less than experience, and in particular, a student Marked out of the Academy can be subject to political manipulation by those more established in the Maze, if you understand me."

"Yes," he said. "I think I do." Of course, Sorn would be just like Father.

"Thus, it would be impossible for him to take anything directly from the senior servant against his will. Ideally, the return of the key should be accomplished by a member of the family who could bear witness to the senior servant's possession of it and leave him free of blame. Your mother's Aloran obviously has his wits about him, young as he is."

"But why wouldn't he just tell my mother?"

Yoral inclined his head to one side. "I can only guess he fears somehow to approach her directly. Perhaps the key touches on a highly private matter where, given his awkward relationship with her, he is uncertain of his rights."

A shudder ran down Tagaret's backbone. "A highly private matter where my father was *spying*."

Yoral bowed. "My heart is as deep as the heavens. No word uttered in confidence will escape it." Then he raised his voice. "Might I request that you return to my Mistress, and send Aloran to me for a moment?"

Tagaret stared at him. Return—and *send*—a question rose in his mind that was almost a scream, but he didn't dare utter it for fear Yoral might change his mind. "Right away," he said. At the brass table, Della had obviously heard the request; her mouth was open, her breast rising and falling visibly.

"Aloran, if you would," Tagaret said hoarsely. Aloran nodded and left them.

Alone.

Was it he who first reached for her hand, or she for his? Oh, gods, it didn't even matter—her fingers were so soft, so warm, and absolutely perfect! Her knee leaned against his, and her eyes lifted, and he fell into their green paradise.

"Della," he whispered.

"Tagaret . . ."

"If I survive this—if I could actually be Heir—nothing anyone could say would matter."

She kissed him.

He clung to her hands as ecstasy flooded his body and washed the entire world out from under his feet. It could not have been long enough, even if it had lasted his entire life—when her sweet lips finally left his, and her hands pulled away, he found tears in his eyes. Yoral and Aloran stood by with understanding, and pity, on their faces.

He wouldn't dare tell anyone about this—not Reyn, not even his mother.

He had to survive Selection. For Della.

CHAPTER SIXTEEN

Ambush

Aloran waited outside the bathroom door, listening to the swirls and gurgles of his Lady in her morning bath. The risk of sending the note had been worth it: his trespass appeared to have escaped Sorn's notice, and Lady Tamelera had changed in the last two days, ever since young Master Tagaret had taken back her key. The difference was subtle—she still didn't permit him *in* the bathroom— but he'd passed all of yesterday with no random dismissals at all.

Della's Yoral had told him he had a new champion, to whom he would owe his gratitude for any change that came.

He would risk his life happily if it meant saving young Master Tagaret again.

Beneath the bathroom door came the rush that meant his Mistress was emerging from the water. He imagined her drying herself unaided, and dressing in the underwear and slip he had laid out for her. The hair dryer hummed. And she should open the door right about—

Lady Tamelera opened the door. "Aloran?"

He stood as straight as he could. "Yes, Lady."

"Please help me into my gown this morning and brush my hair. I'd like to look my best for the Announcement of Candidates and Round of Twelve event."

Blessing of Mai. He bowed deeply. "Yes, Lady."

She approved the dawn gown when he brought it to her. It was an unusual piece: bright yellow orange at the lower hem which he guided down over her head; pale gray blue at the neckline which he carefully slid up over her shoulders. He fastened a button at the small of her back which was almost green—each button faded subtly until they became pale blue between her shoulder blades.

Lady Tamelera took a seat in one of the lounge chairs and shook her hair down over the back. Its red-gold mass fell heavy and damp over his fingers. Applying the brush to it felt so perfectly appropriate—he poured himself into every stroke, making this simple duty a symbol of his gratitude. *See how I serve you, Lady. See me . . .*

"Aloran," she said.

"Yes, Lady."

"You know, how you saved Tagaret from an assassin?"

He kept the brush moving. "I did not capture the man, Lady. I would have been more pleased to save the young Master from the one who sent him."

"Nonetheless, you did well," she said. "And in another way, too—getting Tagaret to return my key."

Aloran flushed all the way to his feet. Apparently, his involvement was not a secret after all. She was kind to sit him safely behind her before saying such a thing.

Lady Tamelera turned her head; her hair shifted through his hands, and he glimpsed her profile—so very Grobal, yet admirably self-possessed in spite of her years of difficulty with the Master. "You are loyal to my interests, Aloran," she said. "I was unfair; I see that now. I'd like to show you how grateful I am, and I believe we have time before the Family gathers."

Breathe. Brush. "Your word is honor enough, Lady. I do my duty gladly."

"I insist. Please take me to the clothing shop Tagaret told me about."

A smile escaped to his face. Aloran let the brush stop. "Yes, Lady."

They went by skimmer to save time. Today he had leisure to notice the shopkeeper's name, Kartunnen Jaia, written in gold script on the front window. Jaia recognized him and kept glancing at him even as she greeted his Lady.

"Welcome, Lady. How may I please your tastes?"

"I would like to purchase a suit for Aloran, who saved my son's life here two days ago."

Strange; she still didn't call him *my Aloran*. But he was thrilled enough just to be here with her, seeing the mannequins for their clothing and not their potential as shields.

Kartunnen Jaia bowed. "Yes, Lady."

"Something innovative, I think. More than just black—embroidery would be nice, if you have it."

"Of course, Lady." Jaia turned to him and smiled with her red-painted lip. "Imbati, sir, would you please come with me?"

Aloran followed her to a rack in the back corner of the shop. To judge by her sudden air of modesty, these must be personal designs—a far better quality than he'd ever choose for himself. He picked one with a black jacket that glimmered blue and retreated to try it on. Before he had put on more than the trousers, however, Jaia tapped at the metal door and her hand appeared above it, holding another suit.

"May your honorable service earn its just reward, sir. Your Lady suggests this piece."

"Thank you, Kartunnen."

Her intervention was well-timed, because the suit he'd chosen didn't fit well across his shoulders. Unfortunately, the new suit was ostentatious. Black silk with a sheen of garnet-red—the romantic color of Sirin the Luck-Bringer—embroidered on the front of the jacket with a fountain of dark fire in shades of red, garnet, and black.

He gulped and put it on. It *was* impressively made. The jacket closed with hook fittings under his left arm, and had excellent pocket design including multiple invisible placements sealed with magnetic closures. It fit perfectly.

"Aloran," Lady Tamelera called. "Come; let me see you."

Now she *asked* to see him. He had to comply. He stepped out with head lowered, breathing a careful pattern to brace himself for her judgment. She'd never approve—she'd never want him so visible . . .

"It suits you," Lady Tamelera said.

Aloran looked up. "Thank you, Lady."

Her head was angled to one side, her eyes gently considering. "The fire was a risk, but it really does match your—" She broke off and blushed. "Well, your hair. Kartunnen, I'll take this one; Aloran, you may as well just keep it on."

"Yes, Lady."

Safe in the dressing room, Aloran shook his head in disbelief. He couldn't argue with her eye for quality. He sorted through the pockets of the suit he'd worn and transferred two heavy handfuls of combat rounders into the lower pockets of the new jacket, where they stayed without altering the fit. His business cards went in an upper pocket. The medications he'd purchased fit in the inside pocket with a pair of treatment gloves, and the adrenaline delivery device slipped easily into a hidden pocket of the sleeve. Heile grant he wouldn't need them, but now, three days after the Ball, the window of doubt would be closing fast. Folding his old clothes, he caught a glimpse of himself in the mirror.

The fire pattern didn't match his hair. It matched his Mark.

His stomach quivered with a sense of invasion—or was it division? How could Lady Tamelera have perceived his Mark as separate from himself? Yet he could hardly say that was not her right. He had nothing to hold back from her, not when those lines of ink carried her name.

Returning with her to the suite, he kept himself on high alert, watching every Grobal he passed for signs of ill health.

"Tamelera, where have you been?" Grobal Garr demanded as they entered.

"Out," Lady Tamelera replied unrepentantly. She strode forward and clasped her son's gloved hand; Aloran kept close in her wake. A small group of nobles had gathered, including young Master Tagaret, young Master Nekantor, Arbiter Erex of the First Family Council, and Grobal Fedron. Aloran silently acknowledged Sorn, Kuarmei, and Chenna—and his heart went cold.

Chenna's crown of hair had been chopped off. She'd clearly rescued it from hideousness by a merciless application of scissors that left her looking like a soldier. Aloran managed not to look at Sorn again, but only he could have gotten close enough to violate her person. And if he knew to punish Chenna, then he *knew*.

"Well, Tamelera," said the Arbiter of the First Family Council, "Tagaret insisted we wait before making any announcements, but I'm sure this will come as no surprise. Tagaret will take the stage today as the First Family's candidate for Heir."

The Lady tensed. "Tagaret, love—I'm sure you'll do a wonderful job."

"Thanks, Mother," the young Master said. "It's making me pretty nervous."

She laughed. "Me, too."

"And me, in fact," said the Arbiter. "Young Tagaret, your new bodyguard will be here momentarily, so make sure you get acquainted. I'll go down ahead and see how arrangements are progressing for the event."

"See you in a few minutes, Erex," said Grobal Garr, rubbing his hands.

"Aloran, you may put away your things," said Lady Tamelera.

"Yes, Lady." With a knot in his throat, Aloran ducked quickly through the Master and Lady's chamber into his own room. He scanned it carefully, and it appeared undisturbed—but might not stay that way. Leaving his old suit on his bed, he locked his Maze door before returning to his place at his Lady's dawn-clad shoulder.

Lady Tamelera wasn't standing as close to her son as she had been, because the Selection bodyguard had arrived. He was an Eminence's Cohort man of maybe twenty-five, built like a crag of granite; his sheer physical presence created a respectful circle around them.

Guests had started arriving in droves—not a bad thing, since it would keep Sorn from acting against him openly. Young Master Nekantor, however, had retreated to the stone wall alongside Grobal Benél of the First Family. Even young Master Tagaret seemed disturbed by the general excitement.

"It's just a bit overwhelming, I guess," he sighed. With one hand, he shaded his eyes from nosy stares. "I appreciate you being here—Arissen Veriga, was it?"

"That's correct, sir. Thank you, sir."

"I expect you'll keep a close eye on him," Lady Tamelera said.

"Absolutely, Lady," Arissen Veriga replied. "It's an honor." The man knew his job well, because his eyes took in the entire crowd without missing the manservants. That personal attention, whenever it came near, felt like the hot crush of a steam press. Aloran began a breathing pattern, and even Sorn stiffened when the Arissen looked his way.

"Well, he makes me nervous," a voice complained—that was the robust young cousin who had accompanied young Master Tagaret to the Accession Ball. "I hate Arissen."

Arissen Veriga raised an eyebrow.

"Pyaras!" young Master Tagaret snapped, turning on the younger boy. "You *don't*. Fine if you hate Nek and Benél for what they did, but you know nothing about Arissen at all."

That was more petulance than expected from the young Master, but it was effective. Grobal Pyaras was shocked into silence.

"See here: Pyaras, this is my new bodyguard, Veriga. Veriga, this is my cousin Pyaras, who just happens to be too strong for his own good. It might help him if he knew what Arissen were really like."

Arissen Veriga smiled and saluted. "When my duties allow, I would be happy to speak to you casually, sir."

Grobal Pyaras flushed and looked at his feet. "Thanks, Arissen."

"*Veriga*," corrected young Master Tagaret.

"All right: Veriga," said Grobal Pyaras. Tears came into his voice. "Tagaret, you know I didn't mean it. I'm tired—I'm going home." He shoved through the crowd and disappeared out the front door, just as a commotion of new guests arrived, including Lady Selemei and Ustin.

"Selemei!" Lady Tamelera called, moving toward her with open arms.

Young Master Tagaret gave an exhausted sigh.

The sound of it stopped Aloran's feet and pulled him around to look. The young Master had his hand pressed beside his eye again, his weight resting on one back heel, and when he turned, there was something uncertain about the movement—a lack of balance. . . ?

Aloran held his breath.

No, no, it wasn't possible. He had worn gloves during the entire Ball. And yet, there had been that short time when his father took them. Had he touched anyone?

Yes, he had. Reyn of the Ninth Family, Fernar of the Eleventh Family—and his cousin Pyaras, who had just left *complaining of fatigue*.

Aloran's heart went frantic. If this was Kinders fever, he might have only seconds to act—but Lady Tamelera was moving away, and Arissen Veriga was on guard, not letting anyone get too close. Aloran tried to be invisible, moving slightly sideways to narrow the distance between himself and young Master Tagaret. Hard to evaluate the boy's breathing just by watching him. What if he was imagining things?

Young Master Tagaret wasn't looking at Lady Selemei or the crowd around the door. He shifted his feet, and his balance tilted slightly past normal.

Aloran tensed, trying to right him by force of will. *No, young Master, no . . .* Oh, let this be something else—something minor—

Young Master Tagaret cleared his throat heavily and gave a cough.

So be it. If he was wrong, he would accept punishment, but ana-phylaxis was final.

"Imbati," said Arissen Veriga. "Is something wrong?"

"The heart that is valiant triumphs over all, sir," Aloran said. He released the adrenaline device into his hand. "I wish to attend to young Master Tagaret. He may be ill."

The Arissen frowned suspiciously. "What's that you're holding?"

"Sir, the young Master—"

Master Tagaret made a wheezing sound; the Arissen turned away to look at him.

Now. Aloran spun past Arissen Veriga and lunged for the young Master's leg, driving the needle in—and then the Arissen's shoulder slammed into his stomach.

Breath gasped out of him. Aloran fell backward into a roll, but there was no point resisting. The room erupted into shouts and screams. The Arissen bunched fists in his jacket, lifted him, and shoved him into the wall. By the time he could breathe again, the entire room was in a fury, and the enraged Arissen was panting in his face, holding him high with his feet dangling.

"I knew it," said young Master Nekantor's voice from the back. "I *knew* that Imbati played games."

Grobal Garr stormed forward with Plis' own anger on his face. "You!" he shouted. "A traitor in my house!" Behind him, Sorn looked pleasantly surprised.

"Aloran," said Lady Tamelera. "How could you?"

The dismay in her eyes was worse than the Arissen's grip. "Lady, forgive me—the young Master is ill."

At the center of the crowd, with his mouth open in an incredulous gasp, young Master Tagaret bent and removed the needle of the adren-aline device from his thigh. He never straightened. He swayed too far; then his long legs gave way and he collapsed on the floor.

"Tagaret!" the Lady cried.

Aloran felt an ache in the back of his throat. Why couldn't he have been there to catch him? He didn't want to be right—but the adrena-line alone wasn't enough to account for a collapse, nor for the way the young Master struggled for air as he lay shaking, clearly unaware of the shocked gazes all around him.

Breathe, Master Tagaret. Oh, Heile's mercy, breathe . . .

Lady Tamelera broke from her position and fell beside her son, her gown deflating.

Aloran cried, "Lady, don't touch him!"

She looked up, straight into his eyes, and her face turned white. Then she gathered her gown in two fists and stood, with all the glorious stature of Mai the Right in battle.

"Selemei, take your party out, *now.* Arissen Veriga, you will release Aloran this instant!"

"Yes, Lady."

The fists loosened on his clothes and lowered him. The moment his feet touched the floor, Aloran ran to his Lady, pulling on his treatment gloves and gathering the medications from his pockets. She looked at him, and for an instant he glimpsed terror and desperation, but then her armor closed again.

Aloran touched his fingers to the young Master's neck. Grobal Tagaret's pulse was racing—probably just the adrenaline—but already he felt hot to the touch. At least he was breathing, his face red instead of blue.

"Young Master," Aloran said, "can you hear me?" It was no use. He'd never drink an oral medicine in this state—it would have to be the needle. He opened the vial in question and glanced at his Lady. She nodded, then raised her voice to the crowd.

"Everyone, we're dealing with Kinders fever here. Fedron, please send Chenna to Administrator Vull's to warn him Pyaras may be ill. Now all of you get out—and for your own safety, go straight home and wash before you go anywhere else."

Chenna flickered out, fast as a flame. The Lady had done well to send Lady Selemei's group out first; the rush that followed was punctuated with cries of panic but resulted in little more than bumping and shoving before everyone was gone.

Aloran rolled up young Master Tagaret's sleeve, barely able to contain a helpless shudder at the sight of the blue veins in his arm. *Give me another assassin instead; I swear, I'd take it!* He clung to his training and delivered the shot. Heile grant he'd given it soon enough to blunt the worst of the fever spike. Now all they could do was get him safely to bed. He slipped his arm beneath the young Master's shoulder and his knees, carefully supporting his head, and carried him toward his rooms. The Lady ran ahead and opened the door.

Grobal Garr thumped after them. "Tagaret, you can't!" he cried. "Merciful Heile, what do we do now? I have to find Erex—where is Erex? We don't have time to convene the Council!"

Lady Tamelera slammed the door in his face and fell against it, sobbing. "Council!" she moaned. "Who in Varin's name cares about the Council at a time like this?"

CHAPTER SEVENTEEN

Players

When the crowd fled in fear, Benél tried to bolt. Nekantor felt the noose of panic. He grabbed Benél's arms and held him pinned against the wall.

"Benél, don't run—whatever you do, *don't run*."

Benél quivered under his hands. "But, Nek, Kinders fever!"

"*No*," Nekantor growled. Behind him, people screaming and swirling, no control, no pattern. The tendrils of chaos were reaching for his back, and if *Benél* ran— Varin's teeth! "Don't you move," he said. "*You* haven't touched anyone. *I* haven't touched anyone. If we move, we'll get hit—stepped on—just *don't move!*"

"But, Nek . . ."

Nekantor only held tighter, pressing his forehead to Benél's until the noises stopped, and the chaos flowed away. Ripples jarred in his mind. He let go of Benél, straightened Benél's collar and shirt where he had bunched it. Better—a little. He began touching his own buttons, but Benél's hand came and grasped his neck, and a wave of power swept the ripples away. He managed a deep breath.

"Gods, Nek," Benél sighed. "You were right. It would have been worse if we'd run." He shook his head. "I still think we'd better get out of here."

Father's voice cried from farther inside the house, "—where is Erex? We don't have time to convene the Council!"

"I want to see what the Council does now," Nekantor said. "If we can beat Sorn down to the Hall of the Eminence, we can do Father a favor and inform Erex." A smile quirked his mouth. "Benél—I *told* you Tagaret wouldn't be our candidate!"

Benél gave a harsh laugh. "Yeah, I remember what you said. Not the way I'd have asked for it to come out, mind you. Let's go."

They ran down the halls. Of course, they might not actually beat Sorn, because they had to pass the security tunnel-hounds. Benél grimaced when one approached, but he didn't change his stride. Nothing ever stopped Benél—nothing but the thought of Kinders fever—and they must stay together. *He* would have kicked the thing, but he couldn't afford to be denied entry.

Guards stopped them at the entrance, more tunnel-hounds wriggling in their hands. Disgusting. Nekantor fixed his eyes on his Arissen. Her brows were straight, her helmet smooth and shiny, her hands strong, holding the tunnel-hound tight. It would be all right. It *had* to be: this was the proper order of things. A woman under the orders of the Eminence controlled the small dark creature. Dark creatures who belonged behind walls might be permitted to emerge, so long as they served the will of gentlemen. *It would be all right.*

Finally, the Arissen passed them in.

Nekantor stopped after only eight steps. He should have hurried on, but he could still feel the snuffling creature. He checked himself, straightened seams, and touched buttons.

"Sorn's going to beat us," Benél said. "What's wrong? Did you lose something?"

"No—" He shuddered. "I can't stand tunnel-hounds."

"I know what you mean." Benél gave a half-smile. "The animals, either."

Ah, to see Benél smile—it made everything better. Nekantor laughed. "Let's try to make up lost time."

Something was wrong in the Hall of the Eminence. Not just anticipation and gossip, but a bubbling, barely contained commotion that tingled on the edges of his nerves. Fortunately, the whole room was roped off into Family zones, with an empty aisle down the center. He ran along it, keeping his eyes on the carpet with its looping Grobal insignias. The First Family zone was at the front, right beside the cabinet members' seating area, but for some reason Erex wasn't there. When asked, not one of his exasperating cousins had any idea where he was.

Nekantor scowled and accosted the nearest guard. "Arissen!"

The man saluted. "Sir."

"Where can I find the Family Councils?"

"In the ballroom, sir, but that area is restricted."

"Fah." Stupid Arissen—stupid security orders. Sorn would pass them, using the Lowers' halls. They'd never beat him now.

"Right, of course," said Benél, and leaned to his ear. "What's the plan?"

The tickle of Benél's breath sent a thrill of confidence down his spine. "We can still do this. Let's run."

He broke into a sprint, with Benél by his side. They arrived out of breath at the right-hand ballroom entrance.

"Arissen," Nekantor said to the guards, "I must speak to Arbiter Erex of the First Family! I have an emergency message from the Speaker of the Cabinet, my father Garr."

"Entrance is restricted, sir."

Benél puffed himself up. "You'll answer to the Speaker himself if Arbiter Erex doesn't receive this message."

The Arissen frowned.

So, now the reasonable move. "We don't have to *go in*," Nekantor said. "Tell the Arbiter about the message, and he'll come out if he agrees it's important. We can speak to him right here, inside the archway."

He waited, counted seconds. One of the Arissen ran off through the passage. The other allowed them to take four steps into the shelter of the arch.

Erex appeared, a silhouette against the light of the ballroom, coming closer with his Imbati woman behind him. He was too weak in his blood to run, but maybe they'd beaten Sorn down here after all, because he looked worried—see how fast he walked? When he saw them, he frowned.

"Boys, what's going on? Young Nekantor, where's your father? The candidates are lining up—where in Varin's name is Tagaret?"

"Tagaret has Kinders fever," Nekantor said.

"Nekantor!" Erex exploded, then controlled himself with effort. "Behave yourself, young man. This is no time for joking."

"Sir." Benél's voice broke. "I swear on the crown of Mai. He's not coming. Speaker Garr is in a state."

In a state— Nekantor blinked. Father wasn't the only one in a state. Suddenly, the wrongness in the Hall clicked into sense. "Erex, you've seen the candidates," he said. "You know some of them aren't who they should be. They're substitutes, when the others have Kinders fever. So does Tagaret. We saw him fall. We want to know who you in the Council have to take his place."

Erex went pale. He swayed, and extended one hand toward the wall. His Imbati woman stepped close to his back and held him up.

Nekantor understood instantly. *There was no one.* Garr, Father of a thousand plans, had prepared no one but Tagaret. Outrageous! What would become of the Family's reputation now?

He whirled to Benél. "Benél," he said. "What I said to you. The First Family needs a candidate—this is your chance. Our reputation depends on it."

Benél gaped and stammered. "N—no, Nekantor, no."

Nekantor almost screamed at him. "But you have power!"

"Not without you—I couldn't be alone up there."

Nekantor looked around, frantic. On the other side of the arch, against the light of the ballroom, the line was already forming. Tagaret was meant to be first, but instead his place was empty, and Menni of the Second Family was there, and the Eminence's fourteen-year-old protégé, Xemell of the Third Family, with the others indistinct figures behind them. The broken pattern wound his chest tighter, tighter. The moment Menni set foot on that stage, the entire Pelismara Society would see the gap. The First Family would be struck an irrevocable blow.

"Fine," he snapped. "I'll do it."

"You'll—?" said Erex. He sucked breath, but then gained some fire. "You'll do absolutely nothing of the sort. When everyone sees what's happened, they'll understand. We'll just delay the Announcement of Candidates."

"They'll *understand?*" Nekantor cried. "Oh, they'll understand, gnash it—they'll know the First Family is weak! We'll have no chance at all in the Selection. The Family's reputation will never recover!" He closed and opened his hands. He could feel the blow looming like an enormous stalactite about to fall. It would crack the whole pattern of the Twelve Families, disarrange everything so it could never be fixed. *No, no, no!*

Erex put his hands on his hips. "There's no way I'm going to let you—"

"Oh, *aren't* you?" Nekantor glanced toward the Arissen guards, now far enough that if he was careful, they wouldn't overhear. He had information on Erex: the skin-tightening sight of Erex naked with a Kartunnen whore. He lowered his voice. "Erex, you're in charge here. The Council answers to you. They rely on you to safeguard the reputation of our Family into the next generation—but they might not be so willing if they knew the truth. About what kind of muckwalker you are."

Benél hissed in a breath.

Erex gulped. He glanced over his shoulder; Menni of the Second Family had started to walk toward them. Erex pressed his hand against his chest and took a step backward.

So he had him. "Contaminating our children with the taint of Lowers," Nekantor sneered. "And with the mark of a fever house? You'll see. I'm Garr's son, too. I'll give the First Family something to be proud of." He shut his mouth; the others were too close. He strode past Erex and his manservant and took the spot in front of Menni of the Second Family.

"Nekantor?" Menni said. "What's going on? What happened to Tagaret?"

"He's not coming," Nekantor said. "Let's go." He lifted his head and set his shoulders back: a dare, but Erex stood silent and let them pass. His Imbati woman stayed close—one hand strong beneath her Master's shoulder, the other light on his wrist.

The lights in the Hall of the Eminence were bright, and the stage steps resonated riches under his feet. They walked up into full view of the faces. No more commotion—the room hummed with power, and here on the stage no one was missing now, the pattern unbroken. The First Family was still first.

The Eminence's throne had been moved to the far side of the stage, before the stairs. That was different, and irksome, but fully explicable. The Eminence Herin, poised there with his white-and-gold drape pinned around his shoulders, was the gatekeeper. Only the chosen Heir would be able to pass him, at the end of this game.

Yes, the game. Nekantor's heart raced. There were places set for the candidates to stand, and he walked to the number one marked on the shining wood, then turned back to evaluate the First Family's adversaries. Beyond Menni and Xemell was Ambrei of the Fourth Family, not quite nineteen yet. The Fifth Family had Innis, aged thirty and almost too old for Selection; his nose was so noble that his entire face sloped back from it. The next man, Vos, was Sixth Family and therefore inconsequential.

"Nekantor!" a voice hissed. Farther down the line, Gowan of the Ninth Family leaned forward, scowling. "What in Varin's name are you doing? You're not fooling anyone—get off the stage."

The Seventh Family's boy winced at that. Herm—he was only twelve, so such weakness was to be expected. The sympathy of the crowd would be his greatest advantage. Between him and Gowan, Sangar of the Eighth Family, a stocky sixteen-year-old with dark hair, bent and whispered in his ear.

Lyaret of the Tenth Family was almost as young as Herm, but he picked up fast and followed Gowan's lead. "Account for yourself, First Family."

Nekantor shrugged. "I don't think I'm the only person here whom nobody expected."

Sure enough, every eye turned to the last two candidates. Eleventh should have been Fernar, the muscle from Tagaret's gang, but instead it was a man almost as old as Innis and Vos, already losing hair. Who was he? Ower, that was it, age twenty-five. And beside him from the Twelfth Family stood Yril. Nekantor wanted to laugh. *He'd told Benél that Yril would be here.*

"Yes, but *we* belong here," Yril said venomously.

Nekantor only smirked. No more posturing. Abandoning Yril to the Arissen had been just the beginning. He turned away from the others and looked out over the crowd. Twelve roped boxes, milling but nicely contained. Those places where excitement bordered on chaos were actually pockets of weakness and suppressed fear. That same fear might hide inside the minds of the candidates beside him, to serve the First Family's advantage. The cabinet members began straggling into their seats below—and there was Father finally, in a huddle with Fedron, Erex, and Lady Selemei at the base of the stairs.

Erex wouldn't stop him. Even Lady Selemei the subversive wouldn't touch him here, not in front of everyone. Fedron would follow whatever Father decided.

But Father wasn't harmless. He could ruin everything.

Father walked closer. Each step slow, heavy as stone; his face gray and haunted, his eyes turned up on the stage. On *him*.

Don't touch me, Father. I know what power is. I know everything you taught me, even the things you didn't. This is for power, Father. Don't make a mistake. Don't touch me. Don't touch me.

"Don't touch me," he murmured.

Menni of the Second Family glanced at him, curious, wary.

Nekantor shut his mouth. With every step Father took, his throat tightened, his fingers ached, and his skin crawled. To look at his watch would suggest impatience. To check or touch would show weakness. It was all right. It *had* to be all right. This was where he belonged, here at the head of the pattern, showing the First Family's strength. Father would never hurt the First Family. *He must not!*

Father stepped to a microphone in the cabinet seating area. His deep voice made the air shake. "I'm proud to introduce the candidates for Heir."

Nekantor held his breath. *Say my name, Father. Show them that the First Family sees no emergency, that we feel no fear. This is for us, and for our power.*

"From the First Family, Nekantor, fifteen years old," Father said. "From the Second, Menni, twenty-one years old. From the Third, Xemell, fourteen . . ."

Nekantor didn't hear the rest. Tension exploded into ecstasy, a single perfect moment whose vibrations chased away every obligation to pattern. They were saved! The order of the world would remain right, and now the game could begin.

He could play games as well as anyone.

The whole Hall applauded. The surge of power felt like the heat of a fire.

At the side of the stage, the Eminence Herin stood and raised a hand to them in welcome. "Candidates," he said. "We will hear your initial statements."

Father looked up at Nekantor.

He knew what that demanding stare meant. Oh, yes—he'd been there for all the preparations, listening hard even when Tagaret was not. Father had composed Tagaret's statement, all idiotic fancy phrases about celebration and the future and the strongest youths of the Race. Father had told them over and over what to expect. *Be graceful, be noble. The Round of Twelve is a simple matter, where the cabinet will smile and nod at one another and vote based on the natural quality of the Great Families.* Today, everyone would desperately want a simple matter—the wrongness in the room told him that, as if it were speaking in his ear. Everyone wanted to ignore the fear, to confirm what they already knew.

That meant everyone was vulnerable. Even Herin. Even Father.

Nekantor straightened his cuffs and stepped forward. "Ladies and Gentlemen of the Pelismara Society, this is *not* a day for celebration. All you have to do is look at the twelve of us to see the entire Race is at risk. Kinders fever has invaded our ranks, and why? Because of contact with contaminated Lowers. This can't be allowed to continue."

He scanned the Hall: Herin was frowning, Father open-mouthed, the entire place seething with fear laid out into the open. He stamped a foot and raised his head. "*We* are the Grobal Race! But if we can't stop this behavior with better law enforcement, our carnal weakness will mean our deaths. I want to know how the other Families propose to win our future against this threat."

The entire Hall was silent. See, how he'd struck the blow just right. When he stepped back, Menni of the Second Family looked at him differently. The glow of real fight shone in the man's eyes. Menni turned away and faced the crowd.

"Ladies and Gentlemen," he said, "this may indeed be the question of our age, but isolation is not the answer. The Kartunnen might carry the vector of our destruction, but they alone can train the doctors who ensure our survival. The cause of this epidemic is not fraternization behaviors as such, but an illness endemic in our population. It can be defeated only through our support of medical advances."

"Wait," Xemell of the Third Family exclaimed. "I object to this entire line of discussion! It's inappropriate to the Announcement of Candidates—this is a time for introductions, not debate. You choose to talk of death when we should be giving honor to the Race and to the noble pursuit we're all entering." He crossed his arms and glanced at the Eminence Herin.

"Yes, indeed," the Eminence replied, nodding. "Thank you, Xemell."

Nekantor gritted his teeth. Herin shouldn't have done that. It wasn't his turn to speak—but he had power, which would protect him from reprisal. Herin knew Garr was watching, waiting to collect a debt. He knew he couldn't afford to let the First Family gain control.

"Ambrei," Xemell said. "Let's get this event back on track."

But Ambrei shrank and didn't say a word. Count the seconds: one, two, three, four— Ambrei stood and let the silence unravel him. A defeat, already? Nekantor started to smile, then discovered that Innis of the Fifth Family was staring at him, smiling back.

This man, now—*this* man was dangerous. The set of Innis' noble face showed the knowledge to manage power; he knew the significance of the move he was about to make. Nekantor closed his fists, with a shiver climbing his back. He could see the scales balanced in Innis' mind: on the one side, the Third Family and the Eminence; on the other, the First and Second Families. Opportunities on either side, for the one who knew how to use them.

Innis turned his smile outward to the listening crowd. "Ladies and Gentlemen," he said, "Nekantor and Menni would have you think that their positions are opposite, but I don't think our solution to the problem of Kinders fever need be as simple as either suggests. We bear a Trust: we are responsible for our people, and *we* must lead. We can enforce stricter penalties on Grobal who transgress—remain aloof for safety, and still bring our will to bear on the University." Underneath it floated another message: *I accept the game you've chosen, because I know how to play.*

Nekantor sucked in a breath. A desire to fight swept over him, and his fists shook with excitement. An enemy Innis might be, but he was a good enough ally for this battle: after that, each candidate stepped willingly into their circle. Sixth and Ninth Families stood with Menni, speaking of cooperation with medicine; Eighth and Eleventh spoke in support of law enforcement. The young boys from Seventh and Tenth distinguished themselves by invoking the Grobal Trust—Herm reciting the part about 'the responsibilities of our exalted station' in a child-like manner that drew sighs from the crowd, Lyaret with just enough talk of economic policy that it became clear he used his youth as a deliberate strategy.

Nekantor watched Yril's gaunt, determined face for signs of weakness, but when it came to his turn, Yril demanded restitution from the Kartunnen with such passion he almost shook. A fascinating way to wring advantage out of his humiliation at the whorehouse—how far it would convince the cabinet was another question entirely.

The cabinet members huddled below, muttering to one another. An Imbati with a bureaucrat's tattoo slowly moved from one to another, entering their rankings into a handheld ordinating machine. Tension reached out from them into the crowd around, stringing one person to the next, binding nerve to nerve in a web of anticipation. Nekantor watched, tense from fingertips to heels. Enough power in this room to shiver all of Varin when they made their decision. The hum of their talk rose finally, and Father moved to the microphone.

"Ladies and Gentlemen of the Pelismara Society," he announced, "We honor all the Great Families for offering us the best of their blood. Will the following four candidates please step back and descend from the stage." He paused, shaking his head.

Nekantor bit down on a scream. He ground his teeth and dug his fingernails into the palms of his hands.

"Herm of the Seventh Family," said Father. "Vos of the Sixth Family. Ambrei of the Fourth Family." He gulped visibly. "Xemell of the Third Family."

"What?!" Xemell shrieked.

Nekantor gasped. Triumph was a slashing knife, severing him from the tension that had bound the room together. The web broke, and the crowd dissolved into a roiling din, full of cries of shock. He whimpered and turned his back on it. Panting, he tried his watch, but won only a scant few seconds before the Eminence himself strode past him, crackling with fury, following his own defeated cousin off the stage.

"Congratulations, Heir candidates!" said Father's magnified voice. "You may now step down. We look forward to seeing you again in the Round of Eight."

Nekantor could not step down. The pattern that had sustained him ran away like sand from under his feet. He panted and shook.

At last Father's arm came, wrapped around his shoulders. "It's all right, son," he said. Then, to others nearby, explained, "He's overwrought—what he's had to go through, you know, after the shock of Tagaret's collapse . . ." The arm closed tighter and pulled him stumbling forward. The ground dropped—stairs. Father's voice a low rumble in his ear. "I'll tell you, Nek, I didn't know you were capable of that. Xemell's failure gives us a chance at the Third Family's cabinet vote, and the Heir's vote as well—it was a coup."

"Nekantor!" Benél's voice.

Benél was here. Nekantor gulped in air and looked up.

Benél was smiling. "You were amazing!" he cried.

That smile was solid when nothing else was. Nekantor grabbed Benél's arm. "Benél—stay with me."

"We have to get you home, son," Father said. "Arissen Veriga is here to escort us."

Nekantor shook his head. "Benél has to come with us."

"Sir," said Benél, "I'll help you get him home."

Father shrugged. "Well, this once."

Step by step, they walked. Nekantor held Benél's arm, and Benél smiled, and Arissen Veriga and Father and Sorn walked with them. Step by step, pieces of the world built back up beneath his feet. It had really happened. No matter the price, the First Family had been saved, the Third Family's bid for the throne cut off. The door to their suite built itself into place ahead.

"Thank you, Benél," said Father.

"No," Nekantor said. "Benél, help me in. Don't leave me."

"Sir?"

"All right."

Benél led him by the back of the neck into his rooms. Nekantor stumbled over to his bed. Benél locked the door, and when he turned, his face glowed—better than when the gang won a fight, better than when they'd escaped the whorehouse unscathed.

"You did it, Nek. I couldn't have done it, but *you did it*."

"Yes . . ."

"Hey, if it were me, I'm not sure I'd be able to stand, either, but everything's all right."

Everything was not all right. "Benél, come here."

"What? Do you have a plan? Do you need a drink?"

Nekantor shook his head. "You. I need you."

Benél came closer, staring with his mouth slightly open. When he got close enough, Nekantor grabbed his arm; Benél dropped on his knees beside the bed. Nekantor found his hand, lifted it, looked at it. Strong hands; Benél was strong, and his hands could chase away shadows; they could hold the world together. *Benél's hands, Benél's lip, Benél's arms, Benél's mouth*—

"Nek," Benél said, breathing hard. "I'm not going to—I—you don't want me to treat you like, well, like I was treated in my last gang. Before you helped me get on top." He coughed and looked away. "I just want—you're amazing, and I want to, to be with you. That's all."

Nekantor took a breath, lifted Benél's hand, pressed his face hard into it, feeling its power put his mind back together. Benél gave a cry and grappled him, strong arms pinning both his hands above his head, strong body crushing down on him. He struggled an instant, but Benél only held harder until he couldn't move, couldn't think—

Couldn't think! Ahh, perfection!

Relief flooded through him: a bliss as sharp as ice. Benél's mouth pressed hard and pushed into his, and he pushed back until the air broke in.

"Is—" he gasped. "Is that—all?"

Benél's face was wet with tears, his voice almost a growl. "No."

"Please," Nekantor said. "I'm yours, Benél. I'm yours!"

CHAPTER EIGHTEEN

Vigil

Aloran woke, half-falling out of his chair. There had been a sound . . . He caught a breath and straightened, trying to orient himself. The young Master's room, dimmed for nighttime—the Lady sleeping in a chair beside the bed—his medical kit on the bedside table, open—and young Master Tagaret tossing in his sheets, panting and muttering while his body tried to go up in flames.

The horrified ache in Aloran's throat started again, and tears rose in his eyes. He longed to fight, to sacrifice himself so that Tagaret might live—as if now that he had stood by Lady Tamelera's side, he received the right to love him as she did. He blinked back his tears, and made another check: pulse steady, fast but not dangerously so. No sign of the hives he'd suffered earlier in the evening, which was a mercy. His temperature, though, was a frightening six degrees above normal.

Aloran checked his watch. Enough time had passed that a fourth dose of medication wouldn't tax the young Master's organs. He shifted him onto his back, and the boy roused, opening bleary eyes.

"Nekantor, don't break my lock this time," he said indistinctly. "Why would you walk on only the black tiles?"

"It's Aloran, young Master."

"Imbati Aloran," murmured Tagaret. "My mother thinks he's a man."

"Hold still, young Master. This will make you feel better."

He steadied Tagaret's arm and delivered the shot, wishing he could give him not just medicine, but some of his own strength to get him through this unharmed.

A soft knock.

Was that what he'd heard? Why wouldn't Serjer just have come in?

Aloran disposed of the needle, removed his treatment gloves, then walked silently to open the Maze door.

Kiit was standing behind it.

Aloran blinked, trying to make sense of her. Her anxious face was newly marked, and she wore treatment gloves just like his own. She carried a paper. Belatedly, he gaze-gestured questioning.

Kiit took two steps back into the Maze.

Aloran glanced over his shoulder, and reluctantly stepped across the threshold.

When she spoke, her whisper was scarcely above a breath. "Update on the epidemic." She placed the paper in his hand.

"Thank you." But she could have delivered this paper to Serjer. Too tired for manners with her, he simply asked. "Kiit, did you need to see me?"

Kiit's eyes flickered over his shoulder. What did she see there? Nothing either of them could have imagined, despite every lesson, every warning. She gestured to her own forehead.

"Just—I'm sorry, Aloran."

How could he even respond? What came out was, "Congratulations. . . ?"

She winced and nodded. "I just needed to tell you. I understand now." She turned and loped away down the Maze hall.

Aloran exhaled. He returned to the room, peering at the note in the dim light, then discovered Lady Tamelera was awake in her chair, gazing at him. She wore a white nightgown, and her face still bore traces of her earlier tears.

Aloran bowed to her. "I'm sorry, Lady," he said. "These are the victims of the epidemic." He placed the list of handwritten names in her hand.

She stared at it for a moment, then spoke in a broken whisper, dropping the paper on the floor. "Forty people, Aloran. Forty of us down."

"Grobal Reyn of the Ninth Family?" he asked, remembering the young Master and his friends at the Ball. "Grobal Fernar of the Eleventh? Grobal Pyaras?"

She swallowed hard. "All of them."

Aloran's stomach clenched. "Lady Della of the Sixth Family?"

She frowned. "I don't think so. I didn't see that name."

"Blessing of Heile," he breathed.

"But ten people have died since this afternoon."

Aloran closed his eyes in grief. When he opened them again, Lady Tamelera was still looking at him. She was pale and graceful in the dim light, and her face showed fear as clearly as if she were an unmarked child.

"Five years," she said, fresh tears running down her face. "Five years. I just got him back . . . if I lose him, I'll die."

The desire to sacrifice himself near-strangled him. "Not Tagaret," he vowed, his voice quavering like a stranger's. "Not if I can stop it. I've failed you enough."

"Oh, Aloran, no . . ." She fell silent, staring at him, long enough that he flushed and turned away. He should check the young Master again. He put on a new pair of treatment gloves. When he touched the boy's neck, Tagaret turned his head, muttering incomprehensibly—the sound of it squeezed his heart. Checked his temperature, though, and it was slightly less; his heart relaxed somewhat to think the medicine was working.

"I remember—" Lady Tamelera said. She paused for a long moment. "I remember, when he was born."

Aloran looked at her. She was gazing at her hands, her fingers wound tightly in her lap. Would she truly confide in him?

"He came three weeks early, but my Eyli knew. I wanted her to deliver him, but she insisted I go to the medical center. She was right. The labor was long, and he was born weak—they took him from me for treatment before I'd had more than a single glimpse of his face. I lay there for an hour, prostrate with exhaustion while the doctors treated me, wondering if that was all I would ever see. If all my efforts had been in vain and we would both die."

Aloran gave respect to her silence, but after a time she flashed him a glance—a clear request for response. "They were not in vain," he said.

"No. They brought him to me at last, and I could see he had grown stronger. I gave him the Tagaret name-line, for strength in adversity, and I promised him we would both survive." She looked up into his face. "I was seventeen years old."

"Ohh—" The sound escaped him on a swell of pity too strong to contain. Imagine her, a mother before she was even as old as Kiit . . . He raised one forearm to cover his face and began a breath pattern before he put it down again.

"Yes? Please, Aloran, tell me."

He couldn't refuse to speak, but he didn't dare look directly at her. He confessed softly to his knees, "I want to make the same promise, Lady. To him, and to you—with all my heart."

"I know you can't."

"Not yet. It's still too early to know—" *If he'll be damaged. If he'll die.* He couldn't say it.

Lady Tamelera hid her face in her hands and sobbed.

Hearing her pain was bad enough; knowing he'd made it worse was torture. He took off his treatment gloves and slipped from his chair onto the floor, pressing his forehead into the carpet at her feet. "Forgive me," he said. "I should not have spoken."

She dragged in a breath. "Aloran, rise," she said. "If you never speak, how can I hope to understand you?"

She wants to understand me? His heart split, one half fearfully insisting he was unworthy of such a gift, the other dizzy with gratitude and devotion. She had commanded him to rise, so rise he must—but Sirin only knew how he could look at her now. He picked himself up slowly.

"Would you excuse me for a moment, Lady?"

"Of course."

He walked away from her, into the young Master's bathroom with its floor of black and white tiles. At the marble basin he ran hot water over his hands and scrubbed them, longer than he needed to. The fire embroidered on his jacket kept her with him anyway.

Somehow, this wasn't at all what he had dreamed of when imagining a Lady who understood the love of mistress and servant. Kindness, yes. Consideration. Not this sudden overwhelming generosity.

But he must not leave the young Master unattended. He wet a cloth with cool water, returned to the room and put on new treatment gloves before laying it on Tagaret's head. The young Master gave a deep sigh, but for the moment he appeared to be sleeping. It was easier to look at him than to risk looking at the Lady.

Lady Tamelera spoke quietly. "When I was alone in the medical center, I was afraid for Tagaret, but also for myself. Afraid of what would happen if he died, and I lived. Garr was dark-haired and handsome at forty, but—busy. When I became pregnant, he changed. He treated me gently, brought me gifts, and told me I was beautiful . . ." She sighed. "He *cared*. I knew in my spine that his care would vanish if I went home alone."

Aloran bent his head. No doubt she was right.

"Garr has always been powerful, untouchable," she said. "His anger is terrifying. He could demand anything from me, and I have no power to refuse."

Aloran glanced at her cautiously. "There are laws . . ."

"Laws are small comfort. He makes me feel so helpless, and I can't escape him. I'm ashamed to say that I have always responded to my situation with fury. This has had some unfortunate, unintended consequences. Aloran, look at me."

He did, and found her leaning toward him. He tried to keep his eyes lowered, but her gaze caught him and wouldn't let go.

"My thoughtlessness has placed you in the same circumstances. Faced with my cruelty, you have responded far more gracefully than I ever did to my partner's. You wouldn't dare say to me what I really deserve to hear, so *I* will: when it comes to someone so gentle, so considerate, who holds my life and that of my son in his hands—Mai strike me if I can't do any better than Garr."

Aloran couldn't move. Blood rushed into his face and burned in his cheeks.

Lady Tamelera stood up abruptly and faced the public door as if she might leave, then appeared to change her mind and walked past him into the young Master's bathroom.

With her gone, he could find a breath to begin a pattern. Surely this was a deliberate kindness, taking her blazing presence away so he could breathe again—she understood him better than he'd thought. He checked his watch: still too soon for any further medications. Checked the young Master's temperature: it was a full degree down now.

Tagaret roused at his touch and cried out. "Mother—Mother, where are you? I'm so thirsty—Mother!"

Lady Tamelera flew out of the bathroom as if to rush to his side, but jerked to a stop two steps away. "I'm here, Tagaret," she cried, shaking her hands helplessly. "I won't leave you—I promise, we're going to be all right!" She turned to Aloran, her eyes desperate.

Aloran slipped his arm under Tagaret's back, lifting him gently. There was a glass of water on the bedside table; he brought it to the boy's lips. Tagaret drank—actually drank, the most positive sign he'd seen in all this night of fear. When he laid him down again, he touched his hand to the boy's cheek before he realized what he was doing. For a split second he froze, astonished at his own presumption, but then he completed the caress.

What was he for, if he could not be his Lady's hands?

CHAPTER NINETEEN

Next Moves

Almost ready to go and play.

Nekantor circled his rooms. He could still feel Benél: a disturbance in the room, a vibration in his body. He touched, checked, straightened, then stopped at the mirror and combed his hair, fixed his clothes, fold by fold. Now the disturbances were hidden from prying eyes, but he could still feel them: they were marks of power, and they made him stronger. He had to be strong to stay in the game for the First Family—he couldn't afford to show weakness again.

The important thing was understanding the pattern. It hadn't disappeared when the candidates left the stage, only changed, and that change was perfectly easy to explain. Just remember that, and there would be no need to panic. The line of twelve up on stage had become eight above, and four below. The eight Families left above would do anything to ensure victory for their candidates, and would pursue assassinations. The other four were supplicants, offering votes in exchange for favors.

The First Family had Fedron and Selemei's votes, plus Father's to make three. The Fifth Family had lost the Eminence Indal, but with two cabinet members, they still had two votes in hand. The Third Family had one cabinet vote, plus the Eminence Herin to make two. And then the rest, for a total of sixteen. He must watch carefully and anticipate the next moves.

The assassination attempts had already begun. Innis of the Fifth Family had been attacked this morning—not killed, unfortunately. The thought of going out made Nekantor's neck feel tight. Made the room feel wrong. One more circle: he touched the door, the desk drawers, the chair; checked the window shade, touched the bed, tapped the bedside table, one-two-three. Touched the wardrobe with its cool drawer handles, and the bathroom door.

Out there, at least he'd have the Arissen man to protect him. He'd be safe with a Selection bodyguard. Yes: time to go find Arissen Veriga.

He took a deep breath and went out, but the drawing room was empty. The sitting room, then. He shoved through the doors.

Arissen Veriga was at the gaming table. He looked all wrong—black hair uncovered, and wearing brown silk? How could he be wearing *brown?* But then, searching Veriga's animal-strong body, Nekantor found the answer: a stripe of cuff peeking from his sleeves in perfect Cohort orange. That was it—he was in disguise, for going out today.

Something was still wrong, though. Veriga was playing keyzel marbles with Pyaras.

"Pyaras, they told us you were sick!" Nekantor said. "What are you doing with my Arissen? Stop it this instant."

"Hello, Nekantor," Pyaras said. "I did have a fever last night, but I feel so much better today that my father had a doctor come check me. You're not the only one important to the future of the First Family." The infuriating baby shot a sly grin at the bodyguard. "I just *knew* you'd barge in and cut us off."

Arissen Veriga laughed. "And this was shaping into a good game, too."

"How dare you!" Nekantor snapped. "Show some respect."

"Yes, sir." Veriga went instantly serious.

Pyaras kept grinning. Nekantor wanted to slap him. If only Benél had been here, they could have schooled that boy.

Arissen Veriga casually held out a silver coin. "Pyaras, sir," he said, "this will pay our wager."

Pyaras stared at the coin dropped into his hand. "You're paying me *real* orsheth? How much is this?"

"That's an eight, sir." Veriga chuckled. "Haven't you seen one? I can show you a one, and a four, if you like."

"Stop it," said Nekantor. His fingers twitched in disgust. "Pyaras, money is for Lowers."

Then Father walked out of his office, followed closely by Imbati

Sorn. "Nek, ready to go?" he rumbled. He looked at Pyaras, and then at Arissen Veriga. "What's going on here?"

"Pyaras is *fraternizing* with my bodyguard," said Nekantor.

Pyaras turned red. "I'm here for Tagaret," he said. "I just want him to be all right, and Tagaret *told* me—he *told* me I should talk to Veriga! It was the last thing he did!"

Father huffed himself up. Nekantor held his breath, waiting for the surge of power, but it never came. Father's shoulders sagged and he waved a hand dismissively. "We don't have time to bother with this. Tagaret's still alive so far—Pyaras, talk to Tamelera if you like. Nekantor, Veriga, let's get on our way."

"Yes, sir."

Nekantor smiled as Veriga came to his side. His own bodyguard— ah, it felt like power. Suddenly, the vestibule and the door were no barrier at all. Time to give the supplicants their hearing.

Grobal Fedron met them at the Conveyor's Hall, where Imbati brought skimmers. Veriga saluted but blocked their way. He checked the skimmers thoroughly before anyone got on. Father huffed in first; Nekantor slipped into the space beside him, while Fedron's skimmer came around on the right.

"Seatbelts for everyone, sirs," said Veriga. "In case we have trouble."

Nekantor buckled his belt and carefully straightened his trousers beneath it. Trouble seemed unlikely—with Sorn standing in front of them, driving, Chenna driving Fedron's skimmer, and Veriga on his own skimmer at the rear, they became a wall of safety against the wide moving air of the circumferences.

"I wish Innis had been taken care of," Father grunted in his ear as they drove. "But I suppose having a knife to the leg prove fatal would be too much to ask. With assassins, you get what you pay for, and Paper Shadows aren't cheap."

Nekantor straightened his trousers again. There were six suspect families, too little information yet to identify which. He shrugged. "Innis is too strong to fall to such a simple ploy. He'll have to be killed with more care."

"Don't rush, now, son," said Father. "Anything could happen in the Eminence's interviews, and the Round of Eight will show us who our real rivals are. Now is the time for negotiating. I wish we had more assets."

Nekantor looked at him. "Assets like your favor to Herin?"

Father pulled at his chin. "Herin's a snake. He'd rather bite you than vote for you, so you'll have to handle your interview very carefully when he calls you up. I mean other assets—if only your mother had performed better, daughters would be a real help. Tamelera herself makes a good distraction, but with Tagaret sick, she looks a fright."

"Fah," Nekantor scoffed. "Mother has no power."

Father wheezed a chuckle. "Ironically, mind you, gloves are now the order of the day. The quarantine measures just came down. We'll have you measured after lunch."

Imbati, touching his hands? Nekantor closed his fists tight against his stomach. "We won't."

"Come now, son," said Garr. "You chose this. I expect you to—"

"I won't fail the Family," Nekantor snapped. "But I will *not* wear gloves. I've survived so far without catching Kinders fever. Arissen Veriga will make sure no one gets close enough to touch me."

"Stop!" Arissen Veriga shouted.

Imbati Sorn braked hard; Nekantor's body jerked forward against his seatbelt, and he clutched the armrest. Imbati Chenna was slower—Fedron's skimmer swung ahead of them. A sizzling energy bolt flew from above, striking metal a finger-width from Fedron's leg. Nekantor screamed; Father grabbed his shoulders and pushed him down, face into his knees.

Look—the skimmer floor—shoes and dust—

Nekantor held his breath, quivering. In the corner of his eye, Veriga's skimmer whizzed past. There was a hum and a crash, and he looked up: a cloud of smoke floated near the top of a nearby building. Out of it fell a weapon, and then a man. The weapon bounced on the sidewalk; the man didn't. Veriga dismounted and pushed through a startled group of Venorai laborers who had ignored the street closures. He shoved the fallen man with his foot, then wrapped the weapon in a cloth and pocketed it. Then he returned to his skimmer.

"Let's continue, sirs."

At the end of the block, Veriga chastised a group of Arissen police officers in rust-red uniforms for failing in their security sweeps, then pointed them back in the direction of the fallen man. At last they drove onward.

Nekantor unfolded himself slowly, slowly. He huddled against Father. The assassin had been killed, so whoever sent him had failed to make his move count. But now he could feel the other Families looming all around, wanting to kill him—and Father had left handprints on his shoulders. He tried to tug his sleeves straight but as soon as the skimmer stopped, Father grabbed him again, dragging him forward into the club that was their destination.

"Let go of me!" Nekantor cried. He pulled away and straightened his sleeves, his trousers, his vest. Then he took refuge in his watch. The round glass gleamed, and the second hand swept a clean curve. A little better at four seconds. Better still at eight. At sixteen he glanced up and down again. Veriga was talking with Father and Fedron in a low voice, about the assassin—but Society Club Five itself was snug and clean: no front windows to expose him, walls striped in white and brown leather, tables clean and perfectly aligned, each manned by its own complement of Household-trained Imbati. A place suited to gentlemen. And finally Veriga came up behind him. Ah, yes, that was it—Veriga would stop them, make it so no one could touch him anymore. Now he could remember the game they were playing: polite friendliness as a disguise for haggling.

He put on a smile, nodded, and exchanged meaningless talk with the four men who rose from padded chairs to greet them—all members of the Sixth Family Council. He even nodded benignly at the Imbati table director who was assigned to their private room. Father claimed the head of the brass table and spoke to a small Kartunnen who carried the liquor menu, so Nekantor took the seat to Father's right and pretended to take interest in the well-being of the Sixth Family.

The head of the Sixth Family Council sat across from him. He was named Doross, and he moved with power—not a muckwalker, this one, though so obviously scared of Father it was laughable. The rest were followers. Weakest was a man named Enwin, who sweated and fidgeted nervously. That might be turned to advantage.

"Have you heard the news?" Doross asked, as his manservant set a plate of food in front of him.

Nekantor looked up—Sorn appeared to be delivering *his* food to

Arissen Veriga. He frowned, but answered, "Innis of the Fifth Family has been wounded. We heard that this morning."

"No, no—this is from just before you arrived. Lyaret of the Tenth Family is dead."

Lyaret of the Tenth—he was the young but smart one who had taken Gowan's side against him. Six rivals instead of seven was excellent news. Nekantor put on a frown. "Oh, that's—"

"Terrible news," Father broke in loudly. "What a tragic loss to the Race. Elinda keep him—how did it happen?"

Nekantor ground his teeth. Gnash Father, did he think he was *that* stupid? Of course, the sympathy move was required here: every measure must be taken to lull the opponent. Enwin was watching him, so he tried to look mournful.

"Lyaret's skimmer crashed," said one of the other followers. "Lost control on a level rampway."

Nekantor sucked in his cheeks. So *that* was why Veriga had been so careful. He glanced to the side and found the Arissen sliding a plate sideways into his place. Oh, mercy, Veriga had taken bites out of everything! Wrong, wrong—the whole plate had hooks in him before he knew it. *A plate must be full or empty.* His throat tightened, and his fingers twitched to throw the whole thing across the room. But that wouldn't serve the game. Don't look; eat. He ate as fast as he could, trying to stare only at the men until the plate was empty.

"So?" said Father after they'd endured some minutes of tunnel-hound admiration.

"The Sixth Family has always had an interest in supporting the First," said Doross. A lie, but he delivered it well. He touched tented fingers to his lips. "The First Family doesn't lack for votes in the cabinet. Neither would they if our Family gained another seat."

What—the *muckwalkers* deserved another seat, did they? "Hm," Nekantor said. "You're certainly ambitious."

Under the table, Father's hand gripped his knee, trying to grind his bones.

To the men Father laughed. "My son is famous for his directness, as I'm sure you already know. I'm afraid it's impossible for us to grant such a request—at least, at this time."

"What about an alliance?" said Doross.

Servants came around, took up plates, and replaced them with tiny glasses full of red liquor. Delivered one to his place also—but not red. It was something else, as if just because he was fifteen, he didn't know how to drink. He did—Benél knew that. The thought made his blood feel hot. What Benél knew . . .

He reached for the glass, but Arissen Veriga slid it aside, away from him. Nekantor frowned.

"We're listening," said Father, and took a sip that left the edges of his lips red.

"Enwin here has a daughter, Della," said Doross. "She'll turn seventeen soon."

Daughter? Nekantor rolled his eyes. "How does that help anything? I won't reach my Age of Choice for more than a year."

Father's hand clamped on his leg again. "A betrothal could be arranged," he said. "Is the girl attractive? Healthy?"

Enwin cleared his throat—an unmistakable sound of fear. And see how he sweated, bending down. He brought up a small painted portrait of the girl: long copper hair, green eyes.

"Lovely," said Father with a smile.

Yes, that was the next required move, but Nekantor hesitated. Fear should be used, but what was this fear on Enwin's face? Fear that the exchange would be made? Or that it would not?

"Nekantor," said Doross, "she would bear you good sons."

Sons.

Sex leapt into his head, twining itself around his mind. *Benél's mouth, Benél's arms pinning him, moving him, every pull of that perfect, delicious power—*

What in Varin's name did he want with a vapid, useless girl?

"I won't do it!" he cried. "There has to be something else."

"Nekantor!" Father barked.

"No!"

Arissen Veriga spat explosively, splattering liquid across the table. "Gnash it all!" he shouted. "Sweet Heile's tits—poison!"

Nekantor stumbled out of his chair and backed against the wall.

Father was on his feet—he slammed both hands down on the table, and the men scrambled away from him. "What in Varin's name do you think you're trying to pull?"

Disorder—he had to keep to the pattern! Nekantor closed his eyes tight. See the lines, see the dance: a poisoning attempt by the Sixth Family wasn't part of it. "Not them, Father," he said. "It wasn't them—couldn't have been."

"Nekantor's drink," said Veriga. "Imbati Sorn, find the Kartunnen who brought the corisi. Figure out who had contact with him. Imbati Chenna, get the table director. I need someone to drive me to the hospital, right now." He thrust shaking hands into his pockets and pulled out a vial of something that he ran about his mouth, then swallowed. "I have six minutes."

The running and rushing were awful. Nekantor put his back against the leather wall and stared at his watch, breathing fast and shallow. Twelve seconds—Imbati Chenna came back with the table director, and they took Veriga away. One minute: Imbati Chenna returned, then disappeared through the door Father's Sorn had taken. Veriga had told him the next moves, and he clung to them. Father stamped and yelled at everyone. No deal with the Sixth Family now, and they would have to get home without Veriga.

How could they get home without Veriga? At least five more Families might have designs for his death, and he needed a new bodyguard—how could he get a new bodyguard if they couldn't get home without Veriga? The questions whirled inside his head. The second hand on his watch was slower. Count the seconds.

"All right, Nekantor? Nekantor!" Father gave an exasperated bark, then lowered his voice, soft and hoarse, close by him. "That's the best we can do for now, son—look at me."

He didn't want to look. He glanced up, and down again, and clenched his teeth. Father and Fedron were both here. Father looked pale, but his Sorn was behind him now, and Fedron's Chenna, too, stood behind her Master.

"How do we get home without Veriga?" Nekantor asked. Slow the questions; count the seconds.

"Son, I *need* you to *do* as I say." Strange bursts of intensity in his voice betrayed panic trying to take over. "We have to leave *now*. The *longer* we stay, the more likely someone finds out we're *here* and Veriga is *not*."

Nekantor's guts wound tight. "Beasts smell blood," he murmured. They had to move; he needed Benél. Where was Benél?

Father wrapped an arm around his shoulders and pulled him away from the wall. No choice now. They hurried to the skimmers, and Nekantor huddled close to Father, buckled himself tighter, tighter, trying to stop his pounding blood from drawing beasts. He kept his head low, breathing hard. Three of them; only two Imbati bodyguards.

"Drive fast," Father said.

Drive fast.

The skimmer hummed and took off, rocking them around the turns—sickening, and worse because his head was down.

"Too close, too close," Father was muttering. "If we get out of this, we need more than a bodyguard. I'll get a tunnel-hound."

Nekantor's stomach lurched; he panted and fought it down. "No tunnel-hounds, Father. I—no tunnel-hounds, they make me sick."

"How stupid *are* you?!" Father exploded, then controlled himself. "Don't endanger a man when you could have an animal instead— what will you do, stop eating?"

"Yes. Yes. I won't eat." How could he, knowing that the next glass, the next plate might kill him? "I'll only eat where it's safe."

"That's ridiculous!"

The skimmer swerved suddenly, and there came the hum and sizzle of weapon bolts. Nekantor pressed his cheekbones into his knees. The floor of the skimmer, shoes and dust; it stopped his breath, but if he lifted his head—

Someone hissed in pain, but the skimmer kept moving, and finally the sounds of shooting faded.

The skimmer jerked to a stop. The others must have stayed with them, because Fedron was swearing loudly.

"We should consider ourselves lucky," Father growled. "Take Chenna across to the medical center. It doesn't look bad, but you'd better make sure. Nekantor, get up, we're here."

Here? Nekantor checked the corner of his eye: black silk, Imbati legs moving past the skimmer. The Conveyor's Hall. His knuckles were white, clenched on his trousers, and didn't want to come open. Opening them hurt; so did sitting up. Just a little farther and he'd be safe. His fingers shook, undoing the seatbelt. The Conveyor's Hall was full of Imbati, moving in regular patterns. Fedron and his Chenna had gone, and it was only Father and his Sorn now.

"Come *on*, Nekantor," Father said, and to the Imbati nearby, "You, you, and you, with us, now."

They walked fast between the buildings but found no one lying in wait. The Household left them inside the entrance of the east wing, and Sorn checked each curtain while they walked. When the suite door finally closed behind them, it was so satisfying. Nekantor felt his chest relax; he pushed into the sitting room and took a deep breath. *Never again*—that must never, never happen again!

"Serjer!" he called. "Contact the Eminence's Cohort—I must have new bodyguards. Tell them to send three, right away."

"New bodyguards?" Pyaras had been sitting in one of the chairs. He stood up, frowning. "What happened? Where's Veriga?"

He hadn't expected Pyaras, but his cousin would be useful now. "What did you learn about Arissen?" he asked.

Pyaras frowned. "Why should I tell you?"

"I need a new bodyguard. You'll help me choose."

"When the sun rises in Pelismara," Pyaras snorted. "Tell me what happened to Veriga!"

Father was out of breath, stumping in behind him. "Veriga's been—poisoned. They took—took him—to the Residence medical center."

"Heile's mercy!" Pyaras looked like he'd been punched in the stomach. "I—I'd better go see him."

Nekantor blinked at him. "Why, in Varin's name?"

"Because I'm nicer than you!" Pyaras dashed through the vestibule curtain, and the front door clicked open and shut.

"He's a fool," Nekantor said.

"*You're* the fool," Father snapped. He paused for breath. "You threw away a vote today. You could have had a fine partner. But instead you acted like a complete idiot. We won't get a better offer from the Sixth Family."

Three votes instead of four. *Only three.* Nekantor closed his fists. "You don't know that."

"What kind of assets do you think we have?" Father demanded, red-faced. "We have no pretty young ladies to offer up in the name of getting this job done. We don't even have Tamelera to flirt with those rock-toads. No one in this house is any use anymore." He started coughing and sat down in one of the guest couches. Sorn stepped quickly out the dining room door and returned with a glass of water. Father drank, coughed, drank again, and sighed, "Much better." But anger still clouded his face.

Nekantor frowned. There *was* a way through this game, into the center. It would require a new bodyguard, and Pyaras would help with that. Something lurked in the assassination attempts—a pattern for sure, so he'd have to get more information on today's attacks. Father was right about one thing: success would require as much currency in the Society as they could muster. But he'd learned something else to-day, too—that partnerships were a form of currency. And if that was the case . . .

"Father, Aloran has no partner yet," he said. "He could be an asset."

Father's face changed: anger to interest. He set down his glass. "That's better, son. That's the kind of thinking we need. Sorn, fetch me Aloran's contract." Then he smiled. "Nekantor, maybe your mother can be useful after all."

CHAPTER TWENTY

Master and Lady

C lean. Aloran pulled on a fresh shirt, and it felt so good—clean at last. He owed a serious debt of gratitude to Serjer for handling extra foot assignments in the last two days, not to mention for bringing him these clothes; also to Keeper Premel for sending in meals to young Master Tagaret's rooms; and not least to his Lady for allowing him to take a shower in the young Master's own bathroom. He started combing back his hair.

"Aloran, Aloran—come quick!"

He dropped his comb on the marble counter and ran out. Lady Tamelera stood with quivering hands stretched out to him.

"Lady, what is it?"

"Tagaret's sweating—he's so wet. Is he all right?"

Could it be? Heart beating fast, Aloran donned a new pair of treatment gloves and sat by Tagaret's side. Lady Tamelera breathed anxiously behind him, leaning so close her long hair brushed the back of his shoulder. He made another check.

The boy's temperature had come down by almost five degrees. Last night, even strong medication had barely reduced it by two. Tagaret was sodden with sweat, but he was breathing deeply now. Was it safe to hope?

"Lady . . ." When he turned, he found her gazing down with such pleading eyes that he spoke in spite of himself. "I think it's good news."

"Oh, Aloran!"

But if she were to be disappointed, the responsibility would lie on his shoulders. He gaze-gestured apology, despite her ignorance of the Imbati codes. "Please, Lady, be careful," he said. "He'll be weak, and until he wakes, we can't test him for damage."

Lady Tamelera gulped and looked aside. "Well, maybe he's lucky he got sick," she said softly. "When I think of what they would have done to him, in the name of making him Heir—maybe the damage would have been worse."

At that moment, the public door opened. Lady Tamelera straightened fast.

It was the Master himself, with Sorn at his shoulder, and young Master Nekantor beside him. The Lady took two steps forward as if to block their way in. Aloran made himself busy with a towel, drying some of the sweat that soaked Tagaret's hair and clothes, but he still kept a cautious eye on them.

"Hello, Garr," Lady Tamelera said.

"Dear, how are you?" Grobal Garr rubbed his chin. "I thought we should bring you the latest news—there were three separate attempts on Nekantor's life this morning."

The Lady made a low sound of discomfort. "That's—not unexpected," she said. "Nekantor, darling, I'm glad you're all right."

Young Master Nekantor shrugged. "The Families are fighting this Selection very hard," he said. "We just now received word that Menni of the Second Family jumped out of the path of a skimmer, and Gowan of the Ninth Family escaped death because the two men assigned to kill him started fighting each other for the privilege."

Aloran blinked in disbelief. The Grobal were terribly determined to kill each other. No wonder it was such a struggle keeping them alive.

"Those young men were fortunate," said Lady Tamelera. "But I know you wouldn't come in here just to tell me *that*. What do you want?"

"No temper, now, dear," said the Master, coming close to her. "How is Tagaret doing?"

"Better."

"Really? That's wonderful!" He put an arm around her stiff body and squeezed. Then he gave young Master Nekantor a confidential smile that sent chills down Aloran's back. "If we're lucky, he might even become an asset."

"An excellent one," young Master Nekantor agreed.

"I see how it goes." The Lady took a step backward, away from them, and crossed her arms. "Garr, *tell me what you want*."

Aloran swallowed. Only days ago he would have found her pose aggressive, the intensity of her voice terrifying. Now it didn't feel powerful enough. Why hadn't he realized that the Master might come in when Tagaret's condition improved? Why couldn't he have dressed his Lady more formally than in a simple gown and house robe? He assumed bodyguard's stance behind her shoulder, but nothing could be done about the fact that he hadn't tied his hair back. Sorn had noticed it—the senior servant was watching with a glint in his eyes.

"I think I'll sit down," the Master said.

Sorn appropriated the Lady's chair at the foot of the bed, and the Master huffed himself down in it, gesturing above his shoulder. Sorn placed a heavy paper, dense with print, into his Master's hand, and the glint in his eyes grew to a vengeful smile.

Aloran couldn't move. Heile help him—Sorn hadn't retaliated before because he'd been waiting for *this*.

The Master said, "Just sign right here for me, dear, that's all."

Tamelera's whole body tensed. "Nicely done, Garr. But Aloran is mine. I suppose now that you've got your paws on his contract, you're not concerned that I got my key back. But you haven't changed anything. The Courts will uphold my right."

His contract? Sorn had used the key to steal *his contract* out of the Lady's diary? Aloran almost clenched his fists, and had to breathe himself back to calm. She was right: *laws are small comfort.*

"This is for the good of the Family, Mother," said young Master Nekantor. "We already know the Sixth Family is seeking an alliance . . ."

"And other opportunities will present themselves," the Master agreed, "even if the Sixth proves a lost cause. I'm sure Aloran will be very attractive to *someone*. We just need your signature to permit the arrangement."

Lady Tamelera's harsh breathing recalled him to his duty. Aloran placed his hands firmly against her back, as he had for young Tagaret when they came under attack in the street. *Lady, I am here to defend you.*

"I refuse," she said.

"Of course you do, dear," said Grobal Garr. "That's because you don't understand how important this is. Families come together during Heir Selection. It's not *me*; any of your old cousins in the Eleventh would demand the same. I'd prefer not to have to forge your signature, but we don't have a lot of time. You may as well leave off the histrionics."

She'd been taught no breath exercises to keep calm—Aloran ached to hear her trying so hard. Suddenly she turned to him with agony in her face. "Aloran," she whispered. "What do *you* want? Would you be willing to—" her voice failed.

Aloran blushed. What he wanted made no difference, but she asked—*she actually asked*. "I will abide by whatever you decide, Lady, and be content," he said. "I have pledged my love to your service. Partnership is only obligation. Love is the jewel locked in the heart."

Lady Tamelera gasped as if he'd hit her.

Oh, by Sirin and Eyn, why had he said that? He wanted to fall at her feet, but didn't dare move with the others watching. *I'm sorry, Lady, I'm sorry . . .*

"Give me the contract," Lady Tamelera said, in a faint voice. "And a pen."

The Master chuckled. "That's better, dear. Sorn?"

Aloran swallowed as Sorn came closer. The senior servant placed the paper in the Lady's left hand, the pen in her right, and took a single step back.

She stared down at the paper.

Don't sign it, Lady. What he wanted might not matter, but he knew already what *she* wanted, and vocation demanded that he make her wishes his own. Should he object? He would be sorely punished. What would young Master Tagaret think, when he learned that his father had pushed his mother to this while he lay by?

Lady Tamelera breathed so fast he feared she might faint. She set her back to Grobal Garr and turned to *him* instead.

"Aloran, take this." She pushed the contract into his hand. "Under no circumstances are you to give it back, either to Garr, to Nekantor, to Imbati Sorn, or any Imbati marked to either one of them, now or in perpetuity. Swear it."

"I—I swear to uphold your command, Lady."

"Varin gnash you to bits!" roared Grobal Garr, surging to his feet. "What is this behavior?"

Lady Tamelera didn't move, but closed her eyes instead. "Garr," she said. "Please don't wake Tagaret. He's been very ill and needs to sleep."

Grobal Garr growled.

"Fah," said young Master Nekantor. "I told you she was useless." He stalked out the door. The Master gave his Lady a dangerous look, then lumbered after him. Sorn went last, pulling the door silently shut.

Suddenly, Aloran realized he was almost in his Lady's face. He stepped away, folded his contract into a pocket against his back, and bowed to the floor.

Lady Tamelera paced the room as though it were too small to contain her. Once, she paused at the head of the young Master's bed, and murmured, "Oh, Tagaret, you'll never believe—" But then she broke off and didn't speak again.

Aloran waited, head down. Dread crept upon him. They had both made a terrible error. He'd always known that an arranged partnership lay in his future—the Master might have bad judgment in such matters, but surely, defying him was not worth the risk. How much of the Lady's defiance had truly been her own, and how much had been her concern for his wishes? What terrible presumption he was guilty of, allowing her to act as if he mattered! Because of him, she'd presumed to deny the Master his will.

Nothing good ever came of presumption.

"Lady," he said. "I beg you, please don't ever consider me again."

She didn't answer. After a minute's silence, he heard the service call bell and Serjer's answering voice.

"Yes, Mistress?"

"Aloran could use your help, if you have time. I'd like to see Tagaret in some fresh clothes, and the bed needs to be changed."

Aloran stood up, but Serjer had seen him in his abject position, and approached with gaze-gestures of concern. Aloran sent back silent reassurances and gave him a pair of treatment gloves for safety. Together, they moved the bedside table out of the way, changed young Master Tagaret into a clean nightshirt, stripped the bed around him, and redid the sheets without causing him too much disturbance. As they tucked a new sheet over him, the young Master smiled in his sleep. That smile leapt to Aloran's own face before he could stop it.

Serjer paused. He wore the same smile in his eyes. "Aloran, sir," he whispered. "We shall never be able to repay you for this."

"It is my duty, Serjer," said Aloran.

"Nevertheless."

It was difficult to be alone with his Lady after Serjer left. Realigning the bedside table didn't take long, and young Master Tagaret needed less tending, which only made it harder to escape Tamelera's gaze when she addressed him face-to-face, rather than allowing him to disappear safely behind her shoulder. Aloran tried hard to find his old silence, but since she now appeared to think nothing of speaking to him directly, both courtesy and service demanded that he reply. At last he bowed to her.

"Lady, would it please you to have me brush your hair?"

Her blue eyes lit. "Yes, please. Would you style it as well?"

"Certainly."

Thank Heile for hairbrushes. Returning behind her at last, Aloran felt the weight of attention lift from his shoulders. He began with short strokes, to chase away the tangles, and shifted to long strokes once all the knots were gone. He nudged her toward a style made popular in the Erin Society, which would require numerous small, interwoven braids.

"There were two days like this in the last Selection," she remarked after a time.

He separated out another of her tresses and divided it with a comb. Fortunately, this wasn't an issue he could speak to.

"Lady Selemei once told me that the day after the Round of Twelve is always bad," she said. "More of the Families perceive that they have a personal stake, and there are only a few free votes to go around. Nobody would ever resort to killing when there were only two candidates left, because no one wants to start over—but last time, there was that second day, after the Round of Eight." She shifted, as if tempted to look at him. "I still shudder when I think of it—they killed my cousin Dest, and almost killed Garr, too."

Aloran shook his head. Grobal Dest of the Eleventh Family already held an uncomfortable place in his memory, but . . . "The Master?" he asked.

"Yes. He was leading the First Family Council at the time. They had a twelve-year-old candidate who was eliminated early, and Garr went out to negotiate with Herin of the Third Family. Garr and I had been fighting because I hadn't achieved another pregnancy, so he left me at home with the boys—Tagaret was only six, Nekantor four and already a struggle. When I heard they had come under attack . . . that was the first time I ever wished Garr might die."

Aloran winced. He tried to immerse himself in the regular motions of braiding.

The Lady sighed. "Of course, when I learned that he'd been shot, I hated myself for thinking it. I took Garr to the medical center, and he cursed Fedron's Chenna all the way there. It wasn't her fault, though. She'd only just been marked. He hadn't taken enough people, somehow—I have no idea where Sorn was."

Aloran's fingers stopped. He forced them to start again and tied the braid off. She had no idea where Garr's Sorn was, on the very day that Grobal Dest was killed? He could practically see Master Ziara's stare penetrating all the way from the Academy. He hadn't sworn, but this was a perfect opportunity for him to investigate—and yet, he *had* sworn to keep the content of their conversation under oath. And he mustn't deceive his Lady . . . He swallowed. "Lady?"

"Yes?"

"The Master's Sorn, he—he frightens me."

Lady Tamelera didn't answer at first. After a time she sighed, "Oh, Aloran. He frightens me, too."

Aloran started another braid. "If you'll forgive me, I think it's because he's so much like the Master. I don't mean to say he shouldn't be his master's man . . ."

"My Eyli used to say that." Tamelera nodded. "*Sorn is his master's man*—and he is, Aloran. In so many ways." She shuddered. "I hate his eyes."

"Lady, the Gentleman's training does teach a person always to watch."

"Perhaps, but not like that. They're like two halves of the same twisted, ambitious man." She shrugged. "I suppose, whatever Garr achieves, Sorn shares the benefit, so why should Sorn ever leave his side if he hasn't been sent?"

"Do you think—" Aloran's throat tightened, but he went on anyway. "Do you think on that day, he might have been—sent?"

Lady Tamelera sat bolt upright and turned to face him. The unfinished braid pulled out of his fingers.

He dropped his chin to his chest. "Lady, I'm sorry."

"Aloran, look at me."

He tried. He couldn't bear to raise his eyes above the level of her mouth.

"I had the same thought," she said. "Especially after we spoke to the police. Garr and Herin both told them that Sorn had been with him the entire time, but Garr has a scar on his arm that says otherwise. I should have said something, but . . ."

"It would have been presumption," Aloran murmured.

She nodded. "I still should have said something. They questioned several Venorai in connection with the murder, I'm not sure why—something about the weapon. Garr still keeps the records in his office files. Dest was a cousin, and a decent man. Once he was gone, Garr shut my family out one person at a time until only Lienne and Doret were left. But then we left for Selimna, and Lienne Fell—and Doret was only ever Garr's friend.

"I *should* have said something, even if I wasn't sure it would make any difference. Even if I knew the consequences." She leaned slightly to one side and raised a hand to her half-finished hair. "This looks beautiful so far. I'm sorry I interrupted you."

"It's nothing, Lady."

"Aloran, may I ask you something?"

"Of course, Lady."

"May I have a pair of your gloves? If I had gloves, maybe you and I could care for Tagaret together—would it be safe enough?"

"It would be safe enough."

Tamelera smiled.

It was during the second time that they cared for him together—well after Aloran had finished his careful braiding and wound the whole into a stylized knot at the nape of her neck—that the Master returned. This time he came without young Master Nekantor, only with Sorn behind his shoulder.

"Tamelera," he said.

Now they would see the consequences of their earlier defiance. Aloran stood, gathering himself to defend his Lady as best he could—but instead of readying her anger, Lady Tamelera shrank. She drew away from the young Master's sleeping form and removed her gloves without touching their outside surfaces, precisely as he had instructed her.

"Yes, Garr?" she said.

The Master said nothing, and Lady Tamelera froze, as if caught in the frigid exhalation of a crevasse. Suddenly she said, "Aloran, you are excused."

Aloran gulped in shock. *Excused*, now? She was even avoiding his eyes—an ache sank all the way from his throat into the pit of his stomach. "Lady—young Master Tagaret?"

"He'll be fine for a little while."

He couldn't reasonably plead with her, though he wanted to. "Shall I run any foot assignments, Lady?" he asked.

She flicked the tiniest glance in his direction. "Yes, please. While I speak to Garr for a few moments, please just fetch what we discussed earlier."

"Yes, Lady." As he turned away, he could feel the Master's eyes, and Sorn's eyes, burning on his back; every step he took tried to pull him back to her side. He stepped out into the Maze hall and shut the door behind him.

Alone in the dim light, he breathed a pattern against his dismay. She trusted him now, didn't she? She knew she was in trouble, so why hadn't she let him stay? And now she wanted him to fetch *what they'd discussed?*

Merciful Heile—was she standing alone against Garr and Sorn so that he could investigate the murder?

A terrible gift, but he could not refuse it. While he still wore treatment gloves, he would leave no fingerprints. He walked swiftly to the Maze door of the Master's office and let himself in. Garr had obviously spent late nights here—the desk was covered with a mess of papers, and a couch against the wall opposite bore a rumpled sheet, and a dent in the shape of the Master's heavy body. Lady Tamelera had said the information was in the Master's files, so he turned to the metal cabinet in the corner and began sorting through. A minute passed too quickly. How long would he be safe in here?

Fortunately, these files were neater than the desk, organized by year, and the Master had made no effort to hide the file, which had not implicated him anyway. The Arissen reports, mostly in print with a few handwritten notes, would have taken too long to peruse thoroughly, so Aloran turned to the back for the photographs.

Three innocent Venorai laborers had had their strange, sunmarked faces captured, and beside those images was the reason why: the murder weapon. He'd heard talk of the long-range crossbows that Venorai used for game-hunting out on the surface, but he had never seen one, nor seen the projectiles they launched.

Except he had.

The last photograph showed a smooth steel bolt, with a tip like a screwdriver—a precise copy of the object he'd seen in Sorn's desk. Mai strike him, *he'd actually done it!*

Aloran shut the file quickly and replaced it in its drawer. Getting back to his Lady was all that mattered now. He shut the Maze door carefully behind him, hurried back to the door of Tagaret's room, and flicked on the service speaker.

Silence.

He waited several seconds, and at last pushed the door open. The young Master still lay in his bed, sleeping. The rest of the room was empty.

His heart faltered. Sirin and Eyn—where was she?

He stripped off his treatment gloves, tossed them into the young Master's garbage chute, and ran out. Taking the Maze corner too fast, he almost stumbled over Serjer when the First Houseman emerged from his room.

"Serjer, I'm so sorry!"

Serjer's look changed quickly to one of alarm. "Is it the young Master?"

"No, no—it's T—it's the, my, Lady Tamelera—I can't find her . . ." The words came out panicked and wrong. "The Master came, she sent me away, and when I came back—Serjer, where is she?"

Serjer's face smoothed to a disturbing calm. "She hasn't left the house, and she's not in the sitting room," he said gravely. "I would guess the master bedroom." He gaze-gestured discomfort, looking aside and down. "But be careful."

Aloran ran. He should never have left her. *How could she have asked him to leave?* Even if she'd decided to pursue the question of Grobal Dest, they could have investigated it another time. She'd known what was going to happen—she'd known it would be bad. Why would she send him away when she knew she needed help?

He dashed into his room. No way to let her know he was here, but if she was on the other side of this wall and needed him, surely she would call. He flicked on the speaker beside the door with the crescent-moon handle, praying to hear her voice, even if it were raised in anger—

Instead, out of the speaker came a bestial, rhythmic grunting.

Nausea swept over him; his entire body shook with rage.

Oh, my Lady! My Lady!

CHAPTER TWENTY-ONE

Change Everything

In this dream, too, Mother was crying.

Not another nightmare—Tagaret shifted, trying to escape it. No more assassins, no more rockfalls, no more, no more . . . Mother was crying, and he wanted to go to her, but his body felt too heavy to move, all his energy drained out of him into the darkness. A low, passionate voice spoke.

"Please, don't try to protect me. Let me suffer before you put yourself at risk!"

The voice was uncanny—it teased him with familiarity, yet somehow he'd never heard anything like it. Mother cried and didn't answer.

"Let *me* protect *you*," the voice pleaded.

Mother struggled with sobs. "Eighteen years," she said, and drew a shuddering breath. "It will never change. You can't protect me."

"What am I for, if not for that? Please let me try. If they punish me, then let me be punished!"

"So what if you *do* protect me? He'll only come for me later when I'm alone. You can't be with me every second."

Was Mother in danger? Tagaret tried to speak, and failed. The effort made his heart pound—a strange feeling, too real for a dream. The voices fell silent. Exhaustion tried to drag him down, but then the pleading voice spoke again.

"Why can't I? I could be your shadow, if you willed it."

After a long while, Mother whispered haltingly. "I—want you to be."

"Ohh," the voice sighed.

"But . . ." She hesitated. "What do *you* want?"

"Why must you still ask me?"

"Because I need to know. Please—please. Tell me what you want."

The voice answered near tears. "Only what I've always wanted. To love you, and to give myself to you totally."

Sirin and Eyn—was someone *real* saying such things to Mother? Tagaret opened his eyes and said, "Who—?"

"Tagaret!" Mother cried. She leaned over him, her beautiful face streaked with tears. Lights were on in the vaults of the ceiling, and a wysp drifted behind her head.

Was he in *bed?* When had he gotten into bed? "Mother?" he said, tried to sit, and fell back exhausted. The nightmare lassitude was real, too . . .

"Tagaret, love, speak to me. Are you all right?"

"What happened?" But then it started coming back: the gathering before the Round of Twelve, the dizziness, the sense of choking—Mother's Aloran stabbing him in the leg . . . His heart started pounding again, and he stammered, "M-mercy—Kinders fever?"

"Oh, my love, my darling . . ." Mother stroked his hair; her hand wore a medical glove. "You're all right now. How do you feel?"

Like his bones were made of water . . . "Bad."

"Aloran, may I touch him yet?"

"Not yet, if you will forgive me, Lady," said Aloran, in that perfectly calm tone that only Imbati seemed to achieve. "Permit me, young Master?"

"Yes."

Aloran sat beside him, wrapped a strong arm around his back and lifted. Hard to believe he couldn't even sit up—the weakness was awful, but at least breathing came easily, and the dizziness was gone. When Aloran brought a cup close to his lips, he sipped. Water, with something medicinal in it. It ran cold down his throat and woke such a thirst that he gulped the entire thing. His stomach felt cavernously empty.

"Gods, I'm hungry," he said.

"Wonderful," said Mother. "I'll ring for Serjer."

Serjer and Premel came together, with such ceremony that they might have been presenting a feast, instead of just broth. The broth was perfect—just slightly hot in his throat, so delicious it woke even the tips of his toes.

"Thank you," Tagaret sighed.

"Oh, young Master, sir," said Premel, "please tell us now you've not gone deaf or blind, and ease us all our worry?"

Tagaret raised his eyebrows. "I don't think so." Glancing past Aloran's shoulder, he discovered disturbing things on the bedside table—bottles of medicine, cloths, and needles. He gulped.

"Blessing of Heile!" Premel exclaimed.

"We couldn't be more pleased, young Master," said Serjer, and smiled at him. He and Premel left through the Maze door.

Tagaret stared at his hands in his lap, grateful for the solidity of Aloran's arm. He wiggled his fingers experimentally. They felt better and better, but they looked different—maybe thinner? This wasn't right. Why was he alone with Mother and the Household? Why was nobody asking him to hurry?

"Mother," he said. "How bad was it?"

"Oh, Tagaret, love." Her blue eyes searched his face; they were tired and red, and she looked about to cry again. "Without Aloran, you would have died. He's hardly left your side for two whole days."

"Two days?" Tagaret turned his head. Aloran looked away, but the support of his arm never wavered.

"The epidemic was transmitted at the Accession Ball," Mother said. "It has affected everyone. Twenty people are now dead across the Pelismara Society."

Horror stabbed through him. "Twenty?" He didn't want to think it, but the awful possibilities multiplied. His cousins? His friends? *Della?* Oh, sweet Heile!

Mother scooted her chair closer and laid her hand in its medical glove gently over his. "We've lost your cousin Inkala," she said. "And we've had sad news from the Eleventh Family . . . your friend, Fernar—"

Tagaret couldn't speak. His mind wouldn't grasp it. Inkala had just been betrothed. And he could still see Fernar's confident eyes, his dark hair swept back for the Ball, the portrait of an Heir candidate. Fernar was strong and fast; he couldn't be dead, he couldn't be . . .

"My Lady," said Aloran. "Perhaps we shouldn't—"

"No!" Tagaret cried. "I have to know all of it. Who else? Pyaras? Reyn? Gowan? Della?"

"Pyaras had a miraculous recovery, and has been coming by every day worried about you," said Mother. "Reyn is—very ill. We have no news of him since he took the fever."

"Gods—oh, gods . . ." His body started shaking.

"To my knowledge young Lady Della has been untouched, as has Gowan, who now represents the Ninth Family in the Selection."

So *they* weren't gone. There was some mercy left. But Fernar! And Reyn, oh, don't let Elinda take Reyn! *When do we get to be together again?* Never, never . . .

His eyes burned, but he had no strength to cry. The grief merged into the awful weakness that held him down. He took Mother's hand tightly in both of his, and closed his eyes.

The sound of the Maze door awakened him. Serjer and Premel carried in a small table, then lifted him to sit, propping him into the corner with pillows. At least sitting didn't make his heart race this time.

"Where's Aloran?" Tagaret asked. "Is this breakfast?"

"Dinner, young Master," said Serjer. "Aloran is serving your mother in her bath."

"As should've been long since," Keeper Premel agreed, his broad mouth quirking in a smile. "We're setting up until they've finished, young Master, such time when they'll join you to eat."

"Oh."

Mother did look clean and a bit less upset when she came in. What a sorry pair they made, with him in bed and her sitting sad and tired at the table. The Keeper had made him some kind of special concoction: a fruit-and-grain porridge that tasted like it contained meat broth. When his arms tired of using the spoon, Tagaret nearly cried in frustration. Without a word, Aloran sat beside him and fed him like a baby.

"Tagaret," said Mother. "I'm sorry to mention this after everything you've had to take tonight, but it's very important that I tell you what's happened in the Selection."

He nodded. "They didn't delay it, did they."

"No. The Families simply scrambled for substitutes—First Family included." She pressed her lips together for a moment. "Nekantor has taken your place."

"*Nekantor?*" He stared in disbelief—but clearly his ears were working fine. His heart started banging against the inside of his chest. "He can't have—Mother, he *can't!*"

She shook her head. "I'd have thought Erex had better judgment, but it's done. Garr seems to have put aside their disputes enough to support him all the way. He's already passed through into the Round of Eight."

"But it's not possible. Mother, Nekantor can't be Heir—he's insane."

Mother looked startled. "Tagaret, what a thing to say about your brother. Nekantor might be—"

"I know. He's headstrong, particular, and vindictive, just like Father. But it's more than that. You haven't been here for the last five years. I swear to you, there's something wrong with him."

"No." Her eyes went wide and filled with tears. "It can't be."

Tagaret frowned. Why wouldn't Mother believe him?

"Forgive me, young Master," Aloran said. "Your brother walks only on the black tiles in your bathroom. Isn't that what you told me?"

Tagaret looked at him. "When?"

"I'm sorry, sir—it was during your delirium. Might I presume to request you tell me more, now that you are well?"

"Yes." Tagaret took a deep breath. "He walks on the black tiles and gets angry if I stop him. He touches his clothes, and counts things, over and over. He doesn't want me to lock my door—he's systematically broken fourteen locks before this one. Once he went around muttering for several hours that his window shade was crooked, and then Serjer discovered he'd taken a knife to it. But the real danger is that he'll hurt people. He bullies and manipulates, is never sorry, and never seems to get caught. He tortures Imbati. I had to warn our caretakers never to enter his room because he would scream and hit them if they changed anything."

Mother wasn't looking at him anymore. She pressed one hand hard against her mouth. Aloran looked grave.

"You know what it is, don't you, Aloran."

"Young Master," said Aloran, "The cruelties you describe are worrisome, but I can't speak to them with any medical certainty. The rest, however: repetitive behaviors, a craving for sameness—these are symptoms of compulsive obsession, which can be treated. Perhaps, if we could get him evaluated—"

"Don't tell your father!" Mother cried out.

Tagaret jerked in shock, and his heart started racing again.

Aloran slid off the bed and folded facedown on the floor.

"Aloran?" Tagaret asked, baffled. "Mother, what's going on?"

"Aloran, please get up," said Mother softly. "It's not your fault—you would see the truth if anyone would." Her eyes turned up to Tagaret. "You have to understand, love. It's far too late to hide him. If that became public, imagine the blow to the First Family's reputation." She sighed. "It would ruin me completely."

Aloran got up on his knees, but kept his face lowered.

"Mother," Tagaret said, "we can't just do nothing and let him win the Selection. With that kind of power I don't know what he might do."

She frowned. "If he's as bad as you say, he won't win anyway."

Tagaret shook his head, with a sick feeling in his stomach. "I wish you were right. Nek might be crazy, but he's not stupid. He schemes. You said Erex is supporting him? Well, there's only one possible explanation for that: Nekantor must have forced him, by some kind of threat."

Mother grimaced. "He *is* just like your father."

"I have to tell Father. Nobody else could possibly withdraw Nek from the Selection. Father would never tell anyone outside the family, but we can't let Nek do this."

"Finish your food," Mother said.

He couldn't argue with that. The food was having a marvelous effect in his stomach, and he picked up his spoon with new energy. No way was he talking to Father while still hungry and unable to move.

But it had to be done.

Mother refused to stay, and took Aloran with her. Tagaret took several deep breaths, and swung his feet down so he sat on the edge of his bed. Stupid, how wobbly he was, but it made him feel better prepared for Father—so long as Father came soon.

He didn't have to wait. Father stumped in the door without knocking, wearing a smile and a pair of new gray gloves; the bed rocked when he sat down, and Tagaret hung on with both hands.

"Tagaret! Son, I'm so glad to see you up and awake. We have business to discuss."

"Yes, we do," Tagaret said firmly. "You have to take Nekantor out of the Selection."

Father burst out laughing. "Jealous, eh? Well, I can't help you there, I'm afraid. Kinders fever made that decision for us. You'll be happy to know that your brother is doing a fine job."

Varin gnash Father! Anger surged through him; when it ebbed, it left weakness in its wake. He should have remembered that dealing with Father was like trying to shovel through rock. Tagaret gripped his knees with both hands. "Father," he said. "You have to withdraw Nekantor from Selection. He can't be Heir, he's merciless."

"Well, so much the better."

"Father, *no*. I mean, what the Kartunnen call it—he's a, a psychopath."

"Tagaret!" Father snapped. "I couldn't reinstate you if I wanted to. I can understand you're disappointed, but that's taking it too far. Mind your manners."

"You're not listening," Tagaret insisted. "Nekantor has mental defects. That's not the only one. You can't tell me you haven't noticed the way he fiddles with his clothes, or the way he's obsessed with breaking down my door."

For a split second, it looked like he'd reached him—fear came into Father's eyes. Then Father lurched up from the bed and roared.

"Gnash you, Tagaret, you will never ever speak to me like that again!"

"But, Father—"

Father swung his arm back. Tagaret panicked, lost his grip on his knees, and tumbled off the edge of the bed onto the carpet. He flung both arms up over his head.

The blow never came.

"Sorn!" Father barked. "Get him back in bed. The fever hasn't fully left him; that's clear."

Tagaret tried to get up by himself—Sorn's help was the last thing he wanted—but Sorn was too fast. With the servant's iron hands under his arms, he made it back into bed and collapsed against his pillows. His heart refused to calm.

"Now, you listen to me," Father said. "If the First Family is going to win, we're going to need your help."

He should say no. Would Father hit him if he said no?

"The Sixth Family has already come to us looking for an alliance, and we weren't able to offer it to them. If we send a message tonight, maybe they'd reinstate the deal."

Tagaret's stomach flipped. "Sixth Family?"

"It's not that bad. The girl is pretty, and a vote is a vote."

"*What* girl?"

"Della, I think her name was. Enwin's daughter."

Tagaret gulped; blood rushed into his face. To say yes would be to cave in to Father—but this was *Della*—but on the other hand, an arrangement like that would only push Nekantor further ahead, and Nekantor must be stopped . . .

Father seemed to take his silence as permission. "That's it, son. You'll be a great asset to our chances." Sorn produced paper and pen, and Father wrote a note. "Run that over to Doross right away, if you would. Stay to relay any reply."

"Wait," Tagaret called, but Sorn didn't turn back.

Tagaret lay limp and guilty, listening to Father talk about oh, how brilliant Nekantor had been in the Round of Twelve, how Arissen Veriga had done a good job, but had gotten poisoned and they hadn't yet replaced him.

Tagaret couldn't stop his mind flying after Sorn, guiltily yearning for Della. Della, Della—her fragrant hair, her strong and graceful hands, her sweet lips—her feet dancing to her sister's yojosmei in a room of lights and gold. Maybe he'd fallen into a real dream, because Sorn reappeared far too quickly.

Sorn bowed. "Master, they say no."

"No?" Tagaret clutched his covers. He might as well have fallen through the cavern floor into the chill waters of the Endro. "*No?*"

"Never mind," Father said. "There are other Families, and more votes will free up after the Round of Eight. You'll be just as useful then."

"Father, wait—"

Father heaved himself up off the bed. "Rest up, Tagaret. That's the best thing you can do right now. Nobody will want to partner with an invalid." He and Sorn walked out.

Tagaret lay shaking. Every thought of Della filled him with anguish. *How could they have said no?* Was it the fever that had ruined him in their eyes?

Someone knocked on the Maze door. Serjer looked in cautiously, then hurried to his side. "Young Master," he murmured. "I've received a message for you."

"All right."

Serjer took reciting stance, but spoke softly. "To Tagaret of the First Family, from Enwin of the Sixth Family, greetings in a difficult time."

Tagaret gasped, "Enwin!"

"It is with joy that I hear of your recovery," Serjer went on. "The Head of our Council will not have informed you of the reason for his refusal. Against my wishes and her mother's, Della has been betrothed to candidate Innis of the Fifth Family. He waits only for success in the Selection to partner with her outright. Forgive my directness, to which I am forced by circumstance. Della loves you, but I can't stop this arrangement unless the First Family makes a more compelling counter-offer. I will appreciate any help you can give me. End message."

"Oh, Della!" Tagaret whispered. His weakened body suddenly felt as heavy as the layers of rock between him and the heavens far above. "Sirin and Eyn help me."

There was too little difference between nightmare and waking. Tagaret sat in bed, staring at the wall; he'd managed to get himself to the bathroom this morning, and after some dozing and some breakfast, into his clothes, but there seemed no point in doing anything else. Grief and fear stalked the corners of the room; whenever Mother opened the door, they leapt upon him, trying to tear him apart.

Mother opened the door again, and his stomach twisted, bracing for a new loss.

"It's all right, love," Mother said, sitting beside him and patting his knees. "I hate to see you like this. Would you like to go out?"

Go where? To watch Reyn dying? To console Fernar's parents? To barter for Della like a Melumalai? He curled away from her. "No. I can't see anyone."

"Not even Pyaras? He'd love to see you—he's been so concerned."

But Pyaras would ask how he was . . . "I can't."

Mother sat silent awhile. "Tagaret, I know Serjer came to speak with you last night. He made a point of telling me he's worried about you, after a message he brought."

"Della . . ." The word whispered out of him against his will. He pressed his lips shut.

Mother's eyes widened. She thought for a long time, and finally frowned. "Aloran," she said. "Where is Garr now?"

"At a meeting with Grobal Fedron, Lady."

"I'll need you to carry Tagaret. Have Serjer call ahead for a skimmer."

Tagaret sat up. "Mother, no . . ."

Mother nodded to Aloran, who bowed, and stepped out.

Soon, Tagaret found himself carried in Aloran's strong arms to the Conveyor's Hall. He tried only to look at the servant's dark hair—not to think of the day the Household had taken Reyn from him. Still, grief churned deep in his guts, remaining long after they had departed.

Aloran drove a long, winding route around any number of Selection detours, so it was impossible to guess what destination Mother intended. They climbed the familiar steep rampway to the fourth level, but didn't turn into the Melumalai districts, staying instead on the westbound circumference and turning off onto another level rampway. This ramp was wider, curving, rising between two melted columnar formations and through a tunnel to the third level.

Tagaret looked around, frowning. Third level neighborhoods were noticeably less dense, with occasional alleyways and courtyards between lines of buildings. They also didn't seem quite—*distinguished* enough, to cater to the nobility.

"Mother," he said. "What are we doing here?"

"Aloran, turn south," Mother said. "But don't pass Fyner Circumference, or we won't be able to catch the next rampway up."

"Yes, Lady."

Tagaret's throat clenched. "Mother—*up?*"

Mother looked him in the eye. "Your father can't stop us this time."

Mercy, she was taking him to see the sky, *now?* When he could scarcely walk?

Aloran drove as if he felt no fear, either for Mother or for himself. On the second level, their road ran beside the limestone banks of the Trao, all the way to a massive metal corkscrew which allowed the river to descend from first level to second. Climbing the rampway that curved behind it, Tagaret tried to stay calm by watching the rushing water, but then the cavern roof came down and they popped through a tunnel onto the first level.

The view here was enormous. What few buildings were visible were barns the length of city blocks, and between them lay raised beds of toremi shoots and river-lettuce, each the size of a whole neighborhood. He'd had no idea there were so many shinca trunks in all of Pelismara—but with walls no longer hiding them, they pierced up to the cavern roof all around. Strangest of all were at least four massive green columns, each as broad as one of the barns, which glowed eerily as though lit from within. Every person in sight wore the black leather belt of the Venorai, and every vehicle was a cargo skimmer. One passed by them, loaded with grain that radiated heat.

Aloran pulled over to the side of the road. "Lady, the Safe Harbor Road isn't navigable by skimmer," he said. "Do you wish to park at the gate and walk out?"

Tagaret shook his head. They weren't really doing this. They couldn't be.

"You'd have to carry Tagaret again," Mother said. "Surely there are other exits?"

"Mother, what if we just went to the gate and looked?" Tagaret suggested.

She frowned at him.

"But it's *morning*," he protested. "What about the sun?"

She studied his face. "Tagaret—when I felt alone and trapped, the sight of Mother Elinda brought me inspiration. Maybe a glimpse of Father Varin can do the same for you."

"I don't know . . ."

"Love, we can only try it and see. While we are still unwatched."

"Lady, I believe I can see where that grain skimmer came from," said Aloran. "With your permission, I'll try another way."

"Of course."

Aloran turned their skimmer left into another road, directly toward the nearest glowing green column. A second grain-filled cargo skimmer passed them. Slowly, the column took on detail. It wasn't really a column at all, but a heavy metal scaffold as high as the cavern roof, bursting with vegetation so its skeleton was near-invisible. As they drew closer, some of the leaves became identifiable. Tagaret gulped—they looked much more threatening here than on a plate.

A pair of hugely muscled Venorai men stood to either side of a bright rectangular opening in the column's base. They approached stiffly with eyes lowered, thumbs hooked into their black belts. Tagaret couldn't help staring: one man was as brown as the Venorai from the Accession Ball, but the other had strange brown blotches all over his face and arms, and even his fingers.

"May your honorable service earn its just reward, Imbati, sir," the blotchy man said.

"Venorai," Aloran replied, with a polite nod. "We wish to ascend."

To *ascend*? Tagaret looked more closely at the opening behind them. It was actually a huge cage, large enough for two cargo skimmers. An *elevator*? Gods . . .

"Imbati, sir," said the brown-skinned man. "Pardon us, but there are dangers above."

Mother flicked at her knee impatiently. "We are aware of this, Venorai."

Both men bowed backward, and Aloran drove straight into the metal box. Tagaret shivered in his seat, glancing at the solid metal roof above, and the glowing greenery all around the railed sides. Were they really doing this?

The cage jerked and lifted. The light flashed to a blinding blaze; the air became an oven. Tagaret's heart pounded, and he gulped huge breaths of heated air. He looked to Mother in a panic—and discovered she had utterly changed. She glowed bright as a goddess, her eyes blue as sapphires, her hair like liquid gold. Behind her, a brilliant emerald space opened—terrace upon terrace of living plants, where Venorai walked, thoughtless of being burned alive. The space widened, and at last the green walls disappeared, revealing golden fields an incomprehensible distance in every direction. The elevator stopped.

Aloran wordlessly engaged the skimmer's repulsion and drove them out of their last protection. The sky looked solid, like a bowl of blue steel. In the molten heat of the sun, even Imbati black wasn't black anymore—Aloran's hair was almost brown, and his suit gleamed with the red of Sirin the Luck-Bringer. It was too much. Tagaret flung an arm over his eyes, blinking tears of pain.

A sweet, shrill tune whistled into his ears, answered by another, fainter and more distant, and then another.

Music?

He raised his arm slightly. The skimmer had continued to move forward, and now the field on his left was full of Venorai. Their heads were covered by broad straw hats, and their arms were bare and muscular. They moved in teams of four across the heat-shimmering space, carrying humming machines that sucked in the heads of the grasses. Fragments of broken grass clung to the sweat on their sun-baked skin—skin in strange colors like deep brown, or splotchy, or red sprinkled with pepper.

How could there be music in a place like this?

The nearest harvest team was only two skimmer-lengths away when something glinted near them, light against light, and one of the team members shouted,

"Wysp!"

Instantly, the team turned off its grain-suckers and froze in place.

Squinting, Tagaret managed to discern two sparks whirling over the team, caught in a breeze that wasn't there.

Light footsteps pattered on the road behind him, and a lanky Venorai girl ran past their skimmer, hat bouncing against her back. She lifted a tin whistle to her lips and played a lilting tune—and the same tune echoed back from the opposite corner of the field.

Tagaret stared at her. Music couldn't possibly come from a less likely source.

The girl turned, and for a second, stared right back at him. Her eyes were the same deep brown as her long, gangly limbs. Then she turned to Aloran and said, "Imbati, sir, you're in fire danger."

Aloran didn't reply—but he did shift the skimmer into reverse, pulling them back slightly. Tagaret looked for fire, but there was nothing except the sun's heat, and the wysps.

"Tagaret," Mother whispered, taking his arm. "Look—more!"

She was right. Another wysp had appeared, and then came two more. *Five wysps*, in a single spot? No one in the Residence would believe it.

The Venorai harvest team split up, walking away fast through the beheaded stalks. A leathery man ran in from another field, taking a place below the wysps; he raised burn-scarred arms, then started walking slowly toward an empty section of the field. Half of the wysps followed him—but the others whirled faster, and suddenly wysps began converging on the spot as if sucked into a vortex. Sparks whirled and flashed, the air shimmered, and the grasses below them started to brown and curl. Wysps could *cause* fire? Tagaret held his breath in horror, anticipating an explosion. In this heat, what would keep fire from gnashing them all like the teeth of Varin? They would all die!

Venorai all over the field started shouting. Whistle girl shrilled an urgent tune.

Out of nowhere, Arissen appeared. Six of them converged on the wysp vortex with backpack fire extinguishers, and away in the distance, several more ran to a spot in an empty field. An electric zap sounded across the open air—the faraway Arissen had used some kind of weapon. Amid the distant, denuded stalks, black smoke billowed upward, full of hungry flames.

"Heile help us!" Mother cried.

"How could they?" Tagaret asked hoarsely. "Who would *set* a fire? Aloran, take us back!"

But before Aloran could react, the wysp vortex broke, venting wysps in a glittering swarm toward the faraway smoke. Whistle girl played another shrill melody, and the distant Arissen responded by doing something that caused hissing and even more smoke. Tagaret could hardly breathe—but then the Arissen extinguisher crew in the nearer field relaxed. Looking about, he could no longer see the swarming wysps, and slowly the faraway smoke began to diminish.

An Arissen woman with brown pepper across her red face left the extinguisher crew and approached.

"Sir! Lady!" she said, saluting. "With respect, I strongly suggest that you leave the fields at once. Harvest is an especially dangerous time."

Unexpectedly, Aloran spoke. "Lady, may we please?"

"Yes, of course, Aloran," Mother said. "Take us back."

They returned to the elevator. The metal cage jerked and started down again through the terraces of green.

Tagaret's heart still pounded. That had been more than a glimpse of Father Varin. How close they'd come to feeling his teeth! But the danger had passed, and they were here, alive, sweating, breathing, returning to a place that suddenly seemed dark and small. He took Mother's hand.

Mother squeezed his fingers and smiled. "We were brave, weren't we, Tagaret?"

"We were," he agreed. Somehow, bravery seemed only natural to this illuminated version of her, and maybe to him, too. He gazed at her all the way down, until the divine light faded from her features. "But, Mother?"

"Yes, love?"

"The Venorai were braver. As brave as the Arissen."

She nodded. "Yes, I think you're right."

"We're so lucky to be alive." A sense of terrible import thundered through his veins. His mind whirled with light and heat, flame and smoke, life and death like a swarm of wysps, dangerous and too fast to catch. The melody of the whistles still echoed in his ears. "Mother, you were right, too," he said. "This changes everything."

CHAPTER TWENTY-TWO

A Better Bet

It was distasteful, how Tagaret looked now—strange, and wrong. Nekantor couldn't stand to look at his too-bright eyes, his too-thin body. Let Pyaras be the one to suffer that view. Yes, let Pyaras cuddle in Tagaret's arm on the sitting room couch—so long as they helped him replace Arissen Veriga.

The inconceivable had happened: Tagaret had offered him a deal. *I'll convince Pyaras to help you, Nek, if you'll help me with the Sixth Family.* He'd told Benél, and Benél had laughed—laughed while pushing him down, while murmuring against the back of his neck, *That silly girl comes with a vote we need anyway! Your brother's an idiot.*

Benél was right. Tagaret was an idiot—but now, weakened by the fever, he'd become a useful one. More useful than Father, who was supposed to be here and wasn't.

"Well?" Nekantor demanded. "You said you'd help me, Pyaras."

Pyaras glared through his dark eyebrows. "They're not Veriga."

"Fah," Nekantor said. Of course they weren't Veriga. Yet they were *like* him, because any of these three could be killed. He needed them all, not just one. *Then* if one was shot, knifed, garroted, poisoned, the others would be there to take him home safely.

Tagaret spoke. "How *is* Veriga?"

Pyaras crumpled a little. "Not awake." He sighed. "He's had a lot of visitors from the Cohort, though. They care about him, Tagaret—and they've been really nice to me. You were right."

Tagaret squeezed his shoulders. "I was too hard on you. But I'm glad it's worked out as well as it has. May Heile bless him."

"Never mind all that, you're wasting time," Nekantor said. "These are Selection bodyguards, too. No better Arissen exist in Varin. Help me, or Tagaret doesn't get his girl."

"Fine," said Pyaras. "Ask them questions, then. That's all I do."

Nekantor snorted. "There are no questions for Arissen."

"Suit yourself."

Tagaret sat straighter. "Actually, I've got one. Do any of you play the whistle? I mean, the signal whistle?"

"Yes, sir," said the middle bodyguard, a woman.

"What kind of stupid question is that?" Nekantor demanded. Really, only one question mattered at all—the one that would show him a safe path to the center of the Selection. He tugged his vest and sleeves until they were straight. Shook off the idea of whistles, and spat out one question—not because it was a question for Arissen, but because it was the *only* question.

"The assassination attempts, Arissen. Poisoning, a sabotaged skimmer. Three shootings. A runaway skimmer. A knife in the leg. There's a pattern." He stopped in front of the first Cohort man. "What is the pattern?"

The Arissen stood straighter, but he didn't say a word. Who would expect intelligence from Arissen? Intelligence wasn't what they were for. Idiot Pyaras, why would he say to ask them questions? This was wasting time, when his interview with the Eminence was in less than an hour.

"Four, actually," said Tagaret.

Nekantor turned and saw Tagaret—back tired, arms tired, legs tired—made a face and looked away again. "What did you say?"

"Four shootings," Tagaret said. "*I* was targeted; Aloran got shot. It was the day after the Accession Ball."

Nekantor clenched his fists. "*Four?*" Gnash Tagaret—four changed the whole pattern. Ripples moved outward, disturbing everything. *Was* there still a pattern? But there *was* one, there had to be, or there could be no way to see where the next knife might come. He paced to the dining room door, to the double doors into the drawing room, around the game table, and back.

Pyaras muttered, "I bet sixteen orsheth whoever shot at Nek is sorry they missed."

One of the Arissen sniggered.

"Varin's teeth, Pyaras!" Nekantor snapped. Pyaras *liked* to make Arissen laugh at him—Veriga and now this man, each with some kind of bet. He wheeled and pointed at the nearest man. "You!"

The Arissen jumped to a salute, right hand to left shoulder.

"You place bets, do you?"

The Arissen gulped. "Yes, sir."

"And you two?" The other two stared into nothingness, silent. Unacceptable. "Answer, or I throw you out!"

The man and woman, in unison: "Yes, sir."

Betting—money, filthy money! He should have slapped them, but didn't want the feel of their animal sweat on his hands. He should have sent them all away, but new Arissen would be no different. Whistles . . . money . . . *He had to have a bodyguard, now.* He growled.

There came a sharp click of boot-heels: the Arissen woman snapping to attention.

"What is it?"

"Noble sir," she said. "All the assassination attempts you mentioned were for violent death, except one."

Nekantor narrowed his eyes. He peered past her perfect orange uniform. The woman's skin was a dark shade of brown, the color of surface work. Guarding farmers before she learned to guard the Eminence, so she knew how to move up, to take power when it was offered. Whistles or no whistles, she was right. All attempts violent except one.

Nekantor sucked in a breath, and the pattern pulled in another piece: one single violent attempt on the First Family had preceded the others, and the single stealth attempt, the poisoning, had targeted the First Family also.

Understanding made his hands shake.

The assassin sent for Tagaret, and the poisoner sent after *him*, had been sent by the same person. A violent attempt preceding, a stealth attempt after. One single person, who had to have known enough, and been scared enough, to attack the First Family even before the candidates were chosen and their worth known. There was only one such person.

The Eminence Herin.

Nekantor circled the room again. Herin would never kill a candidate while they sat face-to-face—he might bend the rules, but he wouldn't be obvious enough to get himself arrested for murder. The danger was before, and after. Especially after. Herin would lash out to cover fear or weakness, and the fear that had begun before the Round of Twelve would be worse now.

Seeing the pattern should have solved it, but now the pattern was clear, the traps visible, and the most dangerous one lay right before him, teeth open, impossible to avoid. How could he take a step? He couldn't count on the Eminence's assassins missing their mark a *third* time. Father knew this game better than any man save Herin himself. How dare he not be here?

"Gnash it! Gnash it!" Nekantor cried. Oh, how he wanted Benél—Benél would grasp him, shake him, cover him in power so none of it mattered!

"So, Arissen," said Pyaras. "While my cousin's busy panicking—which of you is betting on the Heir Selection?"

The three Arissen didn't answer.

"Pyaras, don't pester them," said Tagaret.

"Well, *you* asked about whistles." Pyaras giggled. "Seriously, not one of you has put a bet on the biggest competition in years? Who wants to bet me sixteen orsheth that Nekantor here becomes Heir?"

"Pyaras . . ."

"Sir," said the Arissen woman with a smirk in her voice, "sixteen orsheth would scarcely buy me a glass of bad yezel. Besides which, only a fool would bet against him."

That caught his ear. Nekantor stopped walking. "So which of you *has* bet against me?"

The first man flushed red. "I, sir."

"Get out, then."

Pyaras only laughed harder. "You'd actually bet on Nekantor *winning?* How much for?"

"Eighty orsheth, sir," said the man who remained.

The woman's mouth quirked in a smile. "Four hundred orsheth, sir. I've the note to prove it."

Nekantor licked his lips, a sudden taste of insight in his mouth. Risk, and money: these were the weaknesses in the Arissen, a people who were supposed to have none. Veriga had bodyguarded well, but he did as he liked; because he took no risks, he was untouchable. This woman, who was in deepest, might be led. She might act as part of a larger plan—his own plan—to stop the other candidates.

"Your name, Arissen," Nekantor said.

She saluted. "Karyas, Cohort First, noble sir."

Nekantor smiled. "You're with me, then, Karyas." And to the other man, "You may go."

Now he had a bodyguard. He'd played the right move without Father. A bodyguard was something, even against Herin's threats. She could step into the teeth first. "I'll speak with my Arissen alone," he said.

"Fine with me," said Tagaret. He climbed Pyaras' arm to stand up.

At that moment, a muffled shout came from Father's office. A strange Kartunnen with a medical coat and case burst out, flung herself across the gap between the office and the vestibule, and escaped through the front door. The vestibule curtain kept swinging— Nekantor twitched and turned away from it. Father's fury echoed through the open office door.

"You *presumed*—how dare you try to weaken me! From now on, no appointments of any kind without my approval." Now Sorn backed out of Father's office with hands raised, and Father stomped out toward him, red-faced. "I *am* the First Family, and my success is your success." He stood scowling while Sorn retreated behind his shoulder. "Nekantor, we'd better get picking a new bodyguard," he said, then broke off. His clothes were wrong—rumpled on one side.

"Fix your clothes," Nekantor said coldly. "It's taken care of. I've already picked out my new bodyguard. Father, meet Arissen Karyas."

"Nekantor . . ." Father grumbled. He snapped out his hand to Sorn, who placed his gray gloves in it; Father looked Arissen Karyas up and down while he put them on. "So, you did, did you?"

Father had accepted his move. Nekantor smirked.

Karyas saluted. "Honored, sir."

"*We* helped," said Pyaras indignantly.

Father laid his heavy, gloved hand on top of Pyaras' head and ruffled his hair. Pyaras pulled away, scowling. What a baby—but he certainly could be useful with soldiers.

Tagaret said, "Father, any news? Have you heard from the Ninth Family?"

Father grunted. "Nothing yet. Gowan's finishing his interview right now."

"But what about Reyn?"

"No."

"Have the Sixth Family contacted you?"

"Of course not!" Father snorted. "And I'm not contacting them. You're hardly a good asset if you look half-dead."

"Enough," Nekantor said. "Father, we have to plan our strategy for the interview. Things have—"

"We *have* our strategy." Father waved a hand dismissively. "*You* impress him, answer what he asks, but don't give out any details of our planning. *I* remind him that he owes us, just by being there."

"No."

Father stared at him. "*No?*"

"Father, things have changed."

Father's face reddened and he clenched his fists.

Tagaret made an uncomfortable face; he and Pyaras edged out through the drawing room doors. This much hadn't changed: stupid Tagaret would never learn to play politics when it was good for him.

Father's gloved hand came to his shoulder, trying to grind his bones. "Nekantor, if you continue to disobey me, you'll never survive Selection."

"Herin is trying to kill me," Nekantor said.

"*Everyone* is trying to kill you," said Father. "That's my entire point. Come on, or we'll be late."

Nekantor pulled his shoulder away, flicked off the glove-dimmed marks of Father's fingers, straightened his vest and sleeves, trying to make it all right, to make it safe to go out. The first step outside into the hall was the hardest. But Karyas was here; she answered to *him*, not to Father, and she would protect him. Immediately, she recommended they stay away from the open curved stairways of the grand rotunda, where they might too easily meet a thrown knife. Good idea: that made it easier to walk. They climbed one of the small spiral stairways to the third floor, Karyas in front and Sorn behind. But the real trap was ahead; Nekantor could feel it yawning before him while they stood in the carpeted foyer outside the Eminence's private library.

"That's better, son," Father said. "I've done this before. I know we'll do just fine."

Gnash Father, he was losing his edge. In seconds, the Eminence Herin would invite them in among the teeth. They'd be snapped, no question, if they dared *remind* him of anything. Nekantor's heart pounded; he checked his trousers, his vest and buttons, straightened his sleeves. Not enough. He could feel Father beside him, smug and ignorant; he wanted to slap him, but that move would lose him the game. He took refuge in his watch.

The air moved. The Library doors swung open, and a deep Imbati voice said, "Grobal Nekantor of the First Family. The Eminence Herin awaits you."

"Excellent," Father said. Nekantor looked up: Father was making to walk in, as though the interview were his own. He must not go in. That move would bring the teeth!

"Stop!" Nekantor snapped.

Father's face turned to him; his eyes held a shout he didn't dare utter in such company.

Nekantor stood straighter. "I go in alone or not at all."

Father snorted, as if it were a joke.

Nekantor shrugged deliberately and turned on one heel as if to walk away. Father didn't even blink. Was Father's resolve too strong? Would he *actually* have to leave? It made him sick, but he forced himself to step away from the doors. One step, two . . . oh, he couldn't breathe . . .

"Oh, all right. Go in, then!" Father barked.

Nekantor opened his mouth and gulped air, a rush of power that made him dizzy. He snapped around and followed the Manservant to the Eminence without another word. This was better, oh, this was much better . . .

Then the chaos hit.

The Eminence's private library was a nightmare. The carpet was the wrong shade of green, so deep it squirmed under his every footstep.

Stuffed reading chairs were scattered randomly beneath glass light-globes that hung from bright white ceiling arches. Out of the back wall, a shinca trunk cast silver light at a bizarre angle. Bookshelves poked into the room from either side, creating little pockets of space where anyone might hide, and their shelves were mostly empty. Nothing lined up; nothing pointed anywhere or made any sense. If he hadn't already been checking his watch, he might not have found it in time to stop the scream. As it was, he gave a strangled whimper and walked forward blindly until he bumped into the brass chair. He clutched the cold metal, feeling his way into his seat.

"Nekantor of the First Family," said the Eminence's voice from right in front of him. "Are you—well?"

"N-nervous," he stammered. Stupid thing to say, but a better move than screaming and running out of the room. He had to be able to look up. He *must* look Herin in the eye at least once. Maybe just for a single glance? He lifted his gaze, found Herin—and stopped.

Ahhh . . .

Herin was perfect. How could he have forgotten? Poised in a chair, perfectly dressed in gold silk with sleek golden gloves on his hands and the drape of the Eminence around his shoulders, Herin was an island of stillness when all the rest of the room writhed.

Herin eyed him sharply. "You didn't seem this nervous in the Round of Twelve," he said. "Is it because your father hasn't accompanied you?"

Aggressive question. Nekantor took a deep breath, trying to let Herin's perfection waft stillness into his mind. How straight Herin held his back; how beautifully the four gold buttons shone on his coat . . . "My father—" His voice broke, and he cleared his throat. "My father was bothering me, Eminence. I didn't want him in here."

"Easy enough to say."

"Well, your Imbati saw it, Eminence."

A moment's silence. Herin considering? "Your father is a meddler," the Eminence said at last.

Four perfect points of light, glinting gold. "Oh, yes, sir," Nekantor agreed, nodding. "He really is." And yet, today he'd seized the game for himself.

Herin chuckled. Derision—or amusement? "All right, then, young candidate. Tell me, of you seven remaining, who is best suited to be my Heir? Whom should I trust in this position?"

Nekantor lifted his eyes to Herin's face. "No one, sir."

The Eminence smiled. His fine golden brows rose. "Really."

Nekantor smiled. Now the vision opened up: he counted back along the line of candidates who'd stood by him in the Round of Twelve, removing the lost, and the dead. "Menni has intellect, and hides the spirit of a fighter behind his smile," he said. "Innis will side with an enemy when he has to, but he schemes only for himself. Sangar is distracted by the needs of others. Gowan is too proud. I doubt Ower's intellect, because he is too willing to imitate other people's arguments. Yril is full of envy, and will try to take your power, because he has tried to take mine more than once."

"And what about you?" Herin asked. "Will you tell me *you're* the only one I should trust?"

"Of course not, your Eminence. You distrust me already, and so you should."

"Really."

"Because I will learn your game."

"My *game?*"

"*Always be careful of accepting gifts or favors,*" Nekantor quoted. "*When you accept a gift, you accept an obligation along with it.*"

For a long time, Herin didn't reply. Nekantor tried to cling to scenes of the past, but the present with its strange light began to nudge inward, and the chaos crept closer; he focused harder than ever on Herin, on the Eminence's perfect posture and his gold spider-silk, his buttons, his noble handsome face.

When he looked at Herin's mouth, it bent into a smile.

Wait—that was a pattern.

The more he stared, the more Herin smiled. Not only here, but at the party, and when Herin had spoken out of turn in the Round of Twelve, *attention* was what Herin craved. He loved the stares, the sighs, loved to drink in an adoring crowd or wrap a powerful man around his sleek golden fingers. Father played the game of favors well, but he would never entirely win Herin because he'd never permit himself to be wrapped. A capable boy might threaten Herin as much as tempt him—only an adoring boy would win him over. Better yet would be a boy both adoring and malleable.

So the staring had caught Herin's attention as the behavior of an adoring boy. What would a malleable boy do? Learn his lessons well, yes; also, give favors without hope of reward. Now, *there* was a move worth risking.

Nekantor looked down at his fingers, then up again to Herin's smile. "Eminence, I have to apologize."

The Eminence looked puzzled. "What for?"

"I'm sure you remember how Yril was caught in a raid on the Kartunnen house where the fever began—well, I must confess, I planned that raid myself."

"What?" Herin shifted in his seat. "Are you trying to say we should have banned you instead of him?"

"Not really." Nekantor couldn't stop a smirk. "*He* was the one who got caught. Still, I'm sorry for the trouble he caused, since I planned the raid for you."

"What in Varin's name do you mean by that?"

"You were such an inspiration," Nekantor sighed. "Orn had died of Kinders fever, but you weren't afraid to expose yourself to social contact, and you weren't afraid to tell the Society exactly what needed to be done. And when I realized you *had* the courage to act, but you were restraining yourself for the sake of the future of Varin, I couldn't bear it. I had to do *something*."

"Heh," Herin said. "Did you, now."

"And if it reflected badly on you, I'm sorry."

The Eminence flicked a nonexistent speck off one knee. "Well, never you mind, young Nekantor. You have a lot of years to learn about how to do these things properly."

Nekantor dropped his head and nodded. A lot of years. A lot of years! He *did* know how to play this game.

Of course, Father didn't approve. As soon as they were safely home, Father grabbed his shoulder. "Nekantor, that's the last time I'm letting you behave like a headstrong child. You're throwing away votes right and left!"

Nekantor snorted. Eminence Herin would convince his pet cabinet member, Palimeyn, and that would bring him to five votes. "I'll bet you a thousand orsheth that in the Round of Eight, the Third Family votes for me."

Arissen Karyas let out a laugh that made Sorn twitch.

Nekantor looked at her. "We wouldn't want to lose you any money, would we, Karyas? I imagine you have friends who might not want me to let them down?"

It was the right move: Arissen Karyas' eyes glittered, and she smiled. That meant he could use Karyas to get to her friends, and use those friends for other purposes.

Father ruffled like an annoyed kanguan. "Confident about our interview, are we?"

"Irrelevant, Father," Nekantor said. "Now's the time to plan what comes next—eliminating my competition. Or are you still going to tell me it's not time for that yet?"

Father huffed himself down onto a couch. "Hmph," he grunted. "Say it were—who do you propose I 'eliminate'?"

"Innis of the Fifth Family."

Father raised his eyebrows. "Now, that's where you're wrong, son. You must not understand the appeal of youth and health—our biggest risk now comes from the Ninth Family."

"Gowan?" Nekantor laughed. "He's as harmless as Tagaret. A joke compared to Innis."

"Well, we'll see who wins in the next round. But until you have your own assassins, we'll do it my way."

Gnash Father. Nekantor ground his teeth and cast a glance toward Arissen Karyas, who was looking between them with her sharp brown eyes. She was no assassin. But she was an asset, particularly now that he was running his own game. "Come, Karyas," he said. "We're going to discuss this with Benél."

Benél would give him the relief he needed; and then he could start figuring out how far Karyas and her betting friends could be played.

CHAPTER TWENTY-THREE

The Ninth Family

Alive!

Tagaret hurried to Mother's room, light-headed with relief so terrible he could scarcely speak. Life raced in his blood, as if it could blaze from him like sunlight. Maybe something divine really *had* come down with them from above—something neither Nek nor Father could extinguish, no matter how they tried.

Oh, sweet Heile, *life!*

"Mother!" he cried. "Mother, Reyn's alive!"

Mother stood up from her writing desk. She ran to him in a rustle of carnelian silk, and her arms came around him, warm and tight. "Oh, my darling, that's wonderful!"

"He wants to see me today, before the Round of Eight events. May I borrow your Aloran? *Please?*"

Mother hesitated. "Well . . . how about we both come with you? We can be ready for a social call quite quickly, can't we, Aloran?"

Aloran bowed behind her. "Yes, Lady."

Tagaret grinned his thanks. "So can I."

Dressing was easier now. Today, the Tagaret in the mirror looked almost normal, despite the deathly reminder provided by his white gloves. He met Mother and Aloran in the vestibule, and they walked out together. Excitement and gratitude lifted him so high that he hardly needed help at all. Aloran steadied him only once, while he climbed the spiral stairway.

Imbati Shara answered their knock with a deep bow.

"Welcome, Lady and young sir," she said. "Please be aware that young Master Reyn has just returned this morning from the medical center. He is free of contagion but remains weak due to seizures during his illness."

Tagaret gulped. Fear sank deep into his stomach.

"We understand," Mother said warmly. "It's kind of you to welcome us at such a delicate time, and we don't wish to tax him. Perhaps I might chat with young Lady Iren while Tagaret pays his personal visit."

"Your consideration honors us, Lady," said Shara. She seated them in the sitting room and disappeared into the back.

"Thank you, Mother," Tagaret whispered. Mother always knew what to say.

Mother smiled and squeezed his arm with her soft-gloved hand.

The caretaker reappeared with Iren, who seemed delighted at the prospect of a visitor. She wore a gown of amethyst over which her blonde curls fell to her waist; she giggled shyly at Mother when Shara seated them together.

Finally, Tagaret was able to stand and follow her back to Reyn's private rooms. He breathed deep, trying to loosen his anxiety. But whatever he'd been through, Reyn had suffered much worse. He must be careful, and gentle, and not show horror if his friend were somehow changed.

Reyn lay with his bed-curtains open, gazing at the portrait of his parents, which had been moved to the wall beside his head. He'd always been fair, but now his skin looked pale as steam.

Tagaret took his gloves off and softly touched his arm. "Reyn?"

"Mm?" Reyn turned his head. "Ohhh. Tagaret . . ."

Thank the Twins. Those were just the eyes he knew—clear, undamaged, and filled with their familiar steady sympathy. Tagaret fell on his knees beside the bed and embraced him as best he could. "Reyn," he said, with tears in his throat. "Reyn, thank all the gods—you're really all right."

Reyn's hand came to rest lightly against his back. "Tagaret, you're . . ." he said, and took a breath before continuing. "*Better.*"

He hadn't realized how much better until this moment. He kissed Reyn's forehead. "You'll get better, too," he said. "You will, I promise."

"I heard," Reyn said, and his voice caught. "Fernar."

Tagaret held him tighter. Reyn's hand pressed against his back. Even after several seconds, he couldn't find voice to speak.

"Did you. . . ?" Reyn asked, and paused for breath. "When you, had it," he paused again. "Did you realize, what it would be—to die?"

"Elinda forbear," Tagaret said automatically. But it wasn't Elinda's gentleness that came to his mind—not the fever, nor the relentless and inevitable decline of the Race. Instead came a vision of breathless heat and light, curling grasses, and billowing smoke: Varin's teeth. His heart pounded all over again, insisting he *must live*; and the whistle tune in the heat of his memory sounded like a cry of defiance. He shook his head. He couldn't explain it, even to himself. "Not the way you did, I'm sure."

Reyn's fingers curled closed against his back. "I realized, I might never, see them again." He turned his head toward the portrait on the wall.

Tagaret looked up at Faril and Lady Catenad, smiling down. "Do they know you're all right?"

"Shara sent, a radiogram."

"Maybe they'll come to see you, then." Would they dare? To leave their place of safety, to travel the Road under the sun, with the sky, and the wysps, and the wilderness? But they had gone to Safe Harbor in the first place, hadn't they?

"I can't stay here," Reyn said.

Tagaret looked at him. "What do you mean?"

"Pelismara." He breathed faster. "My parents, won't come back. They don't like it. As soon as, I'm old enough, I'll go. Safe Harbor. No one waiting, to see . . ." He relaxed into his pillow.

"See what?"

"See who dies next."

Someone must have told him about the Selection. Tagaret took Reyn's hand. "There's more to Pelismara than that," he said. "Yesterday, when all I could think about was death, Mother took me to the surface. I saw the sky, and the grain harvest, and fire, and Venorai using music to command Arissen."

Reyn blinked at him. "What? What does that, have to do, with anything?"

"I have no idea; that's the whole point. I had no idea it was even possible. Our life in the Society has never seemed so small."

Reyn sighed. "That's true."

Tagaret squeezed his fingers. "Reyn, there are terrible people here, but there are also people worth fighting for. Worth staying for."

"You . . ." Reyn gazed up at him sadly. "Don't love me."

Tagaret felt sick. "But Reyn, I *do.* Imagining being without you nearly killed me. You *understand* me, like no one else does. You always did." Years ago, in the flood of unbearable congratulations that had followed Father's promotion to Selimna, only a smallish Ninth Family boy had offered him condolences on the loss of his mother. And in all this, he'd lost sight of what Reyn was still going through. Tagaret took a deep breath. "I admit, I've done a bad job understanding you. I'll try to do better. And when—*if,* if you really have to go to Safe Harbor to be with them, then I think you should go."

Reyn didn't answer, but with surprising strength, pulled him down into a kiss. They had no energy for passion, but the feeling of Reyn's fingers in his hair meant hope, and the heavens still turning.

Someone knocked.

Tagaret didn't want to let go. It shouldn't be time to leave—not yet—but he drew away and went to the door. Instead of Imbati Shara, he found Gowan, dressed in a very adult-looking suit of graphite-gray silk and emeralds.

Tagaret startled. "Gowan?"

"Tagaret!" Gowan cried. "Mercy of Heile, you're alive, too?" He hugged him, shook him, thumped him, and then hugged him again.

"Whoa, easy . . ."

"Sorry." Gowan grinned, then wrapped an arm around his back and pulled him into the room again. Reyn got a less vigorous greeting, but still, Tagaret loved that they would include him. He sat down cross-legged on the floor, while Gowan sat beside Reyn on the edge of the bed.

"Kinders fever, and you're both still here," Gowan said, shaking his head. "You're so lucky."

"You're the . . . the lucky one," said Reyn. "You didn't have, to go through this."

Gowan grimaced. "Of course, you're right. And Fernar, Elinda keep him . . ."

Tagaret glanced at Reyn. Silence fell among them like a stone.

Finally, Tagaret steeled himself. "Gowan, we can't blame you for having your own life to look after," he said. "What with the assassination attempts, and the Round of Eight today." Thank all the gods he was no longer part of it—the shortcut to power *had* pitched him into a crack, if not the one he'd expected.

Gowan twisted his fingers. "I thought you might have been too sick to keep track of that, Tagaret."

"Well, no."

"Here's the thing." Gowan looked him in the eye. "I'm really not supposed to talk about the Selection, especially with you."

"But I'm not your rival anymore."

"You're First Family."

"What?!" Tagaret leapt to his feet in indignation, swayed, and had to catch himself on the bedpost. "Is *that* what you think? I thought you weren't seeing me because of safety concerns and the fuss of your candidacy. But have they really changed you? Have you forgotten who I *am?* Now that Fernar is gone, all that's left is *we're-Ninth-and-you're-First*, and I must love my father and my brother so much I'd kill for them, is that it?"

Gowan looked uncomfortable, but he lashed back. "Tagaret, you *know* how dangerous Selection secrets are. You don't understand how important this is to me!"

So, so small . . . Tagaret growled in exasperation. "Listen, Gowan, I *want* you to be Heir. Crown of Mai, I want you to be Eminence! Who else could I trust? I look at Nek and Yril—Ower and Sangar who are total strangers, and Innis—Innis, who's gone and taken my Della while I've become nothing more than another 'asset' to the First Family's chances! My father's trying to partner me to anyone who offers him a vote!"

Gowan lost his angry look. "So is mine," he sighed. "Not that it matters. Lady Inkala was always out of reach."

Mercy—had he set his heart on Cousin Inkala? Tagaret fell silent in another rush of grief and guilt.

"You're not, just, First Family," said Reyn. "Not to us. Is he, Gowan."

"Of course he isn't," Gowan replied gruffly.

"Mai's oath, Gowan," Tagaret said. "There *has* to be a way to get you through to the end of the Selection. I don't have much information to give you, but I do know that my father will plan assassinations without blinking. You should be on the lookout for that."

Gowan raised his eyebrows. "Even after the Round of Eight?"

"Now there's precedent for it. And another thing most people probably don't know is that Father and Nekantor don't work together."

"No?"

"They fight constantly. I wish it were enough to slow them down. But you can be sure that Nekantor is formulating his own plans that have nothing to do with Father's. It's not much, but if I learn anything better, I'll let you know."

Gowan stood and put a firm hand on his arm. "You're a good friend," he said. "I don't know if I can do anything about Della, but if an opportunity comes up today during our question session with the cabinet, I won't hesitate."

"Take Innis down," Tagaret said.

Gowan nodded. "I'll do my best."

Not that he would have traded a minute of his time with Reyn and Gowan, but Tagaret couldn't help noticing that Mother was agitated on the way home. Frustration made sense, with the Round of Eight closing in on them. He'd been lucky for the chance to ask Gowan to act against Nek and Innis. But would it be enough? With the Fifth Family's two votes, plus the vote of the Sixth Family in his pocket, Innis would have to stumble seriously to get knocked out now. On the other hand, it had happened to Herin's favorite in the Round of Twelve . . .

As they reentered the suite, Serjer emerged from his Maze door to greet them, and Mother startled.

"Forgive me, Mistress," Serjer said.

"Of course, Serjer. I'm just—nervous. Has Garr asked after me?"

Serjer bowed. "No, Mistress, but that may be because Grobal Fedron and Lady Selemei have come to call. I believe they all intend to go down to the Round of Eight question session together."

"Garr is consenting to be seen with Selemei?" She glanced at Tagaret; he shrugged.

"Yes, Lady. Though I must remark that both he and Fedron have momentarily stepped out of the sitting room."

Mother's eyebrows leapt high—a reproach Tagaret wouldn't have wanted to be on the receiving end of. "Garr left a guest *unattended?* What can he be thinking?"

Serjer angled his head to one side. "Lady Selemei is not entirely unattended, Mistress. Premel is seeing to her refreshment."

"Thank you, Serjer." She thought for a moment. "Tagaret, love, I'm sorry to ask you this. Do you think *you* could speak with Selemei for a few moments?"

"Me?" After all the Lady had hoped for him, wouldn't she be disappointed to speak to him now?

"The thing is . . ." Mother cast a brief glance back at Aloran. "This isn't what I'd planned to wear to the Round of Eight announcements. Your father won't be pleased if he hasn't seen me ready before he departs. It won't take me much time to change, Aloran, will it?"

"Lady, I'll work as fast as I can."

"Oh, Aloran, bless you." Mother held out her hand, palm-up.

Serjer gasped.

Tagaret had never in his life imagined an Imbati making that sound. He looked from Serjer to Aloran, and found the young bodyguard blushing distinctly. Mother quickly fisted her hand against her stomach. She tossed her head and pushed through the vestibule curtain.

"Selemei," she called. "So good to see you! I hope you'll forgive me, but you've caught us woefully unprepared. Have you seen Tagaret yet?"

His cue. For Mother, he'd handle this—he stepped in. Lady Selemei was standing, and Keeper Premel now bowing away from a flute of drink that she held in one brown-gloved hand. The glass provided a glittering contrast to her gown, which gleamed in colors of jasper. Imbati Ustin was relatively unobtrusive, standing some distance away by the wall, but the intense look in Selemei's eyes put Tagaret instantly on edge.

"Welcome, Cousin," he said. "I'm terribly sorry we were out when you arrived. It was my fault entirely. I insisted on seeing my friend Reyn of the Ninth Family when I learned of his recovery from Kinders fever."

"You'll excuse me, Selemei, dear," Mother murmured, and hurried away through the double doors.

Lady Selemei nodded after her. "It's good to see you, young Tagaret. I don't mind at all that you were out. Elinda's forbearance is worthy of gratitude—and indeed, *you* are looking astonishingly well."

"Thank you. Of course, Father just thinks it makes me a good *Family asset*." He instantly regretted saying it. Either Selemei would be horribly offended, or she might agree with Father. He couldn't decide which was worse.

"One single day," Lady Selemei sighed.

"I'm sorry?"

"You really only missed one day, Cousin. Not that you had any control over it, but that was a sorry day for the First Family." Her dark eyes were compassionate now, full of the same ironic intelligence that always put him off guard.

"Don't vote for my brother," he blurted, then snapped his mouth shut.

The corners of Lady Selemei's lips curved upward. "The First Family Council has fallen into confusion," she said. "One might expect that to weaken our candidate—except, of course, other Families are in the same straits. Your father is driving himself to the brink of exhaustion to get your brother selected, and Fedron now follows him in everything like a tunnel-hound."

"Surely there has to be another way."

"As you say," she agreed. "It's at times like these that I wish I had a better relationship with your mother."

Tagaret frowned. This obviously wasn't about their occasional games of kuarjos. "What do you mean?"

Lady Selemei gave an enigmatic smile and sipped her drink. "I think, if you spoke to her on my behalf . . ."

He stared at her, a horrid feeling stretching his guts. This was Lady's politics. Maybe she didn't consider him an asset, but he'd asked her for a favor, so she expected one in return. She wanted Mother to do something against Father.

"You can't just use me to get to my mother," he said. "She hates politics."

"As do you," said Lady Selemei, unruffled. "But I would have voted you Heir and been grateful to do it. Ladies as intelligent as your mother are not easy to find. You think I should take a more direct approach to your father? A more *gentlemanly* approach, perhaps?"

He flushed. "No. But Mother wants—" *Safety*, his mind whispered. He heard the passionate voice again, begging to protect her, and the image of Aloran blushing leapt into his mind. Uncertainty shadowed him. "Uh, mm," he stammered aloud, "privacy."

"I see," said Lady Selemei. "So I should allow you to speak for her?"

"No!" He looked Selemei in the eye. "Mother speaks for herself— but I speak for *myself*, and I believe *I'm* the one whose help you were requesting. Reach her another way, if you'd like. A note delivered by Household has served you well enough in the past."

Lady Selemei bowed her head. "Well spoken, Cousin—how I wish I might be seeing you in today's question session! Nevertheless, I hope that if you value the goals I once discussed with you, you might mention me to her."

"I'll *mention* you."

"And I'll endeavor to make sure we can announce an optimal result this afternoon."

A thunk came from the double doors of the private drawing room. In walked the new Arissen, Karyas. Nek and Benél came in behind her. Nek looked perfectly arranged, as usual, but his face glowed disconcertingly. Benél was holding him by the back of the neck.

"Benél." Father's voice rumbled through the doorway. "Hands off, or you'll ruin everything."

"Benél's always done that," said Nekantor. "Leave us alone."

"It's too obvious," said Father. "What happened to Sangar of the Eighth Family must not happen to us."

"Yes, sir," said Benél. He dropped his hand. Nekantor's face soured, and he started straightening his cuffs.

Father walked in with Fedron beside him. Father's green suit had the unfortunate effect of making his face look off-color, and he was holding onto Fedron's shoulder. Behind them, Father's Sorn and Fedron's Chenna held themselves with defensive readiness that looked positively dangerous.

Father wheezed a cough and cleared his throat hard. "Nekantor, you're fidgeting."

"Shut up, Father." Nekantor winked at Benél, and Benél smiled.

Father gave a low hiss, but turned his eyes on Tagaret. "Well? Don't stand there like an idiot. Wish your brother good luck today."

Tagaret gritted his teeth. Lady Selemei was right: how low they'd fallen since the gathering before the Round of Twelve! "Nekantor," he said, "may Mai the Right grant you the success you deserve."

Nekantor laughed.

No, he hadn't done enough.

"Well, then," said Lady Selemei brightly. "Seems like we're ready to go. Tagaret, I suppose we'll see you next in the Plaza of Varin, with news on the results of the question session and voting?"

He stood up straighter. "Yes, indeed, Lady Selemei."

"Wonderful. Give my best to your mother."

"Where is she, anyway?" Father growled. "Tagaret, tell her she'd *better* be there on time."

"We'll be there, Father."

Finally, they all swept out, leaving him alone in the sitting room. Gnash it—Nekantor was the wrong candidate, and he knew it. But he also clearly knew that while he had Father's protection, everyone else was powerless against him. Tagaret wandered to the gaming table, where someone had left a game of keyzel marbles unfinished on the obsidian board. He sat and began half-heartedly returning the spheres of lapis and malachite to their starting cradles. If only it were so easy to turn back time. Even just now, he should have defended Mother better. Or maybe he just shouldn't have taken Mother out to Reyn's in the first place. Too late, too late for everything.

"Hey, that's our game."

Tagaret looked up. Pyaras had just walked in.

Serjer announced belatedly, "Your cousin to see you, young Master."

"Thanks, Serjer," said Tagaret. "*Your* game, Pyaras?"

"Veriga and I were playing, before."

"Mercy, I'm sorry." He looked down at the board—no way to re-capture its previous arrangement. "I didn't know."

Pyaras took the chair across from him and smiled almost shyly. "Actually, it's all right. Veriga's just woken up, so we might play again one day. He seemed pretty surprised to find me visiting."

"I'm sure." *Pyaras* had certainly changed. "Good for you."

"What about you? Any news?"

"I saw Reyn this morning, and he's getting better, too." He smiled.

"Shall we play marbles, then?" Pyaras winked. "Bet you eight or-sheth I'll win."

In the end it was a good thing he hadn't agreed to the bet. Pyaras was surprisingly good at keyzel marbles, and quickly took the better strategic position. Tagaret found it hard to concentrate knowing that Herin and the cabinet members were questioning Nekantor, Gowan, and the others at this very moment. He moved a sphere of malachite, certain Pyaras would take it easily.

The double doors swung open, and in walked Mother. Her gown was a blaze of orange and pink with sparkling clouds threaded through it, paling into the bodice and tinged with purple at the shoulders. It made his heart leap.

"Which one is that, Mother?" Tagaret asked.

Mother's face brightened, and she glanced over her shoulder at Aloran. "The sunset," she said, brushing her fingers across her skirts. "Thanks for coming, Pyaras. Will your father be joining us?"

"He hates big fancy events." Pyaras shrugged. "Sunset? You mean, the sky?"

Mother nodded. "When Father Varin departs," she said. "Are you boys ready? Shall we go?"

They walked three abreast down to the Plaza of Varin, where a space had been cordoned off between the front gate of the Residence grounds and the glowing shinca trunk at the Plaza's center. Just before the gold-tipped bars of the gate, a stage had been built, guarded by members of the Eminence's Cohort. Folding chairs filled the rest of the space. Tagaret took Mother's hand atop his own, leading her in among the crowd.

Gossip swirled around them. Here someone said Sangar of the

Eighth Family's commitment to the future of the Race was now in question, since he'd been discovered in intimacy with another boy; there a voice said that the Eminence's partner might appear any second, publicly acknowledging her pregnancy for the first time. Over everything flowed the silver light of the shinca. It reflected off the steel curve of the Alixi's Elevator and gave strange clarity to the swaying of ladies' gowns, to a gentleman tugging at his gloves, to an Imbati smoothly folding and replacing a chair so his master could pass from one row to the next. Lowers had been mostly cleared out of the Plaza; only a few could be glimpsed hanging with nervous curiosity around the edge.

Father had reserved several places in the first row. Tagaret slid in beside Mother, and Pyaras sat on her other side, while Aloran moved smoothly into the second row with the other bodyguards. From here the view was all Arissen, a row of them in the bright Cohort orange that now seemed to be everywhere—the nearest man had nostrils as wide as a herdbeast's.

"Look there," Pyaras whispered. "I know her—that's Dekk." He scooted two seats over, where a whiplike woman in the row of guards nodded a quick greeting to him.

Above, on the stage, four brass chairs sat empty.

Please, oh, holy Mai, let Gowan succeed . . . let Nekantor and Innis fail . . .

Behind the stage, the Residence gates swung open. Someone was coming out, but with guards in the way it was impossible to see. Cabinet members probably, and candidates, which meant the question session was over, the result already foregone. Tagaret's stomach knotted.

Father lumbered into view at the left corner of the stage, with Fedron following, and pushed aside a last couple of people who hadn't yet sat down. He thumped into the chair beside Mother, who shrank away from him against Tagaret's shoulder.

"Father, what happened?" Tagaret asked. Father seemed out of breath and didn't answer. "Father, are you all right? Who are the last four?"

People started walking up onto the stage. First was . . . Arissen Karyas. Oh, gods, Nekantor had made it through. Behind Nekantor, a second Arissen accompanied Menni of the Second Family. The third guard belonged to—oh, no—Innis of the Fifth Family, still limping after his knife to the leg. This was going to be a complete disaster!

But last onto the stage was Gowan of the Ninth Family, who preceded his bodyguard onto the stage. The emeralds on his suit glowed in the shinca-light, and he held himself proudly. His eyes when they found Tagaret's were sober, but full of promise.

Oh, please, Gowan. Two more rounds. Please . . .

CHAPTER TWENTY-FOUR
Bodyguard

The young Master had spoken thoughtlessly, but Aloran's body went cold. *Father, are you all right?* He should have noticed the worsening of Master Garr's condition days ago: his increasing pallor, the fact that he sat in any chair available, his coughing and moments of inappropriate absence—even his breathing now, as fast as running though all he'd done was walk here from the Residence. It all pointed to a single inevitable conclusion.

Aloran leaned forward. "Lady, I must tell you . . ."

"Mm?" Lady Tamelera didn't turn; her gaze stayed on the stage.

The Eminence Herin had taken up a microphone. Now he leapt down from the stage with a flourish and introduced his partner, Lady Falya. She sat several seats away from them, the portrait of late-term fecundity, surrounded by fluttering lady admirers. The Eminence basked in the applause that she received. Only after the applause died down did he climb back up the stairs and explain how he and the cabinet had questioned each Heir candidate in the private session just concluded.

Aloran tried again, speaking into Lady Tamelera's ear. "Lady, your partner is seriously ill."

She made a small inquisitive noise in her throat.

"Lady, he's dying."

She stiffened.

"Forgive me. It isn't the right time to be telling you, but his heart is failing. He might have until next week—or he might die today. If he doesn't see a doctor . . ."

Lady Tamelera turned her head slightly toward him. "But why wouldn't Sorn—" Her voice choked off.

Aloran's heart tried to stop beating. *Sorn wasn't here.* The chair between him and Fedron's Chenna was empty, which meant Grobal Garr wouldn't wait until tomorrow. Someone would die today.

Here. Now.

"From the First Family, allow me to introduce Nekantor," the Eminence announced. The crowd again burst into eager applause.

Aloran tried to begin a breath pattern, but in vain; his body went numb. The Eminence started talking about young Master Nekantor's pedigree in politics, his character, and his performance in the question session.

Aloran forced his fingers to move, feeling in his pockets for combat rounders. Only three—not nearly enough to feel fully armed.

It was hopeless anyway. Sorn's chosen weapon gave him the advantage of range, so he'd be out of reach somewhere, hiding safely beyond the guarded perimeter. And meanwhile here *he* was, hemmed in on every side by the Pelismara Society. He couldn't even leave his seat to investigate, while Sorn might strike at any second.

Think, Aloran. Measured breaths relieve the body. Relief of the body calms the mind. The calm mind is observant and prepared.

With air came logic. A sniper would place himself high, most likely in one of the buildings surrounding the Plaza. The Residence was too far away, behind its gates. The Old Forum stood at a considerable distance behind the crowd, possibly within range for an Arissen bolt weapon, but too far for a crossbow, besides which the bright light of the shinca would make sighting past it difficult. That left the Courts on the right, and the Academy on the left.

"From the Second Family, I present to you, Menni," the Eminence said. In the swell of applause, young Master Nekantor returned to his seat and Menni of the Second Family stood up into the crowd's hungry attention. "Menni is the only son of our well-respected Cabinet Secretary, Boros . . ."

Aloran scanned the stone columns of the Courts, the frieze of Holy Mai the Right and one's petitioners, the roofline. If Sorn was there, he was too well hidden. He turned to the Academy, though, and disgusted certainty filled his stomach. The children of the Academy were always welcome to return, a privilege Sorn would not be granted by the wardens of the Courts. But to use the *Academy*, birthplace of faith and loyalty, to launch an attack? The sheer gall of it was—well, it was utterly Garr's Sorn.

A movement: glinting steel at the roofline rail. Panic tightened his throat all over again. Sorn *was* there. He must have been there for minutes already, waiting. Why hadn't he struck? Gowan of the Ninth Family had already offered him a perfect moment, as the last one to sit down when the candidates first walked up onto the stage. His bodyguard had only chosen to shelter him on the Courts side. So why was he still alive?

"From the Fifth Family, this is Innis," the Eminence said, gesturing to the eldest, sharp-nosed candidate who now rose to stand before his chair. "Innis first distinguished himself at the age of seventeen with his service to Chief Adjudicator Uresin, and he's already shown himself a canny politician."

It had to be something about the ceremony. In the last Selection, Grobal Garr had struck the day *after* the Round of Eight, so there must be a rule in operation here—one that required the ceremony to finish before any action could be taken. That had to be it. And that meant there could be only one best target: the single boy left standing with his head exposed when the last word of the ceremony was spoken.

"And finally, from the Ninth Family, Gowan," said the Eminence. "Son of Amyel, who has served on our cabinet since Indal 3 . . ."

Aloran stopped listening. He watched the Eminence's lips. *What* Eminence Herin said meant nothing, while every word counted down toward death. Whenever he paused for air, Aloran couldn't stop an involuntary twitch; Fedron's Chenna cast him a look with narrowed eyes. Did she know of the plot? Would she try to stop him if he intervened?

The rounders had warmed against his fingers. He took them into the palm of his hand. There was only one possible course of action, and only one moment—the instant when the Eminence's lips stopped moving.

Now.

He stood and threw. The first rounder hit Grobal Gowan in the ankle; the young nobleman leapt backward, clutching his foot, and the second one hit him in his standing leg, just below the knee. Aloran raised his arm for a third, but it wasn't necessary. Grobal Gowan lost balance completely and crashed into Grobal Innis' lap.

The Eminence's partner screamed.

My apologies, sirs, and Lady.

Aloran replaced the last rounder in his pocket and bowed his head as the Eminence's Cohort swarmed the stage. An orange wave surged over the candidates, down into the audience, and over Lady Tamelera and the Master in their chairs. Aloran stood still and allowed them to seize him. The Eminence's partner and her entourage hurried away. Beside him, Fedron's Chenna got to her feet. Chenna's face clearly betrayed her shock—apparently this was one secret about her adversary that she hadn't discovered.

"Imbati!" barked an enormous Arissen now clamping his left arm in mitts of steel. "You are under arrest for assaulting a gentleman of the nobility."

Aloran took a deep breath. "The heart that is valiant triumphs over all, sir," he said. "There is an assassin on the roof of the Service Academy. I couldn't allow him to strike, but I couldn't reach him, so I had to remove his target from a vulnerable position. My weapons are legal and nonlethal."

"So you say," scoffed the woman on his right arm.

A high voice piped up behind her—the young Master's cousin, Grobal Pyaras. "But, Dekk, shouldn't someone at least look?"

"He'll be searched soon enough, sir," the woman replied.

"I mean on the Academy roof."

Lucky thing, that he hadn't thrown the third rounder. He would willingly have shown it to them, but they weren't allowing him to reach into his pockets. Aloran sought after the young man he'd felled, but Grobal Gowan had already been whisked away to safety. There was no sign that Sorn had ever taken his shot. Some kind of stir was still going on in the crowd closer to the Courts, with guards involved, but when he tried to crane his neck to see, his captors shook him straight.

"You'll come with us, Imbati."

Come *with* them? What had he done? "But, sir, my Mistress," he protested. "She needs me."

Lady Tamelera put a hand on the female guard's shoulder. "Arissen, this is my manservant. I vouch for the integrity of his actions."

"Lady . . ." said the Arissen.

"Arissen, I honor your valiance," Tamelera said. "But I guarantee Aloran wouldn't attack anyone if he wasn't certain it was the only alternative. He has saved noble lives three times since the Eminence Herin took the throne."

The woman's hands released his right arm. "Lady," she said, "perhaps we could—"

"Never mind her." That was Grobal Garr. His face was chilling, livid with absolute hatred. "This is an outrage—arrest him already! I see no evidence of any attacker."

The female guard didn't move, but Aloran felt his arm seized again by another Arissen, and his heart dropped.

Tamelera whirled on Grobal Garr, eyes blazing.

No, no . . . Tamelera's courage out on the surface had been frightening, but this was worse. She knew the consequences of defiance as well as he!

Mercifully, she stopped short of direct accusation. "Then find him," she said. "Send guards to the Academy this instant."

Grobal Garr clenched his fists. "Whatever you choose to do, Arissen, this Imbati is guilty of assault and should be held until the Ninth Family has a chance to seek redress for his actions."

"I'll go with him, then."

"Nonsense, Tamelera. You don't belong in the Cohort's station. You're coming home with me."

Aloran found himself gaze-gesturing *stop, stop* out of pure desperation. She *had* to stop before she made this any worse.

Lady Tamelera broke off halfway through a breath with her mouth slightly open.

Bless her for realizing what she was doing. Aloran forced himself into a breathing pattern. He shared that urge—wanted to argue, for her, and for himself—but anything he said now would be perceived as presumption. It could only delay his return to his rightful place at her side. Her intense blue eyes, staring at him full of fear, were enough to tear him apart; he sent her a gaze-gesture of apology because it was the only thing he had left to offer.

Tamelera's eyes moved to one side, then up, then back to meet his—a message delivered slowly but unmistakably: *It's all right.*

He shivered from head to foot. *She knew the code.* Did that mean she'd stopped *at his request?* But how could she know the code? It had to be Eyli; Eyli must have taught her the gaze-gestures, in the same way that she'd taught her how to request a touch, when not even Serjer had known.

Somehow, it made the sense of loss that much worse when the guards led him away.

The two Arissen men took him to the headquarters of the Eminence's Cohort, a stone building behind the east wing of the Residence, directly across the gardens from the Conveyor's Hall. Soon after, more Arissen arrived, roughly escorting a Kartunnen in a medical coat. Aloran stayed away from them and kept silent until a lawyer came to his defense. The lawyer was chosen of Mai, sober and distinguished with a bronze medallion at the shoulder of one's black silk robes, bearing between one's brows the diamond-within-diamond Mark of servants of the Courts. Aloran kept alert to the unspoken instructions in one's eyes, all the while wishing helplessly they could have been his Lady's. He kept his head low, gave the Arissen the respect they demanded, sat when they told him to, stood when they told him to, and answered every question in as few words as possible—that is, every question except one.

Thank all the gods he'd seen only the weapon, and not the man holding it. He didn't have to lie. To give Sorn's name, while there was no evidence to bring him under arrest and while he remained under Grobal Garr's protection, would be tantamount to suicide. Sorn would certainly suspect how much he knew; he must not be allowed to confirm it.

At last, a delegation from the Ninth Family Council appeared to question him—four men who, fortunately, seemed more baffled than angered by his actions. Here, at least, he could divulge his feelings truly. He bowed his head to the floor at their feet, apologized for the necessity, and wished young Grobal Gowan long life, health, and success. He also offered them his last rounder, which they took and discussed with their heads together. Was it enough? Would they accept his apology, or would they insist on prosecution?

They left without a word, and still the Arissen would not release him.

He clung to his Lady's promise: *It's all right. It's all right—oh, gods— let it be all right.*

At six afternoon, to his surprise, Master Tagaret's young cousin Grobal Pyaras walked in with his father the Administrator, alongside the Arissen woman who had first seized him. They went directly to the office of the Cohort Commander. Moments later, the Commander herself emerged from her office—

Carrying the crossbow.

Aloran bowed his head. *Holy Mai, I thank you for extending your hand to me.*

"Can you tell me what this is?" the Commander asked in her silky voice. She held it with disdain, as if she considered it an object of curiosity rather than a real weapon.

"The heart that is valiant triumphs over all, sir," Aloran answered. "It is a Venorai hunting crossbow. It is the weapon that I saw aimed from the Academy roof toward Grobal Gowan of the Ninth Family."

The Commander nodded. "It is also the same type of weapon used to assassinate Grobal Dest of the Eleventh Family, when Herin was selected Heir."

Aloran did not reply, but his heart beat faster.

His lawyer stepped forward. "I hereby petition for the release, upon oath of future cooperation as witness, of Tamelera's Aloran of the Household of the First Family."

The Commander nodded again. "Swear, Imbati, and you shall be returned to your duties."

He would have sworn to anything that won his release. The moment he was free, he ran diagonally across the gardens of imported surface plants, into the west wing of the Residence. Once in the public halls he took more care, but at last he reached his home service entrance, slapped his hand to the glass panel, and slipped inside.

Familiar sounds issued from the kitchen: Premel and Serjer were preparing dinner, but their talk sounded subdued and worried. He had to assume Sorn had escaped capture and returned home—but as he passed the senior servant's room, he could see no light beneath the door.

No need to doubt this time whether his Lady wanted him; he should have been her shadow. He gave a soft knock and opened the door with the crescent-moon handle.

"Aloran!" Tamelera shrieked. "Help me!"

No—Garr had her backed against the far wall; her hair was torn down, her face contorted in pain. Garr limped toward her, his fist raised to strike again, while Sorn blocked any escape through the public door, watching with a faint smile.

Aloran didn't think.

He leapt past the lounge chairs into the space between his Lady and her attacker, spinning to face Garr just as the nobleman's meaty fist swung forward. It was so simple to turn the blow aside—just a gentle nudge, and Garr lurched off-balance, forcing Sorn to jump to stop him falling. Aloran spun and lifted Tamelera into his arms. She flung her arms around his neck.

"You have violated my Master's person," Sorn hissed, readying himself for combat—but he had to keep one arm outstretched toward his Master. Grobal Garr was swaying on his feet; his disarranged clothes showed glimpses of his pasty skin, and he bore livid scratch marks from his hairline down to his upper lip.

Crown of Mai, she was brave! Aloran filled with terrifying, presumptuous pride. He set his teeth and held Tamelera tighter. "Look to your Master, then," he said. "You will not touch my Lady."

Sorn did not attack.

Aloran carried Tamelera into the bathroom, shutting the door and setting his back against it. He wished he knew how to scream or cry. Instead, he let training take over. He set his Lady's feet gently on the floor, locked the door, and guided her to sit on the brass chair to one side of the marble bath. Then he pressed the service call button.

"Aloran, don't," she pleaded. "I can't see anyone else—not now."

Aloran breathed cautiously for a moment until his voice seemed ready to behave. "Lady, I won't let anyone in, I promise. But you're injured. Please, let me take care of you."

Tamelera curled on the chair, pulling her heels up to the seat and wrapping her left arm around her knees. The beautiful sunset gown draped lopsidedly toward the floor. She leaned her head forward and her ruined hair fell over her face. After some seconds she said softly, "Yes."

Thank Heile. When Serjer came, Aloran spoke to him under the door, requesting ice and his medical kit. His Lady's motions said clearly she'd been hit in the stomach, and punched or grabbed on the right arm. That surely wasn't all, but it did tell him that bruising and pain had to be handled now. When Serjer returned, he opened the door a hand's breadth to take the kit and ice bucket, then locked it again.

Aloran brought his Lady a painkilling tablet from his kit, with a glass of water from beside the marble basin. When she held out her hand for it, he stopped breathless. *Touch me*, the hand whispered. But it shouldn't have—it *wouldn't* have, if he hadn't known her eyes could speak! He ignored the whisper, dropped the tablet carefully into her palm, and turned away.

Making ice packs in the available towels was simple. Applying them was far harder, because he had to look at what Garr had done. He unfastened his Lady's gown and lifted it over her head. Her back was unharmed, and despite what had happened to her hair, so were her neck and face—perhaps an advantage of her greater height. But angry red fingermarks ringed her left upper arm, with purple stains underneath betraying deeper damage. Above her ankle, he found a bruise crossed by a red scoreline—a kick from the sole of her partner's shoe. Aloran gave her an ice pack to hold against her stomach, wrapped and iced her arm, then knelt to apply the same treatment to her leg. But he couldn't stop his hands from shaking.

"It was my fault," Tamelera whispered.

He flushed hot. "No."

She sat silent a moment. "I told him—what you told me," she said. "Thinking . . . maybe, that he would appreciate it if I cared enough to save his life? But he went crazy."

The heat crept into his eyes. "It's my fault, then."

"It can't be, Aloran. You had to tell me; it was your duty as my servant."

"So was it *your* duty, as his partner." His fingers stopped on the bandages. "But I made it worse. I resisted when he tried to take you away, and that's why I wasn't here—" The image of violence crashed over him again. He struggled not to hyperventilate. "I vowed to protect you—and I wasn't here—"

"Aloran, look at me."

He did, straight into her eyes, unable to resist a reckless wish that they might speak to him again.

"You saved Gowan's life," she said. "I'm grateful, and not only because of the Selection. He and Tagaret are very close. I don't know how Tagaret could have coped if he lost another of his friends." Her gaze flicked down, and she blinked before raising it again—the gesture for gratitude, performed with the grace of long practice.

His skin prickled in curiosity and fear. Was this the intimacy that she had known with Eyli? Such privilege was almost more than he could bear.

"Lady," he said, trying to tear his gaze away. "May I be excused? I can fetch you fresh clothes—perhaps, something to eat?"

"No—" Panic seeped into her voice. "Aloran, you can't—please, don't leave me."

Aloran bowed his head. As a compromise, he walked as far as the service call button, and summoned Serjer, who brought her nightdress. While she rested from the ice, he called again, for a drink of milk. Then for a second application of ice. A bowl of soup. He took the pins out of her hair and brushed out all signs of the afternoon's fight, watching the tension slowly leave her neck and shoulders. After a time, he no longer wanted relief from her presence. Here was safety, and the comfort of his selfless duty, while outside this room was only danger, and questioning.

"Aloran?" she asked.

"Yes, Lady?"

"Would you ring for Serjer?"

"Of course."

This time, his Lady allowed the First Houseman entry. Serjer maintained admirable control, but his calm was not so perfect that Aloran couldn't read the horror in his eyes.

"Thank you for everything, Serjer," Tamelera said. "Where is Garr now?"

Serjer bowed. "In his office, Mistress. With Sorn, and young Master Nekantor."

"Lock the door of my room, then. And bring a day mattress; set it up next to my side of the bed."

"Mistress." Serjer's eyes flicked over to Aloran's, but perhaps out of a new caution, they gestured nothing. The First Houseman bowed out of the room.

In spite of Serjer's preparations, coaxing Tamelera to leave the bathroom proved to be difficult. In the end, Aloran convinced her to allow him out long enough so he could block Sorn's entry door with the chair from her writing table and lock the door from his own room into the Maze. No sooner had she emerged than she went straight to bed, and asked him to close the curtain at the bed's foot—no doubt, to block her view of the wall where she'd been cornered. He only wished he could have thought of it first.

She didn't ask him to sleep on the day mattress. She didn't need to. Aloran took off his boots and his suit jacket and lay down, staring up at the lights in the vaulted ceiling.

"Aloran," she said. "Are you there?"

"I'm here, Lady."

Her answering sigh of relief lightened his heart, and she fell quiet for a time, but just when he thought she might be sleeping, she gasped.

"Aloran!"

"I'm here, Lady."

She continued to call his name far into the night.

CHAPTER TWENTY-FIVE
Closed Doors

Something terrible had happened—Tagaret knew that much. The scare at the Round of Eight had been awful, with everyone hustled away by the Eminence's Cohort, and he'd had no chance to talk to Gowan, no chance to formulate any kind of plan before he found himself trapped at home again. If he could only have spoken with Mother, they might have found some solace in their memories of sun and courage, but a whole night had passed with no sign of her at all.

This morning, a wysp had been drifting through the suite walls, taunting him with its evident harmlessness. He envied its ability to pass through walls—except, if he really could overhear Father with Nek in his office, or Mother in her rooms, he feared what he might find out.

One thing was beyond question: Aloran would never have attacked Gowan without good reason. When Aloran attacked *him*, it had saved his life! But what could be so bad that Mother wouldn't even show her face?

Soft Imbati footfalls came behind him. "Young Master," said Serjer. "The Arbiter of the First Family Council has come to see you."

Tagaret straightened in surprise. "*Me*, Serjer? You're certain he didn't ask for my brother?"

Serjer bowed. "I'm certain, sir."

Why would Erex have come to see him? Tagaret peered between the double doors into the sitting room. Erex stood with face downcast, pinched in worry. How far had he fallen under Nekantor's influence?

Tagaret took a deep breath, then pushed through the doors. "Erex! What a lovely surprise. Thank you for coming to see me."

Erex instantly lost his pinched expression. "Of course. I was thrilled to see you looking so well at the Round of Eight—I'm glad you didn't come to harm."

"Same to you."

Erex nodded. "I don't wish to be impolite, but we have important business to discuss."

"My future, now that I have one?"

Erex shot him a pointed look. "In fact, your brother."

"Oh." That could be just what he needed—but he glanced involuntarily toward the closed door of Father's office. No; surely after all his years of guidance, Erex was still a man to be trusted. "Let's talk further in."

They pushed through into the private drawing room, and the wysp swirled on the breeze of their arrival. Tagaret chose a seat on the sofa where he could keep an eye on the double doors, just in case. Erex allowed his Kuarmei to guide him into a facing seat, whereupon she moved into protective stance near the arm of the sofa, between the Arbiter and the doors.

"I'm very sorry about my brother," Tagaret said. How many times had he said the same, over caretaker troubles or school discipline? It was deadly serious this time. "You know, he's always been—difficult."

Erex gave a tight smile. "I'm well aware of that. The First Family Council is quite enthusiastic about his candidacy—but, if you'll forgive me, the others don't know him as well as I do. In fact, if he were less, ah, *resourceful*, he wouldn't be where he is now."

So he was right: Nek had done something. Tagaret sat forward, gripping the arm of the couch. "What did he do to you, Erex?"

Erex shifted in his seat. "I'm sorry. If I told you, it would hurt someone whom I love."

Gnash Nekantor. Tagaret took a deep breath and blew it out. "Well, so we both have people to protect. If you're looking to disqualify Nekantor as a candidate for Heir, I can give you something that will do it."

The Arbiter looked at him sharply. "Really?"

"But, sir—first you have to promise that it won't affect your behavior toward my mother."

Erex nodded. "I promise."

Tagaret wiped one hand across his mouth, watching the wysp in the corner of his eye. It felt harder to say this to Erex than it had been to Mother or even Father—hopefully it wasn't a mistake. "Nekantor is weak in his blood."

Erex frowned. "That's strange. His health tests have always been satisfactory."

"Not his body, sir. His mind." He should stick to the obvious, where he had evidence; the rest, Erex no doubt already suspected. "He suffers compulsive obsessions."

At that, Erex paled, and looked away toward the stone wall. "Tagaret, it can't be. I've known him as long as you have. Everyone has—habits."

"Habits like counting buttons?" Tagaret asked. "Like walking in circles touching things? You haven't lived with him, sir. It's not normal. And—and think of what he's done to you."

Erex was panting now, his chest heaving.

"Master?" his servant murmured.

"I'm fine, thank you, Kuarmei." Erex composed himself with an effort. "Tagaret, do you—" He paused for breath. "Do you have any idea how *dangerous* this information is? I don't see what we can do with it short of making your brother disappear. One of the four best protected boys in all Varin!"

"What do you mean, disappear?"

Erex pressed his index fingers together. "I understand you wanting to protect your mother for her involvement, but you'll have no hope if you release this information publicly. There's a reason why Family Councils are so cautious with each choice they make to confirm a child healthy enough to participate in the Society. A revelation like this would have dire consequences, not the least of which would be that your brother would suspect you had betrayed him. This leaves us few options. Attempts on a candidate's life are extremely risky, even for rivals from whom such acts are expected. I'll have to . . . well, I'll think about what to do. In the meantime, I recommend you be very careful."

Tagaret clenched his fists. "When will it be time to *stop* being careful?"

The Arbiter didn't answer.

Tagaret suppressed a snort. "Well, I could hardly be more careful than I am now. Since Aloran was arrested, I haven't even been able to leave the house."

"Ah, Tagaret." A faint smile came to Erex's face. "In fact, I'd been thinking of that. Kuarmei, would you give us the papers, please?"

Tagaret looked up. Erex's sober-faced female servant arrayed a thick set of papers on the low brass table between them. Official print documents, with fancy axis serifs—Tagaret blinked at them.

"Service Academy certifications," Erex said. "These are the current top Service Academy students. I hope you will find one among them possesses the quality you seek." He laid a thinner paper beside the others. "In fact, you'll need to write your own inquiry letter, but you may use this one as an example."

Tagaret swallowed, gathering up the papers reluctantly. "I haven't been in role-play session for a while, sir."

"Tagaret, you need a manservant, and you need one now. Do you want to remain helpless until the end of Selection?"

"No, but . . ." He heard the zap of the assassin's weapon again, then the ping of metal on glass. He felt the dizzy choking, then the stabbing pain in his leg . . . "How can I trust someone new to save my life?"

"You mean someone besides your mother's Aloran?"

Tagaret flushed. The look in the Arbiter's eyes made him feel like a schoolboy.

"You realize any manservant would have done the same," Erex said. "Academy certification means confidence as unshakable as a shinca. You can't afford to let fondness influence your treatment of servants. Given your brother's current position, we need you to be as strong as possible, politically."

He could hear what Erex was too polite to say: *and that won't happen if you're seen as soft with Imbati.* "You're right, sir," he admitted. "But I don't see how I can be strong politically—not at this point."

"Nonsense." Erex smiled. "In fact, you're no less strong now than you were at your birthday party. The rules of the game haven't changed; only the expectations."

How right he was. Before Heir Selection began, the Sixth Family would have been thrilled to see him approach Della, and Father was the problem—now, Father would be pleased, while the Sixth Family wanted their alliance only with the Heir himself. Greedy as Plis, they were. But if Erex was right, maybe this would be easier than he thought. Maybe a simple alliance would be counteroffer enough. "Erex," Tagaret said. "Can you help me speak to the Sixth Family Council?"

Erex lost his smile. "Sixth Family? Why them?"

"While I was ill, they offered Nekantor an alliance."

"Hm. And I gather the girl is one in whom you have interest?"

"Yes," Tagaret admitted.

"I'd be more sanguine if it weren't the Sixth Family," said Erex. "I don't trust the quality of their blood. And Doross is not a man of whose tastes I approve."

"But it's not just an alliance," Tagaret explained. "I *know* this girl. She and I—" He stopped himself. Erex wouldn't care if they'd listened to *The Catacomb* together, or if they'd shared a kiss. "Look, I won't say we're a perfect Sirin and Eyn, but we're well matched. I wouldn't make her miserable for her whole life."

Erex folded his gloved hands in his lap and said nothing.

Tagaret bit back a desperate urge to shake him. "Sir, you and Lady Keir have something special, don't you?" he asked. "You protect each other."

Erex spoke softly. "In fact, we do."

"And you know what my mother's life is like. I can't let that happen to Della. Can you imagine spending your entire life in partnership with the wrong person?"

A muscle clenched in the Arbiter's jaw. "You must not belittle your mother and father's partnership," he said coldly. "Be grateful, for you are their gift to the Race."

"I'm sorry," Tagaret gulped. He'd never seen Erex angry. Even with Nekantor, Erex was more patient than anyone he knew—why was he angry?

"You can't expect to be treated like a child anymore, Tagaret. Our duties to the Grobal Trust, and to the continuity of the Race, have nothing to do with our personal desires. I learned this, and so will you. These are the responsibilities of our exalted station."

And you think that's good enough? Tagaret wanted to shout, but he didn't dare look Erex in the eye. He was still staring at the papers on his knees, mortified, when the doors from the sitting room burst open.

Nekantor was there, flushed and ecstatic, with Benél holding the back of his neck.

"Witnesses!" Nekantor hissed, and Benél whipped his hand away at once. "Tagaret, what in Varin's name are you doing, bringing *him* back here?"

"Hello, Nek," Tagaret replied coolly. "I'll invite Erex in if I like. Seems as if you've invited Benél."

Arbiter Erex stood up and brushed off the front of his jacket. "Young Nekantor," he said. "Didn't you hear about Sangar of the Eighth Family? One might wonder whether you truly care for the future of the Grobal Race. Be careful."

Nekantor growled. "Be careful *yourself*, Erex."

"Nekantor, what a way to speak to the Arbiter of the First Family Council!"

Mercy, was that Mother? Tagaret whirled around. Mother took a single step past the threshold of her room, with Aloran behind her back as close as a shadow. Suddenly, everything felt better. If the others hadn't been watching, he would have run into her arms.

"Arbiter Erex, I'm sorry," Mother said. "Please don't mind Nekantor. It's so kind of you to pay us a visit."

Erex bowed. "Lady Tamelera, what a pleasure to see you. In fact, I was just on my way out."

"I'll take you to the door, sir," said Tagaret quickly.

Nekantor snorted. He left with Benél and stalked off toward his room, with Arissen Karyas a few feet behind them.

"Tagaret?" Mother called. "Could you come speak to me afterward?"

"I'd love to." Thank Heile she wasn't shutting him out anymore. Tagaret bade Erex goodbye as briefly as courtesy permitted, dropped the papers on his desk, then ran back to Mother's room. She let him in, but she didn't embrace him. He heard the door click; Aloran had locked them in.

Everything was not all right.

"Mother, what happened?"

Mother took his hand in hers and led him over to the lounge chairs. There was something tentative in the way she moved. "Love, I need to ask you something."

He sat down in the chair beside her. "Anything."

Mother inhaled to speak, then seemed to change her mind. "Aloran?"

"Yes, Lady?"

"Could you . . . go stand by the window?"

"Yes, Lady." Aloran stood facing the view outside, taut and still in his black silk.

What was that about? "Mother," Tagaret whispered, leaning toward her. "Did he *do* something?"

"Oh!" she exclaimed. "Oh, Tagaret, no. I just—" She lowered her voice. "This is embarrassing, darling, and I didn't know who to ask but you."

He blinked. "What?"

"I want Aloran to sleep in this room."

"You—*what?* Why?"

Mother blushed. "Oh, holy Sirin, it's not—well, Serjer made him up a daybed last night, after Garr . . . But today . . . today isn't the same kind of emergency, and I'm afraid he won't do it. But I really need him to. I mean, I need him to be here."

Tagaret stared at her. The way she blushed—it made the world shift uncertainly. Would she ask him to see Aloran differently now, as she had Eyli? He shook his head. "Mother . . . what are you saying?"

"Oh, I'm saying this badly." Mother leaned so close that her lips brushed his ear. "Tagaret, your father attacked me last night. I don't feel safe anymore."

Tagaret gasped and his stomach lurched. What had he been thinking, even to consider . . . what he'd been considering? Let holy Plis take Father's head—let Varin gnash him into smoldering bits! "Y—you should keep Aloran beside you, then," he stammered, half-choking. "Of course, you should; that's what he's *for*."

Mother took a shuddering breath. "You're right, love. You are."

"If it's not part of his assigned duties, then change them. There are plenty of ladies who require night attention. Pay him more, if necessary. I'm surprised you haven't already arranged it."

She sighed. "It's just—I've been—embarrassed."

"*Embarrassed?*" Her eyes went wide, so he lowered his voice again. "Look—Aloran was with you day and night while I had the fever. He even went with us to the surface! How can this be more difficult?"

"I know, I know, it makes no sense. I'm sorry." She stroked his arm. Her cheeks were still flushed, her eyes guilty. "Love, could you stay while I speak to him? It would be so much easier . . ."

"No problem." What could possibly embarrass her about this was beyond him. *Your father attacked me* was plenty of reason. Heile's mercy, it was enough to make him sick.

"Aloran, could you come here, please?" Mother said.

"Yes, Lady." Aloran returned swiftly from the window. He got on his knees and lowered his dark head until it touched the floor at her feet.

Mother flashed over a grateful glance; Tagaret forced himself to smile.

"Aloran, I will be adding to your duties," Mother said. "I'd like you to stay on night duty, for the next . . ." She took a deep breath. "I'm not sure how long. I hope you will find this change satisfactory. I am happy to pay you extra for the additional hours, as specified in your contract."

"It would be my pleasure, Lady." Aloran sounded relieved. "I would give my life for your safety."

Mother smiled. But whether it was the way she unconsciously rubbed her upper arm, or the emotion that had colored Aloran's response, Tagaret could no longer doubt she needed him constantly.

When he left them, he went straight to his room, to the certification documents which lay on his desk. He copied Erex's model inquiry onto new paper, inserting information where necessary.

It felt mechanical.

He couldn't help remembering Aloran's arm supporting him when he was too weak to sit. He needed *trust*, not anonymous papers. Even in role-play it could take weeks to get past an Academy student's fear for a glimpse of the Imbati's real personality.

Which meant if he wanted protection for the rest of the Selection, he'd have to ask . . . Father.

Instantly he was on his feet, panting, fists clenched. *How* could he ask Father? How could he even *look* at him?

No—there was one other bodyguard in the house. He'd better do this before he thought too hard.

Tagaret marched to the end of the hall, where Arissen Karyas stood at attention beside Nekantor's door.

He knocked.

There was no answer. Karyas raised her eyebrows at him.

Oh, Trigis and Bes, Benél had followed Nek down here, hadn't he? Well, there was no help for it. He knocked again, harder. Waited.

His brother might be too busy to notice. Or, just taking a while to get presentable. That was a better thought; Nek always took time to get presentable.

He knocked again. Waited.

Finally, Nekantor opened the door. He wasn't wearing his coat. Neither was he fidgeting. "Tagaret? What do you want?"

"You owe me," Tagaret said. He refused to look past his brother into the room, glancing instead at Arissen Karyas. "I need you to help me contact the Sixth Family."

Nekantor laughed. "Look, Benél," he said. "Tagaret's come to play politics."

Benél appeared, stroking Nekantor's neck. "Starting to care about the game, is he?"

"Not really. This is about his girl."

Tagaret refused to choke. He was not—was *not*—going to let Nekantor get to him. "Well?" he said. "Are you interested in the Sixth Family's vote or not?"

The Sixth Family Council invited them to meet at Della's house. Tagaret hid his hope, yet he had to imagine that Enwin had influenced the invitation. At last, he'd be able to do *something*.

In the Conveyor's Hall, Nek boarded a skimmer inspected by Arissen Karyas. A second skimmer was in the care of a man as lithe as a cave-cat, who wore plain clothes and a neck scarf in Arissen red. Tagaret approached him cautiously.

"Arissen?" he asked. "What's your name?"

"Don't ask," said Nekantor.

The catlike Arissen smiled a little. "I'm a friend of Karyas, sir. Just helping out for your safety."

Tagaret glanced at Nek, who was smirking. "Well. Thank you, then."

"Sir."

They drove out. When they turned into the mercantile circumference where Aloran had saved him from the disguised assassin, atmospheric lamps faded on the cavern roof, and street lights rose to replace them. Beyond that, Tagaret couldn't recognize the streets—neither the radius nor the smaller circumference where Enwin's house stood. But he recognized the entry door and, of course, the foyer with its servants in black-and-green livery.

Little more than silence issued from the inner rooms now, but he remembered music. The golden room with the yojosmei; Kartunnen Ryanin shaking his hand; Vant, the well-spoken apprentice who played *The Catacomb* as passionately as his master; Della's Heile-touched sister; faint music merging into a kiss that Sirin himself would have envied.

He frowned. That had been after the Accession Ball, yet Della had escaped the fever? It had to be Heile's own miracle . . .

Footsteps were approaching.

Four men with manservants emerged warily from the inner rooms. Tagaret sought vainly for recognition in Enwin's gaze. The four Imbati appeared to be sizing up the danger posed by Karyas. Karyas' catlike friend had stayed outside, ostensibly to guard the skimmers against sabotage—but more likely because he was 'just helping out' and didn't want to be seen.

"Greetings to you," said the dour man who had entered first. "Do you bring business, young Nekantor of the First Family? Where's Speaker Garr?"

Nekantor straightened his cuffs and ignored the question. "Thank you for finding time for us, Doross. I imagine the Sixth Family would still prefer to emerge from this Selection with its influence expanded."

Doross' mouth quirked to one side—not precisely a smile. "Oh, we will. In partnership to the Heir himself."

Nekantor nodded. "Innis, yes, I know your plan. But what if *I* win? Then where will your gamble have left you?"

"You're certainly ambitious," Doross drawled.

Enwin flinched.

Tagaret bit his lip. Why wouldn't Enwin look at him? Hadn't he *asked* them for a counteroffer?

"Naturally, I have the same ambitions as any candidate," Nekantor said. "But the first ambition here was yours. Do you still have interest in a cabinet seat? At the expense of, say, the Fifth Family? Or are you too intimate with them these days?"

Doross grunted.

Nek put on a reasonable tone. "I know I behaved badly when you made your first offer. It was a beginner's mistake—but the fact is, my brother is better suited to partnership than I. In the ultimate test of Kinders fever, he's proven the strength of his blood. And he's a good ten times more handsome than old Innis."

The bargaining made Tagaret's skin crawl. A-girl-for-a-vote felt like a purchase—wasn't this supposed to be an *alliance?* "Sirs," he said, "I don't intend to be merely a partnership placement. In an alliance between us, Lady Della would bring the Sixth Family's interests before the First Family's eye."

Nekantor lashed him with a look of fury.

Nek could glare if he liked. Someone else was listening: Enwin looked up at last, meeting his eyes with a cautious nod. If this offer could convince Doross and the Council, then it was worth a glare, or even three.

"Are you serious?" asked Doross. "That's your offer?"

"Perfectly serious, sir."

Doross snorted. "I'm not convinced, boys. If you could keep your word, that would be one thing."

Tagaret took a breath to object, but Nekantor spoke first.

"How do you know we won't?"

"Doross," said Enwin suddenly. "Young Tagaret has reached his Age of Choice. He is not known for falsehood."

Doross waved him off. "Easy enough to make offers. Harder to keep them. They obviously don't understand the kind of pressures that grown men come under."

"Sir," Tagaret objected grimly. "I believe I understand pressures."

Doross only shrugged. "If you really want us to believe the First Family will consider the demands of the Sixth, let your father come and tell us so himself." He gestured to the servants. "Show them out."

Tagaret walked out numbly. *That wasn't how it was supposed to happen.*

Nek was visibly fuming but held his tongue until they hit the street outside. "Let your *father* come?!" he snapped. "Father doesn't run me. I'll show them, gnash it!"

Tagaret looked up at the high wall of the house. With the street lamp glaring straight down into his face, it was impossible to see any windows. Chances were, none of them even faced the outside. Defeated, he approached his skimmer, but then something moved beyond the lamplight, at the corner of the nearest radius. He froze.

The catlike Arissen man drew his weapon.

A deep, smooth voice came out of the dark. "The heart that is valiant triumphs over all, sir. If I may, I would like to speak to Grobal Tagaret of the First Family."

Yoral. Tagaret grabbed the Arissen's shoulder. "Wait, I know him. That's Della's Yoral of the Household of the Sixth Family."

The Arissen didn't lower his weapon. "Can you trust him, sir?"

"Absolutely."

"Tagaret, don't," Nekantor said.

Tagaret ignored him and ran to the corner. Yoral bowed to him, and without speaking again, turned southward into the radius. Tagaret followed.

The walls here yielded few windows, all of them dark and empty. Tagaret scanned the pools of orange lamplight along the radius ahead, but could see no one. "Yoral," he murmured. "Do you have a message?"

"Della wishes to speak to you, sir."

"She does?" His heart beat faster. "Where?"

"In here." Yoral stopped. Beside him was a dark opening between the outer walls of two adjacent homes—a space not even wide enough to pass two skimmers side by side. Tagaret peered in. It was instantly obvious that he didn't belong there. The narrow dimness was vaguely reminiscent of the Maze at home, except this place smelled of rot.

A shudder ran down his back. "What is this?"

"I beg your pardon, sir," the Imbati said. "We must use the back entrance of the house if you wish to approach unseen."

Behind him, Nek and the Arissen caught up. "Stop!" Nek cried.

"Varin's teeth, Tagaret, you can't, that's—that's—" He made a choking sound and turned his back.

"Sir," said Arissen Karyas, "it's the garbage access. The Akrabitti way."

On the day the assassin attacked, Aloran had told him Akrabitti had their own alleyways. His stomach rolled. "Della's in *there?*"

"No, sir," said Yoral patiently. "She's waiting in the house, near the back entrance. If you will permit me to escort you."

He swallowed hard. "All right."

He walked in, following Yoral closely. The looming walls of the homes on either side were festooned with dark tangles of cable and pipe; the ground was dry in places, sticky in others, and faint movements showed in the deeper shadows. He didn't want to contemplate what might be in the glistening gutter that ran down the center.

At last, a bright doorway appeared on his left. Stepping into the light of a laundry room, Tagaret realized he'd been holding his breath. He gulped in air.

"I apologize, sir," said Yoral. "Are you well?"

Tagaret sucked air and nodded. "Are there many places like this?"

The Imbati regarded him calmly. "They parallel every circumference in Pelismara, sir."

"I'm sorry." His cheeks flushed, but this shame wasn't his alone—it belonged to everyone who had watched the Lowers at the Accession Ball, applauding the Grobal Trust without seeing it complete. He understood suddenly how Aloran had circled behind the assassin at the clothes shop.

"Sir," said Yoral. "My Lady is waiting."

They left the laundry room for a luxurious hall, and from there passed through a white door. Della was here. Her radiance filled the tiny office within; it stole his breath differently from the fetid darkness. She was a marvel.

"Tagaret!" she cried. "You're really alive!"

"Della . . ." His feet tried to rush to her. It took all his effort to stop them. "I'm sorry. I'm so sorry."

"No, *I'm* sorry," she said. "I shouldn't have dragged you back here, but I didn't know how else to see you." She came to him, picked up his hand, softly stroked the back of it. "And I *had* to see you."

A wave of warmth melted down his spine into his thighs. He glanced at Yoral; the Imbati had turned his back, but he didn't dare take her in his arms. Instead, he lifted her fingers to his lips.

"Look at you," he murmured. "You're as healthy as the day we met. I can't imagine how I didn't give you the fever."

"My parents and I are inoculated. Father arranges it every year, to protect Liadis."

"Then thank Sirin I didn't touch her." He shook his head. "Your father must be so angry with me. My counteroffer wasn't good enough."

"Counteroffers!" Della pulled her hand away. "Don't tell me about counteroffers."

The scorn in her eyes burned his heart. "But, Della, I had to—"

"I hate Doross! Demeaning you, forcing you to bargain. And Father! Father *lets* him."

Tagaret shook his head. "It's not your father's fault," he said. "Innis of the—"

"*Innis* doesn't know better. Father does."

"Surely he's doing his best . . ."

"Is he?" Her eyes flared. "He would do anything for Liadis. I thought it was because he loved her, but maybe it was because she had to be kept out of sight anyway. It's easy to break the rules when nobody's watching."

"I'm so sorry," he said. He couldn't deny it; here he was, doing what he was told, conforming to the rules of Selection. Without realizing it, he'd even lost hold of his plans to help ladies. And what had become of the bravery he'd felt out on the surface, that had shaken his world and made anything seem possible? He reached for Della's hands, to stop him falling into the abyss of despair. Thank Sirin and Eyn, she took them in hers. "How *can* I help you, Della? What do you think I should do?"

Della lost her certainty. So she did know it was impossible to escape the watching eyes of the Society. "Stop Innis," she said. "That's the first thing. Don't let him make me his prize."

"And what else?"

She bit her lip. "I don't care if it's hopeless, Tagaret. Don't play their stupid game. You know better."

"I'll try," he said. But what kind of courage would that take?

CHAPTER TWENTY-SIX

Fall

Dirt in the dark, sticky shadows full of Lowers. The alleyway gaped at him from between the walls, the stinking mouth of some awful creature. Its breath reached outward, the sticky shadows reaching toward him like fingers.

"Karyas," Nekantor panted. "Get me out of here."

"Sir?" said Karyas. "What about your brother?"

Tagaret had gone into it. Oh, gods, *he'd gone into it,* and he would come out of it wearing the creature's breath, carrying the shadows— "Karyas, now!"

The Arissen shot a glance at her friend, who shrugged and nodded. In that second, the tips of the sticky shadows touched, and clung.

"Yes, sir," Karyas said. She drove fast, but it was too late, too late, and the shadows crawled up his fingers, to his hands, his arms. They wouldn't let go, even in the light of the Conveyor's Hall, not even in the noble halls of the Residence. Oh, gods!

He ran straight to Benél's suite, banged on the door, and snapped at the Imbati who opened it, "Get me Benél."

"Pardon me, sir," said the Imbati blandly.

He was allowed into the vestibule, at least. Seconds passed. Nekantor clenched his fists, struggled for breath, feeling the scream coming. The shadows tightened, crawling toward his shoulders, onto his neck. He whimpered aloud.

Benél came through the curtain. "Nek?"

"Benél," Nekantor pleaded. "Touch me."

Benél shot a quick glance over his shoulder, but the Imbati had gone. He moved in fast—arms, hands, mouth. A shock of power, relief so overwhelming Nekantor could scarcely stand. The shadows were gone. He murmured, "More . . ."

"Shh," Benél said. "If you want to come in, you'll have to stay quiet."

Nekantor shook his head. "Come out with me? Carefully, this time, mind you."

Benél's eyes flicked to one side, toward the servant's curtain. "Remeni," he said, in a low voice. "I'm going out."

Yes, yes. Only fifty-seven paces left, and he took them fast. Benél didn't touch him again, but they walked together. He could still taste power in his mouth. He slapped the contact pad of his own suite, and walked in.

Father sat on the couch, facing him with Sorn behind his shoulder.

Wrong. Something was different. The scratches on his face, they were . . . no, they were still there. He'd covered them with *paint?*

"You *missed* an *appointment*," Father growled. "You and Tagaret both. The Tenth Family was to meet with us tonight. Arrange an alliance. And just look what you've been doing!"

"You have no idea what I was doing," Nekantor snapped, but he could feel Benél take a step backward. He clenched his fists. "I was on Selection business, since *you're* in no shape to go out. What do you think you are with all that paint, some kind of Kartunnen?"

Father's face darkened. "You'd better send that boy away. He's stolen your face, and if you let him, he'll steal your throne as well."

Suddenly, the front door clicked, and Tagaret walked in. Nekantor leapt sideways, away from the sticky shadows. "Stay back, Tagaret."

"Nek? Benél?" Tagaret said in surprise, and then his voice cracked. "Father?"

Father lurched to his feet. "Gnash you both—where in Varin's name have you been?"

Tagaret answered stiffly. "We were negotiating for the Selection."

"You're both idiots!" Father shouted. "*I* negotiate for the First Family! How many times do you think the Tenth Family will offer us that girl before they tire of our incompetence?"

Tagaret turned bright red.

Nekantor snorted. "So now it's *our* fault? *You're* the one who looks like he lost a fight with a kanguan."

"*Enough*." Power, like boulders grinding. "Young Benél, you're going home right now."

"Yes, sir," said Benél.

"Tagaret, Nekantor, get to your rooms. From now on, you'll go nowhere unless it's with me." Father wheezed and started coughing.

Tagaret said nothing.

Nekantor looked at Benél. That was not defeat in his eyes as he left; it was anticipation. Nekantor shivered but lowered his head. The capitulation move was called for now. That would get him to Benél sooner.

"Yes, Father," he said. Then he ran—ran before Father could catch his breath, before Tagaret could contaminate him again with the sticky shadows. He locked himself into his room and leaned against the door. Ran his finger along the crack between bronze and stone. From there, he moved to his desk, pushed on each closed drawer, and pushed in his chair. Checked the window shade—*I'll come back to you*—ran his hand up the bed to the bedside table, tapped, one, two, three. Crossed to the wardrobe and pressed its doors shut, caressed its cool brass drawer handles. Then the bathroom door, the main door.

Now he could go back to the perfect window shade, open it, and open the window.

"Nek," Benél called.

"Come up," Nekantor hissed.

Benél's hands came to the stone sill, and Benél vaulted up—fell back on the first try, but on the second, he stayed and wriggled in. Nekantor backed off into the center of the room.

Benél picked himself up, brushed himself off. All disarranged. The sight of it set hooks in Nekantor's mind, pulling his hands toward Benél's clothes, straightening, but stroking, too. Oh, Benél was very strong. Nekantor breathed hard, feeling power grow in his stomach. Perfection felt very close now.

Benél moved behind him. Benél's strong hands came over him, electric with power. Nekantor watched his vest buttons come undone, three-two-one, and Benél pulled the vest down off his shoulders and twisted it around his wrists. Jerked him backward, up against Benél's body hard and insistent. Nekantor gasped in relief and delight, and turned, and found Benél's mouth for a kiss—a hot push of permission. The rest of the buttons went very fast, nine-eight-seven-six-five-four-three-two-one. Benél shoved him hard, down onto the bed; pulled his arms up over his head; pushed his legs apart.

Nekantor lay limp and breathless. Anticipation skittered across his naked back. He listened for Benél.

Benél stalked behind him, breathing like a cave-cat, a promise of violence. Power, it was all power! He could feel it now, and it would pound him, penetrate him, echo inside him until there was room for nothing but that perfect relief—no shadows, no Fathers, no brothers, no buttons. Ah, perfection, how could he wait?

"Benél, please."

The cave-cat pounced.

Screaming pleasure filled his body, his mind, until everything was Benél, and there was nothing else.

Nothing left.

Nothing.

When Nekantor woke, his body was nerveless, his mind empty as a drained glass. He drew a slow breath. Sighed, "Benél."

Benél had stayed over. His hand slid under Nekantor's hip, pulled him into a curl, and the strong arms wrapped around him.

"My brother is useless," Nekantor sighed. "He made the stupidest offer imaginable with the Sixth Family yesterday. No wonder they didn't believe us. He should just jump in a crevasse."

Benél shifted against him. "I thought you had a plan for everybody."

"Fah."

"Come on," Benél said. "I'm sure he's good for something. Even Yril and Grenth were good for *something*."

Nekantor rolled on his stomach, pushed himself up on his elbows, and looked at Benél. "But now everyone knows he's not going to be Heir."

Benél shrugged; muscles moved in his shoulders. "He's attractive. He survived the fever. He's First Family. If you keep him beside you, he can make you look good."

"Or he can make offers the First Family won't deliver on, and run off into filthy Lowers' holes when nobody's looking."

Benél snorted. "Nek, who cares what he does when nobody's looking? Who cares what he offers? He might not get you many votes, but you don't need them *all*, just *enough*. Once you win, you could do anything with him. Put him on the cabinet. Make him work for you."

Ah—when Benél understood, he was powerful. Nekantor smirked. "Well, he'd be better than that Selemei creature. Of course, then I'd have to see his rock-toad face all the time. I'd much rather look at you."

Benél smiled and pulled him close.

Rap-rap on the door.

Go away. Knocking would not bother him. Nothing would bother him now; Benél was all that mattered.

Benél's hands stopped moving. "Nek," he said. "Maybe you should answer."

"Tagaret can get lost in an adjunct."

Louder: bang-bang. And still louder: Bang-bang-bang!

"That sounds like your father, Nek."

Father, who did not want him with Benél. Father, who still had power and this one last day to win him votes before the Round of Four. "Oh, fine. But let's get you out of here. No evidence."

They got up and dressed. Father kept banging, but the door was locked, and he could not breach their citadel. Benél kissed him, smiled, and hopped out the window. Nekantor closed the window and the shade, and made the bed. Combed his hair. Remembered his coat. Straightened his cuffs. By the time he opened the door, Father was red in the face, breathing hard. Arissen Karyas was hiding a smirk.

"You've defied me." Father lumbered past him into the room, but now everything was perfect, with no sign that Benél had been here. "You little tunnel-hound!"

"Which votes do you wish me to win today, Father?"

Father only growled and went out to the drawing room. He banged on Tagaret's door.

The locked door. No, no—Nekantor looked away fast, toward the amethyst geode in the corner. He turned inward to the perfection that remained in his body. Then Tagaret's lock clicked open.

"Tagaret," said Father. "You're coming out with us to win the Tenth Family's vote. And you'll have to look good. You've got four minutes to get as handsome as Holy Sirin himself."

"I hate you," said Tagaret.

Abruptly, the double doors opened. The First Houseman walked in and bowed. "Young Master Nekantor," he said. "An urgent message: the Eminence wishes to see you."

Father's anger exploded into a question. "What?!"

The Imbati didn't flinch. "Master?"

"No, I got it," Father said. "Let's go."

Serjer bowed. "The Eminence has requested to see him alone, sir."

Now Father looked over, accusing. "Impossible!"

Nekantor narrowed his eyes. There was no scheduled interview today. This was different, and unexplained. "Herin bends the rules when it pleases him," he said. "Where?"

"In his private library, sir," the Imbati said.

The room of chaos and traps. Oh, yes, Herin was playing a game—a game within the larger game, and one whose shape he couldn't see. It twisted a knot in his throat. "Fine."

Nekantor beckoned Karyas toward the door. Karyas already had her weapon drawn; she knew this summons wasn't within the rules. Father followed with his Sorn, because he still had power enough to insist. Nekantor walked fast, trying not to feel the wrongness of Father following. But it would be all right; so long as Father didn't *enter* the library, he would not be disobeying the Eminence's order, and it should be safe enough.

What *was* Herin's game? Would he ask a favor? That might be good. Just as likely, the room would be full of open teeth. Careful, careful now. Could someone have swayed Herin with another sort of offer?

The library doors opened as they approached. "Come in, Nekantor of the First Family, sir," the Eminence's Imbati said. "The Eminence does not like to wait."

Father caught up, panting and wheezing. Perfect: no breath to argue.

"Thank you, Imbati," Nekantor said, walking forward. "Sorry if I'm late. Father, I'll be out in a few moments." He looked down at his watch. Yes, an excellent first move, and it would keep him safe going in—but inside, the Eminence was not where he should have been. He would have to look up, find where he was sitting.

What if he looked up, and the room strangled him?

"Nekantor of the First Family," the Eminence's voice said.

There, on the left. Nekantor turned and looked up. Herin was seated in a stuffed chair, wearing a suit of glimmering brown and amber, every dark gold curl on his head shaped and perfect. But he was not smiling. Another man stood beside him.

Erex, the Arbiter of the First Family Council.

What are you doing here?

He managed not to say it aloud. "Good morning, your Eminence. Good morning, Arbiter Erex, sir."

"Good morning, young Nekantor."

Erex was the reason he was here. And Erex had arrived here before him, which meant secret games. Information had been exchanged, here among the random chairs, in the presence of the shinca, under the strange lights.

What did Erex have on him? Information about Garr's assassinations? Surely not. Had someone tracked his Kartunnen infiltrator back to Karyas? But she'd said she knew how to be careful . . . Was it the blackmail? It couldn't be the brothel; that, Herin already knew about. Was it Benél? Too many possibilities, each a potential disaster if he let slip his tongue and guessed wrong.

He cleared his throat. "I imagine the Family's Arbiter has come to you with some complaint about me, your Eminence?" He shifted his feet; the carpet squirmed. He tried to look at Erex, and his throat tightened; he took a deep breath and turned back fast to Herin, to the Eminence's handsome face and his gleaming buttons. "Is it that I have bad manners with people I don't like? If so, then he's telling you something you already know."

Herin smiled. "I find your aggression refreshing, young Nekantor. Erex and I have been chatting, and he believes I should disqualify your candidacy. What do you think of that?"

Traitor. Nekantor lashed a look at Erex—mistake. The sight of him brought the chaos encroaching all around. He looked down quickly at his watch, dared count only four seconds, then looked up at Herin again. At least Herin was easy on the mind. "I'm surprised that the Arbiter of my Family Council would want to undermine his own judgment in this manner," Nekantor said. "He approved me."

Herin chuckled.

Amusement? Derision? Nekantor tried not to clench his teeth. If Herin had been told of the blackmail, and forgiven Erex, then this game was already lost. But Erex couldn't have told him. No one could forgive what Erex had done. Impossible.

The Eminence said, "I did tell him he had insufficient grounds."

"I'm sure."

"But still, what he says concerns me. That you would turn down an offer of partnership, preferring the company of a male cousin. Overnight, no less. It's behavior unbecoming an Heir to the legacy of Grobal Fyn."

Holy Twins. This wasn't about Father or Karyas, or the brothel. It was about *Benél!* Anger burned in his face, sparked fire in his chest. He'd been careful, hidden the evidence, even made Benél change his behavior when Father said to— but Erex hadn't come into his house to warn him. He'd been there to betray him!

"The partnership offer was flawed on its own merits," Nekantor said. "Call me sentimental, but I refused the girl because my brother wanted her more. It has nothing to do with—with spying in my house, and slander on the basis of thin suspicion."

Herin chuckled again. "You *do* have bad manners with people you don't like," he said. "But if a boy wants me to support him, he needs to be above suspicion."

He knew what that meant. Herin believed Erex; that was two votes gone, maybe more if Herin decided to talk.

But he had information on Erex: Erex naked with a Kartunnen whore. Erex was tainted. Erex must be removed.

"Eminence," Nekantor said, "I think you ought to know *where* Arbiter Erex first came by his suspicions." He refused to look at Erex, at the weird half-empty bookshelves, the shinca or the lights. "My cousin Benél and I saw him in the brothel raid."

"A ridiculous accusation," Erex burst out. Predictable. "Are you confessing to involvement in illegal activity?"

The Eminence Herin held up one hand. "Arbiter, wait. Young Nekantor and I have discussed this on a previous occasion; I know what *he* was doing at the raid." He frowned. "What were *you* doing there?"

Erex said nothing.

Ah, feel the power shift! "Benél and I both saw him," Nekantor said. "He was in the first room we opened, enjoying the services of a *Kartunnen man.* And when we came in to punish those who dared to put the health of the Grobal at risk, he threatened us." He stood straighter. "Our own Family's Arbiter threatened us, to protect his Lower lover! Bring Benél here and ask him now if you like; he'll tell you the same."

Herin lost his composure. His eyes widened in shock, turning, shifting irresistibly toward Erex. And look at Erex now: pale and shaking, and only his Imbati woman kept him standing.

But he should never have looked at Erex.

Chaos invaded suddenly, pushing through his skin and up his nerves. Gods, the room was closing, he had to get out—no, he had to breathe, he hadn't finished the move. Erex must not bring *him* down— Erex must fall alone! The air tightened; Nekantor gulped it fast, forcing words out with his hands shaking. "Accuse me if you like," he panted. "Say I've neglected the Race for the sake of my brother." The panic hit his backbone, and he clenched his fists. "But I'm not the one fraternizing with Lowers who are conspiring against us!"

He ran. Dodged the chairs, fumbled at the door, stumbled out and into Karyas, bounced off.

"Nekantor! What happened?" Father demanded.

No, not Father—he swerved around him, down the hall. The Arissen woman caught up swiftly.

"Home," he snapped. "Now."

"Yes, sir."

He needed Benél—but it had gone too far, and they had been betrayed.

He ran home, into his rooms, slammed the door, and screamed. He should never have made the bed. The disarranged sheets might have pulled him back into perfection, but now there was no sign left of Benél. He flung himself on the bed, felt for his bedside table, and his fingers found the whore's ring. He traced it in circles, counting. Counting and counting, until the vibrations of chaos slowly—too slowly— began to still.

This was bad. He'd lost two votes, maybe more; his line in the game had been jolted aside. What were the next moves? Erex's disgrace *might* be enough to distract Herin from spreading the Arbiter's accusations, but was it? Had Herin made any note of his last words? There were things to do, moves that had been planned, but were they the right ones now? Without the pattern, he couldn't move.

Father banged on the door. "Nekantor! What happened? Come out—we have to meet the Tenth Family!"

Nekantor didn't answer. He'd lost the Sixth Family's vote because he hadn't brought Father. He'd lost the Third Family's votes because Father had warned him, but he hadn't hidden the evidence quickly enough, completely enough. He needed the Tenth Family's vote, but Herin had dropped a stone into the game, and who knew how far the ripples would spread? If they went out, they would meet the rumors—and how could Father defend him with scratches on his face, and Lower paint, too?

No: he had to stay here, safe, until he found the pattern again.

"Nekantor!"

He would not say Father had been right. He would not ask for help.

"Nekantor, open this door!"

"No!"

Father howled in rage, but he did not have the key, and he could not open a lock with a wire, and at last there was silence.

Nekantor sat alone, searching for the pattern. In Benél's room he had seen it, but to search there was too great a risk. Father's office was a mess of papers; he would find no pattern there.

He would *not* ask Father for help.

No one brought him food. He didn't care. He circled out hours until sleep grabbed him and pushed him down. Morning brought no better vision, only the Round of Four descending on him like heavy darkness. He searched, searched for the pattern.

Behind the curtain on his wall, a door opened. Nekantor whirled on it. "Imbati!" Whoever this was, he would pay for entering where he was not welcome . . .

No one came in. A tray of food slid through onto his floor, and he stared at it.

Dinner?!

He closed and opened his hands. The meal was a terrible sentence. Had he lost so much time? No pattern; and no time, either. He ate—

only because it would not advance the First Family if he fainted in the Round of Four. He bathed. Dressed, hands shaking on his buttons. Circled five times before he dared step out, blind to the pattern and unable to see the line beneath his feet.

Father didn't seem angry anymore, only tired. Nekantor walked, Father and Sorn on his left, Karyas on his right, out to the cabinet meeting room.

"Nekantor," Father said. "The discussion will be about policy, so don't try too hard."

Nekantor looked at him. Father was pulling at his chin, while Sorn stood expressionless. "Father," he began. *I made a mistake. Help me see the pattern.* The words choked him, and he couldn't get them out. "This is my topic. Kinders fever—they chose it because of me."

Father frowned and pulled him down by the arm, wheezing in his ear. "I mean it. Don't try to look better than Innis; he's twice your age and he'll make you look like a fool if you do. Let your youth protect you."

Nekantor shuddered. "Don't touch me, Father."

Now there were people. Cabinet Secretary Boros was coming down the hall, with Menni and an entourage of Second Family bodyguards and cousins. From the other side came Gowan with his Ninth Family crowd, and Innis, who walked commandingly—nose first—only his Imbati and Arissen bodyguards following him. Four candidates, four camps. Soon the game would be engaged. *I made a mistake.* His chest twisted; he listened for the rumors that would destroy him.

"I'll see you inside," Father said. "Remember, this is for the First Family. Don't make a mistake." Leaving their servants behind, he and Boros walked ahead into the meeting room.

Too late: the mistake was already made. Nekantor straightened his sleeves, his vest, brushing away Father's fingerprints. He combed the surrounding talk for names. Garr—Erex—those names were everywhere, so ripples were indeed spreading. His stomach clenched, and his ears burned, searching for his own name, or Benél's. Nothing yet, nothing yet . . .

Down the hall beyond Menni there was movement, and the camps broke and swirled; sounds of a struggle. That couldn't be part of the pattern. Nekantor stopped breathing and pressed his back to the wall, but it was not stable enough. Not chaos—not now! Arissen Karyas stepped in front of him and drew her weapon. Nekantor stared at his watch.

"You're killing yourselves, and you don't see it!" a voice shrieked. "You tie *our* hands, and you're all going to die! You—" It cut off abruptly. The hum of talk swelled in the corridor; everyone was moving now, talking.

An assassin? An assassin had made it this far into the Residence?

The sweeping second hand lost its power. The wall was shifting, chaos creeping . . . Nekantor shut his eyes, clenched his fists. Tried to breathe.

Arissen Karyas' voice whispered in his ear. "You're safe, sir. That was *your* move."

His move?

A piece of the pattern appeared beneath his feet. Yes, he'd asked Karyas to arrange Kartunnen infiltrators. *His infiltrator* had been the one screaming threats.

He was safe. And he could see—only his own line, and only the smallest distance before his feet, but enough.

Nekantor opened his eyes. Before him, the cabinet meeting room door opened, and the Eminence's manservant beckoned. He walked forward on the spindly line, leaving Karyas behind. One step, another, into the windowless stone room. The Eminences, the greatest faces of the Race, looked down on him, and he found the Great Grobal Fyn in his extravagant, heavy wooden frame. Father of them all, but of the First Family first—that ancient, noble gaze felt like power. Courage rose into Nekantor's heart, pounding with the blood of powerful men. He smiled. There was a number one on the floor, and he stood upon it, watched Menni taking the place beside him, and then Innis, and then Gowan, across the head of the brass table. Each one brought with him another glimpse of the game.

The cabinet members watched them from the comfort of silk cushions arranged in high-backed brass chairs, just as they had in the Round of Eight questioning. A face to a vote: there was Father, breathing hard in excitement while Doret of the Eleventh Family watched him anxiously; Fedron with his hands clasped; Selemei cold and closed-faced and female. The Third Family's member, Palimeyn, seemed more nervous than last time, glancing again and again at Herin, who sat like a perfect statue behind the Fourth and Seventh Family's members at the foot of the table. Bald Secretary Boros was smiling. Caredes of the Eighth Family watched him with the staring eyes of a fish. Gowan's father Amyel leaned head-to-head with the Tenth Family's member, keeping generous eyes for his own son. The Sixth Family's member, Arith, was the one whose vote he should have won, but hadn't; he and Ethor of the Twelfth Family sat with the two Fifth Family members, staring at him with disdain. There would be no convincing *them*.

You don't need them all, Benél had said. *Just enough.*

"Welcome again, candidates," said Herin, rising from his chair. "Today we will hear your opinions on the question of Kinders fever, and the role of the Kartunnen in preserving the health of the Grobal Race."

Nekantor rubbed his thumbs across his knuckles. He had information on the epidemic, but only from two days ago. No chance to learn more now—

"The first to speak today shall be the last," Herin said. "Gowan of the Ninth Family, your statement."

Gowan looked startled. "Thank you, sir. With twenty-eight dead of Kinders fever in the past week, I believe we all agree on the magnitude of the problem."

Twenty-eight, not twenty-five. Herin had tried to damage him, letting Gowan go first—and yet, that had helped him. The Eminence was not above his own mistakes.

"Our health is the greatest challenge facing the Race today," Gowan continued. "We need a new approach to the quality of our care. I therefore propose that we allow the Kartunnen to be better informed about our health needs: we must institute a petition process, by means of which doctors can access the health records of their patients."

"What?" Caredes demanded.

Nekantor turned and stared. Gowan wanted to give Kartunnen *more* power?

Gowan straightened defiantly. "It's simple," he said. "Doctors can do a better job if they tailor treatment to our specific needs. The petitions can be written in such a way as to bind doctors to confidentiality."

Innis of the Fifth Family considered Gowan down his nose. "The problem, Gowan, is that Kartunnen aren't *like* Imbati. We can't be certain they won't just turn around and expose our failings to our enemies."

"Kartunnen have their own honor," said Gowan. "They keep oaths of confidentiality to their Lower patients."

Ridiculous. "We're nothing like their Lower patients," Nekantor scoffed. "Lowers don't *die* of Kinders fever."

"They do, Nekantor," Menni objected.

Nekantor shrugged. "Fine, one or two do, but mostly they suffer a bit and then survive."

"We're not disputing medical facts," Menni said. "Innis, what if the information *could* be handled appropriately? If a petition system were modified, say, to assign doctors to each Great Family, so no doctor could accidentally divulge anything across Family borders?"

"You're missing my point," said Innis. "The risk is entirely unnecessary. What we really need here is to hold the Kartunnen responsible for the care they provide. Doctors who care for the Race must be the very best. If anything, we should institute a testing system, to separate mere practitioners from the ones truly endowed with Heile's healing gifts; only those should be the ones licensed to care for us."

A small gap of silence opened, a split second of no argument. Time for the move he and Arissen Karyas had planned; with most of the pattern still invisible, it was a step into the dark, but there was no time for doubt.

"You're all talking about how the Kartunnen should heal us," Nekantor said. "No one has yet mentioned how they hurt us. Kartunnen contact was the cause of this epidemic, and since then there have been no fewer than three direct attempts by Kartunnen to interfere with the process of Heir Selection."

"'Interfere with Heir Selection'?" Innis said. "That's an overstatement, Nekantor. They're nothing but Kartunnen troublemakers, responding to our close scrutiny."

"Perhaps," Nekantor said. "But remember, these are Kartunnen we're talking about. A revolution coming from Arissen would be an armed rebellion—easy to recognize. Have none of you considered the possibility that we may be seeing the Kartunnen version of it? A successful coup at the top, followed by attempts to influence our choice of leadership to their advantage?"

He'd surprised them. They were all staring now: Father, Herin, all the faces in the cabinet, all the candidates, too. Look at Gowan and Menni's shock—and Innis, who was calmer, but whose eyes glittered with frustration. Nekantor kept his breath slow, held his hands still. He'd come this far; whatever happened, he must not let their reaction destroy him.

The cabinet members dissolved into loud argument—too fast, too fluid to follow any pattern. After a few moments, Nekantor had to look away to keep chaos from seizing his nerves; he turned his eyes on the Great Grobal Fyn, while still the chatter and growl tumbled into his ears. It seemed forever before the noise diminished; Nekantor glanced down and found the Eminence's manservant walking quietly around the circle, entering votes into his ordinating machine.

At last, he came to the front corner of the table. "The results of the voting," he intoned. "To Grobal Nekantor of the First Family, four votes."

Four. Only four! So Father had failed to win any alliance with the Tenth Family . . . Nekantor's stomach tightened, and he clenched his fists.

"To Grobal Menni of the Second Family, two votes."

That was Menni down. But there were too many votes left. Ten votes, and if they were split—no, Erex must not win! The filthy Lower-lover mustn't drag him down, too . . .

"To Grobal Innis of the Fifth Family, seven votes."

An exhalation ran around the table. Nekantor counted, counted again. Innis had claimed so many, which meant—

"To Grobal Gowan of the Ninth Family, three votes." The Imbati paused in silence for a moment. "The First Family and the Fifth Family shall advance to the Final Round."

Saved—by *Innis?!* Nekantor gulped a breath as the tension broke; he looked down at his watch with his heart pounding. Just in time: the cabinet members surged from their seats, swirling into Family camps. Bodies came close around him, but his heart still raced too fast, and his throat clamped tight. He didn't dare look up.

"Well, son . . ." Father's heavy hand landed on his right shoulder. "Looks like you're still alive for the next round."

Nekantor risked a glance up. Fedron was grinning at him; Selemei watched him with a faint and maddeningly feminine smile. At his left, Doret let out a short bark of a laugh. "Gods, I need a drink! But that's over, so no more assassinations."

Fedron nodded. "Only one Selection murder—I'll drink to that."

"Thank Heile no one else has to die," said Selemei quietly.

But this game had not been won. Innis of the Fifth Family had taken too many votes. To stand at the center, he'd have to take *all the rest*, every single one. How could he possibly do that?

"Father," Nekantor forced out. "I made mistakes in this round. I'm sorry—I need your help if I'm going to win."

Father pulled him by the arm. Nekantor leaned forward to listen, but Father only clutched tighter, pulled harder, harder, hurting his arm. Oh, gods, what in Varin's name did he want? Revulsion spasmed through him; he screamed and jerked backward.

Father collapsed facedown onto the floor.

CHAPTER TWENTY-SEVEN

Crisis

Aloran felt sympathy for his Lady and young Master Tagaret, untrained as they were in the art of waiting. News from the Round of Four was late, and they'd progressed from silence to tense talk and back again for at least an hour. Tamelera was impatiently twisting a lock of hair she'd loosened from her jeweled pins. Understandable—but his own feeling was more like fear. How might the voting results influence the Master's mood? Would the bedroom door burst open on forced celebration, or on rage?

There was a quiet knock.

Tamelera swished to her feet.

That couldn't be the Master, though; the Master never knocked. Before Aloran could move to answer, the door opened on Serjer. A message? But look behind him: Keeper Premel was here—and his partner Dorya, too?

Aloran caught his breath. There was only one reason the entire Household might leave the Maze empty. He returned to his station, with a horror in his stomach that was almost hope.

Serjer bowed. "Mistress, forgive me for interrupting you with this news . . ."

"What is it, Serjer?" Tamelera asked.

"Master Garr has had a heart attack and been rushed to the medical center."

Tamelera's entire body jerked. But she made no sound, nor did she sway into Aloran's hands when he raised them to support her.

"Mercy!" young Master Tagaret cried, leaping to his feet. "Oh, Mother . . ."

"We must go to him, of course," said Tamelera. Her voice was cold and distant. "Where is Nekantor now?"

"With Master Garr, Mistress."

Lady Tamelera nodded. "Aloran, my jacket, please."

She'd never asked for a jacket before. He picked one to match her dark blue dress. As he slid it over her bare arms and shoulders, Aloran could feel her bracing herself, as if he were girding her in armor. He, too, must become part of that armor: the worst had come, yet Garr was still alive.

They crossed the Eminence's gardens, cutting diagonally toward the medical center building, which stood across from the Grobal School. The windows of the ballroom floated dimly away on their right, and they followed a single bright globe in Heile's green, which hung above the medical center door.

A Kartunnen woman with a matching green lip let them in.

"Tamelera and Tagaret of the First Family, to see Garr," Tamelera said.

"Yes, Lady." The Kartunnen beckoned them forward.

An Imbati recordkeeper, wearing the bureaucrat's pierced oval Mark, sat tucked behind the entry door—but he was the only predictable thing in a facility more advanced even than the Academy's. The triage chairs on either side of their path were hinged and jointed so a noble arrival could be attended to quickly, shifted to lying position at need, and wheeled inward for treatment. The nurses, who stood ready by the walls, were each equipped with a diagnostic unit on a wheeled cart. Aloran glimpsed tubes, wires, even glowing image-screens—specialized classical technology that he would have longed to examine had circumstances been different. They passed beneath a pale gray curtain into a long hall, and approached a treatment room on the right.

"Shall I enter first, Lady?" Aloran murmured.

Tamelera raised her head. "Thank you, Aloran, no." She allowed young Master Tagaret to take her arm, and they walked in together.

Aloran gave a nod to the woman who had accompanied them. "Thank you, Kartunnen."

"May your honorable service earn its just reward, sir."

Aloran closed the door. The entire room throbbed softly with the sound of the Master's heartbeat, projected by the heart monitor. Before he'd even released the handle, Aloran found the flaw: an extra beat at the tail of the pattern.

He turned, and found Garr's Sorn standing up from a steel side table, with a look of personal menace that jabbed him straight in the chest. Sorn now had plenty to punish him for—but he wouldn't attack here. Aloran moved to his Lady's shoulder as she approached the bed.

"Garr?" Tamelera said.

The Master lay in a voluminous patient's gown of green silk that mostly hid medical indignities like the heart monitor's electrodes, the blood pressure cuff, and an intravenous insertion site in his left arm. It didn't hide the oxygen tube under his nose.

"He can't hear you," said young Master Nekantor's voice from the corner behind Arissen Karyas.

Tagaret gently touched his father's hand. "He's cold."

Grobal Garr roused at the touch: the stuttering heartbeat gained speed, and he opened his eyes. He stared up at them.

A muscle flexed in the Lady's jaw. "Gnash you, Garr," she said. "I told you this would happen."

The Master definitely heard her now. His eyes glittered. He heaved a breath, but didn't respond to her. Instead he said, "Nekantor."

Young Master Nekantor startled out of the corner. He walked to his father's head, clasping both hands tight behind his back. "I need *all the votes*, Father," he said. "All of them. How can I get them all?"

"*Nekantor*," Lady Tamelera scolded. "That's hardly an appropriate topic right now."

Young Master Nekantor glared at her. Tagaret stared at his brother in exasperation.

The Master took another breath. "Sorn."

That couldn't be good. Aloran shifted onto his toes as the senior servant moved silently to Garr's other side.

"Nekantor," the Master wheezed. "You must . . . write an inquiry. For Sorn."

Young Master Nekantor stared down, so tense he quivered.

"Keep it with you. If I die . . ." He paused for breath. "If I die— take him."

Take Sorn? Aloran held his breath. As a candidate, Nekantor was eligible for service. Naturally, the man who possessed a weapon as deadly as Sorn would wish to bequeath him to his son. But to *this* son?

"But you can't die," Nekantor said. "You won't. The doctors will cure you, and you'll vote in the final Selection. I need *every vote*."

"Vote—Sorn will bring. If." Grobal Garr coughed weakly. "Write inquiry. Tonight."

"Yes, Father."

Imagine ruthlessness and pathology working together. One letter handed across this hospital bed—that was all it would take.

A knock startled him back to breathing. The door to the room opened, and Grobal Fedron walked in with his Chenna behind his shoulder.

"Lady," Grobal Fedron said. "Tagaret, Nekantor—I'm so sorry."

"Thank you, Cousin," said Tamelera.

"What a terrible shock this has been. How is he doing?"

Aloran felt in his bones the effort it took for his Lady to maintain her air of graciousness. She gave a wan smile. "I couldn't say. He has been awake and speaking." Though he wasn't now—after the effort of his commands, Grobal Garr had closed his eyes again.

Grobal Fedron offered his hand to Tamelera, and when she clasped it, he leaned nearer to pat her shoulder comfortingly. In the instant their convergence blocked his view of Sorn, who had returned to his seat, Aloran found Chenna at his ear with a sly whisper.

"Sorn's awfully nervous, standing on the cliff."

What? Aloran twitched in surprise. He'd noticed only Sorn's anger—but anger could hide fear, and Chenna knew Sorn better than anyone. He turned his head slightly toward her.

Grobal Fedron moved away before he could ask any questions, calling out the door to the doctor for an update on the patient's prognosis. The doctor answered Grobal Fedron's inquiries carefully but optimistically, suggesting the Master might recover enough to attend the final Selection events, perhaps in a skimchair with medical attendants, so he need not be far from his son at such a critical time.

Wait.

Aloran's skin prickled. *Not far from Nekantor at a critical time?*

That was the cliff Chenna meant. Sorn was in terrible danger if

Garr died without Nekantor present. He would lose the cloak of privilege, and could be questioned freely by nobles or by the police. More importantly, until the moment he received a new inquiry, his past acts would become his own—punishable by the Imbati.

That was what Master Ziara wanted. Not information, but justice.

During the hospital visit, Tamelera had wound herself into such a state of tension that she hardly ate or spoke at dinner. It wasn't until she'd said goodnight, and Aloran had escorted her to her room, that the other aspect of this change truly struck him. With the Master gone, his Lady would be safe.

Oh, Sirin and Eyn, *she would be safe!*

To his shock, he discovered tears in his eyes. He covered them by crossing to the bed, closing the curtains at its foot and on the Master's side so his Lady couldn't be reminded of dangers past.

"Aloran," Tamelera said. "Will you brush my hair?"

"Yes, Lady."

She sat in the lounge chair, facing toward the door of his own room. One by one, he took out her jeweled pins and let her hair fall down. He tried to brush peace and reassurance into her hair with every motion. When, after some time, he lifted her hair to brush from beneath at the back of her neck, she gave a sigh and her shoulders finally fell. Thank Sirin his care had allowed her to share his sense of safety—but too soon, some new trouble came to her mind, because she sat up.

"Aloran, I—" She made as if to look at him, but didn't. "I'll be in the bathroom."

"Do you wish to bathe, Lady?"

"No—at least, not now."

While she busied herself alone with the running water, Aloran laid out her white silk nightgown on the bed. He took a place beside the bathroom door and waited. At last, she emerged.

"May I take your jacket, Lady?" he asked.

"Yes, of course."

When he had replaced the jacket in the wardrobe, he returned and found her standing beside her nightgown. Moving to her back, he lightly touched the top button of her blue dress, between her shoulder blades. Lady Tamelera nodded, and he began unfastening the long line of buttons.

While he worked, a strange feeling came over him. Without the Master and his shadow, the room seemed to have grown larger, the air more spacious. Breathing felt easier, each breath deeper and more sweet. He closed his eyes and savored it, continuing the buttons by feel until the last one fell undone. Then he straightened, found the straps of his Lady's dress and slid his fingers beneath them to pull it off her shoulders.

Tamelera shivered.

Aloran froze.

Alarm raced down every nerve. She wasn't supposed to do that. She was leaning into his touch—even her breath had changed. And what of his own? Hadn't it just slipped out of his control without him noticing?

Distance yourself. Your mistress' flesh is the province you guard, whose health and convenience you keep in charge. Distance yourself.

Mechanically, he pulled the dress down; blue silk deflated against the rug, and her feet stepped out of it. Aloran swept it over his arm and walked away. Here was the wardrobe door, made of cold smoked glass. Here was a metal hanger padded with silk. He aligned her dress straps on it. Pushed aside magnificent gowns that he had dressed her in day after day. Hung the dress. It was all service.

Love where you serve—nothing else will matter.

Yes, the Artist was right. It was all service. He must have tickled her accidentally; next time he would do better.

Lady Tamelera wasn't looking at him. She stood perfectly still in her underclothes, as if watching the bedpost. While he removed her brassiere, he focused on making precise movements with his hands. He prepared her nightgown and raised it over her head, but if she sought his eyes, he lowered them beneath her notice; if she was graceful in stretching her arms into the gown, it was only the beauty to be expected of nobility. The silk fell into place on its own, whispering over her hips and down to her knees.

"Aloran," she said softly.

The tone of her voice softened his stomach and sharpened his fear.

This was all service. He began a breath pattern. "Lady, may I be excused?"

"Why?"

He scrambled for a reason, then found one: Garr's Sorn. "I have an errand, if you will forgive me, Lady."

She turned around and looked at him. Aloran kept his gaze lowered, on her skeptical mouth.

"I apologize," he said. "It's an errand I've been unable to complete because of my duty to your safety, but I assure you it is of utmost importance." Indeed, if there was one thing he must do tonight, without fail, it was to take his information to those who could use it—before young Master Nekantor could make Sorn untouchable.

"What is this errand?" Tamelera asked.

The question stung. He tried to be polite. "I don't know."

Tamelera winced and looked away. "You are excused."

Aloran bowed and gratefully escaped to his room. Here it was dark except for the stray illumination of the city coming in the window. He flicked on his service speaker; in the room he'd left, his Lady remained silent. Thank Heile he had somewhere to go, because he was too agitated to sit down. He left through the Maze, found an exit that led into the rock gardens and ran all the way to the Academy.

How long it had been. The gate wardens passed him through, and he entered the main building through its large front doors, crossing the deserted foyer and turning left into the hall of the Masters' offices. Let Mai the Right grant that Master Ziara would be working late tonight. A line of light around her door gave him hope. He knocked.

Master Ziara opened the door. Her lily crest Mark wrinkled between her brows. "Good evening, Aloran . . ."

He bowed. "My apologies for disturbing you, sir. I bring information."

"Then by all means, come in." She closed the door behind him.

Aloran took a deep breath. "Garr's Sorn is guilty," he said. "I saw—"

Master Ziara quickly raised a hand. "Aloran, pardon. You must only speak this once, and not here. I'll call the Headmaster."

He nodded.

Master Ziara entered a code into the intercom unit on her desk. A moment later, a solemn, restful voice answered, "Moruvia."

"Ziara, and Tamelera's Aloran," Master Ziara replied. "Urgent exchange of information, Headmaster."

The Headmaster's restful tone did not change. "Four minutes, please. I'll meet you in my office."

"Yes, sir."

After cutting the connection, Master Ziara took a moment to look Aloran up and down; he kept still, hoping he didn't look as un-Imbati as he felt. "I confess, Aloran," she said. "I didn't believe I would see you pursue this matter. Yet I'm glad, very glad, to see you here."

"My Mistress would wish me to pursue it," he replied. "I'm glad to see you, too."

They walked down the hall together. Master Ziara matched step with him, her strides natural, long and silent. So different from walking with his Lady. Had the unpredictable currents of the nobility dragged him so far from what he knew? The manservant's vocation was not easy: to brave immersion in the swirling water for the sake of those unable to escape it.

Headmaster Moruvia received them in his office off the main foyer. His flawless calm lent him a stature far beyond his small size, and his faded lily crest tattoo, framed with white hair, spoke of a lifetime of service. He had brought another man with him: a man marked with the diamond-within-diamond of the Courts, gray-haired and impressively muscled.

"You'll forgive me," said the Headmaster in his restful voice. "This information is the province of Officer Warden Xim as much as it is mine."

Catching Master Ziara's prompting glance, Aloran bowed. "Yes, Headmaster. I have come to bear witness that Garr's Sorn of the Household of the First Family is guilty of the murder of Grobal Dest of the Eleventh Family, and the attempted murder of Grobal Gowan of the Ninth Family."

The Headmaster glanced toward Master Ziara but said nothing.

"Aloran, sir." That was the Officer Warden—he had a deceptively gentle voice. "We have long suspected Garr's Sorn of breaching his vocation. Please elaborate upon your witness."

Aloran raised both hands before his chest, one palm facing his listeners, the other turned upward in invocation of Mai the Right. "Sir. I entered Sorn's room on an errand, and discovered the bolt of a Venorai crossbow there. This bolt was identical to the one photographed in Grobal Garr's documentation from the Grobal Dest assassination. Furthermore, at the Round of Eight, Garr's Sorn was absent from his Master's side at the same moment that I observed a Venorai crossbow upon the Academy roof, aimed at the candidates. I'm sure you are aware of my actions in the matter of Grobal Gowan of the Ninth Family—and of the current health of Grobal Garr."

"Yes, thank you," said the Officer Warden. "Your information is timely. Headmaster, thank you for contacting me."

The Headmaster inclined his head. "Aloran, Ziara, you have our gratitude. We request your silence as to the matter of this meeting, which has not occurred."

Aloran bowed low. "My heart is as deep as the heavens," he said. Master Ziara delivered the oath alongside him, with a hint of pride. "No word uttered in confidence will escape it."

Afterward, Aloran hesitated inside the iron gates. Here, Xim's wardens protected Imbati from all but their own kind. The sense of peace and order tempted him to return to the dormitory, to try to find his bunkmate Endredan, or Kiit.

No.

This was no longer his place. Instead, he must take something of this place with him: a resolution not to lose sight of his own nature. With that thought, the silence of the night became an embrace of black silk, and he could walk out; when he reached the Maze of the First Family's suite, it felt like home. He must ask his Lady to release him to his own room tonight. And he'd been neglecting his relations with the rest of the Household—no more.

It was too late for Household dinner, but his empty stomach grumbled. Aloran walked into the kitchen, where Keeper Premel was preparing something, swiftly plucking ingredients from the cabinets. At the sight of him, Premel stopped working.

"Aloran, sir! A rescuer you are, returning now."

"Rescuer?"

Premel raised his eyebrows. "You must to the Mistress, sir, she's in a state. I haven't seen such since . . ."

Garr.

Aloran was out the door and halfway down the Maze hall before he knew it. Now he could hear Tamelera shrieking—the awful sound echoed around his bedroom door and struck deep into his chest. He leapt for the door with the crescent-moon handle, half expecting to find her cornered, Garr miraculously healed and lumbering toward her, Sorn watching with perverted pleasure . . .

The corner was empty. But the bed-curtains had been torn down, a pillow flung against the far wall, Garr's watch tray broken and the watches scattered across the floor—

"Gnash you, Aloran! Where in Varin's name have you been?"

He turned around.

Tamelera seized the ceramic rabbit from the windowsill and hurled it at his head.

Aloran flung up his hands as the rabbit hit. Hands stinging, he set it gently on the writing table. Then he fell to his knees and lowered his head to the floor.

"Lady, please forgive me."

"I called you." She breathed hard, half-sobbing. "I *called* you, and you weren't there . . ."

She'd known where he was. She hadn't specified a time for his return. She was too smart not to realize that; clearly it didn't matter. "I was remiss," he said. "I admit my fault."

"You can't *do* that! What if—oh, gods—Aloran, what if he *lives?*"

"I will not fail you, Lady. I apologize for my absence. I thank Heile and Eyn for your safety."

For several ragged breaths, she didn't respond. "I'm evil," she moaned softly. "I want him to die. I'm—I'm inhuman."

Behind his closed eyes flashed a vision of bandaging her: handling smooth pale skin marred with bruises. His throat ached.

"Aloran, won't you speak to me?"

Nothing he could say was safe. He took a deep breath. "You are human, Lady." *So human . . .*

"I'm cruel—as cruel as Plis the Warrior."

"Lady." He spoke toward the carpet. "When we saw the Master tonight, he was at your mercy, yet you took no inhuman action against him."

"You are at my service, and I tried to hit you with a rabbit."

"You would have done the same had I been the Master himself."

She was silent.

He searched for her with his ears, but didn't dare move. Close by, the carpet shifted, and her voice sighed above him.

"Aloran—I need to tell you . . . I haven't been very noble tonight."

He risked a glance to one side. Caught a glimpse of white.

Lady, sometimes we can lose sight of our nature. But he dared not say so; the private thought of a manservant was not the province of his mistress.

"I'm sorry," said Tamelera. "Please come up."

Aloran straightened, just onto his knees. That was her nightgown he'd seen; she was sitting on the floor beside him. On the floor? She didn't belong at his level, and he almost put his head down again.

"When you were gone, I got—impatient," she said suddenly. "I called you, and called you, but you didn't answer."

Why would she tell him what he already knew? And why did she sound like she was confessing to something shameful? He refused to look her in the face, but even her neck was blushing.

"Yes, Lady. I'm sorry."

"I've never been alone. Not like this. There was always someone—if not my Eyli, then Garr."

"I shouldn't have insisted upon my errand."

"It's not that. When you didn't answer I—I handled it badly. Aloran, I *missed* you, and I—" She broke off, and took a deep breath. "I looked into your room. I know I shouldn't have. I'm really sorry . . ."

His mind whirled. Her hand had pushed aside his curtain, touched the handle of his Maze door—her eyes, accustomed to the light, had looked into the dimness . . . because she *missed* him? His chest flushed thick and warm. He began a breath pattern, but the air wasn't cold enough. At last he forced his voice to function. "It is my Lady's privilege."

She pulled back. "My privilege?"

He didn't trust himself to answer.

"What's wrong with you?" she demanded.

He stared down at his knees.

"I didn't tell you that so I could force you into pretending it was normal! I told you because you're my manservant, and I should have no secrets from you. I wasn't even hoping you'd forgive me. How can you have no comment at all? Even Dorya would stand up to me, if just to say what rules I must follow while in servants' territory! Have you returned in body, but left yourself behind somewhere?"

Breath choked him. "I serve you, Lady," he mumbled. *Imbati, love where you serve:* it cut two ways. His love must needs be service, but service without love was false—and now he had failed miserably in both.

"Oh, dear gods—I've hurt and insulted you, trespassed where I must not, and now I ask too much," Lady Tamelera said. "I don't deserve you, Aloran. You are excused. Good night."

Half-blind, he got to his feet. Managed to bow, to push aside the curtain, to open the door and close it again. He sat on his bed with his head in his hands, blood racing too hot and too fast. He tried to feel again the solitary stillness, the comforting embrace of black silk.

He felt only disgrace.

Through the service speaker, his Lady began to cry softly. She did not call his name.

CHAPTER TWENTY-EIGHT

Reputations

It was time to stop being careful. Time to find his courage.

He'd been lucky to escape that arrangement with the Tenth Family, but tomorrow, either Nekantor would become Heir, or Innis would, and take precious Della for his partner. It must not be allowed to happen—and besides, if he had to watch Nek pace that same path around the suite all morning, he might just punch him in the face.

Tagaret grabbed his coat and headed toward the front door.

Erex would help. The Arbiter was clever; by now he'd have come up with some idea. Maybe they could take their concerns to Lady Selemei—or better yet, to the Eminence himself. With Erex by his side, he'd be taken far more seriously than he would alone.

Outside, the hall was crowded with people celebrating the end of the Selection danger, everyone overjoyed no longer to be trapped indoors. Gangs were forming again—a knot of Nek's boys appeared just to have discovered Benél arriving at the base of the spiral stairway. Frustration glittered in Benél's eye, but he joined them laughing.

Tagaret turned his face away as he drew nearer. Maybe they wouldn't notice him.

". . . ment for Erex," said Losli's voice. "Who do you think it'll be?"

Tagaret stopped. Losli was Seventh Family—why would he mention Erex? He braced himself and turned to face the group.

"Hey, Benél, Losli, guys."

Benél narrowed his eyes. "Tagaret."

"So, Losli, what's that you were saying about Erex?"

Losli smirked.

Benél snorted. "First Family or not, he got what he deserved."

Tagaret frowned. "What do you mean?"

The gang laughed. Jiss spat, "The disgusting Lower-lover."

"Stop it!" Tagaret shouted, but the gang only laughed harder. Varin's teeth, if only he had Reyn and Gowan and Fernar with him—oh, holy Elinda, Fernar—

"Go see for yourself what's happened," Benél said.

Gnash them all. Tagaret pushed past into the spiral stairway and panted up to the third floor. At the far western end of the hall, a gawking crowd had gathered outside Erex's door. Somewhere inside, a child was wailing. The door was open, and out swayed a piece of furniture, wrapped in blankets. Tagaret hurried closer, and glimpsing the straining bearers, stopped in shock.

Melumalai were moving the furniture out of Erex's suite?

He pushed into the crowd, trying to find Erex. No one tried stop him—they didn't seem keen to get any closer to the Melumalai. As he neared the door, Lady Keir emerged with tears streaking her face, her young son and wailing daughter clinging to her arms. A Lady who wore her hair in tight pale curls rushed to them out of the crowd and enfolded all three in her arms.

Tagaret's stomach tried to drop out of his feet. Was Erex *dead?* Oh, Elinda forbear! It couldn't be Kinders fever, could it? Everyone said the epidemic had been contained. But Erex also had that heart condition.

What if Erex was lying in a bed like Father's, his small form lost beneath a gown of green silk?

"Lady Keir!" he called, but she'd already moved away in the company of the pale-haired Lady. She'd never hear him now, not with her wailing child between them. And why should she speak to him anyway, when her children needed her?

There was no way he was going back to ask Benél. Vicious rumors weren't worth much.

"Excuse me, young sir," said an Imbati voice. An unfamiliar Household woman had approached him.

"Yes, Imbati?"

The Imbati bowed. "I am First Housewoman to Lady Selemei of the First Family. She requests your presence, if you will follow me."

"Of course," Tagaret said. With Erex missing, this was just the luck he needed. He followed the First Housewoman downstairs. She let him into a suite near the entrance to the Central Section.

Lady Selemei's voice called from behind purple curtains. "Did you find him?"

"Yes, Mistress." The Imbati smiled faintly and pulled the curtains back.

Lady Selemei's sitting room was of tasteful design, with topaz-toned furniture upon a rug of Grobal green. In one corner, the bronze bust of an imposing man stood on a marble pedestal, with a mourning scarf draped across its shoulders. That must be her late partner Xeref, the former master of Ustin. The Lady came forward with one arm outstretched toward him, Ustin following behind her. "Tagaret, thank Heile we reached you."

His stomach dropped. "What happened?" he asked. "I couldn't find Erex—"

"The Family Council fired Erex last night," she said grimly.

"Fired him! He's not dead?"

She winced. "He might wish he were. He was fired for fraterniza-tion with a Lower—a *man*."

Tagaret gaped.

"Honestly, I wouldn't have thought it of him—and since the Coun-cil meeting, he's disappeared." She shook her head. "In any case, we'll soon have a new Arbiter promoted out of the Family Council, and a spot open for a new Councilman. This is a time of opportunity."

He hardly heard her. Erex . . . it was impossible. Unfaithful to Lady Keir, with a man? A *Lower*? But what about his ease with her, how he said they protected each other—had it all been a lie?

Dazed, he found his way to a chair and sat down in it.

Lady Selemei sat on the sofa near him, leaned her cane against the sofa arm, and gazed at him intently. "Do you catch my meaning?"

He blinked. "Meaning?"

"We can get you into politics," Selemei said. "The First Family has suffered losses in this Selection in a way I've never seen. First you catching Kinders fever—then your father's heart—now Erex. But that means new blood. I'd like to take you as my cabinet assistant, Tagaret, and get you into the system. The Heir selects the Speaker of the Cabi-net, so if your brother wins the Selection, we could see Fedron take that position. That means an open cabinet seat, and an opportunity for you—either to become the youngest cabinet member in living memory, or to take a position on the Family Council when one of them moves up—"

"Wait," Tagaret said. "I don't want that. Nekantor *can't* win."

Lady Selemei raised her eyebrows. "I was ready to follow your suggestion when we had other options, but if Innis of the Fifth Family wins, it could set the First Family back by a decade."

"If Nekantor wins, it will be worse. Selemei, he's *defective*."

From the look on her face, he might as well have slapped her.

"Compulsive obsessions," he explained quickly, so she couldn't doubt his seriousness. "Paranoia. And he's completely merciless."

Lady Selemei rose to her feet incredulously. "You never heard him say that," she cried. "Oaths!"

Imbati Ustin knelt with a practiced twitch of her skirts and lowered her forehead to the floor. The First Housewoman adopted the same position. "My heart is as deep as the heavens," they intoned in unison. "No word uttered in confidence will escape it."

Tagaret stared at them. "But, Cousin Selemei—"

Lady Selemei put both hands on the arms of his chair and leaned into his face. "I'm going to assume you're wrong, Tagaret. Don't you see what that would mean?"

He recoiled deeper into the chair. "Mean?"

"What happened to Erex would happen to your family!" Selemei flung up her hands, grabbed her cane, and started pacing. "Your mother's reputation would be ruined, and you would be removed from your home in the Residence." She turned back with a fierce look on her face. "Not only that—everyone thinks *I've* been supporting Nekantor! I would lose my cabinet seat. Everything I've achieved in the last five years would be erased!"

Tagaret gulped. Instead of Lady Keir crying over losing her home, it would be *Mother?* "We can't support Nekantor, though," he whispered.

"This is difficult." Lady Selemei clasped her hands tight together. "I won't be happy supporting Innis; he won't have anything but the Fifth Family's interests at heart, and he's too canny. It's dangerous to give him the Heir's power of appointment at a time when positions are coming open—that's a lot of influence."

"And he'll take Della," Tagaret said. His heart pounded in desperation, but what good was courage in a game he could never win? No wonder Della had told him not to play. "I hate politics," he said. "Don't ask me to work for you, Cousin. I don't want to get trapped in this game."

"Tagaret," said Selemei gently. "You have no choice. Not if you want to see your life get any better. You can't change anything from the outside—if I've learned nothing else, I've learned that."

Tagaret felt sick to his stomach. He stood up. "Pardon me, Cousin. I have to go."

"Please, Tagaret." She reached a hand toward him. "I'll consider what you've said. Just please, consider me as well. With you as my cabinet assistant, we could accomplish so much! The offer still stands—don't forget it."

Tagaret bowed stiffly and walked out. Couldn't go upstairs to see Reyn, because it would mean seeing Erex's life destroyed; couldn't go home, because Nekantor was there. He walked fast in another direction, into the central section of the Residence. The marble nudes supporting the door to the empty Heir's suite regarded him impassively as he turned onto the curved stairs of the Grand Rotunda, descending beneath the dome of white glass. His feet moved on their own, carrying him out into the grounds, toward the Plaza of Varin.

Before long, he became aware of a figure running toward him—fast. He tensed and stopped walking. Maybe this was just a messenger headed to the Residence? But the figure ran closer, and closer—

Was that Erex's Kuarmei?

The manservant stopped before him, breathing fast but quietly. "Grobal Tagaret, sir," she said. "It's my good fortune that you came this way."

"Is Erex here somewhere?" he asked, bewildered. "How did you find me?"

"I waited outside the Academy, sir, in hopes you might choose to pursue your inquiries there." She bowed. "If I may beg your indulgence, Erex would like to speak to you."

Erex? Was she even allowed to call her Master by his name? Tagaret frowned, but followed her, and his own curiosity, out into the Plaza.

As he passed among the Imbati bureaucrats and crowds of tourists, he glimpsed a Kartunnen in a gray tailcoat standing beside the shinca tree at the Plaza's center. He thought instantly of the composer's apprentice, Vant—but this person was older, unassuming, outlined with strange clarity by the silver light.

Five steps away he stopped dead, unable to move.

"Sir?" asked Kuarmei.

The Kartunnen man—*it was Erex*. While Tagaret watched, he moved closer with the same delicate walking pace as always. He had the same hair, the same face, the same way of moving his hands—even the same clubbed fingers, visible now that he no longer wore gloves.

"I'm sorry, Tagaret," Erex said.

"Wh—" Tagaret stammered. "Are you in hiding? Why are you in disguise?" He couldn't bring himself to say the word *crossmarked*.

"I decided it was time to stop being careful," Erex said. "I told the Eminence your brother should be disqualified from Heir Selection."

His stomach clenched with nausea. "Oh, gods, no . . ."

Erex held up his hands. "No, it's all right—I didn't tell him what you told me. In fact, I told Herin about Nekantor and your cousin Benél." He laughed bitterly. "One of the many ironies of my existence. I knew the risks. I'm only disappointed I couldn't bring him down with me."

Tagaret swallowed hard. "But what happened? The rumors, that you . . ."

Erex sighed. "I've never lied to you, Tagaret. The day I met Lady Keir was the luckiest of my life. I'd put off partnership so long it was starting to damage my reputation. But she understood. To find someone like her—a Lady who prayed to the holy Twins for guidance as fervently as I did—it was a miracle. We realized if we accepted partnership in Sirin and Eyn's name, it might take effort to conceive children, but once our duty to the Race was fulfilled, we could more quietly pursue . . . brotherly and sisterly interests."

Of course, he thought instantly of Reyn, and tried not to blush. "But somehow Nekantor exposed you?"

"We made a mistake," said Erex. "Mine far more serious than hers. At least she fell in love within the Race. I met Dois in the Kartunnen house, which is where Nekantor and Benél saw us."

Tagaret couldn't help it—he clapped his hands over his mouth.

Erex's tone softened, pleading. "I never contracted a thing there, Tagaret. I couldn't stop seeing him. For a long time I blamed it on the weakness of my heart—but when you're in love, risks don't matter. Like you with your Sixth Family girl." He rubbed a hand across his mouth. "I was unfair to you about her, Tagaret, and I apologize. Inconsiderate, in fact—too busy fighting to keep my own eyes shut."

"What can I do, Erex?" Tagaret asked. "If Innis wins, he'll take her as his life's partner—I would die."

Erex pressed his hand. "Do anything you must," he said. "It took losing everything for me to see what Dois has been telling me all along: that my future lay outside the confines of the Race."

"Outside?" Tagaret exclaimed. The whole world shuddered, as if the roof had come crashing down. "You mean you *Fell?*"

Erex said nothing.

Impossible—no one could erase the First Family from his features. The coat and Erex could not possibly be one. And yet, Imbati Kuarmei had called him simply *Erex* . . .

Crown of Mai, how could a person be expected to sweep away years of guidance and trust beneath the name Kartunnen?

"I've had an idea," Erex said. He glanced at Kuarmei, who pulled a thick sheet of paper from a hidden pocket under her arm. "As of today, I am no longer able to retain Kuarmei's services, and you need a manservant—someone with proven ability to keep dangerous secrets. If my status had not already been reduced, I would make Kuarmei a gift. Instead, I must ask: please, sir, take her into your protection."

Tagaret flushed and turned away—to hear Erex call him 'sir' was just too horrible.

"Grobal Tagaret, sir," said Imbati Kuarmei quietly. "I would be honored by your inquiry."

Tagaret gathered himself. The fact was, Erex's generosity was inconceivable—there could be no secret more dangerous than the one Kuarmei had kept for him. He turned back to them. "*I'm* honored, Kuarmei. I would be happy to inquire, but I'll just need to . . ."

"Here," said Erex, producing a paper. "This time I wrote it for you. But you will have to sign it."

Tagaret did more than that. He signed it at the Academy, and countersigned Kuarmei's contract with the Headmaster, and with Serjer, who appeared quickly when they contacted him by intercom. Kuarmei vowed service and allowed him to touch her forehead, whereupon he dismissed her from duty—both to allow her to move her things, and to give himself a chance to recover from the shock.

He walked out of the Academy still rubbing his hand. Serjer walked beside him with a subtle Imbati smile showing on his face.

"Serjer, thank you for coming so quickly," Tagaret said.

"It was my pleasure, young Master."

Tagaret pushed his hands through his hair. "I can hardly believe this. I'm really lucky."

"Kuarmei is also lucky," Serjer said. "I have met her off-duty, and I believe she will make a strong addition to our Household."

He should have thought of that. "Well, I'm glad," Tagaret said. "Of course, I'm not sure what to do now."

"I would suggest you speak to your mother, sir."

Tagaret nodded. "You're quite right."

But when they reached the rock gardens, Serjer stopped suddenly, between an obsidian boulder and an enormous swooping formation of sandstone.

"Young Master—while you were out, I received an urgent message for you."

Serjer's head was tilted to one side; a chill ran down Tagaret's back. "Who from?"

"Enwin and Pazeu of the Sixth Family," Serjer said. "If you will forgive me, I would feel more comfortable in paraphrase—perhaps I should have mentioned this when you were sitting down."

Della—oh, Sirin and Eyn . . . Tagaret reached a hand to the shining black rock beside him. "I don't have Kinders fever anymore. Say it however you wish."

"They invite you to their house tonight," Serjer said. "They impress upon you the need for absolute secrecy. They wish you to—" He hesitated. "To render their daughter ineligible for partnership with Grobal Innis of the Fifth Family."

CHAPTER TWENTY-NINE

Complicit

M other. . . !" Young Master Tagaret's voice echoed under the bedroom door, desperate.

Aloran leapt to open the door with his Lady's beryl-green jacket still swinging from his hand. The young Master burst in and ran straight to his mother's arms.

Tamelera held him, stroking his hair. "Tagaret, love, what's wrong? You haven't been to the medical center, have you? We were just on our way over . . ."

Please, no. Aloran held his breath. Surely he would have received word if Grobal Garr had died!

"No," said young Master Tagaret. "I've just received a message, and I don't know what to do. I don't know who else to tell."

Lady Tamelera's fine brows pulled together. "Is it Selemei again?"

"It's from Enwin and Lady Pazeu of the Sixth Family, about their daughter Della," said Tagaret hesitantly. "You won't believe me . . . you'll be angry . . ."

Pity twinged in Aloran's heart. The young Master and Lady Della had been so sweet together—to see their hopes fall apart because of Kinders fever was an injustice that holy Mai should never have allowed.

Tamelera looked at her son seriously for a long time. She raised one hand as if to twist her hair, apparently forgetting that she had chosen a tightly braided style for visiting the medical center. At last she said, "Come. Sit with me."

She sat at the foot of her bed, arranging her long green skirts. Aloran moved to his station beside the bedpost, shifting her jacket over his arm.

Young Master Tagaret seemed too agitated to sit comfortably. He was blushing—a more extreme reaction even than the day Della's Yoral had permitted him a kiss with his young Lady. For several seconds, Tagaret's voice seemed bottled up; then words poured out of him all at once.

"They—want me to spend the night with her tonight."

"What?" Tamelera flung up her hands.

Young Master Tagaret cringed away as if she might strike him.

Aloran bit down on the gasp that tried to escape his throat. Extreme didn't begin to describe this. Such an invitation was unheard of.

Tamelera jumped up and paced to the window. She whirled back to face her son. "It can't be true. Tagaret, it *can't.* You wouldn't lie to me!"

"Please, Mother—I don't know what to do. I have to talk to *someone.* I got the message from Serjer . . ."

Aloran stiffened—*Serjer was in trouble.* Lady Tamelera's eyes snapped to him like a whip of ice. Her voice was just as cold.

"Aloran, fetch Serjer please."

"Yes, Lady."

But surely Serjer hadn't done anything wrong. Aloran hung his Lady's jacket and left the room, crossing the drawing room and sitting room to the vestibule. He cracked the door of the lesser Maze, calling, "Serjer?"

The First Houseman stood up from his chair behind the door. "At your service, Aloran."

Aloran gaze-gestured warning. "My Lady wishes to speak to you regarding a certain message received by young Master Tagaret."

Serjer's body went rigid, and his head tilted to one side, suggesting deep distress. "That message—Aloran—"

"I'm sorry to mention it, but my Lady expresses doubt of her son's truthfulness."

Serjer's eyes widened. He stood unmoving, unspeaking, far too long.

Aloran swallowed. "I apologize. I shall tell her you are unavailable."

"Aloran, wait—"

Aloran turned back.

Serjer took a deep breath. "The messenger was Della's Yoral of the

Household of the Sixth Family. I was unforgivably rude. I questioned him, and when he was kind enough to answer, I realized I should not have asked. He told me the idea for the request was Lady Della's, but that she acts upon it with her parents' joint consent." He paused, breathing hard. Pain came into his voice. "She's a seventeen-year-old girl, Aloran. She's willing to risk her health and social standing, and our young Master's, out of the pure terror of a betrothal to a thirty-year-old man she doesn't know. There's no way to rescue the Grobal from the depths to which they sink!"

"I won't ask you to bear witness before my Lady," Aloran said gently. Serjer had always been so kind to him—he couldn't possibly insist. "I'll speak to her on your behalf."

"Thank you." Serjer sighed. "I only wonder where our Mistress would be now, had she been given the same choice."

Those words felt like a hand twisting in his guts. Aloran tried to hold himself tall, breathing a pattern as he returned to the master bedroom. Young Master Tagaret still sat frozen on the bed, but his Lady's pacing had quickened. Aloran watched her, throat aching. Was it disapproval that goaded her? Or were her frantic footsteps those of the girl inside her, seeing someone else being offered a way out of the prison where she now lived?

Aloran walked into her path and bent to one knee. "Lady, our First Houseman offers his apologies, but has spoken with me on this matter," he said. "The invitation from Grobal Enwin and Lady Pazeu of the Sixth Family was indeed offered with sincerity. According to the young Lady's escort, the young Lady herself was the originator of the plan, and both of her parents have given their consent."

Tamelera swept up to him and stopped. Hands shaking, she bunched her green skirts in both fists. "Tagaret," she said. "Do you *know* what they are asking you to do?"

The young Master broke from his paralysis. "To come at night, to . . . to . . ."

"*To ruin her.*"

"Oh, Sirin and Eyn," Tagaret moaned, and hid his face in his hands.

Aloran bent his head, blushing.

"Even if you're not discovered," Tamelera continued mercilessly, "you won't be able to take her as your life's partner without suffering serious questioning about her value, and about your sanity in accepting an obviously compromised partnership."

Tagaret gained some resolve. "Mother, I would have been questioned anyway, because she's Sixth Family. I don't care about that."

"Easy enough to say, young man."

"I mean it!"

"Then you must do as they ask."

"M–mother," the young Master stammered. "Are you serious?"

"Of course I'm serious!" she snapped. "Will you be offered this opportunity, but sit back and allow her to partner with *Garr?*"

Silence smothered the room. Aloran's heart pounded and his face burned.

"Aloran," Tamelera said sharply.

The hand in his guts had twisted so tight, it hurt to stand up. "Lady?"

Her jaw was set, but tears trembled in her eyes. "If Tagaret is going to do this, he must be able to take her in partnership afterward. All his good intentions will mean nothing if she conceives a child tonight. Could you—access something for her?"

Aloran gulped, seeing lines of bright green Restricted labels in the Academy pharmacy. On the other hand, there was an alternative, if he still had any left . . . "Lady," he said. "May I be excused to check something?"

Tamelera nodded.

Aloran stepped behind his curtain into his own room. Breathing shallowly in guilt and disbelief, he opened the drawer of his bedside table. The bottle in the back corner felt empty to his hand. When he opened it, he discovered he had only two tablets left, unneeded since he'd lost Kiit and sworn off Chenna. For the medication to take full effect by this evening—he checked his watch—the young Master would need to take both of them, immediately. He fetched a clean glass of water and returned with it to his Lady's room, where he offered the tablets to Tagaret.

"Young Master, please take both of these, at once."

Tagaret ran his hands through his hair. "What do they do?"

"They will render you infertile for a period of one day."

Tagaret glanced up nervously. "Are you sure? Only one day?"

Aloran took a calming breath. "Yes, sir. They are both effective and safe; I have taken them myself for more than a year, and I swear by them."

Gingerly, Tagaret took the tablets and swallowed them. "I guess I'd better go," he said, blushing. "I have to . . . make plans."

"Oh, love," Lady Tamelera sighed, but she didn't stop the young Master walking out, or call him back. After a moment she wrapped both arms tightly around herself and shivered. "Poor Lady Della."

Something broke in Aloran's mind. Horror flooded through him. *Look at her.* That retreat, that fear—*that*, for her, was the experience of sex! And that was what she imagined her own darling Tagaret would bring to Lady Della, simply because she had never known anything else.

He couldn't let her be right.

"Excuse me, Lady," he said, and leapt out the door after the young Master, catching up to him just as Tagaret reached the door of his rooms.

"Aloran?" Tagaret looked puzzled. "Does Mother want me?"

This was presumption of the most egregious sort, but he couldn't stop himself. "Young Master, I must speak with you alone," he said.

Tagaret shrank. "All right. Do come in."

Aloran stepped inside the young Master's rooms, just far enough to allow the door to close. There was no natural place for a guest to sit; and since he was no guest anyway, he remained standing.

"Young Master, forgive me, but I shall presume to ask you a question."

Tagaret nodded.

"Do you have any idea how to make love to a woman?"

The young Master sank down on his bed with his head in his hands. "Sirin and Eyn help me," he whispered. "I can't do this."

So it was true: he didn't know anything. It was so horrible, so offensive, that Aloran's nerve wavered, and he almost walked out. But speaking was his only hope.

"Young Master," he said, more gently. "Lady Della will be as frightened as you. Probably more, as we cannot assume she has experience of the same nature as yours."

Tagaret winced, but nodded.

"If you love her, sir, and if you hope to have her love you in return after this, you must always think of her pleasure before your own." Was his advice too Imbati? Selflessness was less than natural for a Grobal, but it was the only right way he knew. "Watch her eyes and her lips as you touch her, especially when touching her sensitive parts. When she smiles, and when she breathes as you breathe, continue. If she stops, or shows any discomfort, stop. For if you can't give her pleasure, you will certainly give her pain, and she will always remember it."

Tagaret moaned, "Oh, mercy of Heile."

"I have given offense, young Master," Aloran said, and bowed low. "I shall withdraw."

"No," Tagaret cried. "Aloran, please—you've done this. You have to help me. I'm not even sure I know . . . which parts are sensitive." He reddened. "Hearsay doesn't count."

In the end, Aloran ran through the Maze to his room, and brought back one of his medical books so they could look through relevant sections together. He left the book, and the young Master clung to it as if it were a rope to pull him out of an abyss.

If only it could.

Aloran returned to his abandoned Lady prepared for the worst— even a flying rabbit wouldn't have surprised him. But Tamelera was standing quietly, gazing out the window.

"Did you speak to Tagaret?" she asked without turning.

"Yes, Lady. I apologize for leaving my post."

"It's of no consequence." She gazed a while longer, and finally turned around. "What did you say to him?"

He should have chosen the polite denial. But the reckless presumption was still too close to the surface. "About how a man need not hurt a woman, in love," he said. "About how to protect her heart from invasion, and not just her womb."

Tamelera wrapped both arms tightly around herself.

Garr had done this to her. Garr had taken the partnership vows, playing the role of Sirin, whose love and trust had so moved the Maiden Eyn that she would return to him, and only him, for all time. And then Garr had forced himself on a tender, frightened girl. For eighteen years, he'd used sex as punishment for his own satisfaction—Mai the Right and Father Varin between them should tear his soul from his body!

Aloran shook with rage; quickly he knelt and lowered his head to the floor, hoping she wouldn't see. "I'm sorry, Lady."

"It was good of you. For her, it's not too late." Her quiet voice took on an ironic note. "If I'm lucky, I'll never have a man touch me again."

Aloran closed his eyes and wished he could sink into the floor.

"Lady, please—" his voice broke. "Please, tell me we don't need to go to the medical center." In this state, he might do worse than Sorn: strangle a half-dead nobleman with his bare hands.

"No," Tamelera said. The rustle of her skirts told him she was walking to the lounge chairs. "I don't wish to trouble Premel by delaying his lunch schedule anyway."

"You are considerate, Lady."

"Could you brush my hair instead?"

"Of course."

Bless her, she must have known how it would comfort him. The meditative calm of removing pins, unwinding braids, holding and moving the brush was just what he needed.

"Aloran?"

"Yes, Lady?"

"You braided my hair a bit too tightly today . . ."

He sighed. "Please forgive me." Nervous as he'd been about their visit to the medical center, that was small excuse for letting his tension creep into his work.

"No, no, I don't mean to criticize." She sat silent for several seconds. "I mean . . . my head is hurting."

"Do you wish medicine, Lady?"

She turned slightly, as if she'd considered looking at him. "Can you rub my scalp, please?"

Aloran blinked. Was this some kind of apology? But no; he was no man in her eyes, just as he was no guest in the room of her son. It meant nothing. He returned the brush to his pocket and softly touched her temples. When she made no complaint, he pressed gently, moving his fingertips among the roots of her heavy hair. Tamelera sighed and leaned into his touch.

Such small comfort he could offer. His throat ached, but he wished the moment might never stop.

CHAPTER THIRTY

Della

It turned out that midnight assignations were one of Kuarmei's specialties.

The small Imbati woman came around front to fasten the new coat she'd purchased for him, while Tagaret tried to keep hold of the thoughts whirling in his head.

Disobedience had never seemed so terrifying. The days when a misdirected glance could invite Imbati retaliation appeared mild in comparison. Yet, Della had the courage to propose it. He'd imagined the trap already closed, but she'd kept her eyes open for one last way out. Those eyes . . . More than emerald, they were as green as the plants that grew in sunlight. Hers was the kind of courage that could brave Father Varin's heat without flinching, and she challenged him now, just as she'd first challenged him with the sound of her voice, and with the promise of music. The risk in this plan was double for her, but she embraced it, and he must do the same.

I embrace it.

Of course, now he had to do it without getting caught.

"I wish it weren't at her *house*," he said. "Everyone knows I've been there before."

"Sir," said Kuarmei, fastening the top button at his left collarbone. "If she met you anywhere else, it would appear she had voice in the plan."

"Oh. Right." Which meant they wouldn't be invited in, either. "There are no windows on the street level in front. I suppose we'll have to break in using the Akrabitti way?"

Kuarmei wrapped a long scarf of slate-gray silk around his head so that it tickled across his face, and one end shimmered to his waist. "With your permission, sir, yes. I'm impressed you know of that method."

"And you can break us in?"

She swiftly applied a black scarf to her own head, hiding everything but her eyes. Even her Imbati mark was invisible. "I believe so, sir. We shall see."

They walked inward along the first-floor hall, fortunately deserted at this late hour. Kuarmei took him to an exit at the juncture of the west wing and the central section. Here, Arissen laughter echoed from a small room off the hall, and no guards flanked the door. Kuarmei pressed herself to the wall. Tagaret tried to do the same, though at his height he felt as obvious as a shinca in the dark. Reaching the guardroom, Kuarmei stole a quick glance in and beckoned; he tried to imitate her silent footsteps across the opening. Then Kuarmei opened the outer door, and he slipped into the dark gap.

The Arissen didn't react. Maybe they hadn't noticed; maybe they didn't care.

Rather than leaving a record of their departure at the Conveyor's Hall, Kuarmei convinced him to remain on foot. It was easier than he'd feared to slip through the skimmer exit when a cargo vehicle passed—but strange to feel like part of the shadows, and not the light. Strange, too, to feel the soft touch of silk across his face. Kuarmei took him on a roundabout route through the northern districts, on streets he did not recognize at all, avoiding mercantile areas and often threading through Akrabitti alleyways. At last, she stopped before a door.

"This is it, sir."

Tagaret's stomach squirmed, but he nodded. *Della, I'm here for you.*

Imbati Kuarmei removed a slender metal tool from one of her pockets and pried on the edge of the door at three points, looking up and down to check its motion. Seemingly satisfied, she hid the tool away and applied herself to the lower of the two locks. It made a horrible scraping noise, and Tagaret's heart started pounding. After far too long, Kuarmei stood up, wrapped the trailing end of her scarf around the handle, and opened the door.

Della's Yoral was standing in the laundry room.

Tagaret gasped—then swallowed it. Yoral was on their side. In all likelihood, he hadn't helped them with the door because to be seen helping an invader was more than his job was worth.

Oh, sweet Heile—was he taking Yoral away from Della just by being here?

"Yoral," he whispered.

"Tagaret, sir," said Yoral resignedly. "I have already vowed not to speak of encountering you here. I'm glad you were able to manage the door without my help."

"Can we—do anything?" he asked. "Somehow, make it look like you resisted and were overcome?"

Yoral's gaze sharpened. "Someone accompanies you?"

Tagaret glanced over his shoulder; obediently and wordlessly, Kuarmei stepped inside.

The relief on Yoral's face was astonishing to see. "Castemate," he said, "to get to my Lady's bedroom, exit this door behind me and take the hall to the right. Climb the first stairway you will see on your left, all the way to the top floor. Continue straight ahead to the corner and enter the door on your left."

Kuarmei gave a sharp nod. Yoral bowed, then turned his back. Kuarmei clamped her arm around his neck. Yoral didn't struggle, but after several seconds his arms moved strangely, as if voicing independent protest. Then he staggered and collapsed onto the floor.

"Gods!" Tagaret squeaked. "You strangled him?"

"I surprised him from behind," said Kuarmei. "He'll waken again soon." She removed her scarf and tied Yoral's hands and feet together behind him. "In case he's found," she said. "We should go."

She'd obviously had no difficulty memorizing the directions. Kuarmei went ahead to the top of the stairs, then motioned him up. Despite the dimness of the light, their dark clothes stood out against the white plaster walls. His heart beat as loud as a drum. If the family wanted him here, surely the Household would have been told to stay in bed tonight?

Kuarmei beckoned him to lean close when they reached the door in question. "I'll stay outside," she breathed. "If there's trouble, I'll knock three times."

Tagaret closed his fists and nodded. Wrapping the end of his scarf around the door handle as she had done, he opened the door and went in.

"Tagaret?"

Oh, that honey voice . . . *I embrace it.* He quivered from head to foot. "It's me," he whispered. He pulled off his scarf and stuffed it in his coat pocket.

The only light came through sheer white curtains on both outside walls. Della sat partially silhouetted in the milky dimness. Aloran had said to watch her face; he crept closer one step at a time, searching for a glimpse of it. Her clothes were pale, her hair tumbling over her shoulders like a fall of dark water. She didn't stand to meet him. As he drew near, she shrugged a robe off her shoulders—hesitated, then pulled it back up.

Something about the gesture stopped him.

"Della? Are you all right?"

"Where's my Yoral?" she asked.

Mercy, what should he say? He gulped a breath. "Downstairs. We—I, wanted to make sure he wasn't seen as helping me."

Della sat up straighter. "What did you do?"

"He asked me to," Tagaret said quickly. "I had my servant knock him out, so he could say he had fallen defending you."

"Heile's mercy!"

"I'm sorry. Della, if you lost him over this, I'd never forgive myself."

She made a small, inarticulate sound.

Mai help him . . . "I'm just trying to protect you. You want me here, don't you?"

"I—" She took a deep breath. "You're right, Tagaret. I do." She shrugged the robe off again and reached toward him.

Tagaret took her hand in his. Every part of him awoke instantly at her touch. When she pulled him forward, he sat down beside her. Oh, the warmth of her fingers, the smell of her, the sweet accidental brush of her leg against his—it was what he'd ached and dreamed for, just what he'd wanted all along.

"You're so beautiful," he sighed, then gulped, instinctively searching the room for a servant who wasn't there. This time it was different. No one would tell him he couldn't speak to her. No one would tell him he couldn't put his arm around her. Kiss her. Touch her. Take off her clothes. Take . . .

It was too much. He trembled just imagining it, but it made him so hard and hot and dizzy he nearly felt sick. She wasn't Reyn. She didn't know him that way—she barely knew him at all.

Start small.

He lifted his hand and pressed her hair back from her forehead, feeling the strands tickle and slide between his fingers. Her head tilted back, and her breath came faster. He followed the sound of it to her lips. Oh, the softness of her mouth opening beneath his—it was like falling into the deeps. Cradling her head in one hand, he reached across with the other and pulled her closer, tighter in. Her hand stroked up his back, and her breast pressed against him, oh, Sirin and Eyn yes, *this*, more of *this* . . . Her fingers tickled buttons loose, and suddenly traced pure, startling pleasure across his chest. A moan squeezed out of him.

Della pulled back with a gasp. "Are you all right?"

At first, he couldn't speak. "Fine," he managed. "It—it feels good."

Next her touch came upon his cheek, and she stroked his neck down to his collarbone, then crept lower—he reached for her again, this time with one arm around her back, and the other hand over the crook of her knees. He pulled her into his lap and covered her neck in kisses.

She wriggled. "Tagaret . . ."

He panted, trying to look at her. He mustn't forget to watch her face, but he could hardly see her face at all. Her breathing *did* sound like his, didn't it? "What's wrong?"

"I don't know." She wriggled again—it felt so good he could have died. He clamped his arm across her lap and pushed her downward, grinding hard.

"Gods—Della—"

Della's breath was fast but uneven, like hiccups. "It's just—ooh— what should I do, Tagaret, should I be—" She clung to his neck, wriggling lower, and her breasts nudged against his chest. He found one with his hand, stroked the nipple that pressed at him through her silk nightgown.

This time they both moaned at once. She gave a strange gulp.

"Tagaret," she whispered. "I feel—strange. There's something wrong with me, my stomach feels . . . and my—" She broke off. "Yoral didn't say I would feel like this."

"Nothing," he panted. "Nothing's wrong with you." He reached for her knees, slid his fingers between them, stroked up along the gentle curve—

"Tagaret, stop."

It was like trying to stop gravity. He clenched his teeth, his stomach, his fists, everything he had, and managed not to touch her there. Half-foundering in the warm wave, he pulled his hands back to the surface of the bed.

"What is it?" he asked. "You're not feeling—bad, are you?"

"No." She slid off his lap. Even in the half-dark, he could tell she was looking down at him. But she'd just been—on there, so she must know—wouldn't Yoral have told her what to expect?

What if he hadn't known what to tell her, good or bad?

Tagaret took a deep breath. "Della, it's *supposed* to feel good. I *want* you to feel good." He reached for her, but she only pulled further away.

"You've done this before."

Oh, no. "Y—no," he stammered. "Not *this*."

"Not this? Have you been with a boy?"

"Holy Twins—"

"You have, haven't you."

Tagaret rubbed his face with both hands. Would she hate him now?

"Tagaret," she said sternly. "You must tell me the truth. If I can't trust you, then why *shouldn't* I take Innis in partnership? He would be the same."

It wasn't fair. Innis *couldn't* be the same—Innis would be like Father, and he could never be like Father, never, never! If he were truly to be her Sirin, he must show he was worthy of his Eyn's trust.

"I have," he said.

"Oh!"

"Please don't hate me. I couldn't lie to you. He's a close friend, but I'm not in love with him. You are everything to me—you've never left my thoughts since the minute I first saw you." The sheets rustled, and her fingertips touched his hand. He turned his hand to hers and held it tightly.

"It's all wrong, Tagaret," Della said. "I wish we could run away.

Live out on the surface with the wysps of the wilderness, where I could want you, and have you, and it wouldn't matter what anyone else wanted." She sighed. "It would *just* feel good. I wouldn't have to feel like I was playing their game."

"You did find a way to break the rules," he said. "If it works, and I can make you mine, we could go to Selimna."

She sighed again. A heartbroken sound. "So we break the rules," she said. "What then? We're still subject to them; we'll feel the consequences. I'd rather play a totally different game."

Out of the dark an idea struck him, so strong and clear, he could not doubt it was a gift—from Sirin and Eyn for undying love, and from Mai for justice. "We can. Della, we *can*."

"What do you mean?"

"We're here together, alone. Who's to say we haven't done as you planned?"

She grabbed his arm. "Oh, Tagaret, would it work? But what if the Council wants to examine me?"

He shuddered at the thought. "They can't examine you *themselves*, can they? Wouldn't they ask Yoral?"

"And he would protect me. Oh, dear Tagaret, he would!" She flung her arms around his neck and kissed him, so hard and long he couldn't breathe. He found the edge of her nightgown and pushed it up. She was naked underneath. He felt up the back of her thigh to her bottom and pulled her closer. As Sirin was his witness, he wanted to forget the whole idea of stopping. She made a sound—a very different sound, blissful and urgent, while her fingers moved from his chest to his stomach, then his hips. He stood up and pulled her against him— how it ached—oh, dear gods, would she consent now anyway, in spite of everything?

Then another consequence dashed him in ice. *Nekantor.*

He fell to sit on the bed, catching her when she tried to fall with him. "Della," he whispered. "What if my brother tries to use us? What if he tries to take your Family's vote?"

For a time, she didn't answer. "Would that be bad?" she asked.

"Yes. He has to be stopped."

"I could tell Father." She sighed. "I don't think it'll do much good.

You can't rely on politicians, Tagaret. If stopping him is that important, you'll need to do it yourself."

"How?"

"Hurt him," she said. "You're the only one who'd know how. He's your brother."

Instantly, he knew what to do. He seized her by both hands. "Della, you're brilliant."

"Now I think you'd better go."

He stood up awkwardly, closed his buttons, and straightened his clothes as best he could. Couldn't get the scarf quite right, but close enough. "I don't want to leave you," he said. "I don't want you to be alone, hearing the things they'll say about you tomorrow. I want to be there every minute."

"You can't," she said softly. "I'll be all right. Don't see me again until an arrangement is made, or they'll know it was you, and everything will go bad. You'll have to pretend you're angry, and that you accept me grudgingly."

His heart hurt just thinking about it. "Della, I love you. I accept you with all my heart."

"I love you, too. I know you can do this." She stood on tiptoes and kissed him. "Together, we will outplay them."

CHAPTER THIRTY-ONE

Benél

The Ninth Family's servant offered Nekantor a drink.

The liquid whispered to him: *poison, poison.*

Nekantor kept breathing. Clear glass; its pale, bubbly contents were probably apple yezel, but his chest felt tight. He needed to count. He couldn't count, with Gowan and his father watching. He imagined buttons in his mind: one, two, three. One, two, three. It wasn't the same. His fingers itched.

Arissen Karyas leaned to his ear. "Shall I taste it, sir?"

Nekantor shook his head. Karyas was too valuable to risk.

He could do this by himself. *Holding* the glass wouldn't hurt him, anyway—it was easy on the eye, cooling on the mind. He took the drink from the Imbati's hand, and his fingers didn't even shake. Clear, smooth crystal. The urge to count diminished.

I can do this by myself. Three more hours, and the game will be over. The First Family can still win.

"Father," said Gowan, "I don't know why you're listening to him."

Amyel turned to his son. Nekantor pretended to sip his drink. Sweet scent touched his nostrils, and the glass remained perfectly full, and he remained perfectly safe. See? He could do this without Father. *He needed all the votes.*

"Honestly, Gowan," said Amyel, "I don't know who else you'd expect to argue the First Family's case at this point."

"Tagaret said—"

"That's not his role," said Amyel. "The final round is where the really difficult decisions get made. I can understand you'd prefer

Tagaret to be here; he's your friend. *I* have to bear in mind our history with the Fifth Family."

Gnash Gowan for his interference. Nekantor wanted to slap that look off his too-handsome face. Instead, he considered his drink—ah yes, pure crystal. The next move drifted up with the tiny bubbles. "Gowan, I'm sorry," he said. "I'm sure you can see why I had to argue against you. That's what Heir Selection is like. Now that we're no longer rivals, I want to honor our Families' history of alliances."

"Alliances that Innis will bear in mind if the Fifth Family wins," Amyel added.

That was better; Amyel was the vote he needed anyway, not Gowan. But if Gowan could be softened, he might be useful later. Father had been stupid to try to kill him. If only he'd killed Innis, then all this fawning would be unnecessary.

Nekantor smiled. "Gowan, I hope you aren't holding our Aloran's improprieties against him."

Gowan glared. "Not *his*."

"We honor Aloran for his actions," said Amyel. "Please also thank your cousin Pyaras for helping to resolve the matter."

Bang-bang-bang!

Nekantor jumped. Liquid splashed over his fingers. Karyas quickly plucked the glass from his hand.

Poison . . .

Nekantor wiped his fingers with a handkerchief. This was apple yezel, not poison. And even if it was poison, it couldn't kill him—there were no contact poisons that could be put into a drink. He was safe. He *had* to be safe! He wiped his fingers again, one by one.

"Aaahmyel!" A voice boomed, as loud as the fist had been on the bronze door. The Ninth Family's vestibule curtain whipped aside and Cabinet Secretary Boros burst in, with his manservant behind him. "News, news! Have you heard?"

"Um, shouldn't we speak in private?" asked Amyel.

"Ah, yes, you have a guest!" Boros laughed, loud enough to echo. "No need—the news is everywhere. Innis of the Fifth Family is in a rage. He's cut off negotiations with the Sixth Family!"

The Sixth Family? Nekantor stiffened against the echoes, fisted his contaminated hand and hid it in his pocket. His chest twisted, but he couldn't run out. He had to hear about the Sixth Family, not to mention keep the Ninth Family's vote, and impress Boros if he could. *He needed all the votes.* He pressed a question between his teeth. "Why?"

"What happened?" Gowan asked.

"This very night," the Secretary made a flourish with his hands, "Innis' betrothed has been *despoiled.*"

Amyel grunted. "What did she do?"

Secretary Boros frowned. "Nothing, so far as we can tell. Her house was broken into and her bodyguard ambushed . . . you can guess the rest."

Sex, behind a locked door. The thought sent a shiver down Nekantor's back. Gods, how he wanted Benél. There must be a way to keep the perfection secret, even now; he could play games as well as anyone. He had to get out of here—but not yet, not yet. A few more moves. He could do this by himself; he *had* to do this by himself!

"Has anyone been arrested, sir?" he asked.

"Not so far." Boros shrugged. "The manservant involved was clearly experienced. And as the obvious motive is political sabotage, the list of suspects is long."

Gowan muttered. "Varin's teeth—Tagaret's going to be pretty upset."

Tagaret? Yes, that was it—the move that would allow him to escape. "If you'll excuse me, maybe I'd better go break the news to my brother," Nekantor said. "He was rather an admirer of that young Lady."

Secretary Boros shrugged. "He probably already knows. Good luck to you, young Nekantor."

"Thank you for coming to speak with us," said Amyel.

Don't scream. Don't run. Nekantor breathed tightly, but managed to bow. "Thank you, sir." He clenched his teeth and walked, step, step, step, through the vestibule and out into the main hall.

"Home," he snapped at Karyas.

"Yes, sir."

There were people in the hall; he shouldn't run, but he ran anyway. Slapped the door lock with his left hand, ran straight to his rooms and stripped down to nothing. He poured hot water over his body, over his right hand. Washed it, and washed it again—the liquid had been on too long, and would not be entirely expunged. Benél, where was Benél? But there was no time for secrecy, for perfection; not if he wanted to reach the Sixth Family and make a deal. He dried his body, but the hand resisted. He washed it again, and again—finally fumbled his cabinet open, took a bottle of cleaning alcohol and poured it over his red, shaking fingers.

He hissed in pain, but finally the last traces of the awful liquid burned away.

Carefully now. Nekantor dressed: eleven buttons, each touched in order with his sore fingers. That was better. He moved into the circle, touching and checking. Yes, better and better. This game was almost over.

He still couldn't see the whole vision in his mind.

But he wouldn't ask for help; Father couldn't help now, anyway. He *had* to do this by himself. All the dancing lines had been cut off, all but two—so close to the center, did he really need to see it all? He could do this by himself, so long as he could see the very next move, the move right before his feet.

Innis' loss was his gain. Innis had broken off with the Sixth Family, and that meant the Sixth Family's vote was back in play.

Nekantor went to his bedroom door. "Karyas."

"Yes, sir."

"Take me to the suite of cabinet member Arith of the Sixth Family."

She nodded. "And your brother, sir?"

"Forget him." A delay with Tagaret's whining might lose him the opportunity completely.

"Yes, sir."

Karyas was a good Arissen and knew precisely where to take him; the Sixth Family's cabinet member also had a suite on the first floor. Nekantor counted paces. Fifty, fifty-five . . .

Wait—there was Benél's door.

At once, he thirsted desperately for perfection. Nekantor shivered, and his hand lifted to his vest buttons, one-two-three, remembering how they came undone.

But there was no time. Karyas walked past the door, and he had to follow.

"Nek?"

Benél's voice, behind him. Nekantor turned around. Benél was here. Benél was strong, and he had power. "I'm on my way to see Arith of the Sixth Family," Nekantor said. "Want to come?"

Benél should have smiled. Benél always loved when they played the game together—but he didn't smile now. "Nek, I need to talk to you," he said.

"No problem." Probably Benél's mother was after him again, or his father, and he needed something explained to him. "Except I have to speak to Arith first."

Two doors ahead, Karyas was already knocking. Nekantor ran to catch up, faced the door, straightened his vest and his sleeves, and touched his buttons. Sent a wink over his shoulder at Benél. Benél's eyes widened.

An Imbati woman opened the door. "Sir?"

Nekantor nodded to her. "I am Nekantor of the First Family," he said. "May I please speak to Arith of the Sixth Family?"

"If you would wait inside, please, sir."

He walked in. The vestibule curtain was blue; in Amyel's suite it had been brown, and in his own, green. He waited, eyes on the second hand of his watch. Finally, the Imbati returned.

"If you would come with me, please, sir."

Nekantor walked into the Sixth Family's sitting room. This house didn't look like a muckwalker's house; it was just like his, with every wall in exactly the right place. Arith of the Sixth Family was waiting for him with an Imbati woman behind his shoulder. He looked as defensive as a tunnel-hound before its den. His long, thinning red hair hung down to his cabinet pin. He hadn't been nervous in the cabinet question sessions, but today his hands were twitching; the recent news must have shaken him.

So much the better.

"You wished to see me, young Nekantor?" Arith asked. He didn't ask for Father.

Time for the sympathy move.

"Yes, sir," Nekantor said. "I wanted to reach out as soon as I heard.

I can't imagine how frustrating it would be to have an alliance come to nothing so close to the final round."

Arith crossed his arms over his chest. "What do you want, First Family?"

Nekantor took a deep breath. Arith was weak; if this had been Doross, the Arbiter of the Sixth Family Council, there would have been sparring, posturing, a game within a game even to get to the point where one might do business. "Sir," he said with sympathy, "I don't imagine you'd still wish to support Innis when he blames you for your own misfortune."

"You think Innis blames me?" Arith laughed bitterly. "Not at all; he blames Lady Della, and deservedly so. She's proven herself a harlot."

Tagaret, and a harlot—he almost laughed, but managed to cough instead. "I know someone who values her rather more than that."

"*You* could have had her," Arith said. "Then it wouldn't have come to this."

"And if I were to have her now, sir?"

Arith's eyes went wide. "You mock me!" he snapped. "You'd look like a fool. It would only prove you had no serious interest in being Heir."

Nekantor pursed his lips and nodded thoughtfully. "You're right, sir, of course—except that I don't mock you at all. I've never had any interest in the girl."

"What—"

He pushed onward. "My brother, though—you should see how he sighs over her! He's devastated at the thought of her disgrace. He's always known he had no chance at a partnership, but he's never been quite sane about her—in fact, I'd wager he might even overlook a bit of harlotry."

Arith was staring. "Your own brother? You must be crazy—Tagaret of the First Family would never consent to be so compromised!"

What, did he think Tagaret was too *strong* to take the girl? Gnash him—there had to be a way to get him to accept the move. Tagaret was weak enough! Nekantor took a deep breath. What did he need to do? What was the next move?

Ah, yes.

"All right," he said, and sighed. "I should have realized you were too smart for me, sir. I confess—Tagaret doesn't know I'm here."

Arith's eyes narrowed. "Young Nekantor, what do you mean by that?"

"Precisely what I said, sir. I came to see you without discussing the offer with him. But that doesn't mean we have no opportunity here. The Sixth Family can't rely on the Fifth to keep its word. I'm here to tell you that the First Family won't treat you so lightly. It's not a direct alliance with the Heir; that's true. But an alliance with the First Family is a thing of value nonetheless, and I don't need to wait for a victory. If you could see my brother's jealous agonies you'd understand—he would be willing to take Lady Della for partner today, in whatever condition."

Arith spluttered, "Even carrying another man's child?"

"Well . . ." Nekantor couldn't help a slight smirk. "Partner them fast enough, and perhaps he won't notice the difference. The Race will prosper either way."

Arith stared at him, one second . . . two . . . three . . . and then the corners of his mouth sneaked up. "You're a practical man, young Nekantor."

Nekantor gave a bow. "I believe it's necessary in times like these, sir. May I consider us agreed, then?"

"Yes."

Behind Arith's shoulder, his Imbati woman bowed. "Witnessed."

"Seconded," said Arissen Karyas.

He couldn't wait to tell Benél.

Nekantor walked out into the hall, hoarding a smile. Benél hadn't gone back in but was standing and waiting for him. Nekantor walked to a careful distance and spoke softly.

"Wonderful news, Benél. I've got the Sixth Family's vote."

"Wow." Benél's answer sounded wrong—uneven and breathy.

"I'm giving Tagaret to that girl."

"What?" Benél exclaimed. "The *used* girl?"

That sounded more like him. Nekantor laughed. "Yes."

But Benél didn't laugh along. He made a face like pain. "Nek, I need to talk to you."

"I know. I don't have a lot of time, or I'd—"

"Just come in for a second."

Strange. Nekantor narrowed his eyes. It was strange, and wrong, but this was Benél. And if he could have a moment—a kiss, a touch— Benél could make anything right. He scanned the hall for watchers, then followed Benél inside. Even unseen in the vestibule, Benél didn't reach for his neck. He breathed like tears, or anger.

Wrong, wrong: someone had done something to him.

"Who's hurt you?" Nekantor asked. "Is it Yril again? If he's done anything to you, don't worry. We'll crush him."

"Gnash it, Nekantor!" Benél shouted.

Oh, feel the power in that shout! For a split second, pure pleasure vibrated through him—but there was also something else in the sound, something that sent cold fear creeping up his nerves. He held very still.

"Nekantor," Benél said. "I can't—see you anymore."

"Of course you can," Nekantor said. "You know how to keep secrets, Benél."

"No. Nek, I can't—I *won't*—see you."

Nekantor stared at him. This was all wrong. It couldn't be true, it was a lie—no, it was a *mistake*. Benél was powerful, but he made mistakes when he didn't have things explained to him. "You don't mean that," Nekantor said. "We're the Twins, you said so."

Benél raised his fist.

Nekantor gasped and closed his eyes, shivering, waiting for it.

Benél didn't strike. "They told me," he growled. "Varin's teeth, Nekantor, they told me what's really wrong with you—you can't fool me anymore."

Nekantor opened his eyes. "Wrong with me?" he demanded. "There's nothing wrong with me."

Benél's gaze was accusing. "You're lying. You're—you're twisted in the head."

"Benél—someone's been lying to you, but it's not me. I'm the only one who sees things as they are! You've told me so yourself!"

Benél gulped. "I was wrong."

Nekantor grabbed him by the shirt. "Who told you these lies? We're on the same side, Benél—the First Family stands together against enemies. You have to tell me!"

Benél looked away to one side. "Just a note," he muttered. "House-hold."

Yril—it had to be Yril; Yril had always wanted his place by Benél's side. But Yril would never win perfection. Nekantor's heart pounded. His nerves hurt, all the way into his fingers, still tangled in Benél's silk shirt. He tightened his fists, pulled Benél close. "Benél," he whispered. "Kiss me."

"No."

"They're lying," Nekantor hissed. "They're wrong, Benél. I'm yours—you *know* me!"

Benél dragged a choking breath. "I do know you," he said. "You should go."

"Benél!"

But Benél ran out of the vestibule, deeper into the house. Nekantor stood shaking, trying to breathe. Without Benél, this was a horrible place, a border place where Lowers moved, and no place for gentlemen. The curtain ahead was restless with Benél's passing, and then the curtain on his left moved, and an Imbati was going to come out—

Nekantor ran. He fled down the hall, slapped the entry pad and ran into his rooms, but his bed loomed ahead, confronting him, whispering of sex. Benél, Benél! Benél grabbing him, kissing him, throwing him down—Benél crushing him, penetrating him, erasing every thought—

"No!" he screamed. "No!" No more perfection, and the Selection was coming fast—Plis' bones, the eyes, the whispers! He had to have all the votes, and he didn't have all the votes, or did he?

Every particle of him screamed for perfection, but Benél was gone. He couldn't see the game, and where was Father? In the Heile-forsaken medical center with traitor doctors who wouldn't heal him enough to let him play—

His chest squeezed tighter, tighter. Breath felt hot, and the room contracted. It was too tight in here—he slammed his fists against the inside of the door, over and over until they went numb. He needed Father—he needed Benél—

"No!" he screamed, "I can do this by myself!"

He fumbled a wire from his drawer, flung his door open, and ran

to Father's office. When the lock clicked open, he stepped inside—
tried to find knowledge and a sense of pattern, tried to see Father sitting at his desk chuckling, full of plans and confidence.

But it meant nothing. Father had never seen the whole game, and
now the chair was empty, the desk a riot of papers, nothing pointing
anywhere or making any sense. Nekantor seized the papers in his fists.
He tore them—gods, it felt good! He seized more, more, and tore them
into pieces, tiny shreds that no longer wanted to be straight because
there was no more edge to obligate them. The floor filled with paper,
and his fingers discovered a long, sharp letter-opener. Just what he
needed—he wheeled toward the couch. Gnash the thing, it had never
belonged! It had encroached here, encroached on Father, taking him
slowly from underneath and ruining his mind and body. He stabbed it,
ripped at it until the letter-opener bent, flung his weapon aside and dug
his fingers into the openings, tearing them outward. The frame groaned
and the rumpled sheet screamed and died; the pillows gave up their guts
and feathers floated in the air until everything whirled in a white fury.

"I don't need you," Nekantor panted. "I don't need you!" A feather
caught in his mouth and choked him, so he stumbled out again into
the sitting room.

He knew where he had to go next: Tagaret's locked door. Even
now he could feel it—those hooks were old, old, and that place never
stopped mocking, every time he walked by. His blood raced madly,
and his body shook. Now was the time. The door would submit, now
that Father could not stop him.

He shoved through the double doors into the drawing room and
went straight to the geode in the corner. It was heavy, unwieldy, but
there was nothing better. This time it would work, even if he had to
break the door down. Tagaret would finally realize there was no use in
trying to keep his secret games.

Nekantor turned around. And growled.

Tagaret's door was open.

The one time he *needed* it to be locked, it was open, and Imbati
Aloran was standing in front of it.

"Gnash you, Imbati," Nekantor shouted. "What in Varin's name
are you doing?"

Imbati Aloran turned around. "Young Master," he said, "Pardon me. I came to speak with your brother."

Look at him: the Imbati who played games. He was playing one even now, or why would he be blushing? Why would his eyes be white with fear?

Nekantor dropped the geode and strode over. "What are you hiding, Imbati Aloran? What's your game?"

The frightened Imbati bowed low. "My apologies, young Master."

"Ha!" Nekantor said. "Deflections, always the deflections! You *will* tell me."

Tagaret appeared in the door. "What are you doing, Nek? Leave him alone. Mother sent him to talk to me, that's all."

"About what, exactly?" Nekantor demanded. "It's wrong, I tell you. He's an Imbati, he doesn't just get to *talk* to you, it's not his place! Imbati, when are you going to learn?"

"Nek, stop," Tagaret said. "Why are you doing this? What's wrong?"

"There's nothing wrong!" Nekantor screamed. *Benél's staring eyes—I know what's wrong with you . . .* He panted, clenched his fists. "Nothing wrong at all. Nothing, except that my brother is an idiot and my servants aren't obedient enough. Imbati, come with me."

"Nek—"

"Give him to me, gnash it, or I'll slap him!"

Tagaret stared with his mouth open. No words, no power. Nekantor pointed the Imbati down the hall toward his room. Slowly, too slowly, the Imbati turned and began to walk down the hall.

"I know what you're up to," Nekantor sneered. "I see your game. It shows in every step you take." He could play games better than any Imbati.

"Young Master, I don't know how I have offended you—"

"In!"

"Please allow me to make amends—"

"Get inside, now!"

The Imbati opened the door of his room and walked in, then turned and made a deep bow. More disguised defiance. Nekantor pushed his shoulder—hard—but he didn't even have the decency to fall down.

"Down!" Nekantor shrieked.

Imbati Aloran got on his knees and put his marked forehead on the floor. Yes, that was wonderful. Probably thought he was safe, the proud little Lower, that deference would make him untouchable.

He would soon know better.

CHAPTER THIRTY-TWO

Apologies

"Mother!" Tagaret shouted. His flailing heart cut off his breath and tried to choke him—he burst into her room without knocking, startling her at her writing table. "Mother, help, Nekantor's got Aloran!"

Mother stood so fast she upended her chair onto the carpet. "Sweet Heile, where?"

"His rooms. I didn't know how to stop him, Mother, I'm sorry, I'm so sorry—"

But words wouldn't help. He turned and ran out again, letting her follow. This was his fault. The anonymous note had done its job too well—Varin knew what would happen if they didn't get there fast. What if he got his wish, but Aloran was the price? Oh, holy Mai!

Down the hall, Nekantor's Arissen woman stood in the hall outside his room as if nothing unusual were going on. Tagaret ignored her and banged on the door. "Nekantor! Let me in!"

No answer.

Mother rushed up beside him. "Aloran!" she cried, her voice edged with terror. "Don't let him hurt you!"

Still nothing.

Tagaret put his shoulder into the door and leaned on the handle, hard. Nekantor always locked his door, Varin gnash him—he'd get Arissen Karyas to *melt* the lock if he had to—

It wasn't locked.

The door gave way. Tagaret half-fell into the room and stumbled straight into Nekantor's back. Nekantor shrieked and whirled, his arm raised high. A leather belt swung from his hand like a whip.

Tagaret threw himself on his brother and knocked him down.

Punched him in the stomach, in the chest. Nekantor curled into a ball screaming, and it was just what he deserved, and Tagaret hit him again, again, in the side, in the back, over and over.

"Tagaret, stop!" Mother's voice.

No— Nekantor would pay, finally would be punished for everything he'd done!

"Aloran, stop him."

Hands under his arms. An irresistible force pulled him upward, and just like that he was suspended in midair, the motions of his fists useless. He cried out in dismay and frustration.

"Young Master, thank you," Aloran said softly. "I'll be all right."

"Aloran," said Mother. "Bring him out."

The strong hands lowered; Tagaret felt his feet touch the floor. Aloran's arm around his back was hard as iron, but he wouldn't have fought it. The terrible anger was gone—only guilt remained, as if his heart had caved in. "I'm sorry, Aloran," Tagaret murmured. "I'm so sorry."

Aloran said nothing.

"Karyas," said Mother. "You are remiss in your duty. Mind your charge."

The Arissen woman twitched, but clapped her right hand to her left shoulder in salute. She went into Nekantor's room and shut the door.

"Mother," said Tagaret. "I'm sorry . . ." What else could he say? But no matter how many times he said it, it was never enough.

"Are you finished?" Mother asked severely.

Oh, the look on her face . . . Tagaret gulped and nodded.

"Now, here's what you're going to do. You're going to pull yourself together, and we're going back in there. You and Aloran are going to apologize to Nekantor."

"What?" he cried. It came out as a squeak. "But that's not fair!"

Mother grabbed his arms. "Fair has nothing to do with this, Tagaret," she hissed. "Nekantor has an important event to attend, and he has to be in the Hall of the Eminence in thirty minutes. You and Aloran have to help him get there."

"But he can't—"

She shook him so hard his teeth clacked together. "You don't understand! Tagaret, he's like your father. If he's late for the Selection, he'll blame you. If he blames you, he'll punish you. If he considers you harmless like Garr has always considered me—he'll hurt you, and that will satisfy him. But if he ever decides you're a real threat, he won't be satisfied until you're dead."

"Mother . . ." He shook his head. But his eyes crept to Aloran standing there silent, his suit disarranged, who knew how many whip-lashes on his back. Aloran was the undeniable proof that she was right—he'd done nothing but stand in Nekantor's path, and this was his reward. If Nekantor ever suspected who had written the note . . . "What can I do?" he whispered.

Mother's grip softened, and she put her arms around him. Tagaret leaned forward against her hair.

"Be harmless," she said. "Tell him it was a tantrum. You were up-set and jealous about Lady Della, and you got angry because it was your turn to have Aloran, not his. Apologize and offer to help him get ready so he won't be late."

Tagaret stepped back and looked at her. His eyes felt hot and his throat raw. "Oh, Mother . . ."

"Keep yourself safe," Mother insisted.

He took a deep breath, then knocked at the door. No one answered—he almost walked away. But he had to do this. "Nekantor, I'm sorry," he called.

There were murmurs inside, and the door opened. Nekantor was there—scowling, but he'd already begun straightening his clothes. It seemed he hadn't yet noticed the crazy state of his hair.

Tagaret deliberately hung his head. His heart screamed, but it wasn't Mai's help he needed now, it was Heile's. "I'm sorry I hit you," he said. "I was a stupid baby. I got too upset over Lady Della, and then you took Aloran when I wanted him, and I lost hold of myself. I guess—I don't know." He forced the words out, though they burned in his throat. "I guess I was too much my—my mother's son."

"You *are* stupid," Nekantor growled. "You don't know what's good for you. That's why I'm in the Selection tonight, and you're not."

At least he didn't have to fake the blush. "You're right. I'm so sorry. Can—" He choked on what he had to say, coughed, and sucked in a breath. "Can I help you?"

Nekantor laughed.

Tagaret blinked at him.

"You already have helped me, idiot," Nekantor said. "You've got me a vote. And I've got you a very pretty, slightly used partner."

"A, uuh," he stammered. "Thank—?" He bit down on the word. *Not thanks, outrage.* "I mean—Nekantor, a *used* partner? What were you thinking?"

Nekantor laughed again. "I knew you'd feel that way. You're welcome. Just make sure you arrange the ceremony as soon as possible so you can take credit for any of her gifts to the Race."

Oh, dear gods! Tagaret's mouth fell open.

Thank Heile, Aloran changed the subject. "Young Master Nekantor," he said, "May I get you a comb before you leave for the Selection?"

"No!" Nekantor shouted. "*I can do this by myself!*" He slammed the door in their faces.

Tagaret stared at the door. Probably he should be relieved that Nek didn't want them—but he couldn't help wondering if Nek would be late and blame them anyway. His body still quivered with the after-echoes of rage. He rubbed his face with both hands.

"Tagaret, darling," Mother said. "You should get ready for the Selection event now, too."

Tagaret grimaced. "But what if Nek wins?" He couldn't have felt more useless—nothing he'd done had slowed Nek down, only made him more dangerous than ever. "I couldn't stand it."

Mother lifted his hand in her warm fingers. "Love, who knows how the votes may have shifted? It may still end well."

He rolled his eyes.

Mother gave his hand a firm shake. "Darling, you need to be *seen*. Were you listening to your brother? Lady Della's plan worked better than we could have imagined—and that means you will have a partner soon, perhaps in a matter of days."

A partner—only from Mother's mouth did the words finally reach his heart. "Sirin and Eyn, you're right," he said. "Do you think I might see her tonight? I can't believe it."

"I don't think you should expect that, Tagaret," Mother said. "You have something else to do—you have to show strength, publicly, for her and for yourself. You're a man now, with responsibilities. No matter what the outcome tonight, you'll have to handle the rockfall that the two of you have brought upon yourselves."

She was right. No matter how clever their plan, they couldn't escape the game entirely. "I'll go, then," he said. "So I won't be late."

He rang for Kuarmei, and she helped him dress in the ocean suit that Mother had given him, deftly handling the long rows of pearl buttons along the cuffs.

As she fastened his coat, he remembered Reyn.

Reyn, who had run his finger down this sleeve, and told him the ocean was the secret behind this shifting pattern of glimmer and blue. Reyn, who had almost died of touching his hand, but would be caught in the changing tide now that Della could be his forever.

"Kuarmei," he said. "Do you have paper?"

"Certainly, sir."

Tagaret sat down at his desk. His chest felt as cold as the blank paper. At last he started to write.

> *To Reyn of the Ninth Family*
>
> *Do you remember the first day we kissed? Then I imagine you must also remember copper and emeralds—I think you always knew she was never far outside my thoughts when we were together. It's not that I ever loved you less, but I suppose there must be different kinds of love. And then there was the fever, and the Selection. And now there's this: I've just learned I will be taking Lady Della in partnership. Nek arranged it, but I'd be lying if I said it isn't what I always wanted. I hope you'll decide not to scorn me—I'm pretty sure everyone else will. It's the worst for you, though, so if you do, then I'll understand. I guess becoming a man happened faster than I was ready for. Now that it's happened, I'd better give it my best. I'm sorry.*
>
> *Tagaret of the First Family*

He almost threw it away the instant he was finished, but what words could possibly serve instead? He sighed and folded the paper closed.

"Shall I deliver it for you, sir?" Kuarmei asked.

Tagaret blushed. "No, thank you. I think I'd better do this one myself."

Mother wished him luck with a smile and a kiss, but his shame only deepened as he climbed the stairs. The letter burned in his inside pocket; he gritted his teeth and forced his feet forward. Kuarmei kept him from feeling exposed—but Reyn had kept him from feeling *alone*. At Reyn's door he took a deep breath and knocked.

Imbati Shara opened the door, but had scarcely begun her greeting when Lady Iren exploded into the vestibule in an amethyst whirl of joy.

"Tagaret?" she exclaimed. "We were expecting Cousin Gowan!"

"I'm sorry . . ."

"No, no, come in. He'll be so happy to see you! We're going out tonight, we're really, finally going out!"

"Won't you come in, sir?" said Imbati Shara, with determination.

He couldn't have said no. When the curtain opened, he discovered Reyn beaming at him, standing on his feet and looking quite together in his ruby suit with the lace collar. If anything, his remaining traces of thinness made him look more mature.

"Reyn!" Tagaret ran to hug him without thinking—then realized what he was doing and blurted, "Reyn, I'm taking a partner."

"What?" Reyn looked stunned. "You can't be serious—who?"

"Copper and emeralds . . ."

Reyn spluttered. "B—but Tagaret, didn't she—"

"No."

"But Tagaret, she did—there was a man—"

Desperately, Tagaret pulled him close and whispered in his ear. "It was *me*, Reyn. I did it. Nek arranged the partnership, but even he doesn't know. I need you to understand."

Reyn stepped back, incredulously. "That's—" He shook his head. "Tagaret, you—that's really—wow. Brave . . ."

Shara spoke from the vestibule. "Sir, your cousin is here."

Reyn waved. "Send him in."

Gowan was wearing sapphire tonight. "Reyn, you look terrific," he exclaimed, then, "Tagaret?"

"Hello, Gowan," said Tagaret. "I'm so glad both of you are alive and well."

"Thank Heile and Imbati Aloran," said Gowan wryly.

"Gowan, Tagaret's brought some news."

Gowan looked at Reyn. "Really, what kind?"

Tagaret cleared his throat. "I—"

"He's taking a partner in the name of Sirin and Eyn," Reyn said. "Lady Della of the Sixth Family."

Gowan exploded. "What?!"

Tagaret winced. "Gowan, don't . . ."

"But Tagaret, she—"

Reyn cut him off. "Gowan, listen. Didn't you say you'd had enough of being shot at? Haven't you told me that Heir Selection is the worst thing that could happen to the Race, that it forces us to kill our own children and tear out one another's throats?"

Gowan's brow furrowed. "Yeah . . ."

"So, what is shunning the Sixth Family going to do for us, except doom us to more disease and dying children? Tagaret is taking a stand against that, for love, and for the good of the Race. And we have to stand by him."

Gowan flushed and looked down at his lace cuffs. "It is forward-thinking, I suppose. One could consider it a sacrifice for the greater good—and a great charity to the poor Lady."

"One could," Tagaret agreed. Gowan had it all wrong, but he wasn't about to object. When Reyn moved closer, Tagaret found his hand and gave it a quick squeeze. "Thank you. Bless you both."

"Let's stick together tonight," Reyn said.

Gowan smiled. "We should—we're going out for an evening event again at last."

Gods, yes. "Here's to Fernar," Tagaret said. "Elinda keep him."

"Fernar," Reyn and Gowan echoed solemnly.

"Tagaret," Gowan added, "I'd like to ask Pyaras to join us, too. He stopped what could have become a serious rift between our Families."

"You're right." Tagaret nodded. "All right, then. Let's go cheer for Nek—and pray he doesn't win."

CHAPTER THIRTY-THREE

Imbati

After she'd seen young Master Tagaret off, Lady Tamelera stood for a moment, perfectly still except for her breathing. Aloran drank in the sudden peaceful silence, watching the gentle rise and fall of her shoulders. His back still ached from the beating—but it would have been far worse if young Master Nekantor had chosen a more dangerous weapon. Or if young Master Tagaret had not immediately gone for help. Or if his Lady had not overridden Nekantor's orders and given him permission to dodge.

Tamelera turned her head slightly, divulging a glimpse of her profile. "Aloran?"

"Yes, Lady?"

She took a breath to speak, but then her brows drew together, and without a word she walked out to the sitting room. She took a seat at the gaming table, arranged her bright, dawn-colored skirts about her feet, and caught him with her gaze.

"Aloran, will you join me in keyzel marbles?"

He hesitated. "You mean, play, Lady?"

"I can teach you, if you haven't played before."

He considered the board: a disc of black obsidian arrayed with blue and green stone spheres. The round table beneath it was solid il-mawood, inlaid with geometric patterns. He pulled out the matching chair but, painfully aware of its magnificence, couldn't bring himself to sit down. "Lady," he asked. "What is the object of the game?"

"To outmaneuver the opponent and cross the board."

He swallowed. "Then . . . must one of us win?"

Her face fell.

"Lady, I'm sorry," he said. "I shouldn't have—I'll try, if you wish it."

"Never mind." She stood up, then suddenly looked into his face. "Aloran, the thing is, you're hurt."

What a strange thing to say. This wasn't the first time he'd been hurt in her service, and it had nothing to do with keyzel marbles. He couldn't imagine how to reply.

Tamelera came closer. "Aloran," she said softly. "May I help you somehow?"

He stepped back, startled. "Lady, please don't consider me—"

"But I *want* to help—I can't stand what Nekantor did to you. Please, let me get you something."

Warmth flushed his face and chest. He began a breath pattern and didn't answer.

Tamelera made a sound of frustration and turned away. When he realized she was leaving the room, he leapt after her. She entered her bedroom and crossed as if to go to her writing table, but didn't stop there—she grasped the brocade curtain over his door and pulled it back.

"Lady, stop!" he cried.

Tamelera turned back and confronted him with a defiant gaze.

She couldn't be serious—she *couldn't*—but her hand on the heavy brocade silenced his every denial. She wanted to open his door, and that wasn't the worst of it. *She wanted to serve him.* His heart pounded as though the floor were about to give way.

"Lady, don't. Please—please don't."

Without warning the public door clicked open behind him, and Serjer hurried in without permission, calling, "Mistress, I've been contacted by the medical center—"

Tamelera dropped the curtain. "Heile's mercy!"

Serjer stopped and bowed deeply. "I regret to inform you that the Master has suffered another massive heart attack. He's—in Elinda's care."

"*Dead?*" Tamelera's hands flew to her mouth. A terrible light came into her eyes.

Serjer looked to Aloran, gaze-gesturing urgency. "Sorn and the Imbati on witness are filling out the paperwork now," he said. "The Master's last act was to record his vote in favor of Nekantor, and he has charged Sorn with delivering it to the Hall of the Eminence."

"He would, gnash him," Tamelera said. "Wherever he is now, he's not in *Elinda's* care."

Aloran's heart went cold. Serjer's message wasn't entirely for the Lady—it was also for *him*.

No doubt Officer Warden Xim had expected Sorn would return home when Grobal Garr died, a route that would send him through the Maze where the arm of the enforcing wardens extended. But young Master Nekantor was no longer at home. And carrying his late Master's vote, Sorn could take all public paths, directly to the Hall of the Eminence.

Xim needed someone else to stop him.

Aloran dropped to one knee. "Lady," he said. "Please excuse me from your presence."

Tamelera stared at him. She glanced to Serjer and back with open suspicion. "Why?"

Serjer said nothing.

"I don't know," Aloran answered, and immediately felt ashamed. The polite denial had never sounded like such an insult.

Serjer murmured, "You will excuse me, Lady," and bowed himself out. The door clicked shut.

"I'm very sorry, Lady." Aloran bent his head. "I beg you, let me go."

"Are you angry with me?" Tamelera asked. "Is this something to do with Garr's vote? Why do you want to go so badly?"

Questions, more questions! He could feel time passing with every breath. Sorn did not have far to travel—how long could the Imbati recordkeeper delay him? "Lady," he said desperately, "do you forget who I am? Please understand the nature of my duty, and don't ask me. Let me go."

Tamelera made a sound, like a stifled sob.

He looked up. She was gazing at him, her blue eyes heavy with tears. "I know who you are, Imbati Aloran," she whispered brokenly. "Go."

He ran, ignoring the pain in his back, risking speed even in the public hallway. Across the Residence, Maze routes were fastest—he slipped in the nearest door he could find. A castemate was standing there beside the door, motionless, out of his way. Aloran sprang past her down the hall. At the base of the stairs he nearly collided with another castemate; the man flattened himself to one side. Aloran had no time to apologize. His frantic footsteps felt too short, too slow. Sorn only had to cross the shrub and flower gardens, enter the grand ballroom, and pass beneath the archways to reach the Hall of the Eminence. The only hope of intercepting him in time was to go straight to the young Master himself. Dim stairs loomed ahead—the ones that climbed above the archway between the ballroom and the Hall. He took them three at a time. Two more castemates stood at the top, one on either side of the stage door reserved for Herin's Argun, Manservant to the Eminence. Both of them wore the diamonds of the Courts. Aloran nodded to them, and they allowed him to open the door.

He slipped through into the space between the curtain and the stone wall, peering out onto the blazing brightness of the stage.

Young Master Nekantor was only three strides away, fidgeting in a brass chair beside Grobal Innis of the Fifth Family, who sat with his head high. The two were flanked by their Arissen bodyguards, and by Grobal Innis' manservant. Between them and the front edge of the stage stood a pair of empty steel podiums. Two guards of the Eminence's Cohort were stationed at each stage stairway.

The Eminence Herin rose from his wooden throne, near the right-hand stairs, and advanced to a stand microphone with his Argun behind his shoulder.

"Welcome, honored members of the Pelismara Society," he said, indicating the seated crowd with an indulgent sweep of his hand. "We've all passed through many dangers to reach this day, but none have faced more danger than our two remaining candidates, Nekantor of the First Family and Innis of the Fifth Family. Let us congratulate and welcome them."

The young Master and Grobal Innis of the Fifth Family stood to their podiums. Fervent applause swelled, filling the space beneath the mosaic arches.

There was Sorn.

He emerged from the broad stone archway that connected to the ballroom. A corner of white paper showed in his right hand—the vote, his Master's final charge. To reach the cabinet members' roped-off seating area, Sorn would have to cross the base of the stage stairs.

"Innis," the Eminence said. "Would you like to make a final statement?"

"Thank you, Eminence," said Innis. "Ladies and Gentlemen of the Pelismara Society, it is an honor to stand before you . . ."

Aloran left the curtain's shelter swiftly and quietly, keeping his eyes away from the candidates, walking as if bearing an urgent message to someone below. The Cohort guards at the base of the stairs allowed him through. He kept his face still, and his eyes away from the white paper so Sorn would read nothing of his intent. *I'm delivering a message to you, Sorn. Nothing more. Let me get close.*

Sorn gaze-gestured questioning; Aloran replied with the code for urgency.

The senior servant hesitated.

Aloran snatched the paper from his hand and walked as fast as he could toward the nearest Maze door.

Sorn's surprise lasted no more than a split second. Aloran had scarcely hidden the vote in a pocket when he heard the senior servant's harsh, angry breathing behind him. For now, Sorn seemed unwilling to make a scene in front of the noble audience and guards—but that restraint wouldn't last long.

Aloran tried for extra speed, but Sorn's hand grabbed his shoulder. He should never have imagined he could make it to the Maze untouched. He spun away, and Sorn attacked, forcing him to block blows aimed at his neck and chest. Plis stand by him—fighting in public?

Guards of the Eminence's Cohort came at them from all directions. Even the Pelismara Society had noticed. Grobal Innis' amplified voice demanded, "What is this business?"

Officers surrounded them, and the largest man said, "Imbati, you're causing a disturbance. Give me your names."

"The heart that is valiant triumphs over all, sir," Aloran replied. "I am Tamelera's Aloran of the Household of the First Family."

Sorn said nothing.

Aloran looked around at the guards. Maybe this was his chance. Surely they were still looking for suspects in the assassination attempt . . . should he accuse Sorn in front of them? But no; everyone knew Mai the Right's embodiment varied, and one's will was understood differently by Imbati and Arissen. If for any reason his witness were not accepted, he would have failed, and Nekantor would wield the most dangerous weapon imaginable.

He could not allow that to happen.

The Eminence's voice now rang across the Hall. "Excuse us, everyone, just a moment while the Cohort gets this small matter cleared up."

Sorn drew himself up. "Arissen, sir. Tamelera's Aloran has interfered in my duty—"

"Sir, my motives in this dispute are privileged," Aloran interrupted. "I will bear no witness without my Mistress present."

The officer frowned. "Is she here now?"

"No, sir. I'm sorry, sir."

The officer swore, then turned to Sorn. "What of your master, Imbati?"

"He awaits me on the stage, sir," Sorn said. "Nekantor of the First Family."

Ice raced down Aloran's back. He could not—*could not*—allow the Arissen to call Nekantor here! "Sir, he lies."

The officer sniffed, looking between them skeptically.

Should he try to explain? But how could he, without landing both of them in Arissen custody?

As if in answer to his prayers, young Master Nekantor's voice cried over the speakers, "That's my father's servant!"

The Eminence replied, "Young Nekantor, please sit and let the Cohort resolve this."

The officer heard; he scowled and crossed his heavy arms.

"Sir," said Aloran. "Young Master Nekantor has said it himself: this is his father's servant, Garr's Sorn of the Household of the First Family. His Master is partner to my Mistress, the young Master's mother."

"You mean you've disrupted the final Selection for a *domestic squabble?*"

Sorn's eyes flashed. "Tamelera's Aloran has stolen my Master's vote for the Selection, sir. You must have him searched and arrested."

"I don't obey orders from Imbati," the officer spat. "Especially Imbati who've lied to my face. You two boys had better work this out on your own. Don't come back in until you're ready to behave yourselves." He glanced toward the enormous bronze-relief doors at the far end of the Hall, the last place where latecomers were being allowed to enter.

Aloran avoided the officer's hand when he reached for his arm, but moved meekly in the direction his glance had indicated. The officer didn't try to touch him again.

Grobal Innis of the Fifth Family resumed his speechmaking. "Ah, thank you, Arissen. As you can see, these are, indeed, tumultuous times. And tumultuous times call for leaders with experience and political acumen . . ."

Under heavy escort, they walked the length of the Hall to the security checkpoint and in among the Arissen with their trained tunnel-hounds. Aloran's chest tightened when he glimpsed the foyer beyond. True, they weren't headed toward the cabinet, or Nekantor, but *there were no Maze doors here.* The doors on left and right were exposed, leading to richly appointed anterooms—the central section's version of a vestibule, to which either Grobal or Imbati might enter. The only direct Maze doors were hidden inside them.

Only speed could help him now.

He kept his weight on his toes, moving between the last two guards. Risked a glance back. Sorn was being loosely held by two Arissen, who appeared to be explaining their dispute to the security team.

Go.

He sprinted for the nearest bronze door, praying the Arissen wouldn't care enough to follow. Pushed it, but it was heavy, too slow to start moving—already Sorn had broken free —

He got the door wide enough to sneak through, but the room within was too big, the Maze door with its promise of safety or rescue too far beyond the chairs. Why hadn't he thought to shut the door behind him? He whirled, but it was too late. Sorn was already in— already *here*, Plis help him—

Sorn's arm locked like an iron bar around his throat.

Aloran jerked his chin sharply downward into the wiry crook of Sorn's elbow, but it wasn't enough. He grabbed backward, found flesh, and twisted hard. Sorn grunted but didn't release. No breath; no time. Already his vision was shrinking. He stomped and kicked backward, but met no resistance—flung himself backward and crashed against the closing bronze door. Sorn barked in pain.

A wave of black rushed inward—

Oh, Tamelera, I'm sorry . . .

The dark swallowed him.

CHAPTER THIRTY-FOUR

Heir to the Throne of Varin

N ekantor gripped the sides of his podium.

He was all pain—his fingers sore from gripping the podium, his hand sore from washing away the poison, his arm sore from punishing the Imbati, his chest and stomach sore from Tagaret throwing his crazy fit. With no more Benél to hold him together, every part of him screamed and squirmed and struggled to crawl away from every other part. Only one thing held him together under the lights, under the hungry eyes of the entire Pelismara Society.

The whore's ring.

He'd found it with his fingers after the fists stopped hitting him, by crawling across the floor to his bedside table. It had reminded him he had power; it had taught him to stand, and to tell Tagaret his childish anger meant nothing.

Even when he was angry—even when he tried to fight—Tagaret was harmless.

Now the ring gleamed, beautiful and perfect in the lights of the Hall. His own piece of power, that he'd found all by himself. It had set his foot on the path to the center of this game. It was why he was here. It was why he had to win.

"Cabinet members, I ask for your vote," Innis concluded. "Thank you." Applause surged through the room, power thundering into every crack and corner, pounding into Nekantor's lungs as he breathed. The pain diminished, and he breathed in more, more, as much as he could hold. Imagine if the applause were for *him*—imagine if he alone could stand at the center. Nothing else would matter at all.

But the applause fell away, disappearing into a tense silence. The room strung together again, and the pain returned, along with the wrongness and the squirming in his body. He watched the whore's ring gleam under the lights, and kept breathing.

"Nekantor," the Eminence said. "Your final statement?"

The eyes shifted to him, and the tension strung itself outward, tugging his nerves in every direction. How he wanted to count, to touch! But that would lose him the game. What was his final statement?

All at once he heard Father's voice. *"Don't try to look better than Innis; he's twice your age and he'll make you look like a fool if you do. Let your youth protect you."* The memory tried to strangle him; he clenched the podium until his fingernails bent.

Father was dead. He was dead, because Sorn had come, and Sorn would only come if Father was dead. Sorn was going to come and deliver the vote, and bow, and receive the inquiry that he kept in his breast pocket. It was planned. Where was he?

He scanned the room, but the sight of the seething crowd made him sick. Sorn had been escorted out by Arissen; he'd seen that much, but the matter was resolved now. What was keeping him? Sorn had to come back—he had to, because it was planned!

"My father is dead," he said aloud. The microphone magnified his voice into the far corners of the room. "Garr of the First Family is dead."

Shocked murmurs wriggled in the crowd, crawling through it like desperate spiders.

The Eminence held up his hand for silence. "Young Nekantor, what are you saying?"

"His Sorn was here," Nekantor said. He struggled to breathe, clinging to the sweet perfect gleam of platinum on his finger. "His Sorn would not have come if he were not dead. Where is Sorn now, Arissen? Why has he not come to me? He was supposed to come to me—my father is dead!"

Herin glanced over his shoulder at his manservant, who ran down the stage stairs into the cabinet area below. Yet another Imbati had appeared there—one who didn't belong to the cabinet members, who hadn't been there before. Wrong, wrong! Nekantor's knees shook, and he held tighter until the steel bit his fingers.

The Eminence's servant came climbing back up the stairs and whispered something in his Master's ear.

"Ladies and Gentlemen of the Pelismara Society," the Eminence announced, "I regret to inform you that young Nekantor is correct. We've just received news that our Speaker of the Cabinet, Garr of the First Family, has taken his place among the stars."

The entire room swayed with a sigh.

Oh, gods, the floor was moving . . .

"Sorn was supposed to come to me," Nekantor cried. "What happened to him? He was speaking to Aloran, and then the Arissen sent him out, but he has to come back. Where is he? Father promised he would come to me. He promised!"

"Nekantor—" said Herin.

"He was supposed to bring my father's vote!" The words tumbled from his lips, and the reality fell upon him like the weight of the city itself. Sorn *wasn't* here, and that meant Father's *vote* wasn't here, and *he needed all the votes.* "Gnash it, Father's not here, and Sorn is missing, and that means the vote is missing, and the whole pattern is broken—"

He choked; his knees gave way and his hands slipped. He sat down hard in the shadow behind the podium.

"Sir," said Arissen Karyas. "Sir."

The room was shrinking down on him. Nekantor fumbled the ring from his finger and took it in his hand, rolled it across his palm, stroked its smooth surface. He clung to it, and it was his, perfect and smooth and his, and he tucked his mind inside it, into that place of power and perfection. Nothing here. No Pelismara Society, no cabinet, no candidates, no votes. Nothing but a platinum circle that gleamed and rolled and felt smooth in his fingers.

Voices spoke around him. The Eminence's voice, loud and strong. The cabinet's voices, small. An Arissen-sounding voice. They were asking what had happened to Sorn. He couldn't stand to listen; couldn't stand to look up or it would all come apart, every nerve would unravel, and he would scream until his body tore itself in pieces.

"Sir," Karyas hissed in his ear. "Pull yourself together. You promised me, sir. We had a bet."

"Karyas—" He risked a glance at her, looked down again. She was strong, like always. Perfect orange uniform, ambitious brown skin, hungry eyes. She believed in power—in *his* power. He looked at her again, and didn't have to look back down.

"Get up, sir," she said. "They'll forgive you for grief. But get in your chair at least."

He gulped air, hissed it out. "Hhh—help. Karyas, help me."

"Yes, sir." She lifted him under the arms.

Nekantor got his feet onto the wooden floor. Slid into his chair. He still had the ring; it was still perfect and could hold his eyes. But the vote . . . "The vote," he whispered. "Karyas, they're missing my father's vote."

"Gnash it, sir, you don't need all the votes. Just enough."

Just enough: suddenly it wasn't Karyas' voice speaking, it was Benél's. What had she done? He sobbed, and burning tears cut down his cheeks.

"One more minute, sir. Just one more."

Nekantor struggled in a breath and glanced up. The Eminence Herin was gazing at him with sympathy. His manservant was no longer visible by his shoulder, but moved instead among the cabinet members below the stage. Gods, they were voting already! And he'd said nothing, given no speech at all . . . Panic climbed his nerves, but he turned the ring in his fingers, and forced air into his lungs. The panic slowed, and breath by aching breath, the room began to open again.

It would not open completely. Feel the tension all around? It webbed across the audience, the cabinet members, the guards, the servants. He and Innis were at the center, bound to one another and to all of them at once.

What must he look like to them? Weak and broken—yet thoroughly unlike Innis, who watched everything down his nose with his head held high.

Gnash Innis. That confidence meant nothing—no one could see the whole game at once.

Even the Eminence showed curiosity now, though he sat perfectly straight in a suit of gold, the white-and-gold drape gleaming around his shoulders, fastened with its shining pin. At last his servant flickered up the stage stairs like a black shadow and spoke into his ear.

Herin stood up, smiling.

"Ladies and Gentlemen of the Pelismara Society," he said into his microphone, "thank you all for giving us the best of your blood. Thank you for risking your own future in the name of the future of Varin. I know the last weeks have been difficult, but your long wait is over. We have our Heir—and he wins by a single vote.

"Nekantor of the First Family, can you come and stand by me?"

Nekantor?

His name?

Every web was slashed at once. Vibrations of power struck him, ringing through him like a bell. The crowd surged to its feet and burst into shouts and applause.

"Sir!" Karyas burst out. She grinned, showing her white teeth. "Sir, it's you! We won!"

"I—I heard." Nekantor found his feet. They shook, so he stood up slowly. How he wanted to look at Innis, to see him miserable in defeat! But it was too dangerous. He might not make it to Herin. Instead, he kept his eyes on Karyas. "You were right, Karyas," he whispered. "We won, and now I can repay you. I can make sure that the Eminence's Cohort fulfills its true potential. It may take some time, but if you work with me . . ."

"Gladly, sir."

They walked forward, one step, another, another. Ahead, the Eminence Herin stood with his hand extended in welcome. Nekantor reached out and took it. It drew him forward, into the humming circle of power. He stood with the Eminence, with the Eminence's hand on his shoulder. Herin's fingerprints were different: see the power rub off on the boy from the First Family, now that he stood at the center? A wave of triumph flooded outward from Nekantor's heart, knitting the last of his nerves back together. He looked out at the assembled crowd and smiled.

"Congratulations, Nekantor," Herin said into the microphone. "I believe the spirit of your father was with us here tonight."

Nekantor remembered to temper his smile with sadness. "This has been a difficult time for me," he said. "I'm grateful for your indulgence and understanding. I give thanks to the Eminence, to the cabinet, especially Fedron and Lady Selemei, and of course to my father, without whom I would not be here. My job as Heir will be to learn from all of you."

Herin waved his hand. "I invite you to join me in the ballroom for a celebration."

Danger—the crowd would break—Nekantor quickly turned his eyes to the Eminence's handsome face, so easy on the eyes.

Herin gave him a smile. "Do you want to know why I changed my mind about you?"

Oh, he knew why: because Herin was far more afraid of Innis than an inexperienced boy. But an inexperienced boy would not already know why; he would ask for his superior's advice.

"Why?" Nekantor asked. "Because I forswore my earlier indiscretion?"

Herin chuckled. "Did you, now? Very good. No, really, I was thinking about our future. Innis is too old. We can't have Heir Selections coming along too often; they're not good for the Race."

Nekantor nodded. "That's true."

Herin squeezed his shoulder. The power made his bones hum. The Eminence meant what he'd said—he *had* changed his mind, and that meant that the Third Family's two votes had both come to the First Family. Of course, with a margin of victory of only eight to seven, that meant some people—people he should have been able to count on— had betrayed him.

Nekantor glanced back over his shoulder. The cabinet members followed behind them through the arch, nothing but relief and jubilation showing on their faces. Lady Selemei held Fedron's arm—Amyel and Boros were laughing, Arith looking gleeful, and even Caredes smiled.

They could smile all they liked. He knew the truth: some of them were playing secret games. Somehow, he'd figure out who had fooled him. He had plenty of time ahead. And when he knew beyond a doubt, then he'd teach them a lesson.

He could play games as well as anyone.

CHAPTER THIRTY-FIVE

Faithful

Something invaded Aloran's nose. A smell, like a punch in the face.

He snorted and tried to move away from it. His eyes blinked open. He was lying on his back. A castemate was looking down at him.

"Aloran, sir?"

Aloran coughed. Officer Warden Xim removed a vial from under his nose, capped it, and tucked it in a pocket.

For a moment, Aloran could only breathe. Where was this place? If Xim was here, it had to be somewhere at the Academy . . . No, wait. This was still the anteroom, but all around him stood a black silk crowd, men and women marked with the diamonds of the Courts.

Wardens. Twenty of them at least.

"Aloran, sir," said Xim again. "I'm so very glad you thought to close the public door."

Aloran shook his head cautiously. The choke had been well-administered, because his neck felt almost normal. "Garr's Sorn?"

Xim looked over his shoulder. Aloran followed his glance as castemates moved out of the way: Sorn was bound and gagged, held tightly by at least five wardens.

"He has forfeited his Mark," Xim said. "He will be excised from the Imbati, and imprisoned casteless. No Grobal will ever recognize him again."

Sorn made a desperate grunting sound, and when Aloran looked at him, gestured urgency with his eyes.

Aloran looked away and shuddered. "You should inform his partner, Fedron's Chenna."

"He was taking this from you when we arrived," Xim said, placing the white paper in his hand. "Before we gagged him, he was insisting that we charge you to fulfill your duty to the First Family, and deliver it."

Aloran slowly unfolded the paper. On it, Grobal Garr had written the words *Heir* and *Nekantor*, and a shaky signature.

"I understand," he said.

"We are deeply grateful for your intervention." Xim inclined his head, and every warden in the room bowed. "Your name will be recorded by Headmaster Moruvia into the Academy lists for outstanding service to the nation."

That was more honor than he'd ever imagined—but he hadn't done it for the nation. He got slowly to his feet. "Thank you, all of you. Now, if you will please excuse me, I must attend my Lady."

He refused to look at Sorn's face again, but walked between the wardens who moved aside for him, and entered the Maze. His hand tightened around the vote. With every step through the dim stone halls, his feet urged him faster.

Tamelera needed him.

He rushed in through the suite, straight to his Lady's side. She sat crumpled on her bed, her tearful face pressed against the bedpost. At the sight of him, she sat up straight.

"Aloran!"

Aloran knelt at her feet. "This is what I was doing," he said. "I deliver it to you, and thus I discharge my duty to the First Family."

A puzzled wrinkle formed between her eyebrows. She took the paper, unfolded it, and gasped. At once, she swept out of the room.

Aloran closed his eyes, waiting for her without moving. He was alive, breathing the sweet air of home. At last came the rush of silk that always accompanied his Lady's entrance.

"Premel was kind," she said. "He let me use the stove."

Aloran said nothing.

"Aloran, I've burned it," she said. "For once, I've silenced Garr. And you've carried out your duty to the First Family."

It was too much. A sob bubbled up in his throat. "I don't want to serve the First Family," he cried. "If I'm to give my life, I want to give it for *you*, Tamelera. Only for you. The Mark on my face I have taken in your noble name. My duty, my honor, my love, and my life to your service!"

For several seconds, she didn't respond. Blushing, Aloran began a breath pattern. At last, very slowly, Tamelera came close and sank to the floor beside him. "The next part," she whispered. "Say the next part."

His throat closed; he shook his head.

"Bestow," she said. "Bestow a touch—please, Aloran, ask me." She lifted her hand toward him. "Let me."

He could feel her touch now, both in memory and anticipation. Half his soul recoiled; the other half trembled. "Lady, I would be remiss," he protested. "My duty requires that I protect you, not endanger you."

"That's why I have to ask."

His whole body flushed hot; he gulped air and shook his head. "It is—"

"No!" she cried. "Sirin and Eyn, Aloran, don't you dare say it's my privilege!"

He snapped his mouth shut.

Tamelera dropped her hands into her lap. "I know you're Imbati," she said, pleading. "And you have your training. But that's not why I trust you. I trust you because you're good, and gentle, and flawless in your discretion." She clenched her fingers in her skirts. "Aloran, you were gone so long, I was terrified I might lose you forever."

A good servant would tell her it was nothing. But it was not nothing. The jealous darkness had only barely released him back to her side.

"I cried, because I thought I'd lost my chance to tell you. That I want—I want to be with you, always. That I would Fall for you, if you asked me."

Her hand, pulling back his curtain . . . Every part of him stilled in focus upon her. "You mustn't," he whispered. "I could never ask you that. I would be damaging the one I have sworn to serve."

Tamelera was silent for a long moment. "Aloran, there are good reasons not to do it. I'd be quite willing to damage Nekantor's prospects, but I've always believed Tagaret will be able to do something important for Varin, and I don't want to take that away from him."

Thank merciful Heile. "Of course not, Lady. I am happy to be yours."

"But Aloran—I want to be *yours*, as much as you are mine. Please look at me."

Suddenly it was so easy. He no longer tried to argue against the compelling character of her nose and her lips—no longer struggled to focus on her blank forehead so he wouldn't notice the grace in her brows and hairline. She was breathtaking. She was close. She was gazing at him—and then her blue eyes lowered, blinked and lifted again in gratitude. *Oh, Tamelera . . .* Returning the gesture sent a thrill deep into his stomach, rousing an immediate physical response. All his training screamed at him to distance himself, to breathe, to look away.

He did not.

"It never felt with you like it did with Eyli," Tamelera confessed. "I've realized now, I'm going to love you whether or not you let me. If the love you say you hold for me is not like mine, then tell me now, and I'll let you go. Gods—" She glanced down. "Maybe I should let you go anyway."

"Lady, no!"

"It's just that—I don't *want* to command you, Aloran. Not in this. I'll kill myself before I force you to act love falsely."

"You're not like him," Aloran said. "You could never be like him. And I could never be false, not to you." His hand seemed almost too incredulous to obey him, but he insisted, and opened it between them. "I trust you."

Tamelera did not place her palm over his. She seized his hand as if it were some kind of marvel, caressing it, turning it, kissing it. The eagerness of her lips was perfect permission, and his body responded with such intensity that even his voice trembled.

"Tamelera . . ."

She looked up in a transport of delight, and began to kiss her way up his arm. Cautiously, so as not to frighten her, he slid his arm beneath hers and pulled her closer.

Tamelera launched herself at him, knocking him to the floor in a deluge of kisses.

The weight of her body was wonderful. Her lips were sweet, urgent, everywhere—on his face, his neck, his chest while he tried with his own to catch them. At last, he caught her against him, and her lips fastened on his.

Closed. Had she never even learned how to kiss?

Gently, he stroked the nape of her neck, and pulled her mouth more strongly against his, letting his lips part slightly. Tamelera caught her breath. On the next kiss he allowed her lips to press his mouth open, and didn't release until a taste of her slipped in. Raising his tongue to it, he discovered she had done the same—such sweetness! Her questing tongue drew him deep into the kiss. He lifted her body more fully over him and tightened his arms around her.

Tamelera gasped and pulled away.

Had it been too much? Aloran sat up slowly, with a gaze-gesture of apology—if Sirin was merciful, then his desires wouldn't have pushed him ahead of hers.

Tamelera reached behind her head with both hands, struggled a few seconds, then dropped one arm and twisted to reach up her back from underneath. She cast him a mischievous smile.

Then it hit him: she was undressing herself.

To sit and watch her do it made his fingers tingle in sympathy, but its very inappropriateness was delicious. She pulled her gown down over her shoulders and pushed it to her waist, then to the floor, shifting it under her bottom. One at a time, she pulled her legs out, so she sat in her white shift in a pool of dawning silk.

"My Lady," he whispered. He ached to hold her again.

She walked up to him on her bare knees. "Sit still."

To comply required some discipline, especially after he determined her intentions. She had no trouble undoing the closures of his jacket, but the feeling of her hands sneaking underneath to push it off his shoulders wound him so tight he could scarcely breathe—and if the shirt was worse, it was nothing compared to the trousers. Thank Heile she let him unlace his own boots, to keep his mind from exploding in sheer incredulity.

The sight of him in nothing but his underwear seemed to astonish her. She stared at him with her breast heaving, hands pressed together over her nose and mouth.

Aloran tried to speak calmly. "I've given you permission to touch. You needn't ask again. Do you—wish, to continue?"

"I do wish," she said. "Gods, just look at you! It's just that—Aloran, I hardly recognize myself."

"*I* recognize you," he assured her. "You've always been passionate. I saw it the day I met you."

She blushed. "That day, I saw—the most beautiful man I'd ever seen. But I was so angry. I tried so hard not to see who you really were. I'm sorry—I see you now." She laid the palm of her hand on his chest and stroked a line down to his navel; her eyes went further. Pleasure thrummed down his nerves and his hips lifted involuntarily. He opened his arm to her.

She moved into it at once, turning her head up for his kiss while he explored her with his hands. He slowed when approaching the lower edge of her shift, but her eager fingers stripped away his remaining clothes, urging him onward. How many times had he removed this very garment of silk? This time she was no longer simply naked, she was his. This soft skin, these full breasts and curving hips—every part of her so familiar, and now a revelation. Slowly, softly, he coaxed her passion with his fingers, easing her down to the floor beside him. Her breath came now with small delicious sounds the like of which he'd never heard. Dizzied, he bent into a kiss that quickly grew to a drink of the heavens, and her hands moved over him, trying to pull him onto her.

But they must not go any further. If there were some limit, beyond which lay pain and fear, he must not find it. It was his duty to protect her—but now her hands took full possession of him, pushing him beyond speech.

Aloran gasped.

Tamelera gave a full-throated moan.

That sound penetrated defenses he hadn't known he had. Before he knew it, he was inside her, blinded by pleasure, locked in a tangle of her, and she was crying out his name. "Tamelera," he answered in confusion, but the pleasure intensified with the word, growing with his rhythm until it poured out of him unbidden, "Tamelera, Tamelera!"

For a long time they rested together, sharing peace in small gentle touches. At last, he convinced her to let him go long enough to lift her from the floor into her bed. She wouldn't release his arm.

"But, Lady . . ."

"Sleep with me," Tamelera said. "I know how to play my part for the watchers. But here in this room you can be safe with me."

"All right."

She moved toward the center of the bed. Aloran climbed in beside her, and soon she fell asleep on his shoulder, her arm draped across his chest. He gazed up at a wysp drifting in and out of the canopy above.

A sudden terrible misgiving struck him.

Safe with her? Oh, Sirin and Eyn be kind tonight, and keep her safe from *him!* Let the time be wrong—even let Grobal Garr have been right that she was no longer able to bear children . . .

In giving the last of his medication to her son, he'd left her unprotected.

CHAPTER THIRTY-SIX

About the Music

Tagaret sat in the audience, watching his brother, holding his breath. At first, it seemed like he'd done it, that the price of telling Benél had actually been worth it. Nekantor came to the podium when he was introduced, but he looked more than half-manic, and when he opened his mouth, he made no sense, talking about Father, and Sorn, and votes and patterns . . . Then he crumpled to the floor, half-hidden by the podium.

That should have been it. That should have been it!

Except then, from the seat to his right, Pyaras murmured, "Poor Nekantor."

Tagaret gaped at him. *Poor Nekantor?* It was the single last thing he would have expected to hear out of his cousin's mouth.

Pyaras' dark brows drew together. "Wait, hadn't you heard, either? I'm so sorry!"

"No," Tagaret said. This couldn't be happening. "No . . ."

Reyn gently squeezed his left arm. "Oh, Tagaret, what a way to learn your father has joined the stars."

"Elinda keep him," Gowan added.

"*No,*" Tagaret repeated. But suddenly it was all so clear: everything he'd done had been for nothing. Nekantor had fallen apart in front of the entire Pelismara Society—and nobody had noticed. When he looked at the stage again, Arissen Karyas had got him up into a chair, and Nek was crying. All the murmurs in the crowd had turned to pity. *Oh, poor Nekantor, what a loss to such a keen young candidate, what terrible news to endure when he was already under such pressure.*

Tagaret clenched his fists. Gnash him, the bastard toad!

Before they even began voting, he knew. *Knew*, with a certainty that made him sick.

"Nekantor of the First Family, can you come and stand by me?"

Tagaret surged to his feet in horror. All around him, others were standing, too, clapping and cheering. There were shouts of dismay, of course, but the First Family had always been well-regarded, and that obviously hadn't changed.

Nothing had changed.

"Holy Mai," he breathed. "Merciful Heile, help me."

"Are you all right?" asked Reyn.

"Tagaret," said Gowan reassuringly, "I know it's not what you wanted, but politics is like that."

Tagaret wheeled on him. "Fine," he snapped. "Clap for him. Gowan, Reyn, Pyaras, all of you clap—protect yourselves, gnash it! Never let him suspect that you doubted him, much less that you hated him, not even for a second."

"Tagaret—hey . . ." Reyn reached a hand to his shoulder.

Tagaret jerked away. He pushed past Pyaras and shoved out of the row, up the aisle and through the arch, took one look at the celebratory decorations in the ballroom and bolted for the nearest outside door. A few steps into the dark gravel paths of the shrub gardens, he stopped and tried to breathe.

"Sir," Imbati Kuarmei said, startling him. Of course she was at her station—he'd simply forgotten she was there. "What may I do for you?"

"Nothing, Kuarmei," Tagaret said. Nothing could be done to change this. He glanced back at the ballroom windows. The Pelismara Society had begun to fill the space in their colored suits and gowns, rejoicing at the end of the Selection, celebrating the beginning of a new era under Eminence Herin and Heir Nekantor. Except nothing about it was new at all. Tagaret's feet moved on their own, faster and faster out of the gardens, then out the northern grounds gate and into the city.

He wanted Della so badly. She'd sacrificed so much, accepting censure and abuse in return for escape from her nightmare betrothal. How could he tell her that Nekantor had won because of the Sixth Family's vote? That the worst had come *because of what they did*? Yet he must, somehow . . .

He found his way to the right circumference easily enough, then hesitated; his memory of the path to find her was too vague. Which radius had the Arissen driver turned into? Ah, this was it—he accelerated into a run as he turned the corner, and nearly collided with a person who came seemingly out of nowhere. A startled face glanced up at him: pale, with a shiny burn scar on the left cheekbone.

"Vant?" Tagaret said.

The person bolted away across the street and vanished—into the Akrabitti way.

Tagaret blinked after him. That *had* been Vant, hadn't it? He must have come here after finishing at Della's house not long ago . . . but what in Varin's name was he doing going down an undercaste alleyway?

Name of Bes, what if this was his fault? What if he'd gone and scared the boy again, and sent him into a panic? If Vant got lost—or hurt . . .

Tagaret crossed the street and ran after him. "Vant! Wait!"

Vant didn't seem to hear. Tagaret ran fast at first, following the boy's retreating back, but soon had to slow to a walk to avoid stinking puddles and tangles of trash. Gods, just look at this place. *This* was Pelismara—it was the truth lying behind every noble house, even the Residence, though no one there would open their eyes to see it. This darkness was the fear in every heart, whispering of illness and death. His own father had smelled like this, festering with the rot of coercion and betrayal. And the tangled pipes on the walls were as twisted as his brother's mind. He couldn't let Vant fall victim to it.

Kuarmei simply followed him as he pushed on.

The alleyway stopped abruptly. A glimmer of silver light grew ahead, and Tagaret found himself dumped into a tiny open space, a sort of courtyard squeezed between the arms of a hulking concrete building that loomed three stories high. A single street lamp stood at the center of the space, but it was eyeless and dark. The only light came from three floating wysps, and from a shinca hidden somewhere nearby, whose light issued from two arched tunnels under the curved body of the building. Silver light cast misshapen shadows outwards through the iron stairs and railings. There was a strange mechanical hissing sound in the air, and a deep rumbling in the ground under his feet.

There were also people.

Three figures in dark hoods emerged from a shadowed tunnel beneath the building's arm, moving warily like feral animals.

"Sir," Kuarmei whispered.

Mercy—Vant wasn't the only one in trouble.

Tagaret turned, but two more Akrabitti blocked his way back into the alley: one awkward and gangly, the other a giant larger than any Arissen he'd ever seen.

Fear closed around his throat. How many people could Kuarmei fight at once?

Then a child's voice cried from somewhere above, in crazed excitement. "Look, all ye look! The gang's nabbed a Grobal!"

The cry set off a rockfall. Footsteps thumped—strange, accented voices shouted—doors burst wide all along the building. Bright yellow rectangles silhouetted hooded people of all sizes who crowded to the railings and peered down.

They were going to die.

"Kuarmei, I'm so sorry," Tagaret whispered. The thought of leaving Vant made him sick, but what choice did they have? "How can we get out?"

"Stay by me, sir," Kuarmei replied with admirable calm. "We'll have to attempt the alleyway."

The giant undercaste man gave a gravelly laugh. "Took a wrong path, all you did," he growled. "Now all we will put that to good use."

"There's nothing all we won't put to good use," a thin voice agreed behind them.

How would an Akrabitti put a musician's apprentice to use? Horrifying thought . . .

"Let's go," said Kuarmei. Hands raised, she advanced toward the pair blocking the alleyway. Tagaret followed close behind, but suddenly another hooded Akrabitti darted from the shadows and placed himself directly in their path.

With his back to them.

The new Akrabitti shouted at the giant man. "Lights and fires, Griss! Have ye wysp-madness now? These folk carry no orsheth!"

Kuarmei stopped, though her hands were still ready for the attack. Tagaret held his breath.

"Let *us* see, then," the giant man growled. "Look and see, now. Highers are rich."

"Ye're a fool, Griss. Melumalai carry orsheth, yes, and Kartunnen, too, but these? Ye'd search all them and find plastic squares, no use to ye or anyone here, only to one by name of Grobal! Or would ye take his coat maybe? And fence it how? One step in the gray market with a prize like that, and Arissen would snap yer family whole. Ye stay all them here, and ye'll soon see how many police swarm after." He stamped his foot. "Not a bargain *we're* keen for, so leave all them be, unless ye fancy to see the Pit too soon."

His words doused the excitement among the watchers. People began to slip back behind their doors; the crowds at the railings thinned and soon were gone. Even the folk on the ground level gradually vanished into the dirty shadows, until the only ones left in the tiny courtyard were giant Griss and their strange defender, still staring each other down.

"Shinca-fire," Griss growled at last. He lunged away to one side and vanished around the stub end of the building at a lumbering run.

The boy who had defended them remained unmoving, breathing hard.

"Akrabitti?" Tagaret said, uncertainly. "Thank you. Is there some way I can repay you for saving us? You're right that I have no money . . ." *Too* right, when he thought about it. How would an Akrabitti know about expense markers, anyway? "Maybe, if you'd give me your name . . ."

The Akrabitti ran.

"Kuarmei, catch him."

Kuarmei flashed him a look, but darted away after the boy into one of the bright tunnels underneath the building. Tagaret ran after, emerging on the back side just as Kuarmei caught their fugitive. Here, barely a skimmer's length separated the back of the concrete building from a vast face of cracked and dripping rock, embedded with an enormous circle of iron grillwork. Incongruously, a shinca pierced upward through the space, filling it with warmth and light.

Kuarmei brought the Akrabitti boy up close to the shinca. He was a pitiful creature in the light. His shoes were falling apart; he wore ill-fitting clothes in a stained, dirty gray, and of course there was the dark gray hood. The boy covered his face with both hands, quivering with such terror that his knees were like to give way.

Tagaret bit his lip. Maybe he shouldn't have asked Kuarmei to catch him—this was an awfully nasty way to thank someone.

"I'm really sorry," he said. "I know you put yourself at risk to help us. All I really want to do is thank you properly."

"Mercy," the boy mumbled. "Have mercy, sir."

"Please, you don't need to hide. Just give me your name."

There was something strange about the boy's hands. Of course they were filthy, shoved up beneath the edge of his dark hood, but their shape was strangely refined. Such long and graceful fingers—

Tagaret grabbed the boy's wrist and pulled his hand away from his face.

There was a shiny burn scar on his left cheekbone.

Sweet Heile have mercy. "Y—you?" Tagaret stammered, disbelieving. "Vant?"

The boy fell limp in Kuarmei's grasp. "Grobal Tagaret, sir, don't hurt me," he begged. "Don't have me killed."

It *was*. The boy he'd thought he'd come in here to rescue—his nose, his scar, even his voice, suddenly changed from the rough accent of his hooded fellows back to the careful diction he'd used in the concert hall, and at Della's house.

"I'd never get you killed," Tagaret said. "You know me—I *think*. How can you be here?"

"I live here," Vant said miserably.

"But how can you?"

Vant gulped. "Kartunnen Ryanin, he—he dresses me in fancy clothes, and paints my face. Calls me apprentice. Takes me places. Gives me orsheth. And p-paper, to write on."

His first thought was that Ryanin was terribly generous. But that was more than generous—it was *dangerous*. Not simply to give charity to an Akrabitti from the street, but to crossmark him and bring him to the Eminence's Residence? "Why in Varin's name would he do that?"

Vant's face filled with despair. "For my music."

Tagaret lost his breath completely. He staggered backward, realizing it was all around him. The black walls of rock. The sounds of dripping, the high-pitched hiss of ventilators issuing from the grid on the cavern wall, and the rumble of the subterranean Endro beneath his feet. The dark ways crowded with desperate people, searching vainly for escape.

"You wrote it," he breathed. "This is the Catacomb."

Vant nodded.

"Kuarmei," Tagaret said. "Let him go."

"Sir."

Released, Vant took an unsteady step back. "Grobal Tagaret, sir . . ."

"Don't tell—" Tagaret began, then realized that even if a hundred Akrabitti reported this incident, no one would believe them. "Kuarmei, we haven't been here. We did not speak to this boy, and you have never met him before."

"My heart is as deep as the heavens," Kuarmei said. "No word uttered in confidence will escape it."

"Vant, you know what that means, don't you?" Tagaret asked. "If we should meet again, as I don't doubt we will, none of the three of us will behave as if we'd met tonight."

Vant nodded, his eyes wide. Kuarmei looked extremely skeptical.

Without saying goodbye, Tagaret turned and strode back through the tunnel, across the now-empty courtyard, and into the alleyway that had brought them here.

"Kuarmei," he said, after a few seconds, "I apologize. I won't ever do that again."

"Of course not, sir." She followed him silently for more than a minute, as if weighing what to say. "But, sir? You should know that Akrabitti are rapacious with information."

"I didn't know that."

They emerged onto the radius again more quickly than he expected—astonishing, how close that other world was to his. But maybe he shouldn't have been surprised.

"Master," said Kuarmei. "I mean they don't keep secrets."

Tagaret shrugged. "This one does. If he didn't, he wouldn't still be alive. Give Vant a chance, Kuarmei. When we meet him again, you'll see what I mean."

He thought the topic finished, but as they walked inward from the grounds gate, she spoke again, quietly. "Sir? What makes you so sure we'll see him again?"

Tagaret stopped and turned to face her. "I met him at Della's house, Kuarmei. Della's younger sister was playing yojosmei, and he was sitting beside her, playing also. That's where we'll see him again. There may be no better way to express our thanks than to protect his secret. His music needs to be heard."

Kuarmei pressed her lips together. "Yojosmei? The Kartunnen instrument?"

"Exactly."

Inside its bright bubble, the celebration of the Selection's end hadn't diminished at all. Clumps of sparkling, jewel-colored people gathered in groups, talking and laughing along the base of the tall windows, and couples had started dancing. As they entered, the sound of a Kartunnen orchestra washed over them.

Tagaret approached the nearest Household servant. "Imbati, can you please direct us to Selemei of the First Family?"

The Imbati bowed and escorted them, skirting the dancers until they reached a tall marble column not far from the orchestra. Lady Selemei was enjoying a drink with Secretary Boros, Menni of the Second Family, and Amyel of the Ninth Family. She raised her glass when she saw him.

"Tagaret! I wondered what had happened to you." Her eyes showed a worry far greater than that suggested by her smile.

"Ah, sorry," Tagaret said. "May we speak alone for a moment? If you would excuse us, that is, Gentlemen."

"Certainly," Amyel replied. "And I should say, congratulations! Tonight we bow willingly to First Family business, don't we, Boros?"

Boros clapped Amyel on the back. "How about we find some of those cakes I was mentioning."

"Congratulations, Tagaret," said Menni, offering his hand. "Your brother's determination really surprised me."

Tagaret shook it. "I'd be happy to renew our acquaintance, Menni," he said. "I hope I can speak with you later."

Menni smiled. "I'll look for you."

At last he was alone—or close enough to it—with Lady Selemei.

"Ustin," said the Lady. "If you'd help keep our conversation private . . ."

Tagaret nodded to Kuarmei, and the two Imbati posted themselves in bodyguard stances, causing the flow of the crowd to retreat. Lady Selemei put her back into the corner where the column emerged from the wall, planting her cane firmly to one side. "I've been very worried for you," she murmured.

"I'm fine, Cousin," Tagaret said. "In fact, I'm better than ever."

Her smile was sad. "You sound like Erex."

"Well, Erex might be happy to know this, too."

Selemei's brows lifted.

"I've changed my mind," he said. "I want to offer you a deal: I'll become your cabinet assistant, if you promise you'll respect my mother's wishes and leave her out of politics for good."

Selemei studied his face, with a smile hovering about her lips. "I can agree to that. May I ask what changed your mind?"

"I've always believed in your project, Cousin. I want to improve life for our ladies."

Her gaze sharpened. "But?"

Tagaret leaned down, speaking into her ear. "But they're not the only ones suffering. We all are—and that means we need a grander project. To improve life for *everyone*."

"The Grobal Trust . . ."

"Is broken. We've been blind—blind to our own place in a game of power as big as all of Varin. It's not only killing the Race; it's killing our people, killing the very soul of our civilization. Honestly, Cousin, I don't know *how* to change it. I just know I have to. But it's like you said: I can't change anything from the outside. If I get in, then eventually I can find somewhere to experiment—someplace where I won't be watched." Suddenly, he understood Reyn's desire to leave. Safe Harbor wasn't his place, but . . . "Selimna," he breathed.

Lady Selemei chuckled in her throat. "Perhaps you may follow in your father's footsteps after all."

He nodded, though the thought chilled him to the core. *Alixi of Selimna*. Yes, that was precisely the kind of power required to change a game so large—and only an Heir could give it to him. Della had paid a high price to change the rules during the Selection, but this price would be higher still. "On that note, there's someone else I need to talk to."

Her intelligent eyes showed him she understood. "Shall I come with you?"

"Thank you, no. I'll need to do this on my own."

He wasn't really on his own, though. Erex had given him the servant at his back; Mother had given him the courage of sunlight; Reyn had given him his direction; and Della whispered in his ear, *we will outplay them*. He hid the memory of darkness deep inside his heart, along with the determination to burn it away, and moved toward the largest, most ecstatic crowd in the room. They clearly recognized him, because they parted as he drew near, opening a way to the center.

The Eminence Herin stood there, beaming, one hand holding a glass of sparkling yezel, the other resting lightly on Nekantor's shoulder. Far from resenting the touch, Nekantor glowed with it. His eyes moved fast, drinking in the adoring gazes around him. His hands were relaxed and still.

"Heir Nekantor!" Tagaret managed a grin.

Nek turned to him. "I'd been wondering when I'd see you, Tagaret."

Then he was here none too soon. "Congratulations," he said, and held out his hand. "The First Family will always be grateful to you for what you've done. I certainly couldn't have done it myself." Every word of it was true.

Nek raised his eyebrows and considered Tagaret's offered hand. "You're in a good mood."

"The best," Tagaret said. "I've got news—not near as good as yours, but I've just got a new job. I'm going to be Lady Selemei's cabinet assistant!" He held his breath and waited for Nek's reaction.

Nekantor burst into a delighted laugh, seized his hand, and shook it, clapping him on the shoulder and whispering in his ear. "Gods, Tagaret, you mean you're *in* with her? This is perfect—you can stop by the Heir's suite any time and report to me."

Nek wanted to use him as a spy. He ignored the familiar flare of outrage. Only if Nek accepted him as a second could he hope to attain his goal. "Not often enough to make her suspicious, of course," he murmured back. "I will have to act the part seriously, you know."

"Most definitely. Father would be proud. Of course, you know what this means."

"I don't," Tagaret confessed. "But I'm sure you do."

His brother's voice quivered with excitement. "It means we'll have our chance. We'll take our time with this game. I'll take Father's allies. You take his enemies. If we work together, we can remake Varin."

"You're right, Nek," Tagaret said. His heart pounded, and he closed his eyes. "Together, we're going to change everything."

CHAPTER THIRTY-SEVEN

Epilogue

Tagaret paced the waiting room of the medical center. The fear had twined around his lungs, and every shallow breath was an effort. "Heile stand by my mother," he prayed. "Sirin and Eyn bless her. Elinda forbear."

Della appeared in his path and put her arms around him, looking up into his eyes. "Have faith, love. Aloran's given her the best care anyone could hope for."

"I know." He took her close, feeling her heartbeat against his chest, stroking her copper hair. But knowing that Aloran had cared for Mother was almost worse—it touched a different kind of fear, a secret certainty he and Della shared, but never spoke.

The door opened, and they both swung around. A young Kartunnen woman stood there, blushing so her green lip stood out starkly.

"Kartunnen?" Tagaret said in surprise.

"I'm sorry I'm not whom you expected, sir, Lady," the nurse replied. "Lady Tamelera would not permit her servant to leave her."

Relief exploded through him. "You mean she's all right?"

"Yes, sir. It is my honor to inform you that you have a healthy baby brother. The doctor will call you when she is ready to receive visitors." The Kartunnen bowed out.

"Healthy!" Della pressed her hands to her mouth. "Heile be thanked, I can't believe it."

"I can," Tagaret said.

Della stared at him, silent.

He shouldn't have said anything. He found her hands and squeezed them tight. "It'll be all right, though," he said. "It has to be."

Far sooner than they expected, the door opened again. The elderly doctor walked in, shaking his hairless head. "Grobal Tagaret, sir, and Lady Della," he said. "Thank you for your patience. Lady Tamelera is asking for you." As they passed him, he murmured under his breath, "Remarkable. Just remarkable."

Tagaret stopped walking. "Doctor—what's remarkable?"

The doctor chewed his painted lip. "Not to trouble you, sir . . ."

"But?"

"I've never seen a Grobal baby receive a perfect health score."

Della squeezed his hand tighter. They hurried down the hall to the treatment room, where Yoral opened the door for them. It was all he could do not to burst in at a run.

"Mother," he called.

"Tagaret, my darling." Mother was lying at an angle in her treatment bed. Tears of joy ran down her face—he'd never imagined she could look so happy. Tiny arms waved out of a bundle in her arms. "Look," she cried. "They didn't take him away."

"Oh, Mother, that's wonderful."

"Just look at him—Della, you come, too. See how beautiful he is."

As he walked to her side, Tagaret stole a glance at Aloran. The Imbati stood silent as always beside Mother's left shoulder. Today he wore a green medical smock over his usual black. His face and hands were perfectly calm, but his eyes smiled down at the child in Mother's arms. Tagaret held his breath and looked down.

The baby had dark hair—but looked like Mother.

"Oh, gods be thanked!" he exclaimed. "Della, look."

"Oh, Tame—Mother," Della sighed. "He's just perfect. May Heile and Elinda grant me your good fortune one day."

"His name is Adon," said Mother. "Aloran suggested it."

Tagaret swallowed. "Aloran?"

"It is an honorable name-line," said Aloran quietly. "With a long history among the Grobal."

"Adon." Tagaret tried the name out, nodding. *My brother.* He reached down and gently stroked the baby's downy head. "I'll do whatever I can to protect him. Have you told Nek?"

"Master, if I may," said Kuarmei, "the Heir sent me a message to deliver, should all go well."

"Yes, thank you, Kuarmei."

Kuarmei took reciting stance. "Dear Mother: I give you honor for your endurance, and congratulate you on the birth of your child. It is a great day, indeed, when we may give thanks for Grobal Garr's last gift to the Race. With love, Nekantor."

Tagaret glanced at Della; she had bitten her lip. No one spoke for nearly a minute.

"Well," Mother said at last. "That was very kind of him."

Aloran smiled.

Deities of the Celestial Family

Father Varin—Source of all life; punishes the wicked after death by gnashing them in his fiery teeth. The sun. Symbolized by gold.

Mother Elinda—Goddess of childbirth and death; brings souls to children, sets the souls of the virtuous dead in the heavens as stars. The moon. Symbolized by silver and the mourning color, pale yellow.

Mai the Right—Deity of justice; takes male, female, and nonbinary embodiments, can see all sides of a problem, chooses humans who share one's nature. A planet. Symbolized by bronze, often worn as a medallion by the chosen.

Plis the Warrior—God of strife and war. A planet. Symbolized by iron.

The Silent Sister—Goddess of earth and agriculture. A planet. Symbolized by any sedimentary stone.

Bes the Ally—God of charity and negotiation; one of the Twins who together symbolize unity, peace, and love. A planet. Symbolized by lapis.

Trigis the Resolute—God of steadfastness and rescue; one of the Twins who together symbolize unity, peace, and love. A planet. Symbolized by malachite.

Heile the Merciful—Goddess of mercy, music, art, and medicine. A planet. Symbolized by peridot, the color light green, and a green lamp.

Sirin the Luck-Bringer—God of luck, youth, and love; one of the Lovers who together symbolize love and faithfulness. A planet. Symbolized by garnet and the color dark red.

Eyn the Wanderer—Goddess of exploration, independence, and beauty; one of the Lovers who together symbolize love and faithfulness. A comet. Symbolized by diamond and the color white.

Cast of Characters
(by caste, in order of appearance)

Grobal

Tagaret of the First Family—son of Garr and Tamelera

Fernar of the Eleventh Family—friend of Tagaret

Gowan of the Ninth Family—friend of Tagaret

Reyn of the Ninth Family—friend of Tagaret

Speaker Orn of the Third Family—Speaker of the Pelismar Cabinet

Nekantor of the First Family—son of Garr and Tamelera

Tamelera of the First Family—mother of Tagaret and Nekantor, partner of Garr, formerly of the Eleventh Family

The Great Grobal Fyn—founder of modern Varin

Benél of the First Family—distant cousin of Tagaret and Nekantor

Garr of the First Family—father of Tagaret and Nekantor

Della of the Sixth Family—a young Lady

Selemei of the First Family—an older cousin of Tagaret and Nekantor

Herin of the Third Family—Heir to the throne of Varin

Dest of the Eleventh Family—distant cousin of Tamelera

Fedron of the First Family—cousin of Garr

Keir of the First Family—cousin of Tamelera by partnership to Erex

Lienne of the Eleventh Family—cousin of Tamelera

Iren of the Ninth Family—sister of Reyn

Alixi Faril of the Ninth Family—father of Reyn, rules in Safe Harbor

Lady Catenad of the Ninth Family—mother of Reyn

Arbiter Erex of the First Family—leader of the First Family Council, older distant cousin of Tagaret and Nekantor

Doret of the Eleventh Family—cabinet ally of Garr, cousin of Tamelera

Caredes of the Eighth Family—cabinet ally of Garr

Inkala of the First Family—cousin of Tagaret and Nekantor

Pyaras of the First Family—cousin of Tagaret and Nekantor

Administrator Vull of the First Family—father of Pyaras

Yril of the Twelfth Family—friend of Nekantor

Grenth of the Twelfth Family—friend of Nekantor

Jiss of the Eighth Family—friend of Nekantor

Losli of the Seventh Family—friend of Nekantor

Amyel of the Ninth Family—cabinet member, father of Gowan

Eminence Indal of the Fifth Family—ruler of all Varin

Tindamer of the Fourth Family—friend of Nekantor

Dix of the Fourth Family—friend of Nekantor

Drespo of the Ninth Family—friend of Nekantor

Boros of the Second Family—Secretary of the Pelismar Cabinet

Menni of the Second Family—son of Boros, former schoolmate of Tagaret

Xemell of the Third Family—a young gentleman, cousin of Herin

Sangar of the Eighth Family—a young gentleman

Herm of the Seventh Family—a young gentleman

Innis of the Fifth Family—a gentleman

Brinx of the First Family—son of Selemei, distant cousin of Tagaret and Nekantor

Enwin of the Sixth Family—father of Della

Pazeu of the Sixth Family—mother of Della

Liadis of the Sixth Family—sister of Della

Ambrei of the Fourth Family—a young gentleman

Vos of the Sixth Family—a gentleman

Lyaret of the Tenth Family—a young gentleman

Ower of the Eleventh Family—a young gentleman

Arbiter Doross of the Sixth Family—leader of the Sixth Family Council, older distant cousin of Della

Falya of the Third Family—partner of Herin
Chief Adjudicator Uresin—head judge of the Pelismar Courts
Palimeyn of the Third Family—a cabinet member
Arith of the Sixth Family—a cabinet member
Ethor of the Twelfth Family—a cabinet member

Arissen

Revett of the Pelismara Division—leader of the soldiers of
   Pelismara
Veriga Cohort First—a bodyguard
Karyas Cohort First—a bodyguard
Dekk—a guard

Imbati

Das—caretaker of Tagaret and Nekantor
Serjer—First Houseman in the Household of Garr and Tamelera
Aloran—a student at the Imbati Service Academy
Kiit—a student at the Imbati Service Academy, Aloran's friend
Min—a student at the Imbati Service Academy
Master Ziara—Health instructor at the Imbati Service Academy
Tamelera's Eyli—servant and bodyguard to Tamelera of the First
   Family
Anin—a student at the Imbati Service Academy
Garr's Sorn—servant and bodyguard to Garr of the First Family
Della's Yoral—servant and bodyguard to Della of the Sixth
   Family
Selemei's Ustin—servant and bodyguard to Selemei of the First
   Family
Jeris—a student at the Imbati Service Academy, Kiit's bunkmate
Endredan—a student at the Imbati Service Academy, Aloran's
   bunkmate
Erex's Kuarmei—servant and bodyguard to Erex of the First Family
Premel—Keeper in the Household of Garr and Tamelera
Remeni—First Houseman in the Household of Benél of the First
   Family

Shara—caretaker in the Household of Reyn and Iren of the Ninth Family

Katella—a student at the Imbati Service Academy

Artist Orahala—the tattoo artist of the Pelismar Imbati

Dorya—partner of Premel

Fedron's Chenna—servant and bodyguard to Fedron of the First Family

Ezill—pharmacy warden of the Imbati Service Academy

Headmaster Moruvia—Headmaster of the Imbati Service Academy

Officer Warden Xim—leader of the Imbati Wardens

Herin's Argun—manservant to Herin of the Third Family

Kartunnen

Tromaldin—conductor of the Pelismar symphony

Ryanin—a famous composer

Yanun—a courtesan

Vant—a musician's apprentice

Jaia—a shopkeeper and fashion designer

Dois—a courtesan

Venorai

Kitrin—elected leader of the Venorai Union

Melumalai

Odenli—chairman of the Melumalai banking syndicate

Akrabitti

Griss—a trash worker

Acknowledgments

I have a great many people to thank—so many that I know I will end up missing someone. So many of you kept up my spirits with kind words or advice, or gave me your precious time for reading, critiquing, and discussing. You know who you are, and I wouldn't be here without you.

I would like to thank my editor, Sheila Gilbert, for her insightful vision in sharpening this book. Thank you to Adam Auerbach for the beautiful cover art, and to Katie Hoffman for her kindness and advocacy. I'm also deeply grateful to my agent, Kristopher O'Higgins, who never stopped believing in this project and supported me through years of work and waiting. A big thank you also goes out to Marguerite Reed, who introduced me to Kris.

Janice Hardy, you've been there every step of the way. Thank you for telling me you cared about this book, and this was where I had to start.

Deborah Ross, I would not have made it through without your mentoring insights, hugs, and gentle guidance.

Among the many people who participated in critique and discussion I wish to extend particular appreciation to Lillian Csernica, Josephine Kelso, Dario Ciriello, Linda Whitaker, and Kyle Aisteach.

Special thanks go to David J. Peterson for the many hours he spent turning my alphabet for Varinin into a real font that could be used in this book.

Thank you to Tim, Niall, and Eagan for all the hours of listening, for telling me I'm awesome when I needed to hear it, and for also being honest about when I needed to fix things. Thanks to Pete and Jen for believing. Finally, I'd like to thank my parents, Eileen and Michael, for all the books they gave me to read, for supporting me through my education in linguistics and anthropology, and for taking me to France where I discovered Varin in the Gouffre de Padirac.